DARKNESS OF DAY

HUNTER'S MOON (VOLUME 3)

RAMÓN TERRELL

TAL PUBLISHING

ISBN: 978-1-9990903-2-6 (Paperback)

Cover painting by Martin Maceovic
Cover Font by Nicole Peschel
Tal Publishing
Published by Tal Publishing Vancouver BC
Edition: January 2017
Printed in the USA

This one is dedicated to Moms, who has joined Pops among the ancestors back Home. Words cannot describe how much you are missed, and how much you are loved. Though I am happy for your reunion with your beloved, we are saddened by your departure. Never could I have known how aptly named this book would be, for it is the dawn of new days for you, but our day was darkened the day you left.

We love and miss you, and celebrate your love, life, and reunion with Pops, who has no doubt been waiting to see you again.

ACKNOWLEDGMENTS

No book is created by one person. And with that, I am so very thankful to Cat Lee, who helped to proof this book. Your sharp eye has been a blessing, as has been your comments on the story and characters.

Karen Pellet. You , my friend, have been absolutely awesome. Your comments and feedback have truly been amazing in helping to make this book even better.

Thank you, Jessica Guernsey, for your help in also cleaning up the book and strengthening weak spots. Your comments were not only a great help, but often quite fun.

1

Ramshackle huts and shacks passed in a blur as Mallika ran down the stained and dirty streets. In the poor district between the temple and her village, each street held its own signature stench. She turned down a street that smelled of humans sweating in the heat, even though it was dusk. Their odor mixed with that of the bovine inhabitants mingling in the thinning crowd as night rapidly approached. Hers was a world of tanners, fishermen, and anything that dealt with death or uncleanliness. For all of her twelve years of life, this was where Mallika lived. This was her place, her life. And it all passed by in a blur of hot, stuffy evening air as she made her way quietly through the cow pie-strewn streets, cradling a bowl of herbs in her hands.

Occasionally Mallika had to dodge left or right to avoid a cow as it meandered lazily across her path. Cows. Considered sacred and not to be mistreated. Cows, with that musty large animal smell. Held in higher regard than her people.

That one stray thought almost caused her to run headlong into a woman carrying a basket of fruit on her head. The woman just barely grabbed the basket to keep it from falling over and spilling its contents onto the street.

Mallika kept running, ignoring the insults and curses spat by the angry woman. She sprinted down the stone street, her bare, dirty feet splashing in puddles of water and crunching through bits of straw and dirt.

At a nearby stream, women and children wearing little more than gray and brown rags washed clothes that looked as though they would never be clean. Despondent men and boys scooped human and animal excrement from the streets for those considered 'better' to travel.

Mallika didn't know what smelled worse, the excrement baking in the relentless night heat, or the scent of broken spirits surrounding her.

Mallika stole a glance down at the tattered hand-woven bowl. She'd wanted to bring some water with the herbs, but she wasn't confident of its purity. Her mother's survival depended on her pleasing Lord Dhanvantari, and she couldn't take a chance in offending the Physician God by offering him dirty water. She hoped the herbs would please him.

As she neared the edge of her village, she slowed and took more careful steps. Now was the time for stealth. During the day, her people mostly slept and remained unseen. It wasn't till night when they went about their business. Unclean business, society had deemed it.

She crept along the side of a stone building and peeked around the corner. She ducked her head back and lowered to the ground, making herself as small and unnoticeable as possible. She heard the footsteps of the night patrolman grow louder. Slow, casual steps. Bored steps. The authorities always had to draw straws when it came to the night patrol of the poor districts. 'Guarding the shit.' That's what they called it, unclear whether they were talking about the actual waste, or the people who shoveled it.

The guard continued on his route, disappearing around the far corner of the building. Silent as a shadow, Mallika slipped from around the building and padded across the street. *Be strong, Mama.*

Lord Dhanvantari won't refuse my prayers or this offering. Just hold on a little longer. Please don't die, Mama.

She zigzagged the street, hiding in the darkest alcoves and lying perfectly still when a guard came near. She hunkered down next to a large basket, drawing her knees up to her chest. A second guard walked by, and Mallika glimpsed the jeweled hilt of the sword strapped to his waist. Her eyes rose to take in the dark blue turban with a single feather on top. His green vest woven with simple yet attractive designs would have been beautiful if not mocking by its very existence. His loose-fitting white trousers only accentuated the jewels in the hilt of that sword.

Her eyes fell on back to that hilt. Head-to-toe, the man's uniform cost more than any possession Mallika and her mother would ever hope to have. Just the jewels alone, inlaid in the hilt of that sword, could buy them food for longer than she could imagine.

She snapped out of her resentment and scanned the area. The presence of such well-dressed guards also meant that she was close to the temple.

She slipped around the basket and made her way in the opposite direction as the guard. Several more patrolled near the temple so she waited, taking note of their patterns.

The moon suddenly appeared in a gap between the sleepy clouds. The pale light held no warmth, but it illuminated the temple grounds brilliantly, giving Mallika a perfect view of the patrolling and stationary guards.

Finally, having established their patterns, Mallika waited till the moon was shrouded once more, then left her hiding place. She skulked along the walls and stopped at the edge of the open ground. About thirty feet of lawn separated the pillars of the temple from her position. That thirty feet seemed like a mile of vulnerability. She would have to be fast and silent.

Her grip on the basket tightened until she reminded herself not to spill its contents and thus her only hope of healing Mama. She closed her eyes and took a deep breath. *She's all I have. I've got to do this.*

Once the guards turned away, she darted out into the opening, sprinting across the lawn. About a dozen feet from the first pillar, her foot caught on a hidden mound. Stifling a cry of pain, she clamped her hand over the basket as she went down. She hit the ground and rolled head over heels, coming back to her feet. Pain burned in her left foot, but she shrugged it off and continued until she reached the pillar.

Chest heaving and big toe throbbing, she slowly removed her hand from the tiny basket to see the herbs disheveled, but still there. She breathed a sigh of relief and started a silent prayer to Brahma, when a guard called out.

"Hey. Someone there?"

Mallika pressed her back to the wall, willing herself to sink into it. She squinted her eyes shut.

"I heard something," another guard said. "It came from over there, near the lawn."

"I don't see anything," a second guard said. "Probably a rat, or some other rodent."

"That's why we're here. To prevent any rodents of the two-legged persuasion from sullying the temple—"

"That's enough."

Mallika's heart skipped a beat. The voice was powerful, commanding. It had to belong to the captain. She'd never seen him, but she could imagine her fate if he found her here.

"Go check it out."

She closed her eyes and arranged her fingers in the mudra of courage, and released her fear. She held still, listening to the muffled footsteps of the guard as he crossed the lawn. She prayed that the moon didn't come back out and send her shadow stretching across the lawn.

The steps drew closer, and Mallika forced her heart to slow, her mind to focus. Mama was depending on her to stay focused and not panic. Strong body odor revealed the guard's close proximity to her pillar. He was coming around to her right. She slowly, quietly, shuffled along the side of the pillar, moving at the same pace as the guard.

The footsteps stopped, and she held her breath. She was facing the row of three pillars that stood between her and the other guards. So long as she remained where she was, they wouldn't see her. But if this guard decided to do a complete circuit of the pillar, she would be forced to slide around it where she would be facing the open lawn.

"Eh. Probably a normal four-legged rat." The guard's voice was nearly in her ear, and she could tell he was leaning around the pillar, giving the area a glance. She barely registered the insult, so preoccupied was she with keeping calm.

She heard the footsteps coming back around the pillar, faster this time, and she matched the steps.

"Nothing there." The guard's voice was father away. She released the breath she'd been holding and waited till she built up the courage to glance around the column. The guards had resumed their patrols. She slipped to the left, darting between pillars until she finally came to the steps at the base of the shrine of Lord Dhanvantari, four-armed God of Health.

She licked her dry lips, glancing down at the basket cupped in her hands. She would have to be quick. There would be no time to go through the full ritual. She would hurry to the shrine, present her offering, say the silent prayers to the God for his blessing to heal Mama, then be gone before the authorities returned.

She waited, eyes darting left to right, feeling much like a mouse navigating a den of cats. The altar and its surroundings were vacant. Despite this, a stab of fear chilled the pit of her stomach. Something was wrong. She shouldn't have come. No. She closed her eyes and concentrated on her breathing.

Just nerves, she thought. *Mama's depending on me. I have to do this.* Of course, Mama didn't know she was here or she would have tried to prevent Mallika from coming. Not that she could have done much in her weakened condition. Better she not know. Mallika would tell her after she had been healed.

Before she lost her nerve, Mallika took a deep breath and got moving. Keeping low to the ground, she silently made her way past the last row of columns, glancing wide-eyed in every direction.

Mallika lifted her foot to take the first step when she felt the tip of a sword touch the back of her neck. She swallowed audibly, foot still hovering over the step.

"What is this?" a voice asked from behind. "So, there *was* a rodent scurrying around here, eh?" The sword slipped around to the front; the flat of the blade pressed against her throat, forcing her to step away from the altar.

"You weren't about to dirty the shrine of Lord Dhanvantari, were you?" The sword pressed harder, and she winced. Even though it wasn't the cutting edge against her skin, it still hurt. The guard used his sword to move her around till he was standing between her and the steps to the shrine.

"What are you doing here?" the guard demanded.

Mallika kept her gaze down, though it grated on her to do so. "My mother is dying. I came to make an offering to Lord Dhanvantari," she glanced around the guard at the depiction of the God of Healing, "that he might heal her illness." The shrine was so close, but impossibly far now.

"And why would He deign to listen to your filthy prayers, let alone sully his hands with laying them on your mother?"

Mallika stole a quick glance at the guard's smug expression and clenched her teeth. She would have killed him with his own sword if she could.

"You've got a defiant streak in you, don't you?" the guard said, eyeing her. "Yes, I can see it. Too bad you were born a girl, and from slums, at that." He jerked his chin in the direction of her home.

"What's going on here?" It was the strong voice.

The owner of that voice moved quickly to them. Adorned with a more intricately designed vest, bright blue turban with a larger feather rising above it, there could be no question of his rank.

"You were right, Captain. There was a rat running around here, and I've caught her." He nodded at her basked of herbs with a disgusted snarl. "She was planning to stain the temple with her filth."

"Take her to the city square for everyone to see, and give her ten lashes," another guard said. "It's the only way those street vermin learn anything."

"You will be silent, all of you! This is a little girl." The captain approached her. "Take your sword away from her neck, Badal. I doubt she's going to overpower you, though with your current skill with the blade, it may be possible."

Chuckling ensued. Mallika glanced around. She hadn't realized two more had arrived.

The guard named Badal muttered under his breath and sheathed his sword. "You think I'm gonna touch this with my own hands?" He nodded at Mallika. "Disgusting."

"You should have more respect for human life, Badal," the captain said. "You could just as easily be born in the same status in your next life."

"So what are you going to do with her, Captain?" one of the other guards asked. "Untouchables aren't allowed in the temple."

"She should be beaten," Badal muttered.

The captain squatted down before her, looking into her eyes. "Why are you here, little one? Surely you know this is not allowed."

Mallika stared down at the herbs in her little basket. "My mother is sick," she said, fighting to keep her voice steady. She would not give them the satisfaction of seeing her cry. "If I don't make my offering to Lord Dhanvantari, she'll die."

"Not such a big loss," Badal muttered.

"Return to your post, Badal. Now." The captain watched him go, then returned his attention to Mallika. "You know that it's forbidden for Untouchables to enter the temple don't you, little one?"

Mallika looked up at him, allowing her anger to show. Just looking the man in the eye could get her executed, but she could hold it back no longer. "So I should let my mother die? I should just do nothing?"

The man's gentle tone didn't waver, despite her insolence. "Perhaps you could offer your prayers in your home."

"Do you believe that would work?" Mallika asked. "If so, can't we all just do that instead of using the altars and shrines and temples the Gods have given us?"

"Shut your mouth," one of the other guards barked. His fist tightened around the hilt of the sword. "Filthy urchins do not question the captain of the guard—"

"That is enough," the captain said. He looked into Mallika's eyes for several tense moments. "Perhaps I can have a priest say the prayers and make the offering for you."

"I should be the one to do it," Mallika insisted. Her pulse raced and her hands grew clammy. There was no time for this. She looked about the dark temple. Outside the many rows of pillars, the moon washed the outer lawn and square white buildings in its pale light. Even that beauty mocked her. She looked back into the captain's eyes. "She's my mother."

"The priests have a closer relationship with the Gods, child. Allow me to take the offering and give it to a priest of the temple. I will have one of them make the offering and pray for your mother."

Mallika felt sick. She should be the one to make the offering and pray for her mother, not someone else. She had little faith in anyone. Those priests the captain spoke of enjoyed an existence far above her own. If they truly cared about the people, wouldn't they pray to the Gods for it to be otherwise?

"You're an angry one, I can see it." The captain smiled at her. "Why are you so angry, little girl?"

"Nobles, warriors, farmers, cows; everyone is above me. Everyone is above Untouchables. You look down on us for having to do the work you don't want to do. You call us names and spit on us."

"It is your karma, child. You were born into this world with your own karma, and this is the life you must lead."

Mallika had no answer to that. She wished she'd been born higher. She and her mother did their best to live good lives, but their karma had cast them into the lowest level of society. She noticed that despite his kind words, even the captain would not touch her. He may have squatted down to her level to speak with her, but he was still far enough away to be careful not to touch her. If it was daylight, he would probably be careful to avoid even her shadow touching him.

After a few more moments of silence, the man stood and signaled to a man with a thick moustache and an angry scowl. "Take this girl's offering and pass it on to a priest to pray for her mother."

The man recoiled. "My Captain, you would have me touch—"

"I would have you do as I tell you."

"Please," Mallika spoke up. "I do not trust them. But I would trust you. If I am not allowed to do this, would you see it done, Captain? Please?"

The captain seemed to think on it a moment, then nodded with a smile. "Of course. I will take your offering to the priests."

Mallika looked up at him; into his eyes. She saw kindness there, and truth as well. She knew he would do as promised.

"Okay." She sat the basket on the ground in front of him and stepped back.

"Go home, child," the captain said, taking the basket from the ground. "And don't do anything like this again. Okay?"

"Yes, Captain."

He smiled again. "Good."

~

It was a shorter trip back to their little shack in the district of the Untouchables. She received a few curious looks, but no one spoke to her. She saw the same look in the eyes of almost everyone she passed. Hopeless, empty, and resigned. There was happiness there as well, when a father lifted his son, or when children chased each other in the street. Mothers teaching their daughters how to weave baskets and carve fruit, while young boys learned how to clean and tan leather.

Mallika had always been taught that everyone was born with karma, depending on their past lives. Some were born as nobles, dignitaries, farmers. Others as Untouchables; the lowest of the low. The simple touch of one of her kind, was said to be unclean. Even her shadow was tainted. Though the latter was a belief from more ancient times, she knew people still believed it.

Despite the teachings, she hated it. She hated being born into such a life. She hated that she couldn't do a thing to elevate her status. She hated not feeling full after a meal, and she hated not being able to pray to Lord Dhanvantari herself. Were the Gods truly so cruel? Mallika's twelve-year-old mind didn't know for sure, but if they were, why pray to them at all?

Her mind clamped shut at that thought. If the Gods could hear her thoughts, they might strike her down, or worse, condemn her to another lifetime as an Untouchable.

Rounding the last bend in the street, she came to a shabby three-walled shack. Home. She stepped through the curtain and stopped to stare at her mother. Withdrawn and wasting away, the woman was half the size she had been when she was healthy. Her full, ready smile and loving eyes had been replaced with sunken cheeks and sunken, dim eyes.

In the darkness of the room her mother lay unmoving, her head turned aside. Mallika moved quietly to her mother's side and rested a hand on her head. She frowned, leaning down for a closer look.

"Mama?" she said, running a hand over her mother's long brittle hair. When there was no response she gave her mother a gentle shake.

"Mama?" she said again, a tiny quiver of fear tinting her voice. Still no response. She placed her hand in front of her mother's mouth, but felt no breath. She leaned down and placed her ear on her mother's chest, waiting. After a few moments, she sat upright and stared down at the empty shell that once housed her mouther's soul.

Tears streamed freely down her cheeks as she continued to stare at Mama; gone to be reunited with Papa.

2

"**M**ama?"

Ever regal, ever loving, ever human, little Saaya's mother looked down on her with adoring eyes. *"Yes, my child."*

"Why do people look at me strange?"

"Don't worry about them."

"Why? I want to know."

"It's because you're different."

"Different, how?"

"You will come to learn."

The little girl twisted her forefinger in her fist. *"I didn't mean to hurt him, Mama. We were just playing."*

"I know. But you must be more careful. You are stronger and faster than they are. Your mind is both the same and different from theirs. You have to learn to live as they do. You have to be careful with them, my child."

"I don't understand."

"You will, my little girl. One day you will understand."

"Will you always be here, Mama? Like Baba?"

"What do you mean, like Baba?"

"Baba told me that he will always be here, forever. He said that you can, too, but that it is your choice."

"Don't worry about that right now."

"Please, be here forever, Mama. I don't want you to go away."

Her mother hugged her close and kissed her on the top of her head, burying her face in the little girl's silky black hair.

"I'm not going anywhere, my child."

"Promise?" She hesitated, and when Saaya looked up into her mother's eyes, there was pain there. "Promise, Mama?"

"I promise, daughter. Now go to sleep. Your father will be here at sunset."

Memories came in a jumble. A flash of children at play. A flash of a boy spinning through the air to land heavily on the ground. Surprise, exhilaration, fear, regret.

More memories. Adolescence. Cuts that healed almost instantly. Hiding her strength and speed. A tall, imposing figure looking down on her with love. A second, slightly shorter and slightly less imposing figure, guarding. Hunger. Hunger for food.

Hunger.

Hunger for more than food. Shock and horror, then sated hunger. Self-loathing, guilt, remorse, fear. Then Baba was there. Love and compassion. Knowledge and understanding. Acceptance and solidarity.

Coming of age. Knowledge. Understanding. No fear, guilt, or self-loathing. Love, understanding and self-perception. She is her mother, but more. She is her father, but less. She is different from all, and alone. No. Not alone. There is one who will always be there. She looks up into those dark brown eyes. They look down at her and there is amusement and love. The eyes glow lavender. Hers do the same. Saaya smiles. Her brother winks.

～

J elani awoke. It was not an exceptional event, if it could be called an event at all. It felt more like a return to consciousness. He opened his eyes and looked around. The room's solitary window was closed, the drapes pulled tight, shrouding everything in darkness.

A darkness where everything was perfectly visible to him.

"The dead finally rise again."

Jelani didn't move, though he knew the voice. Saaya.

"You look like a possum trying to play dead, *jaan*."

Jaan. It was a word in the language of her mother—her Indian heritage—that meant love, or, my love. For the first time that word actually brought him comfort, though he couldn't say why.

"Don't look so paranoid, *jaan*, it might hurt my feelings."

"Where am I?"

"Where do you want to be?"

"An hour or two before that jog in Stanley Park."

Jelani put a hand to his head, but there was no warmth to comfort his clean-shaven scalp. His skin was so cold. And what was that dream? Some little girl and her mother? It felt so familiar, like he was directly experiencing these things but outside of it all at the same time.

"I'm afraid I cannot send you back in time, love, but I can assure you one thing. Time will come to have a different meaning to you," her lavender eyes glimmered in the darkness, "in time."

Those words brought everything crashing back into place. Being able to see in utter darkness, the strange dreams, his cold skin. He ran his hand back and forth over his head as was his habit. He forced his mind in another direction.

"How long have I been asleep?"

"You have slept for a little over a month," came the reply.

A month. Impossible!

"Was I in a coma or something?"

There was a stretch of silence before the answer came.

"I think you know the answer to that."

Jelani raised himself up on his elbow, and a rush of dizziness passed through his head. He held his head between his hands and squeezed his eyes shut.

"You surprise me, *jaan*. I hadn't expected you to rise so soon."

"Will you quit using words like that?"

"Like what?"

"Rise." He swung his legs over the side of the bed, but didn't trust them enough to hold his weight just yet. "Can't you just say wake up, like any normal person?"

"Like any normal person." Saaya stepped fully into view, moving out of a deeper shadow he hadn't known was there. "Is that what you think, Jelani? That I, or even you, now, are like any other person?"

"I don't want to talk about this," he said, putting his face in his hands. This could not be happening. It was impossible.

"What happened to Daniel and Alisha? And Wen?"

"They live."

"Was Alisha…" he couldn't bring himself to finish the question.

"No need to worry, love," Saaya replied, sitting down beside him. The warmth from her body was both comforting and confusing. "She still walks in the sun."

"But he bit her."

"A bite is nothing more than that. To turn a human takes a little more … effort. He had been sipping from her for a time, but not enough to kill her. He was saving that for your final torture."

"Where is everyone now?" Jelani found that his voice was oddly calm. Calmer than it had ever been since this whole ordeal had begun months ago.

"They remain together in your home. Kafeel watches over them, though I may owe him a considerable favor for doing so. I think he is a little disgusted with me."

"They must think I'm dead," Jelani said. "What with me being asleep for a month, as you say."

"Do not worry," Saaya said. "I told them that you were grievously injured and that only my help could revive you."

"I'm sure they readily swallowed that one."

Saaya smirked at him. "It is actually true. Your fate was colored with a darker tone until I found you."

"And you saved me from what?"

"Being compelled to serve a foul creature who would torment you for ages to come." She shrugged. "To tell the truth, I cannot recall such a thing ever being done; one vampire imbuing their essence into a human who had already been turned."

Turned.

Jelani held up a hand. "I can't deal with this yet."

"You will have to find a way to deal with it," she replied, and there was firmness in her voice. "You don't have the luxury of time to digest your new state, or the situation you're in. This matter with Remy is not finished."

Remy.

Jelani felt his blood light on fire at the mention of the one he hated. Remy had done this to him. Had forever altered his life.

"So what now?" he asked.

"I will let your friends know that you are awake when you are ready to see them again."

"Then let's go."

He heard her chuckling softly in the darkness. "*Jaan,* I will admit that you have recovered swiftly considering the special circumstances of your re-creation, but I'm not certain you are ready to meet your friends yet."

"My re-creation." There, he'd said it. Though a large part of him still denied it, he'd said the words. "This can't be real, Saaya. It can't."

She placed a hand on his shoulder. "You will come to accept

your life, Jelani. You will come to understand and you will live on, and become so much more than you are now."

Jelani stood and started toward the door, then turned back. "I didn't want this. I was perfectly fine the way I was."

"Of course, but what you wanted and what you were are now irrelevant. I am sorry to be so harsh, but you must understand that there's no going back."

Forcing his legs to hold him, he stood and walked away from her, running both hands over his head. Instinctively, he reached for the switch on the wall and turned on the light. His eyes adjusted immediately, which was both amazing and disheartening at the same time.

He looked down at his hands, still the same color, but he could feel a strength that wasn't there before. He turned and looked around the room, his gaze resting on a full-length mirror. He looked at Saaya but the *dampeal* simply sat in a chair across from the bed with her hands folded in her lap, watching him patiently.

He crossed the room and stood before the mirror, and let out a sigh of relief at the sight of his reflection. A disgusted snort drew his attention back to Saaya, who rolled her eyes.

When he looked back to the mirror, the person looking back at him seemed unchanged. Same nose, head, skin. Same eyes. But beneath the surface, there was a difference. Something powerful and unnerving projected from him.

When he looked again at the reflection of his eyes, he retreated a step. Tentatively, as though he feared his image would reach out of the glass and throttle him, he leaned forward and studied his eyes. They were almost black. He leaned closer, his face almost touching the glass. His eyes *were* black.

"What the hell?"

Saaya came to stand beside him. "What do you see?"

He looked at her, and she nodded. She was about to say more when a sudden cramp hit Jelani in the stomach. He doubled over, gasping. The pain was like a lance of fire or acid shooting through him, shredding his intestines. The pain shot through his arms and legs, neck, head, fingers and toes. Even his teeth.

"What the hell is happening to me?" he groaned, dropping to his knees.

Saaya crouched beside him, resting a hand on his back. "The thirst is upon you," she said. "You must feed."

"I need some food," Jelani said, shaking his head. He didn't need to feed, he just needed food.

"You will find your definition of food is quite different than what it once was."

"No."

"Jelani, look at me." She put a finger under his chin and lifted his head. He looked into her eyes and saw something he had never seen before. A hint of sympathy. "You must trust me. If you go out of here now, trying to find food, you will attack someone. Can you live with that?"

As if in answer, another jolt burned him from inside. His blood was like lava, coursing through his veins.

"What choice do I have?" he groaned. "It feels like I'm being burned alive from the inside out."

"And as the pain increases, so too will your desperation to quell it."

She left him and a minute later, returned and handed him a thermos. He looked at it. It looked like it should have hot chocolate or coffee in it. He went to unscrew the lid, but she placed a hand over his.

"I would not recommend you look inside until you drink for the first time."

"If this is what I think it is, I'm not drinking—" he nearly dropped the thermos when another spasm hit.

"You were saying?" she replied, arching an eyebrow at him. "Jelani, you must drink. If you do not, you will eventually surrender to the thirst and it will become primal. You would attack the nearest person. Many before you have tried to deny the thirst."

"And what happened to them?"

"The Hunters."

Jelani looked at the thermos as though it were a poisonous snake.

"Shake it first," she said.

"Why?"

"To liquify it again. It begins to clot—"

"Okay, okay," Jelani said, patting the air. "I wish I hadn't asked."

He shook the thermos and took a sip. Revulsion gave way to relief, and he drank the rest of the contents in one gulp.

"How do you feel?" Saaya asked. The fact that she'd even asked indicated her relief.

"More," was all he could manage.

3

J elani listened to her receding footsteps and soft laughter as she went back into the kitchen with the thermos. He didn't know what disgusted him more, that he'd just downed a thermos filled with blood, or that he was sitting here in anticipation of her bringing another one.

Moments later, she returned and handed it to him. Again, he emptied the thermos in seconds, wiping a stray crimson drop from the corner of his mouth. He looked at red smear on his finger.

"My god. What have I become?"

It was a rhetorical question, of course. He knew exactly what he'd become. The true question, however, was what it meant.

"Are you planning to pray while you're down there?"

Saaya's voice drew Jelani out of his thoughts. He blinked, realizing that he was still on his knees. With an ease he hadn't expected, Jelani rose to his feet. He placed a hand on his stomach which not only had stopped cramping, but felt like the pain had never been. He looked again at his arms and hands. No pain anywhere. Quite the opposite, in fact. He felt stronger than he'd ever felt in his life.

"Better?" she asked him.

He nodded, blinking as he took in the room. Colors were more vivid. He could hear everything around him. He closed his eyes. Two people in the neighboring room playing cards; soft breathing of someone asleep in a room across the hall.

He even heard an insect buzzing around the window in the next room. Countless sounds and smells all around him. It was amazing and maddening at the same time.

"Too much." Jelani pressed his hands to the sides of his head and clamped his eyes shut.

"Focus," Saaya said. "That is how you stay sane and avoid sensory overload. Focus your mind and your senses. Hear and smell and perceive only what you need."

Jelani forced himself to narrow his senses to a more manageable degree. After a few moments, he no longer heard the person sleeping across the hall or the insect in the next room. He still faintly heard the people playing cards next door, but that wasn't so bad. A few more minutes passed, and Jelani finally succeeded in reigning his senses in to a manageable level.

Saaya studied his face, smiling that beautiful half-smile. "Very good. You learn quickly." She walked around him, and Jelani got the impression of someone assessing a prized pedigree. "I do believe immortality suits you, *Jaan*."

Immortality.

Jelani closed his eyes. He took a deep breath and opened them again, forcing himself to look the *dampeal* in the eyes when he said his next words.

"That's it, then. I'm ..." He bit his bottom lip and looked aside. Then he looked back at her again. "I'm a vampire." There. He'd finally said the word. He was a vampire, a monster. He was a creature out of myth.

Saaya stepped in front of him and placed her hands on his shoulders, looking up into his eyes. "Yes, love. You are a vampire.

Age will never touch you again. You are now outside the cycle of life, and only through some form of violence can death ever claim you."

"And, I now have the pleasure of watching those I love age and die." Jelani walked to the window and peaked around the side of the curtain. Darkness. He pulled them open and gazed out into the night. "If I ever choose to have a relationship, I now get to watch her grow older every day, while I remain the same. I get to watch her wither and expire before my eyes." He turned to look back at Saaya. "I get to experience this time and again."

"You have a new life ahead of you filled with endless possibilities, and endless time to experience it all."

Jelani turned back and stared blankly out the window. "I am dead."

"You are reborn."

"Into a creature of the night."

She sighed. "How poetic, you are." She grabbed his hands and turned him to face her. "You have a knack for seeing the darkness of the day."

"Day," he echoed. "There's another thing I'll never see again. The sun."

Saaya started toward the door. "Come. Now that your thirst has been satiated for now, I feel confident you won't kill anyone."

"Where are we going?" Jelani asked.

"I haven't preserved you this long for you to make some silly mistake and have an entire coven of Hunters after you again. I mean to make your transition as smooth as possible."

He followed her up a narrow flight of stairs to another door. When they stepped out onto the roof, he closed his eyes and basked in the crisp fresh air. He opened his eyes again and took in the sprawling city lights of Vancouver. The sphere of Science World glowed like a huge green golfball, while the circumference of the arena shone blue, then green, then purple, each color zipping around the building as it changed.

He ran a hand over his arm, studying it as though it were a foreign object. "This is weird. I know it's cold, but I don't feel it. I mean, I feel it but I'm not cold."

"Welcome to the paradoxical world of vampirism, love."

"Is that why you dress so skimpy in the cold weather sometimes?"

"You never seemed to mind." She took a step toward him, arching her back just enough to subtly push her breasts out. He felt a burning in the pit of his stomach and an involuntary grin escaped him.

"See something you like?"

"Yes," he said. Then, with a great effort, he forced his eyes away from her. "So what are you planning to teach me?"

"A great many things, *jaan.*"

If temptation were personified, its name would be Saaya. He gave himself a mental shake. "I doubt that is essential for my survival."

"Ever try to go too long without it?"

"I'm feeling like I can be far more disciplined than ever before."

She glided closer, circling him while trailing her hand across his chest, his arms, his stomach. "Don't be so uptight. We all feel the urge to merge, love. You will find you have not even broken the surface to the depths of passion."

"So I didn't satisfy you?"

Saaya grinned at him. "Just because I know greater depths of pleasure than you could possibly imagine doesn't mean you did not bring at least one or two aspects of it to me." She stopped behind him, wrapping her arms around his waist and pressing herself against him. He could feel her medium-sized breasts pressed against his lower back. Her hand drifted lower and his body betrayed him.

"Feels like you're ready for a different first lesson, hmm?"

"Only if it involves staying alive, Saaya."

She huffed, and released him. When he turned around, she was already at the edge of the rooftop.

"You insist on being no fun, so fine." She crossed her arms and glared at him. He smirked. Even when she pouted, she was stunning. "What are you looking at, fledgling?"

He frowned. "Fledgling?"

She chuckled. "Oh, dear Jelani. That is exactly what you are. You are a fledgling, little more than a month old and less than a day awake."

"Okay?" He spread his hands.

"First lesson is your speed." She tapped the chest-high stone wall next to her. "Come here, next to me. And get here as quick as you can."

Jelani's frown deepened as he thought of the many times he'd seen her in one place, then someplace else in the blink of an eye. Could he really be that fast?

"Alright," he said. He placed one foot back and lowered his body. He looked at Saaya, but her expression gave nothing away. "Alright," he repeated, and sprang forward. Before he knew what happened, he was dangling over the side of the wall, looking down at the ground at least seventy feet below.

"Part of lesson number one is control," she said casually, holding him by the back of his shirt. With a flick of her wrist, she yanked him back from the ledge and sent him flying into the air.

Reacting on newly sharpened instincts, Jelani performed a backward somersault and landed on his feet. He sprang forward again, this time managing to stumble to a stop right in front of her. To his satisfaction he saw a flicker of surprise and approval. A fleeting reaction, but he saw it.

"Not bad. So quickly you learn." She turned toward the balcony. "A normal *shaquora* would only be several times stronger than a human. I've given you a greater gift, but it is up to you to learn its depths." She pointed down toward the sidewalk. There's no one around but there is always someone looking. Never take a chance of being seen when doing something a human would consider ... abnormal."

Jelani shoved his hands in his pockets, chewing his bottom lip. "Like?"

She pointed at the clump of trees across the street.

Jelani looked at them, then back at her. "Yeah. I see a bunch of trees far away. And?"

"Think you can get that far?"

"What?" He eyed the distant 'goal'. Jump? It may as well be a mile away. "Um. Yeah. That's pretty far."

Saaya responded with slow, lazy blink. "You can jump pretty far."

Jelani rubbed his hands together. "Okay. I guess I can try—"

"Good."

Jelani was suddenly launched into the air. He clenched his teeth together in terror as he glided high above the ground, then started his descent toward the trees.

I ... am ... dead, he thought.

He crashed into the trees, bouncing off branches on his descent like a ball in a pinball machine.

Somehow, he got his bearings. He landed on one tree limb and fell away, but was able to flip backwards to get his feet under him. He gained some measure of control with each landing until one branch broke underneath him. He fell to the ground and landed on his side with a thud.

Quick as a cat, Jelani hopped to his feet. He looked at his arms and hands, then felt his chest.

"Damn," he breathed.

That first landing should have crushed his chest, but it didn't. If he'd earned any scrapes or cuts on the way down, none showed, and he felt no pain from the rather harsh impact with the ground. He remembered crashing through the trees back on Grouse Mountain not too long ago, and thought of the pain in his ribs long after the battering descent.

"I hope you say that in the sentiment that you have all the grace of a sea lion on land."

The woman's fast, Jelani thought. *I just hit the ground and she's already here.* He ran his tongue along the inside of his cheek. "A sea lion on land is out of its element. They're more graceful in the water."

She arched an eyebrow. "And you are out of your element?"

"For now," Jelani said. The casual remark he'd just made sent a shiver of fear through him. He looked up at the trees to hide it.

"Jelani." Saaya came beside him. "You are not the first human to be re-created. It will take some time."

She was too close. He breathed in her scent. If every flower in the world came together to produce a single fragrance, that would be the smell. He wanted her. He wanted Alisha. Melinda crept into his mind. *What the hell is going on with me?*

Saaya saw the confusion in his eyes. "You are conflicted." The look she gave him said she knew exactly what he was conflicted about.

"I don't know what to think. Everything is slamming into me all at once. It's like I have nothing solid to grasp."

"That is because you fear to grasp what is before you."

He looked at her, and to his surprise, she looked genuine. He felt a pang of guilt. Whatever her motivations, Saaya was taking the time to help smooth his transition to this new life. This life he didn't want. This life that both fascinated and terrified him.

Jelani took a deep breath. "You're right. I appreciate all that you've done for me and continue to do, Saaya. In a sort of back-handed way, you've been a true friend."

"Of course I have," she said. The cheer in her tone suggested she'd just helped him bake cookies. "So," she said, her voice going sober. "How do you feel?"

"Well, I'm not hurt if that's what you mean."

"The thirst?"

Jelani paused for a moment, then shook his head. "I'm fine. I don't know how long 'fine' will last, but I'm good for the moment."

Saaya looked into his eyes for several moments, then nodded.

"Perhaps I can take you to see your friends."

4

Yako studied the streets from his perch atop a high-rise. Though he had been careful not to give away his presence, Remy would surely know that he was back in the city. Massius would have contacted him, and he'd have to be a complete fool not to take the threat seriously.

He had been tracking Remy for the last month and had not yet found an opportunity to dispatch him. It seemed the craven had a sharp intuition for danger. When he thought about all the trouble Remy and Massius had caused him these past months, and the irritation Remy had caused him for years, Yako looked forward to sliding his sword in the middle of the troublesome Hunter's chest.

Yako narrowed his eyes. He might need help, as the coward was too good at avoiding danger. More than once, he'd questioned his wisdom in ordering Mariska to remain in Peles Castle, but it was the right decision. With Mariska there, he had someone he could trust to keep an eye on things and inform him of who may side with him when it was time to deal with Massius.

His thoughts strayed to the *dampeal* and her pet. Now that he had been turned, Yako wondered if her interest in the former human would endure. Given her brother's occasional presence and hers and the *shaquora's* absence, Yako guessed that she was watching over him during the change. A month had passed but it would be some time until the human had fully undergone and finished his re-creation.

As he knelt at the edge of the high-rise, well over a hundred feet above the city, Yako knew that he would see both of them again soon. The *dampeal* would not have spent so much effort keeping the human alive only to see him executed by a Hunter for doing something stupid. Most newly turned vampires tried to fight the thirst, which ultimately led to their undoing. One could only deny the thirst for so long before the urge to feed became undeniable. What followed was a human witnessing a newly turned *shaquora* feeding.

It happened so frequently that Yako wondered if this was what kept the vampire population relatively small, given that the job of Hunters was to exterminate reckless vampires, and human witnesses as well.

He spotted a man amidst the clumps of pedestrians, hands in his pockets with a friendly smile on his face. Solid, measured steps. Average build, solid posture.

Yako watched pedestrians give him plenty of space without realizing it. The more oblivious humans he effortlessly slinked around, like water flowing down a winding path filled with rocks.

The Eldest Hunter walked along the edge of the building, keeping directly above the figure. The man stopped behind a woman at a crosswalk and waited. When the light turned green the two, along with a group of other humans, crossed the street. Despite the outwardly normal situation, Yako kept the man in view.

He leaped to another nearby rooftop and continued to pace the man from the rooftops. The woman turned away from the group of pedestrians and continued down another street. The man continued to follow at an inconspicuous distance. Yako narrowed his eyes. It wasn't his job to stop a vampire from feeding so long as they were discrete, but his instincts were one of the reasons he was Eldest Hunter.

He watched as the woman made one mistake after another. A woman alone late at night was not such a dangerous thing until she turned down a street with practically no other pedestrians. Combined with not being aware of her surroundings, and it was no surprise when, as she crossed a street that led to an alley, the vampire attacked.

Before she could so much as cry out in surprise her stalker clamped a hand over her mouth and the other around her neck. In the span of a heartbeat he had her more than halfway down the alley and in the shadows of a declining driveway. Yako crouched low and watched.

The woman tried to struggle but the vampire just snickered at her. Yako focused his hearing. The woman screamed through her attacker's hand, but it came out as nothing more than a muffled sound.

"Now, now," the vampire said. "Don't go straining yourself. You're gonna need all those vocal cords and tears for when I'm done with ya. If you're alive, that is."

He turned her head aside and looked at her neck. "Mmm. You look good enough to eat." He leaned back just enough to give her a once-over. "Not bad. Why don't I see what prize is under all this wrapping. What do you think?" He leaned his ear close to her as if listening. "Ah! You agree too. Great!" He then lifted her chin and grabbed the neck of her sweater. There was a thick tearing sound, as he ripped the sweater down the middle.

The woman's eyes widened and she kicked and thrashed. The vampire continued to laugh at her.

"I'd thought to just drain you and be done with it. Buy you're just too damn enticing." He licked his lips. "How could I resist, hmm? How about a little fun?" He braced her against the wall and stuck his fingers in her pants.

Though he had his back to Yako, the Eldest Hunter could tell by the woman's even wider eyes that her attacker had just revealed his true nature.

Enough. Yako leapt into the air. Legs straight and arms out at his side, he glided into a forward somersault, closing the distance across the street. He landed silently behind the vampire, drawing his sword at the same time his feet touched the ground.

The sound of steel being drawn alerted the attacker, and he half-turned. His flaming red hair matched his eyes, and his pale skin was practically translucent, giving him an almost ghostly look. Once he recognized Yako for what he was, he sneered.

"You got no business with me, Hunter," he growled. He narrowed his glowing red eyes. "Last I heard, we were still allowed to feed to survive."

"Survival is not dependent upon rape," Yako replied.

"Who said anything about me raping this?" His hand still clamped around her neck, the man gave her a little shake. The woman clenched her eyes shut, no doubt in pain. Yako's only response was to narrow his eyes.

"What do you care, anyway? I'm gonna empty her out and she's gonna be dead anyway. What difference does it make if I play with my food first?"

Yako's stoney expression tightened further. "Blood is for survival. This is defilement."

The vampire visibly cringed at the sight of the Yako's murderous glare. "So who are you then, the enforcer of morality?"

"Release her."

"Release ..." this time he frowned with a confused smile. "So what, you're gonna just let her run free? I thought you all didn't allow that, once they've seen us."

"Her fate is her own. You should be concerned with yours."

There was a tense moment before the man threw her to the ground. Beside his foot, she coughed.

"There you go," the man said. He spat at the ground. "Your fair maiden has been rescued. Am I free to go now, or are you gonna lecture me on ethics or something?"

The woman had stopped coughing and Yako saw her eyes darting between himself and the other vampire. She started quietly crawling away.

Yako never took his eyes off of the vampire standing in front of him. "Stay where you are." She froze. Once again, that familiar mask of terror seized her features when she found herself compelled to obey him.

After a moment of silence, the other man spread his hands. "Well?" he said, leaning forward a bit. "What now?"

"I'm going to kill you."

"Kill me? But I just let your little bitch here go—"

Yako closed the distance between them. Vampires were fast but Hunters were faster, and Yako was Eldest Hunter. Before the other vampire could react, Yako drove his sword through his chest, withdrew it, then swept a horizontal cut, severing his head.

Yako swiped the side of the blade across the clothes of the headless body, then sheathed it. The body fell.

"I'll tell you why," he said to the rapidly decaying corpse. "Humans are our lessers, but as the lion feeds on the gazelle, so too do we feed on them, if we make that choice. Committing bodily defilement and torture is not our way. We will not sully ourselves by becoming creatures as base as you, and never will you vermin be allowed to bring dishonor upon us before the illustrious *Ancestors*."

He glanced at the woman, who lay where he'd stopped her, trembling. He walked over and stopped, glaring down at her. "Stand." She stood immediately.

For a moment he simply stared at her, seeing the fear in her light brown eyes. Her sandy hair hugged the sides of her face, cut short into a forward curving style to her chin. That tiny pointed chin quivered, and tears welled in her eyes. He could see the plea in those eyes. So delicate. So vulnerable. So oblivious.

"Your carelessness is more dangerous than my sword. How have you survived so long?" He stepped closer. Terror wafted off of her. He stared into her eyes, concentrating.

"You tore your sweater at work. It has been another uneventful walk home. You are always careful of your surroundings." He watched her eyes go out of focus as he spoke. He continued to focus on her eyes. He was barely proficient at this and had to concentrate. "Walk back to the street and do not look back. Once you turn the corner, you will remember nothing of this. Leave my sight."

The woman turned and made her way back to the end of the alley. By the time she rounded the corner Yako was already gone, and all that remained of the altercation was the clothes of the red-haired vampire lying on the ground.

Yako cared little to involve himself in the plight of humans, but such an attack was beyond his level of apathy. He hadn't saved the woman from being raped so much as prevented a fellow vampire from dishonoring their species. Though he could not abide the rape and torture of anyone, he rarely involved himself in situations that did not concern his own kind. What humans did to each other was between them.

He had to admit to himself the irony of this night in relation to his former target. The fact that mind manipulation was not one of Yako's strong points played a major role in Jelani's situation. It took Yako time to concentrate on a human to influence their mind beyond a simple command, such as paralysis. The circumstances of that fateful night in Stanley Park had not afforded him the opportunity to wipe Jelani's mind of the incident, and Yako didn't truly care enough to try. If the opportunity arose, fine. But he wasn't about to go out of his way.

The stray thought of humans reminded him of why *shaquora* were so disliked among purebloods. Vampires disagreed and occasionally fought with each other, but rape and torture was extremely rare. A death was dealt cleanly, and the act of merging was always between consenting parties.

But these *shaquora*, these turned vampires, were once human. They retained their human memories, tendencies, and thought processes. Amongst purebloods, *shaquora* were not considered to be trustworthy until they saw at least a hundred years through the eyes of immortality. Conversely, they rarely lived that long.

Yako stayed to the less travelled streets. Mingling with humans was not a problem, but the sword strapped to his back made him more conspicuous.

Eventually he made his way to Coal Harbour. He doubted he would find Remy lurking around the humans' building, but he knew that the big and powerful pureblood would be nearby. Perhaps Yako could glean some information by watching the *dampeal's* elder sibling.

Once he reached the boardwalk he began scanning the rooftops. Within minutes he spotted a tall, imposing figure atop an apartment building. Yako continued walking, glancing up at the figure. The big man could have been a statue; the only movement about him being his long cloak blowing in the ocean breeze.

Yako knew the man was watching him. He continued around the building till he came to the space between it and the neighboring hotel. He leaped the fifteen feet to the balcony overhead, then to a windowsill on the building across. Back and forth he zigzagged until he made it to the roof of the shorter hotel. The top of the building in front of him was another thirty feet so he sprinted for the wall, using his momentum to run half the distance up the side, then jumped the rest of the distance, gliding well clear of the top.

He landed on the far end of the roof from the towering vampire who remained where he was, back turned and staring in the direction of the home of Yako's former target. He started toward the other pureblood, not trying to hide the sound of his approach. Once he was within a dozen feet, a baritone voice stopped him.

"I wasn't aware we still had business, Eldest Hunter."

5

Yako said nothing and stood where he was. The big vampire seemed to be equally inclined to silence. For a time both parties remained as they were, the blood of an *Ancestor* watching over the building containing the three remaining humans, and the Eldest Hunter watching him.

The boardwalk lights of Coal Harbour illuminated the bike and jogging paths with a soft ambiance attractive to humans. Every night, joggers took to the path, couples went for a leisurely stroll, cyclists rode home from work or just for a quick ride. A scenic and peaceful environment. A hook ladened with a fat, irresistible worm.

"You continue to guard my remaining targets," Yako finally said.

"You come here to inform me of my own actions."

"I observe something odd."

"But make no move against it."

Yako went silent again. Skilled though he was, he doubted he could overcome the man. Size was not a problem, but in the case of dealing with this one, his size only decreased Yako's chances of winning, should it come to a fight.

"I have no need to move against you."

"That is fortunate for us both, then."

That caught Yako by surprise. "How so?"

"I sense true nobility in you, Eldest Hunter. Your sense of honor is beyond what most of your kind can conceptualize."

Yako did not sense an enemy here, so he moved to stand beside the other man. It was like standing next to a giant. The only other person Yako could think of comparable to this one's height was Braggus Rayne, Eldest Reaper of the Peles coven. He mentally smirked at the thought of a titanic struggle between those two.

"Most of my kind? Are my kind different from yours?"

A sharp breeze whipped across the roof and billowed Kafeel's long cloak. The sudden flap seemed an expression of the man's mood; not quite derisive, but that of finding amusement in conversation with a lesser. "That you must ask such a question betrays your limited knowledge of the *Ancestors*."

"Perhaps you will enlighten me."

"Find a library in one of your many covens."

Yako thought of the libraries and research offices in Peles Coven, as well as other covens across the world he'd visited. Some well kept, others dusty and strewn with cobwebs. Many with information leading back to the earliest records of the Elders' exploits. All with gaping historical holes. "I find the information there … lacking."

"Then you place yourself yet one more level above your kind, who are little more than singularities of a whole, following those who are simply older than they. I have heard the term 'lemming', used to describe this type of condition." He turned his head ever so slightly to regard Yako. "And just like lemmings, you would follow yourselves to your mass destruction."

"You speak as though we are on the brink of annihilation."

"You misinterpret. I'm simply addressing the possibility you have opened yourselves to."

"And still you speak of us as though you are something apart."

"The *Ancestors* do not their time with you, and rarely expend much energy imparting wisdom to a collective that is more concerned with living among and trading with humans in such a mundane capacity."

"What would the *Ancestors* propose as an alternative?"

"Find one and ask. I have no intention of detailing global possibilities with you. Nor do I believe that is why you are here."

"And why have I come?"

"You tell me."

Yako wondered if he was this intractable with his subordinates. Not that it mattered.

The honking of a gaggle of geese pierced the night, followed by the sound of flapping wings. A moment later, several gentle splashes of water.

A human couple trotted to the edge of the boardwalk and leaned over the rail. One pulled out their phone and switched on the flashlight function. After several passes, they finally spotted a light gray harbor seal, its round head bobbing just above the surface. It turned in their direction, then plopped back into the ocean.

The female gasped. "So cute!"

Humans.

"Perhaps we can start with introductions. I am Yako Shimamoto, Eldest Hunter."

There was a stretched silence, and Yako thought the big vampire might offer offense by not returning the gesture. But finally he spoke.

"I am Kafeel Omari, blood of the *Ancestor*, Count Omari."

Count Omari. Yako had never heard that name before. Though not every *Ancestor* carried a notable status, the presence and power that radiated from the man beside him suggested Kafeel's sire preferred solitude, or detachment from vampiric society. Given the way Kafeel spoke, Yako suspected the latter.

Finally, he turned his attention to the building that Kafeel had been watching. They had an almost direct view, and inside, one human male and two females sat on a couch. They ate in silence, the mood in the room subdued. Certainly they knew that because they had knowledge of the existence of vampires, they remained targets.

As Yako watched them, he couldn't decide if he cared enough to pursue their elimination beside his determination to be rid of Remy and Massius. Both would be trouble enough without him having to deal with Kafeel and his sister in order to get to these three humans.

Kafeel spoke again, and it was as if he'd read Yako's mind. "I do not pretend to understand my sister's interest in these pets of hers, but she compelled the promise from my mouth, and I will watch over them … for a time. If you try to move against them, I may kill you."

Yako found that interesting. The choice of words suggested the towering vampire might not wish to fight.

"I have no desire to engage you again, Kafeel Omari. I trust you understand what I mean."

"Of course. The one time I saw the eyes of that other Hunter, I saw an inherent fear of uncreation. I see no such cowardice in you."

"Then I may be confident we share a mutual respect."

"That you continue to actively write history instead of having become a part of it answers that question." Another pause, then Kafeel looked at him directly. "You aren't entirely interested in killing those three." It was not a question, but a statement of fact.

"Other matters that outweigh three humans are occupying my mind at present."

Kafeel returned his attention to the building. "The cravenly Hunter."

Yako nearly chuckled. "I've been tracking him for weeks. My efforts have yielded no fruit."

"I have never seen a coward who was easy to catch."

Yako nodded. "He is intelligent, and there are some who fail to see his contemptible level of cowardice. I mean to put an end to him." They were silent for a while, and Yako decided to risk the question that had been on his mind.

"Do you know anything of the newly turned human? My original target?"

Kafeel gave him a sidelong look. "My sister deals with him. By now he has arisen. That one has a will of steel. I would not be surprised if you end up in a race to catch up to the other Hunter. He may well beat you to it."

Unless we encounter one another first, Yako thought. It was all too likely that the newly turned vampire might hold a lasting grudge against him. Some humans forgot old grudges after they were turned, some did not. It would be a shame to kill him. Yako saw a warrior's spirit in that former human, as well his friend, who had just finished dinner with the two females. Another interesting thing was that he had already arisen. A human normally took two months before rising to the night.

"Have you come here to offer me your undying friendship?" Kafeel asked, interrupting his thoughts, "or is there another reason for your presence?"

Yako found that he could come to like Kafeel. He was direct and spoke plainly. "Have you seen Remy in the area?"

"And so the little mouse has a name. No. If he has been here, I haven't seen him. I suspect he has seen me, though, and is probably watching us now. I also suspect I know what his *talent* is."

Yako nodded. Kafeel was correct. Every vampire possessed at least one *talent,* an ability unique unto them. Remy's *talent* of guile and evasiveness was the very reason he was so hard to catch. It was also what made him so dangerous.

"I continue my hunt, then." He turned away, then stopped and looked over his shoulder. "A question."

"Speak it."

"Why? Regardless of your sister's desire to keep those humans alive, why do you agree?"

"My sister has an uncanny ability to insert herself into rather interesting situations. Despite my apathy for humans and their issues, I find myself interested in this. My intuition tells me that when this drama unfolds completely, some very old members of your coven will become aware of their own self-overestimation."

Yako arched an eyebrow. "And you find that amusing."

"I find that entertaining." He looked over his shoulder at Yako. "Do you not?"

Yako made a noncommittal sound and continued to the edge of the building. Without hesitation, he stepped off the side and disappeared over the edge, but not before he saw a hint of movement on the building directly across.

6

L ying behind a three-foot wall on the roof of the neighboring building, Remy didn't know whether to praise his luck or curse it. He couldn't believe what he was seeing. Not only was he watching that towering fool standing sentry over those three humans like a giant mother hen, but then Yako shows up. He almost felt sorry for the two of them. They were hopelessly outsmarted, and didn't even know it.

On the other hand, Remy found that the two of them could pose a problem should they decide to work together against him. Was that what they've been talking about? Despite his amusement at constantly eluding the big vampire and the supposedly most skilled Hunter in their ranks, a fissure of doubt snaked through his wall of confidence. Remy had heard about how the tall one and his sister had prevented Yako from eliminating the targets more than once, which explained why Remy had found the job equally difficult.

So why were they speaking with each other? Despite having acute hearing that was innate in all vampires, the statuesque sentries spoke too quietly for him to glean any information.

Finally, the Eldest Hunter turned in Remy's direction and

started away from the tall man. Remy ducked behind the short wall and waited for a few minutes until he believed the Eldest Hunter was gone. Guessing the coast was clear, he peeked over the side ... just in time to see Yako dropping off the side of the building closest to him. He hurriedly ducked back down, but the look on the Eldest Hunter's face was undeniable. He'd seen Remy. Whether he recognized him or not, Remy couldn't be sure, but he had definitely been spotted.

"Shit!" he growled. "Dammit!" If he got to his feet and ran, the tall vampire would spot him. If he stayed where he was, Yako would be on him. "No time!" He rolled over onto his stomach, then crawled along the wall until he was out of the tall vampire's periphery and more to his back. He carefully stood and took a few steps back, still watching the statuesque figure. Sure that the other man had taken no notice, Remy sprinted away.

He took one last glance over his shoulder. The big one still hadn't noticed. *Oblivious idiot.*

Remy turned forward again and his eyes widened. He dropped to his knees and leaned backwards, sliding on his back and narrowly avoiding the sword that swiped over his nose on his way down.

Acting on instinct, he rolled on his side, just in time to avoid the tip of a black sword driving into the stone beside him. Remy came to his feet and ducked another horizontal swipe. He straightened and kicked out, trying to connect with the Eldest Hunter's midsection. He missed completely and had to duck and roll yet again to avoid being beheaded. Remy lashed out with a clawed hand and Yako grabbed it. With a twist of his wrist, the Eldest Hunter sent Remy head over heels onto his back.

As soon as he hit the ground, Remy twisted his right leg around in an attempt to trip his enemy. Yako simply lifted his foot and brought it back down on his hip. Remy's neck arched as he growled in pain, just in time to see the Eldest Hunter's sword lined up with his mouth. Remy was sure it was his end, but before Yako could deliver the killing strike, he brought his sword around and down, fending off one of the other Hunters Remy had posted in the area.

Took you long enough, he thought as he struggled to free himself from the Eldest Hunter's iron grip. Despite fending off the new threat, Yako still hadn't released him his wrist.

He tried to turn on his side and kick Yako in the ankle, but it was like the bastard could read his mind. A squeeze and a twist of the wrist, and Remy was forced on his side. He curled around and swiped at Yako's leg just as the other Hunter brought his sword down.

This time, Yako was forced to release him. The Eldest Hunter spun away from his lashing claws and ducked under and around the cutting sword in one fluid movement. As much as he hated Yako, Remy couldn't deny the skill and grace at which his enemy moved. Once he came to his feet, Remy started circling around behind him.

There wasn't a place on earth as cold as Yako's expression. With little effort, the Eldest Hunter immediately had his opponent backpedaling. He turned his icy gaze on Remy, a gaze that promised his swift uncreation. "Your method of fighting betrays cowardice," Yako said.

"You go ahead and fight valiantly with all that honor you talk about. I'll see that it's remembered for as long as it takes you to decompose at my feet."

Yako made a derisive snort. Remy snarled and lunged at him. At the same time, the other Hunter—now bleeding from a half-dozen places—came in, the tip of his sword leading. Together they attacked the Eldest Hunter, and together they managed only to keep from dying.

Remy saw the glint of fear in his underling's eyes, and he could despise him for it. Despite their best efforts, they were gaining no ground and Yako had not once brought his sword to bear in a block or parry. It was a silent fight atop the roof of the building, and to

Remy's mounting fury, he realized that Yako hadn't bothered to block, not because of the other Hunter's lack of skill, but because the big vampire on the other rooftop would hear. Yako wanted this fight for himself!

"So you think you can take us both, eh?" Remy said. "Okay. Then let's go." He redoubled his efforts, coming at Yako with every bit of speed and skill he possessed. "Quit playing around and kill him, already," he said to the other Hunter, who flashed him an incredulous look before nearly being disemboweled by a swipe at his midsection.

They coordinated their efforts and struck at him, one after the other. Remy would strike from behind, and while he retreated the other Hunter would wade in for an attack. For a moment, Remy dared believe they were slipping past the Eldest Hunter's defense, but then Yako spoke.

"You are a sad example of a Hunter, and you have led another with moderate skill to his death. You are a disgrace."

He ended the statement by sidestepping a stab by the other Hunter and grabbing his wrist. In that same motion, he pulled him in close and turned, causing the already lunging Remy to score four deep slashes across his ally's chest. The Hunter cried out, then his back arched as the Eldest Hunter's sword came through his back and out his chest to stab into Remy's shoulder.

Urgh, dammit! Remy clenched his teeth at the burning pain and stumbled away. He turned and ran. No need for his underling's sacrifice to be in vain. His death would ensure Remy's survival.

As he neared the edge of the rooftop, he heeded his screaming instincts and darted left just as black steel came down, swiping the air beside him.

Remy cursed again and leaped high into the air, gliding the twenty-foot distance to another rooftop. He kicked a piece of the short wall and sent it flying at Yako. Not waiting to see the result, he continued his flight, reaching the other end of the roof and leaping over, gliding away and down to another building across the street.

He continued his zigzagging retreat, turning and leaping, dropping and gliding, till he ran out of buildings and had to take to the street. He sprinted down the sidewalk, knocking pedestrians out of the way, rounded a corner, then another. After he had turned several streets, he came to a closed restaurant and jumped up to grab a steel bar in the awning.

He curled his body up and into the awning and lay on his stomach. The black material with the solid front concealed him perfectly; just another of the infinite sushi joints across town.

For a long time he waited. Yako could be just as patient as he was, but Remy knew he could outsmart the Eldest Hunter. Feeling it was finally safe, he dropped out of the awning. After a quick check for any witnesses and seeing none, made his way toward Stanley Park.

~

Mere seconds after Remy had concealed himself in the awning of the sushi restaurant, Yako arrived on the rooftop of the supermarket around the corner. He crouched low, studying the intersection and every corner. He knew enough about Remy to realize that if the slippery Hunter had escaped his sight, it was unlikely that he would find him.

He replaced his sword in its sheath, controlling his anger at being so close to finishing this and missing the opportunity. This was the one chance he could have dealt with Remy easily. The fool had either been overconfident or it was simply coincidence that he had been watching Kafeel when Yako arrived. Either way, the next time they met, Remy would be sure to have as many Hunters that were fool enough to be convinced to aid him.

Yako cursed in his native tongue, then turned on his heel and made his way down the sloping rooftop. He needed a few minutes to collect his thoughts. Those powerful siblings wouldn't be a problem so long as he ignored the humans, but Kafeel had hinted that he would not guard them indefinitely. Yako stored that bit of information in the back of his mind for later.

His pure silver sword hadn't pierced Remy deep enough to deal any lasting damage, so he expected the coward to be healed by dusk tomorrow and lurking the streets again. Yako frowned. Would Remy even bother to pursue the targets with not only Yako, but possibly Kafeel and his sister after him?

Yako didn't like where his line of thinking was going, but it seemed more plausible by the second. Remy might flee back to Romania where he and Massius could devise some way to further undermine him.

I must be done with this, he thought. *I don't have the time to fool with him or risk his alignment with Massius.*

He made up his mind. The three remaining humans were no longer his concern. He would focus all of his attention on his current target before he could flee back to Romania. At least he didn't have the original target to worry about. Ironically, Remy had taken care of that for him …

In one fluid motion, he straightened and spun around, drawing his sword. The figure standing before him was a surprise, but not wholly unexpected.

"So, what? You're not going to say hello?" the figure said. Yako remained silent. "Oh, that's right. You probably never bothered to get my name while you were trying to kill me."

7

The Eldest Hunter's stony features were intimidating, Jelani had to admit to himself; especially with those hard, cold eyes narrowed at him. What he'd found interesting was that the eye color of every vampire he'd seen changed when they felt any type of strong emotion. This one was different, though. Even when this guy had been incapacitated by Saaya, his eyes had remained the same.

"Is there something you wish of me?" the Hunter asked, interrupting his thoughts.

"Something I *wish* of you? Can you really stand there and ask me that question? You've had me running for months. Had me living in fear and guilt. Why don't you tell me what you think I wish of you?"

The man's expression never changed. "I don't care."

The bluntness of the statement caught Jelani off guard. He was expecting a threat, or the old 'it's just business, not personal' garbage. Of course, he knew this whole situation hadn't been personal, but that didn't make it right.

"I no longer have business with you," the Hunter continued.

"So because I'm one of you, I'm no longer your business?"

Jelani felt the pit of his stomach grow hot. His hands clenched to fists at his side, and he took a deep breath to wrestle his temper under control.

"Hardly one of us, *shaquora*. You have been turned from the light, but that does not make you what I am."

"So what the hell are you, then?"

Yako's dark-eyed gaze shot straight into Jelani's eyes and seemed to see right into his soul. "More than your small mind can begin to understand. Should you manage to survive a century or two, you might; though given your choice to find me suggests your survival unlikely."

"Oh really." Jelani drew two silver daggers from his belt, mentally thanking Saaya for giving them to him before they'd left. Where was she, anyway? He'd suddenly taken a detour once he spotted this guy, but Saaya should have caught up to him by now.

He spun the blades in his hands, feeling their weight in his palms, flipping them with his fingers. His hands were the same hands he'd used his entire life, but now they were different. His fingers were so much more dexterous than before, his hands so much stronger. He had been good with daggers and short swords, preferring the smaller weapons to the lengthy ones that were difficult to conceal.

He and the Eldest Hunter circled each other. The more he moved, the more Jelani began to feel his new body. He felt the strength in his limbs, the toughness of his skin. His eyesight, hearing, and reflexes were so much sharper than before. Even here on the roof of the Safeway where there was little light, he could see his former stalker perfectly.

"You are a newly turned fledgling," Yako said, holding his sword out at his side, tip pointed toward the ground. "All fledglings feel indestructible when they first discover their re-created bodies. You would be wise to take time and contemplate your new state before you challenge me. You may find the effort not worth the risk."

"The risk of my life?" Jelani asked, studying the way the Hunter moved. His steps were measured, his posture erect. Everything about this vampire was perfectly honed. With new eyes, Jelani began to grasp just how formidable his opponent truly was.

"The risk of your newly acquired immortality."

"You seem pretty confident," Jelani said. They were circling closer to each other now.

Yako shook his head slowly, giving Jelani a look that suggested an adult making a futile effort to reason with a child. "I will only say this once more. You are no longer my concern. I have no desire to fight with you. Attack, if you must."

"Thanks for the permission," Jelani said, closing the remaining distance between them.

He held his left-handed dagger in a forward grip, and the right one in reverse. He swiped right, and the Hunter simply leaned away. He then stabbed with his left, going for the midsection. Yako thrust his hips back to avoid the thrusting silver. The Eldest Hunter countered by bringing his sword around and up.

Jelani snapped his arm back, and felt the wisp of air that followed the blade up. With a turn of his wrist, Yako angled the tip of his sword down toward the left side of Jelani's chest. He brought his right dagger around and spun away, while parrying the stabbing sword down. It was a close call.

"Nice," Jelani said, as they parted and circled again. "You're fast."

"You're slow."

"Guess I'll have to pick up the pace, then."

"Can you?"

A half smile crossed Jelani's face. "You be the judge." And then he was on the Hunter again. His blades of pure silver whirled and spun, slashed and stabbed. At first, Yako simply avoided the attacks, but as Jelani pressed, Yako began to block and parry.

"I will admit that I am impressed, child," Yako said as he leaned away from a swipe at his throat. He leaned left, away from a stab, then spun around to the right, avoiding another thrust by the opposite dagger, and brought his sword around and down with the turn. "You've adjusted quickly."

The skilled maneuver would have taken his arm off at the elbow, but Jelani followed through with his body and spun to his right, bringing his right-handed dagger around and stabbing backwards. The move sent him in a sideways role, avoiding the descending blade by a hair's breadth. He thought he'd had the Hunter, and his surprise was complete when the black clad vampire brought the sword back up and over his head, parrying the stabbing dagger away from the back of his right shoulder.

Jelani had no choice but to reverse his movement and fall backwards to the ground. He'd been quick, but the Hunter was there, his sword descending toward his exposed neck. Jelani turned on his back and brought his blades up in an **X**, stopping the sword in the space where the two blades came together. He got an up-close view of the perfectly honed edge of that silver blade.

Jelani's arms bowed slightly. This guy was not only fast, but strong. He snarled and kicked his foot up, but Yako simply used his own foot to stop it. Jelani then tried to trip the Eldest Hunter, throwing his legs out sideways in a scissor motion.

Yako jumped straight up, reversed his grip on the sword, then brought it straight down. Once again, Jelani narrowly avoided being impaled. He rolled to the side just as the sword came down, sliding effortlessly into the concrete roof. Yako snatched the blade free and resumed the offense.

The Hunter was too fast for him to come to his feet, so Jelani parried the descending sword, rolled, then stopped when the Hunter came at him from above again. He rolled back in the other direction, splashing through a small puddle on the flat rooftop. *Ugh. Disgusting.* He blocked another downward cut, then stabbed out at Yako's ankle. The Hunter simply stepped away from the dagger and turned toward Jelani's head, again reversing his grip and stabbing down.

Jelani saw the silver tip coming straight for his forehead and he rolled away again, swiping his left leg around and using the momentum to flip his body back to his feet again. He spun the dagger around in his right hand into a forward grip and brought them both down, again forming an **X**.

The blade was deflected down, but not far enough. Faster than he would have thought himself possible, Jelani's feet left the ground. He tucked them in, his knees touching his chest, and he kicked out. Both his feet scored a solid kick to the right side of the Hunter's chest.

Yako was thrown into a backward spin. The Hunter followed the motion around, drawing a concealed throwing knife from his hip and sending it spinning.

Jelani leaned back and to his left, and the blade whizzed by, scoring a cut on his shoulder. That thin cut burned like nothing he had felt before and Jelani's concentration was broken for an instant.

That instant was enough time for the Eldest Hunter to kill him.

When Jelani looked back, the tip of Yako's sword was at his throat. He brought both his daggers up to deflect, throwing the blade wide as he backpedalled.

After he'd put a comfortable distance between himself and the Hunter, he stopped. Yako hadn't pursued him. They stared at each other, Jelani in a defensive stance, Yako once again with his sword at his side, tip toward the ground. Several long moments passed before Yako sheathed the blade and turned away.

"I don't have time for this. I have business that doesn't involve schooling a foolish fledgling."

Before Jelani could respond, the Hunter was over the edge of the roof and gone.

"Well done," he heard from the far end of the roof. Saaya approached, her hips swaying hypnotically with every step. "You've adjusted quickly, to your re-created body. Most fledglings have to grow into their speed and strength, and go through a brief clumsy phase.

She stopped beside him, and Jelani eyed her. "You watched all of that?"

"What else would I do?"

"You could have ..." he trailed off. She could have, what? Helped him? She knew that he wouldn't have wanted her help.

"You men always have something to prove, even if it means your untimely demise. I'm sure you do not have the lie on your lips that suggests you wanted my help?"

"No," Jelani grumbled. "You're right." He frowned at her. "You would have let him kill me?"

A breeze drifted across the roof of the supermarket, causing a few stray strands of raven hair to sway in front of her face. Saaya closed her eyes and nodded, opening them again and smiling at him. "This was your business with him, not mine. It was your choice to challenge him. If it led to your uncreation, then your destiny would have been completed." She tilted her head as she regarded him. "Not that I wouldn't have cursed you for a fool."

Jelani lifted his hands and let them drop to his sides. "Might as well do it anyway."

"Oh? And how does it feel to be dead, yet alive?"

Jelani rubbed the hollow of his neck. The area where Yako's sword had touched him.

"Humbling."

8

F or a long time, Jelani stood in silence. Amused but patient, Saaya waited behind him. Jelani's hand unconsciously went to his throat. Saaya's words couldn't be truer. He'd never seen or fought a person with more control than that Hunter. Even with his new-found speed and strength, Jelani saw the other man's skill for what it was. Even if they had both been human, Jelani would have lost the fight no less decisively.

"But why?" he asked himself aloud. "I attacked him. Whether I live or die has no bearing on him." Jelani thought back on the fight. He could argue with himself about whether Yako could have killed him when he was on the ground, but there was no doubt about those last few moments.

If he had desired it, the Hunter could have driven his sword through Jelani's throat. "Color me confused," he muttered.

"You speak as though you are not relieved to be alive," Saaya commented.

"And you speak as though you don't know why I'm confused," he replied.

Saaya arched an eyebrow at him. "Ah, my handsome fledgling is still undergoing the change."

Jelani looked sidelong at her. "What are you talking about now?"

"Your personality, *jaan*."

She moved to the edge of the building, and Jelani found himself shamelessly admiring her every curve. Whatever he saw when he was human, it was in sharper detail. Even the *dampeal's* skin seemed more vivid and perfect.

"As you continue to change, your personality will shift, here and there."

"So, what? I'm going to be a different person entirely?"

"Not entirely. You will always be who you are, but some parts of your persona will become more pronounced, while other dormant parts of you will become active."

"That sounds ominous," Jelani said, joining her. They stood near the edge of the roof for a while, watching the occasional pedestrian pass underneath them. They seemed so fragile; so vulnerable. In his new state, there was not a doubt in his mind that Jelani could drop from the roof and kill every one of the people who passed below. A simple blow to the head, or quick snap of the neck, or simply grabbing them by the throat and dragging them helplessly to a secluded spot to empty their veins.

Jelani shook his head, horrified at the thoughts that had entered his mind. Beside him, Saaya, nodded, reading his expression.

"This is the time when you will remain who you are, or become someone or something else." She nodded her chin down at a woman passing beneath their position. "You have power unlike anything you could have imagined. You could kill the strongest, fastest human with little effort, and unless you continue down such foolish paths as you have tonight, you will live forever."

Jelani listened. Despite what he knew in his heart to be true, his mind did not want to accept it.

"I'm immortal," he said. "I have to live on blood, avoid daylight, garlic, and silver. Everyone I've ever known will age and die while I remain the same." He looked down at his hands, as if they held the truth of his words. "I don't know if I want to endure this."

"So dramatic," Saaya replied, but there was a hint of sympathy in her tone. "The death of loved ones is not something you could escape, even in your human life. Trust me when I tell you that the passage of a century or more helps to sooth the ache."

"How would you know that? You were born an immortal."

Saaya held up a finger. "You forget. I am only half a vampire, love. My mother's family is human. When she chose to accept my father's offer of immortality, she was forced to endure the very thing you fear."

"How did she deal with it?"

"She did not come to the choice of immortality easily. She considered everything my father warned her of, and thought about it for a long time. What ultimately decided the matter for her was the idea of not remaining alive to see her child grow, or to continue sharing her life with my father."

Jelani nodded. "Love. At the end of it all, when nothing else matters, it always seems to come back to love."

Saaya nodded again. "Yes. Even my father was not immune to it. Kafeel tells me that he has taken more than one human woman to his side, but it was more out of fleeting interest than anything substantial. He was always kind to them, but with my mother it was different."

Jelani was thinking of Alisha, but he kept it to himself. Not the best subject to broach with the *dampeal,* to whom he owed a great deal. Not only had she agreed to help him save Melinda, but she had also saved him an eternity of servitude to Remy. Aside from the fact that Saaya would not want to hear about the human woman, Jelani wouldn't ruin the night by mentioning the woman. He owed her that much and more.

Still.

"So," Saaya nudged him in the ribs. "Unless you're planning

on having another go at being destroyed in the first night of your re-creation, shall we go see your friends?"

Jelani wasn't sure if he wanted to or not. "Why are you so willing to take me to see them?"

"It will ease your transition." Saaya started toward the opposite side of the roof, facing the alley. "Your friends are your anchor to your human life and who you are as a person. It isn't necessary for everyone who has been turned to undergo this process, but for your personality I think it's a good idea." She narrowed her eyes at him. "And besides, if I don't take you to see them, you'll continue trying not to mention that little human girl of yours."

She dropped off the edge of the building, leaving Jelani standing there with his mouth hanging open.

"Well, alright then," he muttered to himself, and stepped over the side.

I f there was one thing Jelani got used to quickly, it was the ability to jump and fall very far. He reveled in the thirty-foot drop from the roof of the Safeway to the alley below. Though the descent only took a handful seconds, the fall would have killed him in his human life. Now, he landed with a bend of his legs, stood, and walked away.

"Looks like someone is starting to enjoy this," Saaya said, eyeing him.

"I can't deny the fun of dropping off of a roof like that," Jelani agreed.

"Allow yourself to enjoy your newfound abilities," Saaya said. "You are just discovering a new world and a new life. Not all about your new existence is filled with darkness. These few things you've discovered are but a glimpse of what you will be capable of."

"You think so?" Jelani asked. "I mean, I'm only a *shaquora*," his mind gave a little shudder at the realization that the word he spoke had a much clearer meaning to him than before. "I thought turned vampires were only a bit stronger and faster than a human."

"That is true to an extent," Saaya replied. "A turned vampire is physically superior to a human, but not by a great deal. I believe you've already experienced this first hand."

Jelani nodded, remembering the attacks on him while he was still human. "Yes, but I can't deny that a bit of luck played into my survival."

"I'm sure it did." She smiled at him. It was a delicious, seductive smile. "As for your re-creation; you are more than most, since you carry some of my essence in you."

"How so?"

"Would you have me ruin the fun of your self-discoveries?"

Jelani nodded. "I like surprises, but not when it comes to my survival."

"Smart," Saaya replied, "but I think it best that you discover your differences on your own. Besides, I'm not the hand-holding type. You wouldn't want me to bore you." She winked.

Despite his situation, he found that he did not want that to happen. How had his feelings toward her changed so much? She could still kill him relatively as easily as before, but he felt no fear toward her now. Perhaps it was the result of a better understanding of her on a subconscious level?

"Wouldn't want that," he said.

"Good," she replied cheerfully. "Then let us go to your friends and be done with it."

Jelani shrugged. "If you say so."

9

W hen the reality show Daniel had once described as the most annoying crap to mar television continued without comment, Wen knew that her fiancé's mind was someplace else.

"Babe?" She leaned on the back of the couch and peeked over his shoulder. "This show growing on you?"

"Hm?" Daniel glanced up at her, then at the television. He frowned and picked up the remote control. "Ugh. This garbage again." He changed the channel.

"You okay?" Wen poured water into the diffuser on the mantle-piece, shook several drops of scented oil into it, then replaced the lid. The room quickly smelled of spring rain by the time she came around the couch to sit next to him.

Daniel draped an arm around her shoulders and she leaned in to him, resting her head on his chest. Outside, rain fell hard enough for them to hear it pattering on the windows. It was perfect ambience for a night of TV by the fireplace, with the living room filling with the scents blowing in the mist of the diffuser.

"Yeah, I'm okay," he replied.

"So now we're lying to each other," Wen said, looking up at

him. Those light brown, half-moon shaped eyes could always melt his iciest mood.

"Alright, you got me." He leaned down and kissed her on the forehead. "Yeah, I'm a little bummed out."

"Jelani?" He knew Wen hated to mention it, but she knew that was what was on his mind.

"Yeah," he said, his frown deepening. "Saaya keeps giving me the runaround, saying that Jelani would be okay soon, and that he'd be back. It's been over a month, and still nothing."

"When was the last time you spoke to her?"

"About a week ago. So far, she's been stopping by once a week to let me know how he's doing. It's actually kind of surprising, considering who she is."

"I won't say that she doesn't creep me out, but there's a level or morality in her that's either unfamiliar, or she doesn't understand it." Wen shrugged. "I also don't think she's figured out how she feels about him."

"Do you think he's dead and she just hasn't told me?"

Wen could see the barely concealed desperation in his eyes but she knew better than to lie to him. "I don't know. But I don't think she would go to all this trouble to lie to you about it. That wouldn't make sense."

Daniel nodded. "True. And why would she need to, anyway? It's not like she would need to be afraid of me being angry or anything. The woman could snap me like a twig."

Wen's eyes widened. "Don't say things like that!"

"It's true."

"I don't care. Just don't say things like that. I don't like it."

Daniel squeezed her shoulder. "I'm sorry."

Wen poked out her bottom lip playfully. "It's okay. I think Jelani is alive, but I hope he'll recover from whatever was done to him."

"Yeah. I wish I could say I knew what happened, but Melinda dealt me a pretty solid blow to the head. I've never been knocked out before, but the headache afterwards was enough to let me know I didn't enjoy it."

Wen shivered. "I still can't believe Melinda is …" she leaned closer to Daniel, "a vampire." She whispered as though just mentioning them would bring vampires crashing through their window. Daniel couldn't blame her. For all he knew, that might just happen.

"I know. It's pretty unbelievable. First Claire, then Melinda." Mentioning her name had Daniel thinking about his longtime friend, and short time girlfriend who had been found dead in the woods near Electronic Arts, where they worked. She had been found with violent trauma to the neck, and almost empty of blood. The police had been puzzled about the situation, but of course Daniel knew better.

He sighed. The news of Claire's death had hit him hard and it was still a sore spot. Melinda had been more of an acquaintance than a close friend, but Daniel still had known her. For a short while, she and Jelani had dated before his best friend realized that his feelings were for Alisha.

Whatever Daniel had felt for Melinda's fate couldn't possibly compare to what Jelani must have felt.

Man, where the hell are you?

The sound of keys rattling outside the door, followed by the click of the door lock interrupted his thoughts. The door opened and Alisha stepped in.

"Hey, Wen. Hey, Daniel." She sniffed the air. "Spring rain. Nice."

"Hey, girl," Wen replied, leaning away from Daniel to half turn and look over the couch. They hadn't heard Alisha's normal cheerfulness since Jelani's disappearance."How was your day?"

"Same as yesterday, except it's today."

Wen got up from the couch and went over to give her closest friend a hug. "How're you holding up?"

Alisha glanced at Daniel. Getting the message, he got up from the couch and grabbed his keys and a book. "Been wanting to start this since I got it last week. They started turning on the fireplace in the lobby, so I think I'll just head down there."

"See you in a bit, babe," Wen said, giving him a hug and a kiss. "Please don't leave the building."

"You know you don't have to worry about that," Daniel replied. He stepped out the door and caught a glimpse of Alisha's shoulders trembling, and Wen reaching up to give her a tight hug. Wen saw him hesitate at the door, and waved her hand at him to go. He closed the door and went down the hall to the elevators.

While waiting, he thought about what he was going to do. He remembered Jelani mentioning that he'd finished all of his projects, which was good because Daniel had no way of checking his friend's email to see what jobs he hadn't finished.

The bigger problem would be Jelani's family. If his friend didn't turn up soon, or at all, Daniel would have to figure out what to say to Jelani's family back in the States. This whole situation could get really complicated if Jelani didn't make an appearance soon. His family would become rightfully concerned, the police would be involved, and everything would go downhill from there.

He stepped out of the elevator and found a comfortable leather sofa chair right next to the fireplace. "I sure hope you show up soon, man," he said. He'd been speaking to himself, so his heart nearly stopped when he heard a response.

"Now's as good a time as any."

Daniel was up and out of his chair. By the time he turned around, he was on the other side of the room.

"Dude, you nearly gave me a heart attack! Don't do that shit!"

Over a dozen feet away, Jelani stood behind the sofa chair. Daniel watched him, waiting for his heartbeat to slow. He liked to think he wasn't the easiest person to sneak up on, but despite the quiet of the room, Jelani had come up directly behind him.

Daniel tilted his head and studied the man on the other side of the chair. "You alright?" he asked. Jelani looked the same, but there was something different about him that Daniel couldn't place. "You look healthy enough, but from what Saaya told me, you've been through a lot this past month. You been in a coma or something?"

Jelani smiled. It was a regretful smile. "Coma? You could probably say I was in a coma, yeah."

"You seem different." He didn't know why, but Daniel felt the need to keep his distance. "Anything happen to you that you wanna share with me?"

"Unfortunately, yes."

There was a stretch of silence.

"Um," Daniel tried again. "So, what happened? We've all been worried about you. Alisha's up there probably crying right now. She's been crying almost every night since you disappeared."

Jelani looked up at the ceiling as if he could see the two women, ten floors above. "I feel bad about that." He looked back at Daniel. "I've just awakened. It's been a long night."

"Awakened?" Daniel smirked at him. "I don't think I've ever heard you say awakened before. A little unusual, don't you think?"

"Yeah, well things like that seem to be happening to me lately. I don't know how far it will go."

Daniel's palms were clammy and his heart beat rapidly. Jelani closed his eyes for a few seconds and Daniel could have sworn a look crossed his face like someone who had just smelled something particularly delicious.

"Look, man," Jelani said. "We've always been straight up with one another, right? I don't see any reason for that to change, now."

Daniel slowly shook his head. "No, man. No. No. You're not going to tell me what I think you are." He hadn't realized he was backing away until his back touched the wall. Behind the chair, Jelani hadn't moved.

"What do you want me to say?" Jelani spread his hands. "What *can* I say? All I remember was that the son of a bitch bit me and drained so much of my blood that I eventually blacked out. I'm

having weird dreams that I think are Saaya's childhood or something, and next thing I know, I wake up with a massive headache
and probably more confused than the day I was born. I open my
eyes to see Saaya standing next to the bed I'm lying in, in a room I
don't recognize, only to find out I've been asleep for over a
month."

Daniel saw the same sincerity in his eyes there had always
been. "Stay over there if it makes you feel more comfortable,"
Jelani said, leaning on the back of the sofa chair Daniel had been
sitting in. The move seemed more an effort to appear normal than
an actual move for comfort. "But as far as I'm concerned, you're
still my best friend. I have no intention of harming you."

"It's not your intentions that have me concerned," Daniel said,
thinking of their earlier encounters with Melinda. She had done her
best not to kill them, but in the end she couldn't fight the will of
the one who had turned her. If Saaya hadn't been there, they would
have been dead.

Jelani must have been thinking along the same line. "I've
already ... eaten." When he saw the horrified look on Daniel's
face, he chuckled. "Let me clarify. Saaya has some packs of um,
food, in her fridge. I don't know if it's donated or synthetic or
what, but it satisfied my appetite. If that wasn't the case, I wouldn't
have come here and she probably wouldn't have let me anyway."

"You'll have to pardon me if this is just a little too much,
Jelani."

"We can pardon each other, then. How do you think I feel
about all this?"

"How *do* you feel?" Daniel asked.

Jelani hopped over the back of the chair and dropped onto the
soft cushion. "Got a minute?"

10

J elani sat watching his friend mentally argue with himself on whether or not to trust him. Though he hadn't said the words, Jelani had all but confirmed that he'd been changed. He thought about all the challenges and triumphs and fun he and Daniel had shared. Part of Jelani was hurt that his friend didn't trust him, but he had to remind himself that the circumstances were unique, to put it lightly.

Finally, Daniel spoke. "I hope you understand that I'm a little uncomfortable at the moment."

Jelani nodded. "I know, and I don't blame you one bit. I'd feel the same if the situation was reversed."

Daniel seemed to come to a decision and crossed the room, sitting down in the chair opposite Jelani. Daniel never took his eyes off of him, and there was a slight stiffness to his posture. "Guess I'll get comfortable. It's not like I could get away from you anyway."

Jelani flinched at that. "Now that kinda hurt, dude. Despite all that's happened, I'm still relatively the same guy."

"I know, and I don't mean to be this way toward you." Daniel shook his head, but still didn't take his eyes off Jelani for even a second. "But all that we've learned so far suggests that not every-thing could be in your control."

Jelani shrugged. "Fair point."

"What does it feel like?" Daniel asked, and Jelani saw that his friend was relaxing a little.

"What does it feel like?" Jelani repeated. "It feels like nothing you can imagine. It's hard to put into words. My body feels the same, but much stronger and lighter and faster that it's ridiculous."

Outside, raindrops started to patter against the glass, then a few minutes later it came in earnest. Jelani looked out the tall windows at the roaring showers. "It's really coming down out there."

"Is it just physical changes that you've experienced?" Daniel asked, ignoring the weather.

"No." Jelani still gazed out the windows, his thoughts both far and near. "My mind feels sharper than it's ever been, and my emotions are pretty solid, if that's a way to describe it." He looked back to Daniel. "It's like I have every part of myself under tight control." He didn't want to say what he was about to, but he had to be honest with his friend. "There is one exception, though."

"Blood," Daniel said.

"Blood," Jelani confirmed. "It's referred to as the thirst, and believe me when I tell you, it's a debilitating experience. When I first awoke tonight it didn't hit me for about ten or twenty minutes, but then I was doubled over in a pain like nothing you've ever experienced. It was like acid or lava was coursing through my veins and my stomach. It's enough to drive you crazy."

"So if I'd been there when you first woke up?" Daniel asked.

Jelani was expecting the question. "Look, man. I don't want to go down the road of 'what ifs' and speculating my resistance to the thirst. You weren't there, and Saaya is helping me adjust." He sighed. "I don't like what I've been turned into, but if I thought for a minute I didn't have control of myself, I wouldn't be sitting here in front of you. Despite the stories and the movies, this change doesn't make you evil."

"Why can't you say it?" Daniel asked. "Why can't you just say that you're a vampire? You keep tap dancing around the word."

Jelani held up a hand as if to stop him. "Just … just don't say that word to me, please."

"Why not?" Daniel pressed. "It doesn't change who you are, does it?"

"If you want my honest answer, I don't know." Jelani looked Daniel in the eyes, and willed his nature to come to the surface. The only thing that kept his friend from jumping out of his seat was the vice grip he had on the arm of the chair.

"What do you see, Daniel?"

"Your eyes. They're … glowing. They're glowing in a kind of purplish color. Like lavender."

He was unsettled. Good. "Look, man, I want you to be clear about something. I am and will always be your friend, but you need to know what's happening and what I am." He looked back out the windows again, seeking comfort in the sheets of rain falling from the sky.

"In time, I'll gain a stronger level of control. I know because I can feel it. But for now, I've got to be careful. All of this is new and sometimes a little confusing. I can't take any chances around you or anyone else."

"I get you," Daniel said. An uncomfortable silence stretched for several moments before Daniel cleared his throat. "Uh, what are you going to do now?"

"I'm going to kill the one who turned me," Jelani replied. He saw that the flat, matter-of-fact way he'd said it had caught Daniel off guard.

"I've never heard you say anything like that before, Jelani."

"That's one part of me that's changed. I've only been awake for several hours, but it seems like as time passes, my thoughts and actions are becoming more direct." He changed the subject. "How's Wen?"

"She's doing ok," Daniel said. "Worried about you."

"You're a lucky guy. You really are."

Daniel nodded. "I know. I can't tell you how much it's stressing me out, worrying about her safety with that guy out there." Jelani's expression darkened, and Daniel recoiled. "Dude, you've got to stop doing that."

"Doing what?" Jelani asked.

"Your eyes. They're glowing in that purplish color again. It's really kind of scary."

"Sorry." Jelani willed himself to calm down. "Sometimes I forget things. I'm still getting used to all this."

"I still can't believe it."

Jelani nodded. "Yeah, I know. I promise you this, though. I won't rest until I get ahold of that son of a bitch. I'm going to handle him real proper for what he's put all of us through." He ran a hand over his clean-shaven head and leaned forward, propping his elbows on his knees. "I've been going back and forth with myself all night trying to decide whether or not to come see you all. In the end Saaya convinced me."

Daniel's eyebrows rose. "Now that's a surprise. I would have thought she'd try to whisk you away or something."

"You sure about that?" Jelani responded. "If she was planning to do that, she wouldn't have been keeping you in the loop about me, would she?"

"Good point," Daniel conceded. "You um, want to come see the girls? It would do them good to see that you're ok."

"I don't know," Jelani said, holding his head in his hands. "I'm not sure it's a good idea for them to see me like this yet. You're still not all the way comfortable with me. Imagine them."

"I'm getting there," Daniel replied.

"I know. And believe me, it means a lot that you're even sitting here with me, given what I am, now."

Daniel thought about it. "Well. Maybe you can let me talk to them first, and give them a heads up."

"That would probably be best."

"I think after the initial shock, they'll be fine."

Jelani looked at Daniel, thankful for having such a good friend. Not many people would trust him after the change he'd undergone. When it came down to it, Jelani had become an apex predator, and his friends were lower on the food chain. That thought sent a mental chill through him that he had to shake off.

"I appreciate that. I really want to see Alisha, but now I don't know what's going to happen. I doubt we can be together. I don't know how that would work out."

Daniel sighed. "I honestly don't know what to say."

Jelani glanced out the windows. The rain was starting to lighten. "What time is it?"

Daniel pulled his phone out of his pocket. "Quarter to midnight."

Never in the deepest corner of his imagination did Jelani ever believe his life would depend on getting indoors before daylight.

"I'd better go," he said. Though he didn't say why, Daniel's expression said that he knew.

"Yeah. I guess you should." They stood. "Oh, hold on a sec." Daniel pointed at the ceiling as if they could see through it. "You need your computer. I've had no way to check your email and stuff, so I don't know what's going on with your web business. I've been covering for you at EA, but that's all I've been able to do."

In the midst of discovering his new existence and the night's events, Jelani had forgotten all about his business. "Yeah, I guess I still need to make money. Not planning to just dig a hole in the ground to live in."

"What about those things they live in?"

Jelani was already shaking his head. "No. Never. They're called covens, and I will never live with a bunch of vampires. Ever."

A sad look crossed Daniel's face. "Jelani. I'm really sorry this happened to you."

"Yeah. Thanks, man. I don't know what all this is going to mean, or what's going to happen, but right now my focus is keeping you all safe."

"You know I've got your back."

Through the rock that Jelani's emotions were becoming, he felt a surge of gratitude toward his friend. "I don't think I've got any words for how much I appreciate that, Daniel. Thanks. I mean it."

"I know. Just hold on a sec. I'll go grab your computer and throw some clothes in a bag for you."

Jelani smiled. "I wish I had something else to give you instead of just one thank you after another."

"Don't worry about it. That's what friends are for." Daniel left in the elevator, and Jelani went to the tall windows. The rain had lightened, but it still came down heavy enough for large droplets to spatter against the glass. Saaya was out there somewhere. She'd told him she would be nearby, just in case, but he could feel her, just as she could feel him.

When she had passed some of her vampiric essence to him to counteract what Remy had done, it formed a connection between them that he still didn't fully understand. He could sense her when she was nearby, and to a small degree, feel what she was feeling.

What's my next move? he thought. After his encounter with Yako, Jelani thought it best to leave that situation alone, at least for the time being. He appreciated that the Hunter hadn't followed through with the stroke that could have killed him, but Jelani still hadn't forgotten about all those nights running and living in fear.

Remy was going to die. That was a given. Jelani planned to go after the Hunter that had done this to him as soon as he was ready. Was Remy as skilled and powerful as Yako? Jelani couldn't say, but he doubted it. He could sense Remy as well, and he hated it. The last thing he needed was that one in his head, but there was nothing he could do about it, save killing the bastard. Jelani planned on settling that matter soon.

His mind went to Melinda. What would he do about her?

Perhaps after Remy was dead, Melinda would be freed and could attempt to lead as normal a life as was possible. Maybe … maybe what? Jelani searched his feelings. Had fate pushed the two of them in front of each other again? Would Melinda forgive Jelani for what had happened to her? Given the circumstances, would it be a good idea to at least try to contact her?

All of these thoughts fell away when he heard the ding of the elevator, and turned around to see the doors open, and Alisha standing there.

11

T he sun rose and fell, and with it came the dawn of a new day and dusk in its departure.

As was his habit, Yako had been up long before the sun had disappeared below the western horizon. The power of the fiery orb in the sky did not touch him in the twilight hours that linked day with night. As a pureblood, Yako had been born a vampire, and this was the most he would ever see of daylight.

High above the city of Vancouver, atop the Royal Bank of Canada building, he saw the far-reaching hands of darkness stretch from one end of the horizon to the other, enveloping the world in its lightless grasp.

On rare occasions when he allowed his mind to wander, Yako wondered what daylight actually looked like. There were paintings and television that depicted the day in all its splendor, but those were superficial experiences. What did it feel like to walk in the light of the sun without being incinerated?

He had heard the occasional story of a newly turned *shaquora* that committed suicide by walking into the sun, not able to endure an endless life of darkness. Most purebloods scoffed, thinking of the burned fledglings as weak and undeserving of the gift of immortality.

In his youth Yako had believed the same. But after only a few years into his life as a Hunter he had learned differently. Not all humans endured the change in the same way, and things that were most important to them often carried over into their re-creation. Those that revered the sun found eternal separation from it unbearable. A *shaquora* fledgling had once told him, "better to die in the sun's light than live an immortal life without it."

Yako had respected him for that. Death was not something everyone embraced. Even among the warrior class many fought more to not be killed than to achieve their objective. Not that there was anything wrong with not being killed.

He returned his attention to the northwest; the direction of the home of his former target. He still didn't have much to go on, so he figured it might do to stay near this location in case Remy appeared. There was really no other reason for the other Hunter to be in the city, except to eliminate the remaining targets.

"Are you hunting humans, or a quick route to Sinaia?" he thought aloud. The more he thought about it, the more it seemed likely that Remy was indeed waiting for the next flight to Romania. Yako's lycan friend Darren had agreed to keep watch on the airport, specifically for flights to Romania. So far there had been no sign of Remy.

"How long can you hide in your little hole?" he muttered under his breath. It didn't matter. Yako was patient, and if he needed to wait for a year till Remy resurfaced to get on that plane, then Remy had a year to live before Yako sent him to oblivion.

From the corner of his eye, he saw movement on the rooftop of a building across the street. It was that girl again. The first time he'd seen her, Yako had thought it was just another vampire who might have taken a casual interest in him. The second time he knew it was a fledgling that belonged to Remy. One of Darren's pack had informed him that Remy had abducted a female who'd had an intimate relationship with Jelani. It was a classic but effective tactic. Lure the target from hiding with something or someone important to them. In this case, a lover.

Yako kept still and looked over at her, moving only his eyes. Darkness meant nothing to a vampire's sight, and since she was only across the street Yako could see her well enough. She was barely concealed around the wall of the building, leaning out and stealing glances at him.

It seemed comical that Remy had sent such a deplorably unskilled woman to track him. But as the nights passed, the woman had continued to spy on him, showing little ability to hide herself. Yako narrowed his eyes. Even a human could be better than this. Remy probably wanted her to bait him into following her into some trap the fool had lain.

It was tempting. The fledgling was the only active link Yako had to Remy's whereabouts, but he was not about to walk into a trap like some simpleminded idiot. Perhaps he would have one of his subordinates that was better at mind compulsion extract some information from her. Not all vampires were vulnerable to mind compulsion but most were; a newly turned vampire even more so.

Thinking of the fledgling *shaquora* brought his thoughts to the former target, Jelani. Yako had surprised himself by holding the killing stroke. Never had Yako allowed someone who'd attacked him to live. The Eldest Hunter was not given to mercy but perhaps something else had stayed his hand. Respect.

When he'd thought about it, the fledgling had come after him to stop Yako from killing his friends as much as for revenge for being hunted. He nodded to himself. He respected Jelani for challenging him on behalf of those who could not, and also because the young vampire had skill. Although there was no way he would defeat Yako, Jelani had demonstrated remarkable skill in only his first night reawakened.

The Eldest Hunter found that he hoped Jelani would not challenge him again. He had no intention of holding back a second time, and Yako found that he was very much interested in seeing how the fledgling would develop.

What was odd was that Remy had not asserted control over him, as was normally the case when a vampire turned a human. Yako could tell that Jelani was acting of his own volition, and this was curious.

He grunted. A fledgling to lure him into a trap, a cravenly Hunter to kill, another fledgling running loose, and an Elder to un-create. It seemed that Yako had a mountain to climb and he wasn't sure where to start. He felt the phone strapped to his upper arm vibrate and he clicked his earpiece on.

"What have you found?"

"Massius has called on Remy to return, but only when it is safe to do so." It was Mariska's voice on the other end of the line.

"Why?"

"Massius believes that if he can get Remy to issue his verbal report that you have betrayed the North American coven and the High Council, he can have you condemned to uncreation."

It was plausible. Vicken and perhaps Lemanda, may hold him in their favor, but they were not the sole voice of the High Council. There was only so much Vicken could say, or do, in his position. Besides, if Yako couldn't demonstrate his ability to keep his affairs in hand, he was not suited to the position to begin with.

"The others?"

There was a stretched silence before Mariska spoke again. "Hunters Lydia and Barakus have gone to the ancient library as you suggested. They discovered the history for themselves, and Barakus's fury has been tempered by Lydia, but barely. Both have too much fire."

"Their fire will remain contained by the Elders' superiority," Yako said. "They are not fools."

"But they are not patient, either."

"Their fate is tied to their patience. They will live or die. What of Reed?"

A longer pause. "He has also visited the library, and has since sought to meet with me several times. He is reckless and inexperienced, and it will lead to his uncreation."

Yako heard a hint of irritation in Mariska's voice. "You think it a mistake that I laid claim on him?"

"It is not for me to question the Eldest Hunter's motives or actions. I only inform."

Yako watched the female fledgling leave her hiding spot and head east. Whatever else may be the case he was certain Remy had taken up a temporary residence somewhere in that direction, and possibly not far away.

"Inform me of your opinion."

"He is reckless. Mostly due to his inexperience. Still, there is potential. Should he survive this he may be an asset. You may also like to know that Massius had not expected nor was pleased to see Reed alive. And when informed that you had laid claim on his life in exchange for Nikko's sacrifice, he was visibly angered."

Livid, was more likely the case. It was an audacious move, considering Yako had left the country without their consent and had sidestepped protocol in not bringing the matter before the Elders. Yako imagined Vicken's amusement disguised as irritation. He imagined Lemanda was just simply amused.

"Reed is eager to prove himself an asset," Mariska continued, "But his efforts must be curtailed if he is to survive and not bring ruin upon our efforts."

"You are Second," Yako replied. "In my absence, you are in command. Reign in his efforts and temper his impetuousness. If he proves to be resistant and poses a threat, eliminate him."

"It will be done, Eldest Hunter. One way or another."

Yako switched off the earpiece and stood. He knew that Mariska was taking a risk in contacting him at this hour. It was night where he was, but across the ocean, it was the middle of the day. Unless there was some pressing issue, vampires slept through the day. Mariska would be discrete, of course. It was one of the reasons he trusted her.

He considered his options. If he left for Sinaia to wait for Remy, his underlings would spot him and report back. Or he could simply let Remy escape back to Sinaia and have Mariska move on him. Aside from himself there was no one better suited to the job than his Second.

It was a viable option, but Yako didn't like leaving a job to someone else. He cast that notion aside as a last resort. Better to take Remy before he managed to get back across the sea.

He looked back to the east, in the direction the fledgling female *shaquora* had gone. Logically, he knew he was being baited. But his instincts were leaning on him that there might be more to her appearance than Yako had considered. He made up his mind to have answers from her the next time she appeared.

Having made that decision, he cast the woman from his mind and turned his attention back to Remy. Yako didn't bother to consider visiting the coven for any news. Although he'd heard of Remy's disgraceful failure on Grouse Mountain that had resulted in the uncreation of six Hunters, Yako was certain the coward still had allies who would take note of the Eldest Hunter's sudden appearance. He was on his own against a foe who was unrivaled at evasion.

A thought occurred to him. The new fledgling, Jelani, had come after him on his first night of awakening. It might not be inconceivable that the impetuous *shaquora* might go after Remy as well.

Yako allowed himself a hint of a smirk. What made that possibility humorous was that Jelani was already so well adapted to his new existence, he may already had the abilities to kill Remy.

Still. He doubted the fledgling would actually catch Remy, but Yako might be able to use the situation to his advantage and cast a larger net to ensnare the cravenly Hunter.

He liked the idea, but there was one snag. It meant he would have to keep watch not only for Remy, but Jelani as well. It was already enough of a chore trying to catch up to Remy. The last thing Yako felt like doing was trying to track both of them.

He stood and looked out at the brightly lit city below. There were some missing pieces to this puzzle that he had not yet found. Why had Remy had not asserted control of his newly turned fledgling? How had Jelani awakened so soon and become this dangerous already? Regardless of how skilled Jelani had been in his human life, he should not have been as deadly this soon after being turned.

Yako stared down at the streets below without seeing them. He thought of the blow Jelani had landed on his chest. The kick was harmless enough, but it had been a long time since anyone had been able to make solid contact with Yako in a fight.

He made up his mind. Like it or not, coordinating his efforts with an unwitting Jelani was his best option.

12

I f there was one thing Remy disliked, it was being hunted. It was a new experience and he absolutely hated it. A Hunter was not supposed to be the hunted, but that was exactly what was happening to him because of that bastard Eldest Hunter. Remy had always been confident that he could best Yako in a fight, but he'd been forced not only to call for help but to retreat with a stinging injury, another dead Hunter from his command, and wounded pride.

Remy scowled. He might be forced to admit that he couldn't kill Yako in a straight up fight, but he still had no doubts that he was smarter than the fool. Fine. Let him revel in his physical superiority. Remy would defeat the idiot with his mind. There was no such thing as playing dirty, only surviving.

He felt a wave of resentment targeted at him and knew that Melinda was close. He delved into her mind as much as he could, feeling the strong resistance from his newly turned fledgling. He had to give her credit. She had a strong will to fight him every time he entered her thoughts, but the only thing she ever really could hide from him were the trivial things from her former life that he cared nothing about anyway.

His amusement at her futile efforts at privacy reminded Remy of his newest turned fledgling. He wondered if that female half-breed had found a way to shield Jelani from his influence. Her brother, perhaps? A simple *skiek* had no such power, so it had to be her full-blooded brother who was causing the interference. The only other explanation was that Jelani was far enough away that Remy could not establish control over him.

Remy still couldn't puzzle out the source of the two siblings' interest in a simple human; an interest that would place them in direct conflict with a Hunter.

Remy pursed his lips. Purebloods typically had no desire to be involved in Hunter business, yet here was a half-blood female and her pureblood brother involving themselves in this business, risking their immortal existence for a simple human.

Somewhere in the back of Remy's mind, he knew that those two had taken little risk to themselves, given his multiple encounters with them. That they were unusually strong was a point he couldn't, in good sense, deny, but it mattered little. After he dealt with Yako and the rest of the targets, he would unravel the mystery of those two. If he was still interested, that is.

A strong wave of hatred penetrated his musings. "Ah, my dear Melinda has returned." He didn't bother to look at the woman standing behind him. "I take it you've failed me again?"

"Yes I have," she said, not shrinking from the truth.

That's interesting. Remy turned around. He couldn't deny the woman's strength of will, even if it did amuse and annoy him at the same time.

"You haven't forgotten that I'm not inclined to react positively to failure, right?"

"I must admit that I am unsure," Melinda replied. "You appear to have a fair amount of self-esteem, yet your recent track record would suggest a self-loathing unparalleled."

In an instant, he was right in front of her, left hand crossed over his right shoulder. In the moment of pause they stared at each other and he saw no fear in her eyes of what was coming. His hand whipped out in a backhanded slap, and she spun to the ground. When she started to rise, he kicked her.

"Lie there," he commanded. "Lie on the floor like a worm and think about how I could crush you with little more effort than if you were still a useless human."

Remy felt her mind. A seething hatred boiled in her that was enough to throttle him if made physical. He smirked. "If only you were more competent at the little errands I assign you, I wouldn't be forced to punish you so." He tilted his head. "Perhaps after fifty to a hundred years of servitude, you'll become more proficient at your duties, hmm?" A spark of fear shot through her mind, but it was quickly stamped out. Remy was impressed with the woman's discipline and mental strength.

"Of course," she purred, causing Remy's smug expression to slide away. "I've got an eternity to learn how better to please you." Her hair obscured her face, but her tone was clearly mocking.

Well, he could play her little game too. "Why not start now," he said. "With you learning how to please me, that is." He crouched over her and threw her onto her back. Her eyes pulsated with crimson hatred. He leaned over her until the tips of their noses touched. "We need not have so formal a master and servant relationship. Why not have fun?"

Her eyes narrowed, but she smiled. "Lie on your back and close your eyes, and I'll give you a big surprise." Her lips twitched and the tip of an elongated fang dipped below the left corner of her upper lip. It was like looking into the eyes of a succubus.

Fury overtook him and he slapped her. Melinda's head snapped to the side, then she looked back at him with an expression mixed with pain and amusement. Remy's nostrils flared and he slapped her again, then again. It went on for several minutes and by the time his anger was fully spent, bloody streaks were scattered across Melinda's face. He sensed pain in her thoughts but also, what? Satisfaction?

He ripped her blouse off, and studied the woven designs of her bra. "You'll please me now," he said. Whether or not she wanted it was irrelevant. He would take satisfaction in forcing her to submit to him.

Melinda's eyes smoldered. "Mmm. It's been a while, love. I suppose I can envision Jelani while you gyrate through your little love seizures."

He roared and lifted her, slinging her across the room to crash into the wall. By the time she had crumpled to the floor he was looming over her, red eyes glowing. "If it is death you so desire, I will oblige you soon enough." He grabbed her by the throat and lifted her off the floor. He felt the reflex in her mind to reach up and grasp his hand but he compelled her to keep her hands at her sides.

For several heartbeats he held her aloft, feet dangling several inches above the dingy carpet. He brought her face close to his and smiled. "I promise I will make your reunion with the sun a memorable one." This time there was no retort, no defiance. She might not fear un-creation, but all vampires feared the sun's burning kiss.

"The day has come and I don't want you here with me. Go. Sleep in the sewer or dig a hole and jump in it. I don't care which, but return with the night." He looked her up and down. "And make sure you're cleaned up and looking pretty." With a casual flick of his arm he tossed her aside and went to sit by the window. He made a lazy motion with his hand, dismissing her. "You may go now. I look forward to seeing that," he leaned his head sideways and cast her a bored look, "rather average little face of yours soon." Oh, how the woman wafted abhorrence at him. He sniggered.

"And see that you do your hair and nails. Just because you're a filthy little *shaquora* doesn't mean you have to look like one." He waved his hand again and looked out the window. "Begone. The stench of your recent humanity clings to you like the grime of an unwashed street urchin."

He heard the door open and slam shut and he grinned. She was strong, he had to grant, but he would eventually break her. He had all the time in the world and it was too much fun. While he gazed out the window his satisfaction was shadowed by her mention of Jelani. The fact that he was somehow outside of Remy's influence and that Melinda still desired him chafed at the Hunter. No matter. Once he was able to exert control of his other fledgling he would have hundreds of years of touting them in front of each other and denying them what they wanted most.

The smug expression returned to his face. That was a game he didn't think he would ever tire of.

13

J elani lost himself in the eyes of the beautiful woman who stood staring back at him. He wanted to go to her and he could see the same feelings in her eyes, yet they both hesitated. It was like there were two magnets between them; one pulling them toward each other while the other pushed them away.

The trance was broken when the elevator doors started to close. She blinked, then stuck her arm out, causing the doors to open so she could step out. For a time, they stood silently facing each other in the dimly lit lobby, the pattering rain outside the only sound between them.

Jelani searched his mind for something to say but came up with nothing. Finally, after a few moments longer Alisha found her wits enough to break the silence.

"Hello, Jelani," she said hesitantly.

"Hi Alisha."

Silence.

Alisha slid a nonexistent lock of hair behind her ear, then chewed her bottom lip.

"You look great, as always," Jelani said.

She looked down at herself. "I'm wearing pajamas and slippers."

"And you work 'em like a champ."

A tiny smile creased her nervous face and the tension eased a bit. She glanced at the strap of the backpack on her shoulder as if remembering it was there. "Daniel came to get this for you, but I wanted to bring it down." She unslung it and stood there. With his newly sharpened senses Jelani could feel the fear drifting from her like a vapor. The predatory nature of his new existence wanted to taste her blood; all of it. Jelani shook his head, doing his best to hide his self-revulsion.

"If you would feel better leaving it there, I can wait till you're gone before I come get it."

Alisha rolled her eyes, but the fear was still there. He appreciated her show of confidence in him, lightly felt or not. He wasn't sure how much he trusted himself, which scared him. A lot.

"That's ridiculous," she said. "I didn't come down here to just say *hi,* drop the bag, and run back upstairs."

"You could toss it to me, then."

This time she laughed. "Quit being silly."

"You like it when I'm silly."

She looked at him with those beautiful hazel eyes. Even from across the room he could see the tiny details of her eyes. The way her pupils expanded and contracted to regulate the amount of light to the retina. Unconsciously, he looked closer and saw through the tiny, dark opening in the center of her left eye, all the way in.

He shook his head and gasped. Too much. That was just too much to see. If he looked hard enough, could he see every blood vessel, every neuron? Her brain? He shook his head again.

"What's wrong?" she asked, frowning.

"Um, nothing. Just a random thought."

"You looked like you were about to be sick."

"Don't worry about it. How have you been?"

Alisha leaned forward as if to take a step, then stopped. Still hesitant.

"We could have this conversation by phone, if it would make you feel safer." Jelani held out his hands. "I totally understand."

That seemed to make up her mind. Alisha made a visible effort to cross the lobby. He watched her set his computer backpack on one of the sofa chairs and stand there, waiting.

Several heartbeats passed, then he took a careful step toward her. He saw her lean backward, and she took half a step away. He doubted she was even aware of the movement. He stopped, held out his hands, and waited. She took a deep breath, then straightened and gave him a nod.

He took another step, then another, approaching her as though she was a deer. Finally, he stood in front of her, and they looked into each other's eyes. He saw fear and hesitance in those hazel orbs, but he also saw the same love he'd seen before his transformation. She leaned forward, stopped, then reached out. He stepped in and she crushed her body into his. He held her as her shoulders trembled while she sobbed into the side of his chest.

Minutes passed and he heard her sniff, and her shoulders finally stilled. She pulled away and wiped her eyes. They stood for a moment, then she raised up on her toes and kissed him. They embraced once more.

"You must really love me," he said over her shoulder.

"Not really," she said, voice muffled in his chest. "It's just that I moved into your room and your stuff is in the way." She leaned away from him and smiled, and they both laughed a little.

Jelani smirked in mock conceit. "Gurl, please. You can't fight it. You know you lurve me." She giggled, relaxing a little more.

They found a spot in front of the fireplace and sat down on the couch. Alisha scooted closer until she was right up against him. Jelani draped his arm around her.

"It's true, then?" she asked, looking up at him. "Daniel didn't say it, but I saw it in his face.

Jelani sighed and looked at the flames of the gas-powered fire-place. After a while, he nodded. "I'm afraid so."

"You seem the same, but there's something different about you that I can't put my finger on."

"Oh yeah?" he said. "What's that? Luminous, perfect skin? Sparkling white teeth?" He offered a toothy, cartoonish smile. "Long, oily slicked back hair?"

"Your head is shaved," she said, giggling.

"I could grow it out, then slick it back." He pulled his shirt over his nose and crossed his arm over the bottom of his face. "Bleh! Bleh!"

She laughed, shoving him. "You're so silly."

Jelani continued. "Bleh, Bleh! I drrrrink your …" he trailed off and her laughter faded. He lowered his arm and pulled his shirt back down. "Sorry."

"It's okay," she said. "Maybe we both have a lot to get used to."

"Yeah," he said. *Good job, homeboy. You managed to wind all that tension back up in a mere ten seconds.*

"What are you going to do now?" she asked, interrupting his self-chastisement. "You're pretty lucky you have an internet business, so you don't have to change that. And the work you do at EA, a lot of it is at night, or at least dusk most of the time anyway."

Jelani thought about it. "I don't know what I'm going to do," he said. "I can't just continue things as usual, that's for sure."

"Why not?" Alisha said. "I know plenty of people who work graveyard shift careers and hardly ever see the sun aside from their weekends."

In theory she was right, but there was more to it than that. "Alisha." He sighed, more out of habit than the normal human function. "It's not quite that straightforward. I can't even tell you how yet. Plus, I'm still new at all this and I have to be careful; with myself, and with you all." She nodded and he continued. "Then there's that jackass who's been after us. I still need to deal with him."

"He'll kill you, Jelani." A note of fear crept into her voice.

Jelani shook his head. "I'm a little more equipped to deal with the situation now than before, trust me."

"Which one do you plan on going after first?" Alisha asked.

Jelani frowned. He had been talking about Remy, not the Japanese Hunter. Being honest with himself, he wasn't totally sure he wanted to have a go at that one again. Not for a while, at least.

"Remy," he answered. Just thinking about the Hunter who had turned him into what he was caused the anger in him to simmer. He heard a gasp and Alisha recoiled and scooted away from him. He looked at her in puzzlement. "What? What did I do?"

"Your eyes," she whispered. "They're glowing in this ... lavender color."

Jelani closed his eyes, willing his temper under control. When he opened them again he was sure they had gone back to their usual brown, but the fear in Alisha's face hadn't diminished. A cold sinking feeling froze his stomach, and in that instant Jelani knew they would never be together. It was more than he could stand.

Just then, the elevator gave a soft ding and the doors opened to admit Daniel, holding Jelani's big bag.

They both stood.

"Hey," Daniel said, looking from Jelani to Alisha, his expression asking if the coast was clear.

"Hey, man," Jelani said. "Good timing. I was just thinking I should probably go."

Daniel crossed the lobby and the three of them stood in an uncomfortable silence. Finally, Jelani reached out and grabbed the bag from Daniel, who released it somewhat mechanically. It hurt. Though he knew that his best friend was making a valiant effort to appear at ease, Jelani could see and feel the fear in him. Him and Alisha. It hurt him more than he thought possible.

"When you coming back around?" Daniel asked.

Jelani shook his head. "I don't know. I'll email you my half of the rent as soon as I fire up my computer."

Daniel snorted. "Don't be stupid, dude. Your half of the rent is the last thing I'm thinking about right now."

Despite his sinking heart, Jelani smiled. "Just thought I'd throw it out there. It's only right." He slung his backpack over his shoulders then draped the long strap of the duffle bag over his right shoulder.

"That's not heavy?" Daniel said. You've probably got close to a hundred pounds there. I stuffed everything I could into it, and I know your backpack has your computer and books in it."

It felt like nothing. "I'll manage," Jelani said. He waved. "Guess I better get going. I still got a lot of things to figure out." The truth was that dawn wasn't far off, but Jelani didn't want to say anything to remind his already skittish friends of his new nature.

"Try to come by again soon," Alisha said.

"Don't know if I should."

Her lips twitched into a smile. "I think you should."

Jelani thought about it for a moment, then shrugged noncommittally. "Maybe I will." He waved again, then turned toward the front door. Alisha came around in front of him. She wrapped her arms around him in another crushing hug that made his heart ache. Her blood was racing through her veins, rich with repressed passion and fear. He could practically hear it, smell it. He had to get out of there.

She released him and Daniel reached out his hand. Jelani took it and they pulled each other close in a half-hug.

"Take care of yourself," Daniel said.

"You too," Jelani replied. "Whether you see me or not, I'm watching out for you all."

"I know," Daniel said. "Oh, and Wen says hi. She wanted to come down, but she had just gotten out of the shower and—"

Jelani held up his hand. "Neither she, nor you owe me any explanation. Tell her I love her like the sister I never had, and I've always got your backs. Alright?"

Daniel shook his head. "This isn't fair at all."

"Neither is life." Jelani started for the door. He was reaching for the bar when Alisha's voice stopped him.

"I love you."

Jelani clamped his eyes shut, clenching his teeth. After the agony passed, he looked over his shoulder. "Love you too."

He opened the door and disappeared into the night.

14

M elinda slid the key in and turned it. The lock clicked open and she turned the knob and stepped into the darkened apartment; the apartment she hadn't seen in over three weeks, but still paid rent for.

Remy had insisted that for now, she maintain a bit of her human life to avoid any complications. She was to continue on at her job and maintain the rent at her apartment.

Considering her new existence, the concept of keeping a mundane job was ludicrous but Melinda had little choice in what she did with her life these days. Every bit of free-will she was able to exercise was a small triumph.

She stepped in and closed the door, standing in utter darkness. It was the darkness of a human night; the darkness of a vampiric day. For a long time she stood there and let the irony of her situation settle over her shoulders. She had always loved living in Vancouver but oftentimes the dark and rainy days would drag her mood down. She'd spent many a gray wet day wishing the sun would come out, and wishing it didn't rain all the damn time.

She clicked her tongue behind her teeth. Now the day was her darkness, the night, her day, and the very thing about this city that made her occasionally depressed now made it more livable.

Vampire.

That's what she was now. A vampire. A couple months ago, if someone had told her vampires existed she would have laughed and rolled her eyes. Now those same eyes were seeing in the dark as easily as if she had the lights on. She walked through the darkness, taking in the last remnants of her human life. A tennis racket. A yoga mat, workout bands, a medicine ball, and clothes everywhere.

Her life hadn't been the most exciting, but she enjoyed it. Her downtown apartment was only seven hundred thirty square feet, but it was all she needed. She'd worked five days a week and had weekends off, and could pretty much book time off whenever she liked as long as she gave notice in advance. She had plenty of money in the bank and lived well below her means, enabling her to take vacations and pamper herself occasionally.

Remy had taken all of that from her. That thought brought on a round of laughter that held no mirth. *I guess if I don't laugh, I'll rip this place apart.* She dropped onto the couch and let her head fall to the side. Well, he'd taken almost everything; her social life, her recreation, the sun. But in his generosity, Remy had allowed her to retain her job, her apartment, and bills. Just thinking about the bastard set her blood on fire. Oh, how she would love to jam her hand into his chest and crush his heart.

The vicious thought made Melinda weep. She thrust her elbow into a pillow beside her. Despair turned to anger; she couldn't even cry properly in this new condition. She didn't know if it was because vampirism permanently dried up the tear ducts or what, but her eyes were as dry as the Sahara.

"What did he make me into?" Melinda whispered into the darkness.

She had always thought that vampires were supposed to be these mythical creatures neither living nor dead, yet retaining all of their memories and mental functions. Not to mention the whole gaining 'supernatural powers' thing.

Well, some of it was true and some of it was not. She couldn't deny that it was all very interesting. Her heart still beat, but at a much slower rate, so she could understand the whole undead thing if someone happened across a sleeping vampire that suddenly woke up.

And then there were the myths. She looked to her left at a painting on the wall with a glass covering. Her unhappy reflection stared back at her. "I wonder who thought that up," she muttered, thinking about how vampires were not supposed to have reflections.

She went into the kitchen, grabbed a saucepan from the cabinet and set it on the stove. After turning the stove on, she opened the refrigerator and grabbed a plastic bag filled with a thick red liquid. Blood.

Refrigerating it preserved it for longer. She gave the bag a shake to re-liquify it. Melinda thought about how squeamish she used to be at the site of blood. Now she needed it to survive, and could barely control herself if she let the thirst become too strong. That lesson, she'd learned the hard way.

Remy had warned her about waiting too long, but she had thought it was just another of his endless games of tormenting her. Now that she thought about it, he probably knew she wouldn't have believed him, so he'd told her the truth. He'd reveled in denial, and watching her take her first victim.

That thought nearly made her knees buckle. The man's face remained burned into her memory, likely forever. He just left the gym, duffel bag slung over his shoulder. She remembered flirting with him, taking him just enough away from the doorway in the parkade and snatching him clean off his feat.

Melinda took a deep, shuddering breath. She'd grabbed him by his blond, spiky hair and forced his head back. She remembered feeling him squirm in her unbreakable grasp, hearing his deep voice as all he could do was gurgle in response. She'd tried to stop, hated herself even as she basked in the revitalization his lifeblood gave her. A primal urge had taken over, and all she could do was continue to drain him. It was like she had traveled across a desert where the sun burned her on the inside. That man's blood had been the water that rehydrated her body, her cells and organs. Where a desert traveler sought water, she had needed blood.

She sighed and opened the packet, emptying the contents into the saucepan. She'd watched the life fade in that man's eyes. The first person she had ever killed. She didn't think she would ever forgive herself for that, no matter the circumstances. Through the memories in the cells in his blood, memories she had gained for a time, she knew that he had a family; a wife and two daughters who would never see him alive again.

She clamped her eyes shut, willing herself to calm down. She was shaking with sadness and rage. After bringing herself back under control, Melinda stirred the blood until it was warm, then poured some into a coffee mug. It could be drunk cold but blood was best warm, like in the body in which it flowed. It was never the same as when it came fresh from an exposed neck, but Melinda would do everything in her power to avoid attacking anyone else.

She took a sip from the mug, then drained it. "I'm going to kill you, Remy." She grabbed the saucepan and poured the rest of the contents into her mug and drained that as well, then washed the dishes and put them away. "I'm going to kill you for what you've done to me."

She wondered if it was true what he said about Jelani. Remy had told her that he'd turned Jelani as well, and that the three of them would be one happy family. Of course he was being sarcastic. Melinda didn't need Remy to tell her that he intended to torture her by keeping the two of them close but never allowing them to be together.

Not that Jelani wanted her anyway. He'd chosen that other girl. Deep down Melinda couldn't begrudge Jelani his decision. He'd been straightforward with her from the start, but that didn't make it any easier to deal with. The thought of having to look at him every day and not be able to touch him, or worse, to have to make love to him in the shallowest experience possible while Remy watched them. That was more than she could bear.

She'd caught the images in his mind. She'd felt the intentions he had toward them both. Remy had a sadistic sense of entertainment and he was planning to enjoy centuries of tormenting her and Jelani.

She smirked. "You just keep thinking that, you son of a bitch." The sound of her own icy tone surprised her, but the strength made Melinda feel confident. Remy may be good at evasion and deviousness but she had inherited some of those qualities in being turned by him. That, in addition to her natural ability to play mind games, and it would be interesting to see how much fun Remy would really have with her. As a human she'd been good, which was what earned her the nickname, Melinda 'the-tease' Reese.

Tonight, she was thankful for that title. It saved her from being raped. Remy had intended to force himself on her. She'd seen it in his eyes every night for weeks, but he had been so preoccupied with that Eldest Hunter Yako, and those siblings, that he hadn't given her much thought. That was changing. She wouldn't be able to escape his lust indefinitely.

The thought made her shiver, and she wished Jelani would show up. Maybe together they could find a way to overpower Remy and be done with him.

Melinda ran her thin fingers through her long, sandy brown hair. Jelani had run his fingers through her hair every time after they had been intimate. He had such gentle and caring hands, attentive to every curve and detail. A tiny voice in her mind hinted at the possibility that they might be together. Surely, he couldn't expect to try to live a normal life with a human woman. That seemed impossible.

She snorted. Knowing Jelani, he would give it his best effort. A heavy, drowsy feeling settled into her body, telling her that dawn was near. Strange, the things that were inherent in this new existence. She would never be caught off guard when dawn approached because her body would tell her in time for her to find sanctuary.

Melinda went into her bedroom and checked the curtains. Shortly after being turned, she'd gone to buy the thickest black curtains she could find. They were a bit on the ugly side, but they blocked out all sunlight. She'd bought three sets, and nailed them to the wall, covering the window. Not even a sliver of sunlight came into the room.

"I almost wish a seagull would crash in and put me out of my misery," she said dryly

She lay down on the bed, staring at the ceiling. Jelani was out there somewhere, settling down to sleep through the day as well. She needed to find him, and then find a way to kill Remy. Or, she needed to find a way to get that Eldest Hunter to do it for her. She had to be careful with that one, though. *Shaquora* such as herself ranked at the bottom of the vampire hierarchy, standing only above *skiek*; half-breeds. And since half-breeds were somewhat rare, that placed her virtually at the bottom of the food chain. That Eldest Hunter might sooner dispatch her than think twice about it.

Melinda thought about the Indian vampire that had saved Jelani from her a month ago and felt a pang of regret. Too bad things had gotten off on the wrong foot. She would have been a good ally against Remy. Maybe Jelani could convince the woman to bury the hatchet anywhere but in Melinda's head.

She laughed at the macabre humor and pushed all of these thoughts into a part of her mind that held little of importance. If she could focus long enough before falling into sleep, she could convince herself that Jelani, his friends, and the Eldest Hunter were all unimportant to her. Remy had no interest in anything that seemed trivial to her 'small' *shaquora* mind.

15

As if to punctuate Jelani's mood, the rain intensified as he navigated the streets of downtown Vancouver. Saaya must have sensed his feelings, for she did not appear once he'd left his former home. Now he walked the wet streets in silence, melancholy his sole companion. He turned a corner, making his way toward Stanley Park; the place where all of this began.

He huffed and a puff of air clouded in front of his face. Who could have thought that a simple nighttime jog could so alter his life? One minute he was enjoying a brisk run around the seawall, the next he was running from the night itself. Jelani puffed another cloud. His friends dragged into his mess, one of Daniel's friends killed, and Melinda turned. Now Jelani shared her fate.

He came to the seawall and made his way through the darkened woods of what he had often referred to as the micro-rainforest that was the interior of Stanley Park. Normally the woods at night would be frightening, but he was a creature of the night now. There were few things that could threaten his life and werewolves didn't hunt here.

He increased his pace, passing through the trees in a blur. His sadness burned away in the fire of his anger, and he wished another vampire would appear. Saaya had told him that turned vampires were the second lowest class in the hierarchy, and that older or purebloods would often attack and kill them.

"Uh huh," he muttered under his breath. After spending months running and cowering, fearing for himself and his friends and flinching at shadows, he'd had enough.

If not for the circumstances, he would have found it humorous that Remy had given him the ability to defend himself and his friends. Thinking about that, and the fact that he could feel this weird little tingle in the back of his mind that was Remy attempting to connect with him, Jelani almost laughed. The idiot had no idea that Saaya had intervened and spared Jelani the fate of living under the Hunter's control.

He came out of the woods in a dead run, crossed the street, then leaped off the cliff. He glided over the fifty-foot drop to the paved paths below, and landed in a crouch on a boulder two dozen feet out into the water. He closed his eyes and felt the splash of the waves as they collided with the rock. The cold air, pouring rain, and crashing waves all washed over him but he felt only the wetness. If he had been susceptible to the cold, the heat from his rage would have kept him warm.

That first vampire who had been after him was dead. What was his name? Jake? Jack? Jelani couldn't remember. It seemed years ago. He couldn't kill who was already dead, but Yako and Remy still lived. Oddly though, when he thought of Yako, there were no distinct feelings there. He didn't like the vampire, certainly, but he didn't necessarily hate him, either. Yako had hunted Jelani and his friends because that was his job. Jelani didn't feel the need to be friends with the Hunter, but now he understood the situation for what it was.

When he thought of Remy there was no confusion. A white-hot anger seared his insides when he thought of the arrogant vampire that had taken everything from him. To Remy this was simply a game. He sacrificed other lives for his own amusement and thought nothing of needlessly involving others if it suited his ends.

Jelani longed for the moment when he slid one of his silver knives into Remy's heart and let him die slowly. The cold thought was unnerving. Jelani had never been a person given to violence. Well, he had thought about punching out a person or two, but not doing mortal harm. Now, he could think of little more than killing Remy.

Still crouched like a statue atop the bolder, Jelani clenched his jaw, his eyes narrowing as another wave crashed over him. He was long past waterlogged by now, but it hardly mattered when you didn't feel the cold.

Remy would be difficult to catch, but Jelani would find a way. A feeling deep in the pit of his stomach warned Jelani of dawn's approach; yet another attribute he had gained since his re-creation. Jelani considered remaining where he was and awaiting the day. It would be the last time he witnessed the sun's glorious emergence from the east before he burst into flames and disintegrated. It would be agonizing, but Jelani found that the prospect didn't scare him.

No. Death was not an option. Because of him, Melinda was under Remy's control. Because of him, Alisha, Wen, and Daniel were still in danger. And because of him, Daniel's friend, Claire McMahon, a woman he had never even met, was dead. Jelani leaped backward off the rock and landed on the paved seawall, then headed back toward Saaya's home.

He owed Saaya his gratitude, he owed Melinda freedom, he owed Claire retribution, he owed his friends protection, and he owed Remy a slow and painful un-creation.

16

The sun rose and fell, and once again Jelani opened his eyes to darkness. Darker still, were his thoughts.

He sat up on the bed and looked around. Saaya was home. He could hear her, smell her. Not for the first time he wondered what this was going to cost him. That the *dampeal* had been kind and hospitable was no question. What she would expect in return was another matter.

"I see your re-creation has not diminished that rather annoying human trait of yours." Saaya stepped into the doorway, staring sultrily at him.

"And that is?"

"You still worry too much."

"I just got up, Saaya. How do you know I'm worrying about anything?"

She tapped the side of her head and he remembered their connection. She could feel what he was feeling. It felt like an invasion of privacy, but when he considered the alternative of having Remy in his head all the time, Jelani could hardly complain. Besides, he was privy to Saaya's feelings as well, although to a much smaller degree. Jelani suspected he only felt what she allowed him to feel from her.

"I apologize for being a worrywart, but I've got friends that are a lot less durable than you are, Saaya."

"Do you doubt Kafeel?"

"I doubt the endurance level of his interest," Jelani said. "I'm sure you know better than I, that he isn't too happy about having to watch over a bunch of humans because his little sister wants him to."

"Yet, he still watches over them."

"For how long?" he asked. When the *dampeal* shrugged, Jelani shook his head and stood. "What do you want with me, Saaya? You've saved me numerous times from Yako and Remy, and then saved me from an eternity of torment as Remy's servant, or whatever I would have been to him. I appreciate it all, so if I sound ungrateful I apologize. But what is it you want of me?"

"Ah, my poor appreciative Jelani. You appreciate Kafeel's help. You appreciate my help. You appreciate all of the difficulties you have imposed on your friends, though it is through no fault of your own. You appreciate so much."

Jelani closed his eyes and ran a hand over his face. "Saaya. I'm not in the mood—"

She was right in front of him. "You think, you calculate, you worry, you plan, you consider, you appreciate. But have you lived? How much of life have you actually lived, *jaan*?" She was close. Very close. All he could do was take in that sweet, intoxicating earthy rain scent. Now he smelled orchids, which was strange because orchids had no scent. Then, he smelled wildflowers. Then the forest, waterfalls, the sky, plants. He smelled things that couldn't possibly have a fragrance.

"What are you doing to me?" he whispered.

"Nothing yet," she purred. She moved closer, her breasts brushing gently against his stomach. She looked up at him with

those light brown eyes, infinitely deep with knowledge and experiences. "Is there something you wish me to do to you?"

"Yes."

"What?"

"I …" he shook his head. "You're doing that thing to me again,
aren't you?" He backed away. "Are you telling me I'm still vulnerable to that dazzle thing you do, even now?"

She giggled, matching him step for step until his back touched
the wall. She placed a tiny hand on his chest and looked up at him
again. Those round, brown lips had been so enticing when he
looked upon them with human eyes. Now he saw details that his
mind couldn't begin to describe to his still lingering human sensibilities.

"Jelani, you are newly turned. You are a great deal stronger
than a human and I suspect you will soon be formidable, even to a
pureblood. But to me that means nothing at all. I am descended
from an *Ancestor*, love. You already have an idea of what that
means. After you have more adjusted to your new existence, you
will understand the gift I have given you."

Her hand slid up his chest, the side of his neck, his cheek. Her
touch was warm and soft, and Jelani resisted the urge to surrender
to the flood of desire she was pumping into him.

"I won't repay your generosity with lies," he said, struggling to
keep his mind from falling into a daze.

"Of course not."

"I love her, Saaya."

"Of course you do."

"I … I …"

"Hmm?" She looked into his eyes.

His mouth opened and closed several times, but a haze had
settled into his mind; all he could see or think of was Saaya. He
closed his eyes and her hand went from his cheek to his shoulder.
Then her other hand went to his other shoulder. He felt her full
weight—which wasn't much—as she climbed up his body and

wrapped her legs around his waist. When he opened his eyes, he saw her light brown orbs, inches from his.

"That's better," she breathed. "I'm not too heavy?"

The corner of his mouth twitched. Even if he was still human, she would have been light. Now she might as well have been weightless. "No," he replied. "Not heavy at all."

"Good. So you were about to tell me something?"

"Yes."

"Mhm?"

More out of a sense of decorum than her need of assistance, Jelani placed his hands on the sides of her thighs as if supporting her weight.

She glanced down, then looked back into his eyes with amusement. "Are you telling me you're still trying to be a gentleman? Do I really need to tell you that I don't mind if you enjoy my dimensions a little more fully, silly boy?"

"You don't need to tell me that," he said.

She blinked slowly at him then leaned forward. "You have a strong mind." Her face was so close, her lips brushed his as she spoke, and his body responded. She brushed her supple brown lips over his again and part of him surrendered, enjoying the kiss. She wrapped her arms around his neck and pressed her body into his, kissing him even deeper.

Jelani fought not to lose himself in the contact. She tasted like everything delicious in the world, all at once. It was a sensation he'd only had a hint of before but felt more fully now. He felt more intimacy with her in this contact than when they had actually coupled, months ago. He couldn't tell if it was his newly acquired senses, her influence on him, or a mixture of both.

Finally, hesitantly, their lips separated and Saaya leaned to his side and pulled herself upward till her lips were touching his ear. "Very strong," she breathed, this time in his ear. "I am impressed and a little irritated." She leaned back and looked at him again. Her expression was serious but her eyes held a hint of playfulness.

She straightened her legs and he lowered her to her feet with unnecessary gentleness. "You should go out and enjoy the night, Jelani. There are many things to learn, and most of them are best done through experience." She turned and practically glided to the door. The way her waist swayed and her hips twitched with each step invoked images in his mind that he could almost feel.

"Girl," he said, frowning in disbelief. "How long have you spent perfecting all that?"

She half turned, smiling at him. "Some must work for perfection. Some are perfect."

"Nobody's perfect."

"Then come find my imperfections."

Jelani's mouth fell open and she laughed, disappearing around the bedroom door.

For a while he stood where he was, staring at the last spot Saaya had been. The image of those curved hips and that tiny waist were burned into his mind. *Did I just deny myself that?* He shook his head. *Did I really, seriously, just deny myself that?*

The sound of the door opening and closing jarred his mind back to the present. He took a deep breath and blew it out. "Guess I should get out for a while." He grabbed a light jacket and was out the door.

$\sim$

The Shangri-La. The tallest building in the city of Vancouver. As a human, Jelani hadn't necessarily been afraid of heights, but he'd never had a desire to acquaint himself with them either. Mountains were okay. Nature made those. Tall buildings? People made those, and Jelani had a little more trust in structures that said "made by nature", so to speak.

Now he didn't much care. If the building fell beneath his feet right now, he would simply drop with it and walk away. Maybe a little dirty, but still walking. He crouched at the very edge of the rooftop of the Shangri-La and enjoyed the view with a sense of wonder he had never experienced before. Even the climb up here, leaping from handhold to handhold, had been fun.

Jelani could smell the rain in the air. He would probably be wet in minutes. He looked around at the still lights of buildings, and the moving lights of the vehicles. Everything was small from this vantage point. Tiny moving specks milled along the sidewalk like ants. They may as well be ants, as fragile as they were. Jelani tilted his head. An odd thought to have since it hadn't been that long since he was one of those ants.

He wondered how many of them were vampires, or lycans. He blew out an irritated breath. The way his world had been turned on its end, he wouldn't have been shocked if a Martian had walked up and introduced itself.

A raindrop spattered on his shaved head, and he looked up at the sky. In the absence of any substantial wind, the drops were falling straight down. He looked back at the city below; at the life he'd once had. Somewhere down there, people were living their lives oblivious of the predators who walked beside them. Couples held hands, hugged, kissed. People went to work, friends went to the pub, or a restaurant, bars, nightclubs.

Jelani's eyes narrowed. It was still spring, but summer was coming, and the days would get longer until nighttime wouldn't come until ten o'clock.

He'd planned to take Alisha whale watching when it got hot. He loved the salty smell of the ocean on a hot day. Nothing could beat an ocean breeze to cool the air, and refresh the soul. They'd planned to go hiking every week when the weather grew dry enough. Alisha had never ridden a scooter. He'd planned to rent a couple and take her to Vancouver Island, where they would spend the day riding and exploring Victoria and some of the outlying areas. Jelani's eyes narrowed into slits.

Lots of things he'd had planned for them. He had actually been able to see them building a life together. Now? Gone. How could he live a life with her? They could try, but to what end? She could walk in the day while he could not. She would age while he would not. She would eventually die while he would endure. It would be a torturous life.

Remy.

Jelani's eyes flared purple. Remy had taken his life away and still threatened the people he loved. He clenched his fists and he gnashed his teeth, unaware that his fangs had fully extended. Damnable vampires had caused all this and created all this suffering. He hated them.

At that moment, all Jelani wanted was to kill every vampire he could find. He didn't care who they were or how they had come to be what they were. He just wanted to kill them. He scanned the streets below and saw a woman follow a man down a quiet street. Newly turned though he was, Jelani knew a hunt when he saw one. He leaped off of the building, gliding into the sky, then falling.

Oblivious to the black wings of death descending on her, the woman said something to the human male in front of her and he turned around, smiling. She must have revealed her true nature, for a look of horror twisted his features. Before he could cry out, she snatched him off his feet and took him in the small space between two buildings. Jelani landed quietly on the low-rise apartment behind her, then dropped the remaining thirty feet.

His descent was silent, but her hearing was acute. She half turned, her hand still clamped around the man's throat. "There are thousands of humans on the street tonight. Find your own …" she trailed off, studying him. "You're a fledgling," she said, her face brightening. "You just made your biggest mistake, handsome."

"You are *shaquora*, like me," Jelani replied.

The woman clicked her tongue and shook her head. "Poor brainless beauty. Didn't your master teach you that the only other who stands as low as a half-breed, is a newly turned *shaquora*?" Struggling for breath, the man looked from her to Jelani, eyes wide with fear and desperation.

Jelani stared at her. Purebloods disliked turned vampires, turned vampires disliked newly turned vampires. And all of them disliked half-bloods. How the hell do vampires endure as a species?

"Look, kid. I will allow you this one time to live because I have the thirst, and I already have dinner in my hand." She gave the man a little shake and looked at him, grinning. Get out of here and I promise I won't leave you in a decomposed pile for the rain to wash away—"

Jelani closed the distance as she said the last word, and punched her in the face. The blow was hard enough that she released the man, who fell to the ground coughing. Her head snapped back but she recovered, hissing and slashing out at him. Jelani easily dodged her attacks, sidestepping and circling, ducking and slapping her clawed hands aside.

Out of the corner of his eye, Jelani saw the man trying to sneak past them. He maneuvered the still attacking woman around and stomped his foot in front of the crawling man's face. At the same time he slapped the woman across the face and sent her spinning to the ground.

"I'd stay put if I were you," he told the man.

Jelani heard the woman scrabbling back to her feet. He turned, then ducked as she slashed her clawed fingers at his eyes. He deflected her arm up and punched her in the underarm, dislocating her shoulder. She grunted and staggered away. He matched her pace, slapping and punching, kicking and shoving till she fell help-lessly to the ground.

Jelani snarled and grabbed her by the hair and yanked her back to her feet. To his irritation, he saw the man quietly crawling toward the street again. He growled and threw the woman at him. She crashed just in front of the scampering human, and Jelani was there before she stopped rolling. He grabbed both of them and lifted them off the ground.

"I told you to stay put," Jelani hissed. He hurled the man back down the alley, then leapt a dozen feet into the air. He turned his body and brought the woman around and down, slamming her into the ground. The concrete cracked beneath her and she groaned. Jelani stood, circling her as she struggled to rise.

"Why?" she asked, coughing up bits of blood.

"Sucks to lose even a little blood when you're thirsty, doesn't it?" Jelani asked her. A tiny part of him recoiled at the malice in his voice.

"Why?" the female vampire asked again. "Why did you come here? You can't be a Hunter. You're too new, and you're not a pureblood." She finally made it to her feet and Jelani kicked them from underneath her. She fell hard to the ground again and glared at him. "What the fuck do you want?" she demanded. "I haven't broken any laws of discretion, here. Not that I owe you any explanation."

"I don't care whether you've broken any laws or not," Jelani said.

The woman winced at the flatness in his tone. "Didn't your mama teach you not to strike a woman?"

"You're not a woman."

"What?" She started to climb to her feet, then hesitated. When Jelani made no move to attack, she carefully straightened, still keeping her distance. "I'm very much woman." She gave him a once over. "Under different circumstances I wouldn't have minded proving it to you—"

Really? I look that stupid? Jelani was on her in a flash. He grabbed her by the neck and slammed her into the wall. He tightened his grip on her throat and saw her pale red eyes alight with fear.

"You can't be more than a couple months old," she growled. "How can you be this strong?"

"It won't matter to you soon."

"Why do you want to kill me?" she asked, and he hesitated.

She saw the flicker of doubt and clung to it. "What have I done to you? I don't remember you. I'm just trying to survive."

"By killing him?"

"You know a better way?"

"I've come to understand there are blood banks."

She looked like she would have laughed if her throat wasn't on the verge of being crushed. "You ... ever ..." she could barely speak, so he loosened his grip. "You ever had that stuff? Yeah, if it's fresh it's okay. That synthetic shit is just like a microwaved TV dinner. You're full, but it's disgusting."

"You kill for a better taste, I kill you because I don't like you. Not much difference."

"You're not like that," she said. "I can see it in your eyes."

"You see your death in my eyes."

"I see anger and hurt."

The truth of it hit him. "Why don't you shut up?"

"You know I'm right," she pressed. "We all go through it at first. Your world is turned upside down. You have to leave those you love, or you may have killed those you love in a fit of blood thirst and came to your senses to see what you'd done. Then you feel alone, but the one who turned you has control over you."

She slowly reached up and grabbed his hand and urged him to release his grip. "That's it, isn't it? Did you kill the people you love when you awoke to that hellfire burning in your veins, demanding you sate it?"

"No."

He released her, and she took a step toward him and pointed down the litter-strewn alley at the man who sat on the ground, transfixed with fear. "We have no choice but to feed on them." She tilted her head and looked up at Jelani. "If it's any consolation to you, they would overpopulate and ruin the world in no time. We're just like any other predator. We maintain balance."

Jelani's eyes lit with rage and she retreated a step. "Don't blame me for your anger. Find a way to kill the one who brought you to the night."

"What if I see vampires like you as predators who kill out of preference instead of need?"

"You have no idea what it's like, fledgling. You are how old? Two months? Three? Given time, you'll understand why many of us prefer a fresh neck to a cheap brown bag."

He would have laughed at the liquor store 'brown bag' reference if he wasn't still on the edge of uncontrolled rage.

"I'll offer you a trade," Jelani said. She tilted her head at him. "You tell me where I can either find a coven or a place where vampires congregate, and I'll let you walk out of here."

She laughed. "You want what? A lone crazy fledgling, you are. You want me to send you to a coven of not only older vampires, but purebloods at that? You know most covens have either an Elder or a very old pureblood at their head, right?"

"Let me worry about that."

She gave him a doubtful look. "You're good, but you'll die as soon as you step foot in a coven."

"What do you care? Trade other lives for your own."

She shrugged. "There is a *dark rock* going on, actually. It's at the outdoor theater in Stanley Park. It's mostly vampires, but some humans who don't know what's good for them tend to show up as well. Plenty for you to kill before they kill you. And before you ask, I would prefer you not to attack a coven because they would find out who sent you, and I don't want that on my head."

"*Dark rock?*" Jelani asked.

The female vampire shook her head at him. "As strong as you are, I still can't believe you're so new. A *dark rock* is our version of a concert. Elders and most purebloods have nothing to do with them, but *shaquora* enjoy them. Think of it as a wild party." She grinned.

"Fine." Jelani stepped back. She looked hungrily down the

alley, then back at him. "Take one step toward him," Jelani warned, "and I'll kill you."

"He knows about us, now. If we leave him, the Hunters will find out and we're dead. Trust me, you do not want one of them on your trail."

Jelani smirked. If she only knew. "Let me worry about that."

She mistook his smirk for arrogance. "You think a little too highly of yourself. Fine. It's on your head."

"Don't let me find out you've attacked someone else tonight."

"I will not guarantee you the future, but I will promise you this night. I will go home like a good girl and have one of those repulsive TV dinners. She turned away. "I'll think of you with every disgusting sip."

She disappeared around the corner and Jelani went to the sitting man.

He looked up in fear. "Please don't kill me. I won't say nothing. I promise."

"I know," Jelani said, circling him.

"Don't kill me, man," he pleaded. "Please, just don't kill me."

Jelani studied him. A blow to the head at the right spot with the right amount of force could create amnesia. "Sure you won't say anything?" he said.

"I promise on my life," the man said, and Jelani heard the desperation in his tone. He didn't trust that it was the truth, but it was certainly sincere at the moment.

"Stand up."

The man rose hesitantly, keeping his eyes on Jelani. "I promise. I swear I won't—"

Jelani was suddenly behind him and struck him in the back of the head. When the man crumpled to the ground, he stood over him and watched his chest rise and fall. Satisfied, he turned and exited the alley.

～

After Jelani had gone, a figure dropped down at the other end of the alley and approached the unconscious man. He drew a long knife as he knelt and lifted the man's head. His eyes began to glow pale red and his fangs extended. He snarled and bit into the man's neck.

The human's eyes popped open and he tried to struggle, but only for a few seconds before blood began to dribble from his lips. After the death spasms ceased, the black clad Hunter rose and stared down the other end of the alley. He pulled out a handkerchief and wiped the blood from around his mouth and chin. Remy would be interested in this.

17

A vampire concert, or *dark rock*, as that female vampire had called it. Jelani sprinted across the rooftops alongside Georgia street till he came to the street-level bridge that passed over the bike path below. He jumped over the railing and glided toward a towering redwood tree. He caught a low-hanging branch and easily hoisted himself up. He heard a gasp and figured a pedestrian must have spotted him. Jelani didn't care. Let their sense of reasoning tell them it was just a large bird or an animal.

Jelani wondered how many of the outdoor concerts held in Stanley Park were in fact, vampire parties. He wondered if they were monitored. That thought brought him up short and he stopped just as he was about to leap to another tree. He looked around, scanning the woods for signs of Hunters. He saw nothing, but his instincts warned him otherwise.

Jelani closed his eyes and went still. He could feel the wariness of the woods. The small animals and birds that lived in the area were on alert, but whether it was because of him or the giant mass of vampires concentrated in one area, he couldn't say.

He was still trying to get a feel for the surroundings when he heard someone speaking softly.

"I saw him come this way and head in that direction."

"He was moving fast," a second voice said. "She said he was abnormally strong and fast for a fledgling, but I don't believe it. We couldn't keep pace with him."

"You think she lied to us," the first voice said.

"Possibly."

"Why would she? Why would a *shaquora* seek us out, only to lie to us about being attacked?"

"I don't think he is a fledgling, and I'm doubting if he's a *shaquora* as well. He moves too well to have once been human."

"Yet he's heading in the direction of the *dark rock*."

Jelani's narrowing eyes smoldered in hot, purple anger. That woman betrayed him to a pair of Hunters after he'd let her go. Apparently, mercy was a weakness. Very well. He was new and learning, and he would remember this mistake. The voices drew closer.

Silent as the night, Jelani leaped straight up from his position, grabbing hold of a branch ten feet above. He made his way through the treetops, circling around where he judged his pursuers to be.

Jelani made his circuitous route to position himself behind the voices, then quietly and slowly made his way forward, hopping from branch to branch. In seconds, he saw them. Both were of average height and held semiautomatic handguns with silencers attached. Jelani remembered being told that no firearms were permitted, because even the muffled whistle of a silencer could be heard. Only bare hands and bladed weapons were supposed to be allowed. Maybe the rules were different in an area such as this, surrounded by trees and foliage.

Jelani drew his silver daggers as the Hunter on the right spoke. "Go a little in front and I'll be close behind and to the right."

Mistake.

The other Hunter had not gone more than five feet when Jelani dropped onto the branch next to the one who had spoken. Seven stabs from lower back to neck left the Hunter descending to death and Jelani leaping past. Before the rapidly decomposing body hit the ground, Jelani was gliding at the back of the Hunter ahead. While airborne Jelani tucked away one of his daggers and upon impact, wrapped his legs around the Hunter's body as they were knocked from the tree.

They turned a complete forward flip and as he came back around, Jelani placed the silver blade at the vampire's throat, reached out with his free hand, and grabbed a nearby branch. The Hunter tried to raise his gun, but Jelani pressed the blade further into his throat. There was a sizzling sound, followed by a coughing gurgle.

"Drop it," Jelani ordered, and the Hunter complied.

For a few moments, they hung suspended nearly forty feet above the ground, held aloft only by Jelani's inhumanly strong grip on the branch. Never in his wildest dreams did Jelani believe he could be capable of such feats.

He looked down at the Hunter. "You were looking for me?"

"We … were monitoring you," the other man grunted.

"Why?"

"It's our business to do so."

"To monitor newly turned vampires like me? Or to monitor turned vampires in general?"

"Argh!" The knife cut a little deeper, and the sound of sizzling flesh intensified.

"Better hurry up," Jelani said. "I know this has to hurt. Answer my questions fast, and I'll release you."

"*Shaquora* in general are to be monitored, but you looked suspicious—"

"Noble of you to protect the woman who told you to find me," Jelani interrupted. He looked ahead in the direction of the faint sounds of music. He looked back down at the struggling Hunter. "How many are there?"

"What the hell are you? How can you be this strong?"

Jelani tightened his legs around the other's torso, and heard the resulting gasp. "You already know what I am. As far as my strength. I dunno. Now, an answer for an answer. How many are there?"

"How many what?"

"Hunters," Jelani said impatiently. "Are there any Hunters monitoring the *dark rock*, and if so, how many?"

The Hunter hesitated till Jelani tightened his grip further and dug the silver blade into his neck a little more. "Ah! Six. There's six of them, okay? One on each side of the stage, one on each side of the front of the crowd, and one on each side of the back."

"Are they visible."

The Hunter hesitated again, and Jelani drew the dagger from his neck and stabbed it into his shoulder and held it there. The pain was sufficient and the Hunter babbled out all the details.

"No. They aren't visible but everyone knows they're around. They'll be in the trees. You don't cause trouble, you won't have any trouble."

"Six, you say?"

"Yeah, yeah. Ah! Yeah, six!"

"Alright." In one motion, Jelani yanked the blade out of his shoulder and slashed it across the Hunter's throat. He let go and the corpse fell decaying to the ground. "You are released." He lifted himself onto the branch and continued toward the sound of the music.

J elani followed the sound of the music, continuing in the direction it grew louder. He stayed hidden in the trees, searching. Soon he found the first Hunter standing in a tree. Jelani closed the distance swiftly, clamped his hand around the vampire's mouth and buried his dagger in his neck. One down, five to go.

He hid behind the trunk of the tree and peeked out at the mass of dancing, hopping, flailing bodies in front of an open stage. There had to be at least a two hundred down there. Jelani would never have guessed there were so many vampires in the city. He wished he could kill them all but he would take as many as he could.

He looked down toward the stage where five band members practically mutilated tone and melody in a symphony of noise and loudness. The sound screeching out of the eight foot tall black speakers surrounding the crowd and on stage only made Jelani angrier. From his position, he was to the left of the stage, so he went right, making a wide arc and coming behind another sentry. Just as before, he took the watching Hunter quietly and continued on. In ten minutes, he'd circled the area and killed all but one. He crept up and, on instinct, clamped his hand around the other's mouth and pushed the tip of a dagger into his back.

The Hunter stiffened, but kept still. "How many of you are there?" Jelani asked. "Are there any more?"

"Just me," came the muffled reply.

"Really?" Jelani replied. "I'm assuming you Hunters are skilled, yet I just got the drop on you. Do you really think I'm stupid, or are *you* just stupid? Oh, and by the way. Five of your friends aren't feeling so well." The Hunter was silent. Jelani let the moment linger for a few more seconds then said, "you care to come a little cleaner with me?"

"We're all there is," he finally said.

Jelani started to speak, but stopped. A burning feeling crept into the area behind his sternum, then spread upward and downward. The burning crept through his arms, his fingers, his legs, up his throat and behind his eyes. The thirst was upon him. Jelani looked around, desperate. He didn't know if he was ready to feed on anyone. Then again, he had already killed eight people, though he wasn't sure if they could be called people, since they were vampires and two of them he was sure would have killed him.

Thinking about that dimmed his anger for a heartbeat, then

rage replaced it. Rage at what he had become; what Remy had made him into. His eyes burned, and the rage inside him danced and coiled with the thirst, creating an uncontrollable bloodlust. His fangs extended, and he buried them into the Hunter's neck.

In less than a couple minutes, he had completely drained the vampire in front of him, and the skin of the corpse began to flake and float away in the night breeze. Energized and angered, Jelani looked down at the mass of vampires writhing in an intoxicated cesspit. Seeing the erratic dancing and flailing bodies, Jelani better understood purebloods' general distaste for *shaquora*.

"Fine," he said under his breath. "I'll send them to wait for your pureblooded asses in hell."

He dropped out of the tree and stalked into the crowd. One vampire dancing at the edge turned and looked at him. His red eyes glowed wildly and Jelani wondered if a vampire could be influenced by drugs.

"Late to the party—"

Jelani cut him short with a roundhouse slash across the neck. He continued the motion and spun around the dying vampire as he fell to his knees.

Jelani milled through the bouncing and swaying crowd, dispatching all in his path. So discrete were his movements, that at first, no one took note of him. *It really is like they're high or something*, he thought.

Once he'd made his way nearly to the middle of the crowd, the dancers began to slow with the music in what felt like a buildup. At first Jelani thought he'd been discovered, but then all eyes lifted to the sky. Jelani glanced around, wondering what the hell was going on. Slowly, arms started rising, and every vampire on the grounds was reaching toward the sky with clawed hands and curled fingers.

Still looking around, Jelani followed their gazes and saw a patch of clouds drifting across the sky until a gap revealed a bright full moon, tinged with orange. Jelani's mouth fell open. *What the hell is that?*

The music built to a fever pitch and all the vampires around him hissed, mouths opening wide to reveal elongated fangs. Jelani felt something stir within himself as well. His blood felt like it was lighting on fire, not from the thirst, but a different kind of feeling. The base in the music deepened until the thump could be felt on the grass-covered ground. Arms and bodies swayed, and glowing eyes were fixed on the moon.

What the fuck is this? Am I surrounded by vampires or were-wolves? He felt the heat rising inside him as surely as the revelers were. The music made a sound that made Jelani think of wind passing in every direction across a turntable, blowing, scratching, spinning. The crowd stopped swaying and stood in place, shaking. All around him was the sound of sighing, hissing, and moaning. Jelani's eyes were still fixed on the moon. Then the clouds drifted away and the moon was revealed in its full splendor. It was the most frightening, alien, and empowering sight he had ever laid eyes on. *Beautiful*, he thought.

The music finally exploded in a cacophonous burst, and the reveling crowd was swept in the energy. Bodies swayed and flailed anew, swinging arms and bouncing to the fast beat of the loud music. They scratched and bit, shoved and hissed in a monstrous celebration. What they celebrated, Jelani didn't know or care. The power of this strange moon had taken him as well.

His fangs extended, the nails on his fingers elongated, and he felt within him a primal bloodlust that pushed his rational sensibili-ties aside. He drew his second blade and, in the midst of the whirling mass of violently dancing bodies, went to work.

His hands were a blur of silver. Low and high, left and right, straight and diagonal. Wherever there was a vampire within reach, they died. Tirelessly he worked through the crowd, dispatching all in his path, sometimes as many as three at a time. The situation was a perfect storm of death, and Jelani its messenger.

One vampire noticed his actions and turned toward him, bearing his fangs. Before he had taken a step, Jelani dealt a right-to-left slash across his throat, and a left-to-right slash across his chest. He came back again for another right-to-left slash across his abdomen, then followed the motion around, spinning his body. He hopped straight up in the midst of the turn, reversed his grip on the dagger, and drove it into the side of the vampire's head.

His snapped up his left leg and wrapped it around the other vampire's throat and bore him to the ground. He was up again before his unfortunate victim had begun to decay, and two more vampires had noticed him. They tapped others to their sides, and more took notice.

No thoughts came to Jelani's mind as he faced the seven vampires converging on him. A circle had opened up, and many of the dancers had stopped to watch the spectacle. Jelani would give them one.

One of the vampires thought to take Jelani down by himself and rushed in with quick, slashing claws. He was fast but Jelani paced his movements, half studying half teasing. It seemed that most vampires, while lethal to humans, were relatively unskilled, unless they were Hunters. This guy attacked in the same manner as that woman in the alley. Mostly punching, slashing, or grabbing actions.

"How long have you lived?" Jelani asked, ducking a slashing claw at his face.

"Shut up," the larger vampire answered.

Jelani dealt him a knee to the midsection and when he doubled over, placed his blade over the back of the exposed neck. "How long?" he repeated.

"Seventy years," was the growling response.

"Pretend you're still human and have lived a full life."

"What—"

Jelani drove the blade down through his neck and spun to meet the other six. They came at him as one, and he met them, step for step. A claw came at his left, scoring a cut the entire length of the side of his face. Jelani's left hand snapped out and he severed the hand before the attacker could fully retract it. Spinning with the motion, he stabbed a female vampire that was reaching for his back. He pulled the blade free and spun again, driving his left elbow into the side of her head and bringing his right hand around and slashing the dagger across her neck.

He felt the burning sensation of claws digging into his back, and spun around yet again, and brought both his daggers around and down, slashing another enemy from face to torso.

In the span of a dozen heartbeats seven bodies lay on the ground, death rushing to claim their decomposing bodies. Still bouncing and swaying to the music, the spectators seemed as if they didn't know whether it was personal business between Jelani and the others, or whether they should attack him. Despite his injuries, Jelani made the decision for them.

He leapt forward, driving both his daggers into the chest of a large male vampire. He curled his body and planted his feet beside his hands and pushed off, freeing his weapons and sending the dying man falling backward. Midair, Jelani turned and slashed another spectator downward across the chest, then kicked his feet from under him, slamming him to the ground with a dagger to the chest.

His instincts nudged at him and he stood, turned, and slashed downward, catching another enemy across the face. After raining a flurry of attacks Jelani kicked him away, spun and dropped to one knee, then whipped his hands out, launching his daggers into the necks of two more spectators.

They had been rushing toward him but now they fell backward and Jelani ran forward, reclaimed his weapons, and continued on. Now spectators gave way before him. Those that were too slow, died.

18

H unger sated, Melinda sat on a park bench looking out at the dark ocean of English Bay. Though she wished she could subsist on the synthetic, or legally harvested blood that most of the older vampires drank, she couldn't do it. For a time, she had thought something must be wrong with her, and that perhaps Remy's filthy essence had turned her into an insatiable monster.

Oddly enough, she'd learned the truth from a woman she'd developed a hesitant friendship with. "Don't be stupid," she'd told Melinda. "If every vampire tried to live off the human population like that, we would have long ago been discovered, and it would be war. Just try not to be stupid with who you take out, and you'll eventually get it under control. And if it makes you feel better about it, become some kind of stupid vigilante, or something."

Despite her 'friend's' rather colorful way of speaking, Melinda found those words comforting. She had taken the jibe to heart, and started hunting for prey who exhibited no moral values. Though it had been a bit of a challenge to get used to feeding on people, Melinda found it easier to kill those who killed others.

"Maybe I can be some kind of superhero," she thought aloud, sarcasm dripping from her tone. "Clean up the streets by feeding on the scum of society. Champion of women who walk alone at night." She blew air out of her thin, pink lips and rolled her eyes. It could be worse. She could have been killing just anybody.

"Guess you were right about that, Scarlet," she muttered to herself, thinking of the other woman. She was just about to get up and search for that Eldest Hunter Remy was so afraid of—though he pretended otherwise—when she heard excited voices. She half turned her head, listening.

"... already started an hour ago," a female voice said. "I wanted to get there early so we could get close to the stage."

"Who cares about the stage?" another voice said; this one male. "The view of the moon will be the same no matter where you're standing."

Melinda frowned. She'd only seen a werewolf once, during that ordeal on Grouse Mountain where she'd nearly been eaten by one of the disgusting things. She couldn't imagine them talking so freely about it out in the open, nighttime or not.

"Typical fledgling," another female voice said. "Only once every couple hundred years, a hunter's moon appears, and she's worried about getting close to the band."

They laughed and continued on. Melinda was curious. She let her gaze linger on the trio, but there was nothing about any of them that was indicative of a lycan. None of them exhibited the overtly aggressive demeanor, gruffness or overall wildness that was typical of their kind.

Intrigued and with nothing else to do, Melinda decided to follow the group. She stayed a good distance away, keeping them just in sight. After several minutes, she realized they were moving in the direction of the Stanley Park outdoor theater. *This is getting interesting,* she thought.

A few minutes later she heard the music, then she saw more of what she guessed to be stragglers making their way to whatever it was that was going on. Finally, she came over a little hill and around a bend to see a huge crowd. More disturbing than the fact

that she had never seen the outdoor theater so full, was the mass of
pale, flailing, and bouncing bodies packed onto the grassy field.
Even if she had still been human she would have sensed the
wrongness here. It was a mass of writhing vampires at what looked
to be some kind of twisted concert. They curled their fingers and
bent their limbs while turning and swaying, rising and lowering to
the music.

Melinda's gradually diminishing human sensibilities were
horrified, but her new nature was intrigued. She reminded herself
that she was low on the food chain, so to speak, so she sought a
place overhead to watch the festivities.

Carefully jumping from branch to branch and loving every
second of it, Melinda finally found a comfortable spot and settled
down to watch. The tempo of the music was starting to slow down,
then suddenly all of the dancers looked to the sky and lifted their
arms. The music became more bass heavy, and it felt as if it was
building to create a mood. Every gaze turned to the sky, and all of
the swaying arms and writhing fingers were starting to make
Melinda nervous.

Then, something amazing happened. The clouds parted to
reveal the full moon. It shone brilliantly, not only in its usual white
but with a tint of orange to it. Melinda sat transfixed at the sight
and felt a growing power within her, though she couldn't identify
it. Had she not already fed on the jerk who had tried to slip her a
date rape pill earlier that night, she would have been overcome
with the thirst, and likely attacked anyone in sight. Now she felt
charged, energized.

When she'd first reawakened, she had felt so much stronger
than when she was human. Staring at this strange moon right now,
she felt almost as strong again as she had in comparison to her
former human life. Was this temporary, or a permanent thing? And
what did it mean?

The music took another turn, building energy until the moment
finally came and it released, the tempo practically shooting off like

a drawn arrow. The beat sped up and all of the reveling vampires went into motion. It was a violent, off-putting, yet enticing sight, and Melinda had to consciously resist the urge to jump down there and take part. *I may be a monster now, but I'm still not ready for that.*

She just sat there watching, shaking her head in disbelief at the morbid world that had claimed her. "What the hell is all this?"

The words had barely left her lips when a figure on the other side of the field dropped out of the trees and walked purposely toward the crowd. That walk was familiar. Melinda watched, wondering how this could get any stranger.

She got her answer. The new arrival began systematically cutting down everyone in his path, moving to the rhythm of the music and with the movements of the crowd. He was so good that no one noticed what he was doing for a long time. If not for her overhead vantage point, Melinda doubted she would have noticed him either.

After about five minutes passed—plenty of time to rack up a large body count, if the bodies didn't disintegrate—the attacker's luck ran out and he was spotted. A group of dancers parted and formed a circle, and Melinda nearly fell from her perch. That was Jelani down there!

"What the fuck is he doing here?" she whispered.

He faced off with seven vampires and Melinda was sure her former lover was bound for death. To her surprise, he dispatched his first attacker in less time than it took her to be surprised. His skill was shocking. She had never seen Jelani this way. She'd had no idea he possessed such skills. It was shocking, but it also set her blood afire.

With one of their friends dead, the remaining six vampires attacked him together, and he fought them all at once.

Melinda couldn't believe what she was seeing. Jelani was like death personified. It was like she didn't know him at all. That there was this side of him, a side of him that knew how to kill so skill-fully, set off mixed emotions in her.

In seconds, six more vampires lay dead, and without missing a beat, Jelani resumed killing anyone within reach. What was he doing, and why? He couldn't have some kind of vendetta with all of them?

Melinda thought she knew the answer. If he was going through what she had when she was first turned, he was feeling rage at the loss of his former life and was targeting anyone who walked the night.

Melinda shook her head again. She definitely knew the feeling and had entertained the same thoughts, but it never crossed her mind to attempt something like this. Not that she would have survived longer than a couple seconds. Despite his skill, there was no way he could kill every vampire on the field. There had to be at least two or three hundred. Well, minus twenty or thirty, if she had to guess Jelani's murder tally.

"He's going to get himself killed," she mumbled, watching Jelani blaze a bloody trail toward the stage and leaving swiftly decaying bodies in his wake. She wanted to help him but what could she do?

Melinda wasn't helpless by any means, but this was beyond her. "Ah, love. I guess this is goodbye, then." She figured she would watch until the end. She admired that he would die his own way, on his own terms. How he'd resisted Remy's influence was something she wished she could find out. Looks like she would never know.

As she resigned herself to watch her former lover die in a blaze of glory, she noticed that his path straight down the middle of the crowd veered toward the left.

∼

One of Jelani's strong points as a human was his stamina, but that was nothing compared to this new existence. He felt like he could go on like this indefinitely. He moved faster than he'd ever thought possible and had taken down more bloodsuckers than he could count. Whatever that moon had ignited within him was still burning hot, and he reveled in the slaughter of all the monsters that represented what he had become. They preyed on those who could not defend themselves. They were monsters who deserved to die. They were just like him.

As if awakening from a daydream, Jelani snapped out of his trance. The moment of hesitation almost cost him, and he had to roll backward to avoid being disemboweled by a slashing claw. He avoided the worst of it, but still suffered four deep cuts that stung. Thinking she had him dead, the female vampire rushed in and leaped the distance between them, slamming into him.

Just before the impact, Jelani brought his daggers up, tips facing out, and the female impaled herself on the weapons. She screamed as he tossed her aside and came back to his feet. He looked around and saw that the left side of the crowd was a little thinner. He turned and made his way in that direction, cutting down anyone who moved to stop him.

His bloodlust was fading, and all Jelani wanted was to get away. He ducked and dodged and shoved his way through the crowd. A big male vampire stepped in front of him and Jelani skidded to a stop.

"What's the rush now, little man?" he said. "You've caused all this trouble, I'm gonna break your neck for it."

"Get outta my way," Jelani growled.

The big man snarled and grabbed for him. Jelani sidestepped and slashed down. He was fast for his size, and he pulled his arm away before Jelani's stroke fell. He kicked out, but it was slow and awkward. Jelani slapped the big foot aside and punched him in the stomach, putting as much force behind it as he could. The big vampire grimaced and bent at the waist. Jelani jumped over his head and planted his feet on the other man's back. With all his strength, he launched himself away, gliding over the crowd until he finally crashed on top of a group of dancers.

He bore them to the ground, but rolled with the impact and came up running. He ignored the injuries he sustained and kept moving. More enemies came before him and they died. He turned in one direction and another vampire blocked his path. He brought his dagger up, reversed his grip, and brought it around for a slash across her face. The fear he saw in her eyes sapped his will to follow the stroke through, so he pulled up short and shoved past her. Soon he was out of the crowd and sprinting for the trees. He heard sounds of pursuit and increased his speed, then zigzagged his path. He took to the trees, then dropped back to the ground. There was no pattern to his movements, but it was as if a new set of skills were available to him. Instinctively, he knew there was no way anyone would catch him.

He didn't stop until he had made it to back to the rooftop of the Safeway grocery store on the corner of Denman and Robson Street. Out of habit he started in the direction of home, but thought twice about it. He didn't dare lead any vampires near his friends.

He crouched atop the sloping roof and eyed the dark surroundings. Only oblivious humans milling about the quiet streets were present. Jelani stood and turned to the high-rise apartment building behind him, deciding he wanted to be higher.

Minutes later, he knelt on the edge of the forty-story building, gazing down at the brightly lit city below.

"What the hell just happened?" To his own ears the question was rhetorical, but to his mind it was legitimate. "What did I just do?" He inhaled a deep breath and blew it out. "What the hell am I?"

The voice that replied made his heart stop.

"What's wrong, baby?"

19

On a hunch Yako had gone to watch over the Hunter's Moon celebration, hoping he might spot Jelani. Luck had been on his side, but he hadn't expected this. That a newly awakened fledgling could wreak such controlled havoc, and on a host of vampires older than he, was something the Eldest Hunter never thought he would see. What would this child be capable of in a few years, a few decades, a century? If he managed to survive his anger and cease with the self-destructive behavior, it would be interesting to see him develop.

To his surprise, Yako found himself wondering if he could make an ally out of an enemy. The warrior in him saw a great challenge, but the pragmatist in him saw greater opportunities. With some direction, Yako thought Jelani might grow as capable as himself. That too, was a dangerous thought. Little could be more dangerous than a patient grudge.

Figuring there was nothing left for him here, Yako was just turning to leave when he saw a figure several hundred yards to his right, turn and jump back into the trees. It was Remy's female. At first, he'd thought she was watching him again, but she was focused on something else. Why was she hiding in the trees instead of the down there with the rest of the *shaquora* if she wasn't spying on him?

Yako shook his head, wondering if his luck was this good. Could that female have some kind of connection with Jelani? That possibility could make things even easier. He moved back into the trees and followed after her.

~

J elani's daggers were in his hands at the same time he turned to face Melinda. For several moments they stood there, staring at one another.

"You're breaking my heart again," Melinda said. "First you tell me you don't want me, now you're drawing weapons on me."

"Nothing personal," Jelani replied. "I'm just a little high strung right now. And if you consider the last two times we saw each other—"

"I know," Melinda said. She looked regretful. Jelani wanted to believe she was sincere. She blinked at him. "You've become very suspicious, baby."

"Can you blame me?"

"It's been a pretty hard time for me, too, you know."

Jelani relaxed a bit but didn't put his weapons away.

"When you've got someone in your mind most of the time," Melinda continued, "it can be difficult to be your own person." She took a step toward him and he tensed. She stopped, then took another step. "When he first kidnapped me, I didn't know why or what was going on. He had an inhumanly strong grip and nothing I could do to him made any difference. I may as well have been trying to stop a bear from attacking me."

She wrapped her arms around herself. "At first I thought he

was some crazy guy hyped up on drugs, but then he showed me his true nature. I'm not ashamed to say it was terrifying."

"Trust me," Jelani said, "I know what it feels like."

"He played so many games with me," Melinda continued. "He let me believe he was going to let me go, then told me he would never let me go. He told me he would let me go if you cooperated. Other times, he'd tell me I had to make a choice between my own life, or yours." Her voice went hard. "In the end, he just turned me." She spread her hands. "And here I am."

"And why are you here?" Jelani asked.

"I saw you," she said. "I saw you at the outdoor grounds."

A look of alarm shot across his features. "I wish you hadn't seen that. I really do."

Melinda shrugged. "Why? It's nothing I hadn't considered doing if I could manage it."

"I don't know what happened," he said. He lowered his daggers a bit more. "Something just came over me. I was already angry about what's happened to me and I wanted to take it out on anyone who drank blood. But when I saw that moon, it was like whatever I was feeling intensified tenfold."

Melinda was nodding as he spoke. "I know. I felt it, too."

"What was that?"

"I don't know, love." She had finally gotten close enough to touch him. She reached a hand out but stopped when he flinched. After a few more heartbeats, she touched one of his hands and lowered it. "I'm not going to hurt you, baby." *Not that I could,* she thought, with a mental smirk. "When we last saw each other Remy was nearby and had deprived me of blood. I'm sure you know by now what the thirst is like. Combine that with him controlling my actions, and that's what was happening to me."

She stepped in closer. "So how long have you been dealing with the shock?"

He sighed, putting his daggers away. "Two nights. I feel like I just tainted my soul. If I still have a soul, that is."

Melinda responded with a sad smile. "I know what you mean, but I think you don't have to worry about still having a soul. I always thought vampires were supposed to be undead, but my heart still beats. Less frequently, but it beats."

"There's times when I feel like I should still mine," Jelani said, and his gaze dropped to the ground. "Especially after tonight. In the course of a few hours I managed to smack around a woman …"

He winced at the admission and Melinda mentally smiled. Ever was Jelani the gentleman. If he'd attacked a woman, she could guess it was probably because she attacked him, or some other unusual circumstance.

"… and kill more people than I can even count," he continued. "And not to forget that I left a guy unconscious in an alley after I knocked him out."

She placed a hand on his chest and he shivered. She felt his heartbeat increase a little and closed her eyes. There were still feelings for her in there. "If it makes you feel any better, you may have saved a lot of people tonight."

"How so?" Jelani mumbled.

Melinda placed a finger under his chin and lifted his head. She met his earnest brown eyes. Such genuine eyes; even now. "I don't know what's going on, or what that moon is all about, but I have a feeling a lot of them," she nodded her head in the direction of the outdoor grounds, "would have probably gone out and attacked people."

Jelani snorted. "I doubt it. The Hunters that lurk around the city ensure that mass feedings like that don't happen."

Melinda shook her head. "You're still learning, love. Let me help you out a little. Most vampires who've walked the night for at least a few years are capable of a basic kind of mind manipulation. It's almost innate." She moved past him, walking toward the edge of the building to look out at the lights below. Jelani turned and watched her, remembering that walk all too well. She glanced over her shoulder and gave him that same seductive smile that had always set his human blood afire.

"When a vampire finds someone they want to feed on, they release a sort of pheromone into the air. I don't know if it's actually a pheromone or not, but that's the best way I can describe it." She laced her fingers together and put them behind her neck, stretching. "It makes the nearby human practically helpless in that they can't think clearly, and it also attracts them to you. The aftereffect is a loss of memory of the encounter. This particular trait is inherent in all purebloods, and many who've been turned, though not all."

"That sounds all nice, but how do you explain when a person wakes up and looks in the mirror to see two punctures in their neck?"

Melinda gave him a curious look. "You really must have been in shock when you woke up. Didn't you look in the mirror?"

"Yeah, but—"

"You didn't even glance at your neck?" Melinda said, grinning at him. "The first thing I did was check my neck."

Jelani ran his fingers over both sides of his neck and felt nothing. Melinda walked back to him, leaned her head to the side and pulled her hair back. "This is the side he bit me on."

Jelani's eyes widened. Her neck was as smooth as it had ever been. "How is that possible?"

Melinda shrugged. "Can't say I know the answer to that one, but they should bottle the shit and sell it."

They shared a chuckle. "What do you plan to do now?" she said, moving closer. He saw the desire in her eyes and fought to control his own. He knew she saw through the facade, though. "Why are you so hell bent on denying how you feel? Did someone tell you it was a sin to be with me?"

He laughed insincerely. "Of course not. It's just that," he spread his hands. "I told you before,"

She held up a hand to stop him. "Just, don't, okay? I really don't need you to say it right now."

"Okay," Jelani said. "I won't say it, but you know I'm going to always be straight up with you. I don't know how to be any other way."

"I know, I know," Melinda said. "I … just don't need to hear it." She looked in his eyes, and he saw a flicker of guarded hope and pride. "I don't know why I'm so caught up on you anyway," she said.

That hurt, he thought. He didn't begrudge her, though.

"There's a million guys. I don't know why I waste so much energy on you." When he didn't respond, she stared at him. "Nothing to say?"

"There's plenty I could say, but I doubt any of it is the right thing."

Melinda laughed. "I guess that's my answer. Only you could say something like that." Before he could react, she slipped her arms around his waist and pressed her body against him. She lay her head against the side of his chest. "The stupid girl in me that wants to be in love still hopes we can be together," she said. "The proud woman in me wants to slap the shit out of her, then slap the shit out of you."

"I get you," he said. "If it would make you feel better to take a shot at me, I can take it."

She leaned back and rolled her eyes at him, then stepped away and slapped him across the face. His head remained turned aside, and she could tell that it had hurt his heart rather than his face.

Finally, he looked back at her with kind eyes. "Feel better?" he said, forcing a smile.

"No," Melinda said. "Come here." She leaned in close.

"Melinda, you know I—"

"Shut up, will you?" She grabbed the back of his head and forced him down to her. Before he could object, she rose to her toes and kissed him.

Her slightly thin, reddish pink lips were just as soft and sweet as he'd remembered. Part of him wanted to pull away, to not betray his love for Alisha. Another part of him knew that Melinda needed this. She needed his touch, his caress, his kiss. He couldn't begin to imagine what she'd endured in her servitude to Remy.

If he was honest with himself, he would know that part of himself craved her as well. Melinda was a feisty, spirited, and insatiable lover that Jelani had found was a similar experience to riding a raft down a river rapid. Her hand behind his head was strong, but still gentle. Her kiss was rough and urgent, but also soft and exploring. Her tongue flicked in and out, teasing, testing. Knowing he would regret it, Jelani relaxed, and allowed himself to enjoy the contact.

For some time, they stood there, kissing on the roof of the supermarket. When Jelani thought she would break away, she wrapped her other arm around his waist and kissed him more deeply, more urgently. Finally, when Jelani was beginning to think she would try to rip his clothes off right there, she broke away. For several long heartbeats, they stared at each other. Jelani didn't know what to say that wouldn't ruin the moment, so he didn't say anything.

"Cat got your tongue?" Melinda asked, putting her hands on her hips. "Am I that good of a kisser that I've left you speechless?"

"You've always been a good kisser, and you know that, Melinda 'the tease' Reese."

That drew a wistful smile. "Seems so long ago when I got the nickname I wasn't supposed to know about." She ran her slender fingers through her sandy brown hair, leaning her head to one side and providing Jelani a clear view of her neck. He thought not about biting that neck, but kissing it.

She smirked at him. "See something you want?"

"Yes."

"I'm not stopping you."

"I know."

She shook her head. "Only a samurai could take their honor more seriously than you, Jelani."

"Oh, I wouldn't say that."

"Why not?"

Jelani raised an eyebrow. "Well, I have no concept of honor in comparison to a samurai, for one. Secondly, I did kiss you."

"Correction," Melinda said. "I kissed you. And thank you for not stopping me. I needed that."

"I know."

"How could you?" She blinked at him. "How could you possibly know what I need?"

"We're both standing here on a rooftop in the middle of the night, are we not?"

Melinda narrowed her eyes at him. "I'm sure your little Shiva Goddess treats you a lot better than Remy treats me."

Dangerous ground, Jelani thought. "That's true," he ventured, "but despite that, I can still feel the control there, that my free will could be snatched away as quickly as it would take for her to think it."

"Do you think she would do that to you?" Melinda asked. Jelani almost thought he heard a hopeful tint to her voice. It was always easier to share your plight with another when your circumstances were similar.

"I wouldn't be surprised if she did. Even when I was human she would do this hypnotic thing that would leave me dazed. Remember that pheromone thing you were talking about? I don't have anything to compare it to, but I imagine it's much stronger with her."

"Interesting friend you've got there," Melinda said dryly. "Sounds like she's got you right where she wants you."

"I doubt it. I'm too confused about all this for anyone to be anything other than frustrated with me." He indicated Melinda and himself. "Case in point."

Melinda smiled at him. "Your biggest frustrating trait is always trying to do everything right. It's impossible, you know?"

Jelani shrugged. "Maybe. I can always try, though."

"What are you, obsessed with karma or something?"

"Couldn't hurt," Jelani said, grinning.

Melinda wasn't buying it. "Oh? Look where it's gotten you so far." She waved at their surroundings. "It's the middle of the night and instead of having mind blowing sex with me, you're standing on the roof of a Safeway. You're a vampire, I'm a vampire, we're not together, and you can't even be with the girl you dumped me for, as I'm sure you've concluded by now."

Melinda sighed at him. "Let's not forget that the son of a bitch who turned me had been out to kill you and your friends." She indicated him with her hand and let it drop, slapping the side of her hip. The motion drew his eyes downward and he absolutely did *not* find her hips distracting. Not even a little.

"You listening to me, or fantasizing about my lower body, Jelani?"

"No, I'm listening," Jelani lied. "I just look down sometimes when I'm concentrating."

"Concentrating." Melinda rolled her eyes, but she smiled. "Well, here's something else for you to concentrate on. Remy wants me." She waited till the statement really sank in. "He's only tried to take me once, but I managed to piss him off enough to stop. I don't think that'll work forever." She turned her back on him and went to stand at the edge of the roof, gazing past the buildings, past the water, at the bright lights of North Vancouver. "I know we're not together or anything, so it's not really your concern. I just thought you'd like to know."

Jelani was moving to stand beside her, but the comment stopped him. For a few minutes he stood in silence as she continued to stare out at the city on the other side of the water. "Well," he finally said, "if you wanted to hurt me, you just did."

"I'm just stating fact, Jelani—"

"Stating fact," he interrupted, "yeah, whatever. I hate Remy with every fiber of my being. I hate what he's done to you. You knew that would hurt, you said it. You're pissed off at me, I get that. Believe me, if I had any way of knowing that going for a simple jog around Stanley Park at night would have caused all this, I assure you I would've made a different decision."

Melinda ran a hand through her light brown hair, her thin lips pressed into a line. "I'm sorry. Sometimes I just feel mad at everything. Mad at him for making me into this. Mad at life, because this had to happen to me. I don't feel like I've led a life that deserves this." She turned back to face him. "Sometimes I'm mad at you, too. I know it's not fair, but it's the truth."

Her face softened and Jelani didn't know how to feel. So many lives—his included—turned upside down because of one, seemingly innocuous decision.

"None of it is fair, but at this point it doesn't matter." He took her hands in his. "Some gifts come with a curse, and some curses come with a gift. Maybe this is a curse, maybe not. But we did get a gift or two in the bargain. We're immortal and can do things we only could have dreamed of before."

He let go of her hands and turned toward the view of North Vancouver. "I'm going to track him down and kill him." Jelani's eyes glowed. "I don't give a damn if I have to go through his entire coven to do it. I'm gonna lay him down cold, and that's what's real."

Melinda giggled. "I love it when you talk dirty, baby."

Jelani laughed. "Quit doing that. I'm trying to be serious and determined." He turned back to Melinda and grabbed her shoulders. "Do you want to work together on this?"

"Love to," she said. "But he has a grip on my will, so I can only do so much. When I'm within a certain proximity to him, it's game over. If he willed it, I'd attack you without any control over myself." Her face went hard. "I hate him for that more than anything else. I might be able to live with the blood-drinking thing, and I can definitely get used to immortality and the strength that comes with it. But not having my own free will is crushing."

"We'll work on that," Jelani said. "Can you stay out of his reach indefinitely?"

"No." Her hands balled into fists. "He'll pick up on my intent the moment he realizes the distance increasing. If I try to resist his call, it becomes stronger until it's physically painful to ignore. When I return to him, the pain in my mind has company when he gets his hands on me."

Jelani's eyes widened. He knew he shouldn't have been surprised, but still, the thought of some guy putting his hands on Melinda infuriated him.

Melinda smiled that sexy slanted smile. "Oh, be calm, my dark savior. I do plenty to irritate him, and in the end, it'll be worth it when he's dead."

"I'll be sure to prolong the process of removing his head from his shoulders." A part of Jelani was horrified at what he'd said, but it didn't change what he intended to do."

"You may actually have to fight me for that pleasure, love. I want to be the one to kill him."

"We'll see," Jelani said.

Melinda started to smile, but it turned into a grimace. "Speak of a worm and it crawls out of the dirt. Son of a bitch's calling me. I have to go." She turned away, then stopped and looked over her shoulder. "Try to remember all the details, but don't tell me too much. When I'm close to him he can touch my thoughts, so I try my best to forget what I can and make important things feel unimportant. You get my drift?"

"Gotcha," Jelani said. "Take care of yourself."

"You too." She went to the opposite side of the roof and stepped off, descending to the dark alley below."

Jelani watched her go, then sighed and turned away. He thought about what he'd done tonight, and what he intended to do. He delved within himself and found a coldness that wasn't there in his former life. Could his re-creation have changed him so much, or did it simply awaken what was already there? "What the hell have I become? And how many times am I going to ask myself that?"

He caught a whiff of fresh roses, summer rain, and lilacs. Jelani's gaze fell to the ground in front of him, and he half sighed, half chuckled.

"Hello, Saaya."

20

E very side of the roof of the Safeway had about two to three feet of overhang; perfect for one who might be strong enough to hold themselves in the narrow space, staring at the ground below. An unusually strong and confident human could achieve such a feat for a short time. Even among his own culture, Yako had found some of the stories about ninjas amusing. That they could be capable of some of the things depicted in stories was simply comical. One of the more impressive feats—by human standards—was a ninja's ability to hold themselves upside down while spying on or waiting to descend on their target. That part was actually true.

His arms, core, and legs taut, Yako hung upside down beneath the overhang, his back pressed against the piece of roof above him. He held on to two handholds, as still as the building itself. The impossibility of the position would have left a gymnast envious.

He had remained where he was for the entirety of the two fledglings' conversation. What he heard had confirmed his suspicion; that the one named Melinda sought a way to kill Remy, and that Jelani was also on the Hunter's trail. Cold and calculating as he was, Yako couldn't help but give a tiny shake of his head. That Remy could inspire such hate in so many was in itself a *talent*.

"Disgraceful," he muttered. Often a re-created human would arise in shock to their new existence, but then come to be thankful to their re-creator, whether it was through genuine recognition of their enhancement or through subtle manipulation of the still fresh and humanlike mind. Not making the mystery of Jelani's resistance to his influence a top priority was mistake enough, but for Remy to so abuse his other fledgling while being hunted by the Eldest Hunter himself was idiocy. He had created an enemy out of one that might have been an ally—willing or not—and his newest creation was plotting against him as well. Fool.

Impressed as he was at Remy's ability to create enemies, Yako had no issue with using the situation to his advantage. The easier route would be to speak with the female and perhaps reach an agreement. Unlike most purebloods, Yako was more concerned with efficiency than status. *Shaquora* or not, he would work with them if it suited his goal.

Yako thought about what he'd witnessed not long ago. Jelani was already an efficient killer. Under Yako's training, he could be truly lethal. There was just the matter of the standing grudge that the fledgling held against him. That thought led him to the second and less desirable option. He could enlist the aid of another Hunter more adept at mind compulsion and use the two *shaquora* as fodder against Remy.

Well, perhaps not fodder. Yako was confident that Jelani was already Remy's superior, judging by what he witnessed at the *dark rock*. Whatever happened between those two, Yako would have little trouble in dealing with what remained of Remy's resistance.

He heard the conversation end, and saw Melinda just as she landed in the alley almost directly below him. After she disappeared into the darkness, he was just about to release his grip and depart when he heard the voice of the *dampeal* and was reminded that he needed to tread carefully.

The Eldest Hunter had no use for ego, so it was simply a matter of fact that he recognized the woman as superior to him. One of her parents may have been human but the other was an *Ancestor;* a Count or Countess. Purebloods like him were strong, the Elders were stronger. *Ancestors* were the oldest and strongest of them all. Most vampires thought the Counts and Countesses of history were no more than that; history.

The Elders and some few purebloods like Yako knew better. The *Ancestors* were very much still in existence, and though they generally shunned most of the world at large, they still held a great deal of influence within the hierarchy.

Yako listened as the two conversed. Having learned long ago that the *dampeal* had a special interest in Jelani, he wondered if she might be convinced to play a part in not only Remy's demise, but in Massius's uncreation as well. Yako intended to send Remy to oblivion by the bite of his own sword, but Massius's demise would be more difficult.

He cast the thought aside. From what he knew about the half-breed spawn of an *Ancestor*, Saaya likely shared much of her parent's apathy for vampiric affairs. He made up his mind to stay clear of the female. He was powerful, but she was beyond him.

Again, he was about to depart when the sound of his name gave him pause.

"... want to cast aside your little vendetta against the Eldest Hunter, Yako, and work for the cause you both have in common?"

Despite hearing the passionate objection voiced by Jelani, Yako was amused.

21

J elani couldn't believe what he was hearing. "Just to further clarify; you want me to ask for the aid of the guy who would have killed me, my best friend, his fiancée, and my girlfriend?" He turned away, then turned back. "Please excuse my language, but you got me fucked up." He turned away again, and ran a hand over his head as he looked out over the city.

"She wasn't your girlfriend at the time."

Jelani opened and closed his mouth several times. Did she hear anything he'd just said? Of course she did. She simply didn't care.

"You know, Saaya, I understand that you come from a different world and all, but could you try to care, or at least pretend you do?"

"Why?"

The question was asked with such an innocent tone that Jelani found himself stumbling over the answer. "Why? What do you mean, why?"

"Seems like a straightforward question to me. Why should I care about your little friends, *jaan*? Their lives are their own, and have nothing to do with me."

"But I—"

"You," she interrupted, "as I've explained more than once, were the only one I took interest in on that fateful night. I have preserved your life because you interest me and I find myself drawn to you."

"So, if I ceased being interesting to you, you would just what, leave me to my fate?"

"Does this fact upset you?"

"Of course it does!"

The *dampeal* tilted her head at him. "Why?"

"Because it means you don't care. It means that you only help out of your own self-interest and that if I was not interesting to you, you would have left me to die."

"How different is that from when a human helps someone?"

"We help each other because it's the right thing to do, Saaya." Jelani was becoming exasperated with the woman. "We do it because it's right."

"I see." She tapped a finger to her smooth brown cheek. "When you help someone, it does not make you feel good to do so? It does not make you feel as if you've done a good deed and that you are a good person for it? Is that not a good feeling? A desirable feeling?"

"It's not the same."

"How so?"

Jelani raised his hands and let them drop. "I ... for starters, it's not always desirable to help someone. They may smell offensive, but they need help. A person may be in a situation that requires pain and possibly risk of life to help, but you still do it because they need your help, and it's what's right."

"And that does not make you feel good when you've done such a thing?"

"In the moment? Sometimes not. And in some cases, you might not live to see the results of whatever the good deed is that you've done."

"Why would you risk uncreation needlessly?" A tiny frown creased Saaya's brow as she gazed up at him, genuinely curious. Even that expression made him want her right then.

Jelani spread his hands, then let them drop. "You know, for someone who is half-human you seem to have little connection with what it's like to be human."

In response, Saaya looked to the east. "The sun approaches, my lovely Jelani. It's almost time to sleep."

Jelani turned his regretful gaze in the same direction. "What does it matter to you? You're a *dampeal*."

"I sometimes sleep in the day."

"You planning to sleep today?"

She looked him up and down. "Perhaps." Before he could speak, she was right in front of him. She pressed her tiny hand across his mouth, and looked up at him with glowing lavender eyes. "And if you so much as speak her name, I will incinerate every memory you have of her. It will be as if she didn't exist."

Jelani stared at her. Was she serious?

"I am quite serious, my love," she said in that playful tone of hers.

"I don't respond well to threats, Saaya," he said. She shrugged. He sighed. "I appreciate your helping me out and all, but just try to have a little more patience and not threaten me with the prospect of a memory wipe. That's not the best way to nurture a friendship."

"Friendship," she said, as though the word amused her. "I like you, Jelani. Do you not like me?"

"Of course I do. Are we not friends?" Her face went serious, and despite himself a sliver of apprehension crept down his spine like an icy finger. "Saaya, you know if the circumstances were different I'd be all into you." She arched an eyebrow. Jelani swallowed. "You sure know how to twist words into a perverted context."

"You said them."

"Fair enough. Can we drop it?"

"For now." Saaya stepped in close, then turned away, allowing all of her complimentary dimensions to brush against him. "But we will explore it again."

Jelani stood frozen for a few heartbeats, willing his body under control when Saaya glanced back at him. "Your lips tell the story, but the body tells the truth."

She smiled.

He grimaced. "You sure know how to make things hard on a guy." Her lips twitched. Jelani gritted his teeth. "Ahem, let me rephrase that. What I meant to say was that you know how to make things difficult for a guy."

Saaya stepped to the edge of the roof and looked over her shoulder at him. Her lips parted and her long eyelashes fluttered when she blinked at him. "You are mistaken, *jaan*. I may make things," her eyes flicked down then up again, "hard on you. But you are the one making things difficult." She stepped off the roof.

Jelani was left standing there, his mind, body, and heart all at war with each other with the specter of daylight looming over his shoulder. "Probably be easier to just walk into the sun than deal with all this," he muttered. He stepped to the edge of the roof and gazed longingly to the eastern horizon.

An eternity without ever again feeling the warmth of the sun. Jelani didn't know how long he could endure it. Was this the reason vampires were so callous toward humans? Was spending immortality in the absence of the sun's cleansing warmth the reason for their apathy to what most of humanity would consider morally acceptable? Jelani found that he liked the possible answer to that question even less than he liked asking it of himself. Would he become this way in fifty years, or a hundred?

He shook his head. Alisha, Saaya, Melinda, immortality, and morals. It was all too much to think about. But what he could focus easily on was Remy. His frown eased, and he relaxed. Yes. He had forever to think about everything else. For now, he would focus on removing Remy from existence. With one last glance at the brightening eastern horizon, he ran toward the edge of the roof and jumped off.

22

The morning light penetrating the blinds woke Daniel. He opened his eyes to see the golden dawn seeping through the gaps. If there was one thing a Vancouver resident appreciated more than most, it was sunlight.

"Three days of sun in a row," he said with relief.

"Supposed to rain later today."

Daniel looked down at the woman curled up next to him. The woman that would be his wife soon. Her long black hair was disheveled so perfectly he wondered if she had arranged it that way while he slept.

"Mmm," she hummed, shifting against him and placing a delicate hand on his chest. "How did you sleep?"

"Well enough, I guess."

She opened her eyes and looked up at him. Those beautiful brown, half-moon shaped eyes were one of the things he loved most about her. Those genuine eyes held more love for him than he'd ever experienced from anyone.

"What?" she croaked, rubbing her eyes. "Why're you looking at me like that?"

He smiled. "No reason. Just looking."

"You're weird."

"You know, your voice is deeper than mine when you're still waking up." She shoved him in the ribs and he laughed, then coughed.

"Quit talking so much and go brush your teeth." She wrinkled her nose. "I won't mind if you take a long time."

He raised his eyebrows at her but got up. "I'll remember that when you want to run your hands over all this." He flexed his chest muscles then half turned his torso, imitating a bodybuilder.

Wen giggled. "Quit being weird. You're so silly. Save all that when you're with your friend …" she trailed off and Daniel froze, then dropped his arms. For a moment they just looked at each other, then Daniel turned and went for the bathroom. A tiny voice spoke from behind while he was brushing his teeth.

"I'm sorry, babe. I didn't mean—"

He held up a hand to stop her while he rinsed his mouth. "Don't apologize, he said, grabbing a towel and wiping his face. She leaned in the door in nothing but a silk pale pink slip. The way her uncombed hair fell down the sides of her head and over her shoulders set the pit of his stomach burning. He took her hands in his. "You don't have anything to be sorry about. It's nobody's fault."

"I know, I just … It's still hard to imagine he's not around, you know? You two were best friends."

"*Are* best friends," Daniel corrected. "That hasn't changed."

Wen considered him for a moment before she spoke again. "Are you sure? A lot has changed in the past month. You said yourself that just being near him made you nervous."

Daniel moved past her and back into the bedroom. He went to the nightstand beside the bed, opened the drawer, and retrieved a six-inch rod. It was smooth polished onyx, each end worked to a blunt tip. Daniel dropped onto the bed and ran his fingers over the beautiful piece.

"He gave this to me a year after we met," he said, twirling it in his hand, then flipping it round and round between his fingers. "When he found out I'd learned to fight with long daggers as well, he gave me this. Fun to flip in your hands, especially the non dominant one." He glanced at her. "You ever meet someone for the first time and it's like you've been best friends, or brothers, your whole life?"

Wen sat down beside him and put a comforting hand on his back. "Maybe you were, in a past life."

He shrugged. "Maybe. It was like we'd been friends forever and were just catching up on lost time. Been my best friend since then." He flipped the rod in the air and caught it with his other hand, flipping it just as skillfully.

"When we met for the first time at work, one of the first things he said to me was, *look at this ole pretty, Russell Wong-lookin' ass.*" They laughed, and Wen rubbed her hand across his back.

"You're much more handsome than he is," she said.

Daniel rolled his eyes at her. "Babe, you were obsessed with Russell Wong for years."

Her hand stopped. "No I wasn't."

"Oh?"

Wen's cheeks started to color. "Who told you that?"

"Who do you think?" Daniel replied, chuckling.

"Ooh, that girl." I can't believe she told you that."

Daniel rested a hand on her leg and gave it a squeeze. "If Alisha hadn't told me that, I might not have approached you."

"Why not? I liked you."

"Yeah, but you had that other guy drooling all over you."

Wen leaned away and wrinkled her nose again. "Charles? Eew! His pants were always crooked and he had that nasal voice that made my skin crawl."

"Yeah, but he always wore that big sexy net hat with the adjustable button clip strap on the back."

Wen laughed and gave him another shove. "Don't judge poor Charlie. He was a good enough guy. Just not my type." She tilted her head at him. "You thought he was a threat?" She leaned around his arm and looked up at him. "Or were you just shy?"

"I wasn't shy," he said, looking away.

Wen smiled at him. "Daniel Ng, you don't lie well at all."

Daniel smiled helplessly. "Yeah. He must've worn off on me more than I thought."

The mention of Jelani sobered the mood again. They sat in silence for a while, each wrapped in their own thoughts.

"And speaking of Jelani," Daniel said, breaking the silence, "I've got to figure out how to help him."

He felt Wen go rigid beside him, and he stopped twirling the rod and looked at her. She looked terrified.

"What makes you think he needs your help?" she said, and he could tell she was struggling to keep the fear out of her voice. "He should be a lot more capable now than before."

"He's also in over his head with a bunch of vampires who've been around for who knows how many ages."

"What about that girl with the magical hips? Isn't she helping him?"

Despite the discussion, Daniel almost laughed. Though Saaya was no threat to their relationship, there had been a tiny bit of jealousy from Wen since the *dampeal* had first appeared.

"I don't know if I completely trust how much she's going to help him. They don't think the same way we do."

"And now that Jelani is one of them, don't you think—"

"He's still Jelani," Daniel said. "He's still the same person on the inside. He's just … changed."

Wen nodded. "But think about what he's been changed into."

"I *know*," he said more harshly than he intended. He took a deep breath and blew it out. "I know, babe. As hard as it is for me to admit, I know. He's a vampire. I'll only ever see him at night. But he's still Jelani, and he's still my best friend. He's out there dealing with at least two Hunters, a new life, and whatever games Saaya is playing with him. I have to help."

Wen gave him a sympathetic look. "Yes, Daniel. He is still Jelani. He is still your best friend." She stood and went to the door, stopped, and turned to face him again. "But if circumstances place the two of you together when he gets thirsty and there's no other way for him to get what he needs, will your friendship give him the strength not to kill you?"

~

Only three phone calls could interrupt Daniel when he went for an evening jog; Wen, Alisha, or Jelani. Despite that fact, he was still caught off guard when Jelani's ringtone sounded in his pocket. He fumbled around in his pocket and fished out his phone.

"Jelani?"

"Yeah, it's me."

"Good to hear from you, man. I can't say I'm not surprised, but still good to hear from you."

Silence.

"Um, you there?"

"Yeah."

"Uh, so what's up? What's going on?"

"Can you meet me in Coal Harbour on the boardwalk? Maybe around seven?"

The fact that his friend had chosen a place that would be heavily populated was not lost on Daniel. It gave him hope, yet made his heart ache at the same time.

"I trust you, dude. We don't have to meet in a public place."

"You shouldn't trust me. You only have an idea of what I am."

"I only have an idea of what you are, but I know who you are."

There was silence for a few heartbeats before Jelani spoke again. "I would feel more comfortable if we met in a public place. The things I've got to tell you won't make you very comfortable, but you need to know."

"Alright. Seven, then."

"Daniel?"

"Yeah?"

"How's Alisha?"

"A little distraught about this whole thing, but she's tough."

"Thanks. See you at seven."

The line went dead. "Well that was different," Daniel muttered, shoving the phone back into his pocket. Jelani had always been so anal about proper manners. *I guess the circumstances are a little difficult,* he thought. He pulled the phone back out of his pocket and checked the time. Six. Just enough time to get home and clean up.

He started back into his jog when a particularly large crow glided alongside, then banked a left turn in front of him. Daniel leaned his head away from the large bird, frowning at it. The bird flapped its long wings and glided around him again, then landed a few dozen feet in front of him in the middle of the path. It flexed its shimmering black wings and cawed.

The bird's voice was much deeper than a crow's, and its call sounded a little different. "Raven," Daniel whispered, coming to a stop a few feet away.

He looked around. Though many people went for afternoon jogs in the interior of Stanley Park, it was still easy to travel the entire length of a trail and not see many people at this time of day. Today was such a day. "Alright, Saaya," he said, having long ceased feeling foolish when talking to one of her messengers, or whatever the birds were to her. "What's the deal?"

"That is a cold way to greet a friend."

That sweet, seductive voice practically floated on the air around him. Daniel had encountered several vampires over the course of the last half year or more, but none had ever exuded anything close to the power that the tiny *dampeal* had. It always changed. At times her presence could be so enticing, he had to concentrate on not losing himself. Other times, it was over-whelming and intimidating.

Today was the former. Saaya exuded a presence that made him want to surrender to her. He shook his head. "Do you enjoy doing that to people?"

"Doing what?" Her tone was so genuine that he couldn't be sure if she was toying with him, or was simply unaware of the power she exuded.

"Never mind. What's up? I'm assuming the reason you're here is because it has something to do with Jelani?" Why did that thought make him feel a little jealous?

"Why would you think that, Daniel? Have I been neglecting you?" The small, graceful figure of Saaya stepped out of the trees and moved toward him. The woman made something as simple as walking into a dance.

"Do you wish me to pay more attention to you, lovely boy?"

Daniel swallowed. "Uh, no, that's not what I meant."

"No?" She stepped closer. Close enough to touch. Close enough to kiss. She looked up at him and those light brown eyes were a world that he could fall into.

He blinked and gave his head a little shake, then Wen came into his mind. The thought of his fiancée made him feel guilty. He let the guilt wash over him and it swept away the desire for the woman in front of him. Mostly.

Saaya tilted her head. "Ah. Love. Such a strong thing, love is. That little girl holds your heart completely. She's a lucky one."

"Are you testing me?" Daniel felt his confidence building.

"Are you feeling strong?" Saaya replied winking at him. His confidence trembled.

"Uh," he cleared his throat. "Wanna tell me what's going on? Why are you here?"

"Maybe I just wanted to see my other favorite," she replied. "You two are quite a pair, you know. He is just a little faster, but you are a little stronger."

"That used to be the case," Daniel replied. "It should make sense, though, since I'm bigger than he is. Not that it matters anymore, I'm sure." She shrugged as if it didn't matter, and Daniel asked again. "Why are you here, Saaya?"

"I think your friend may benefit from a visit with you."

That was surprising. Daniel had assumed Jelani would be practically under her thumb since his change. She read the surprise in his face. "You think he is my slave."

To his further surprise, her tone suggested she was insulted at the notion. "I don't think that."

"But you think I have exerted some kind of control over him, do you not?"

"Saaya," Daniel ran a hand through his hair. His body heat was dropping and he was starting to feel the cold. "Every time I encounter you, it's like I'm trying to hold onto myself. It's hard not to think he's in your thrall, or something."

Saaya reached up and stroked his cheek. The contact sent warm shivers through his body, and he found that he no longer felt the cold. "My dear, dear Daniel," she said. The air became her voice. The wind, the sky, the ground. Everything was the sound that came from her lips. "I only draw out what is already there."

Daniel's eyelids drooped. Heat radiated from her hand and flowed through his body, filling him. Her words were a whisper that swept into his ears and touched his bones, his organs, his blood, his cells. "Desire is not forced. It is not thrust upon another. It is willingly and willfully experienced. I only see what is there and magnify it. Is that wrong, my lovely?"

A tiny voice in the back of his mind demanded that he focus. He found the voice, like a tiny flicker of light in a void of darkness. He went toward it and willed it to grow.

"Jelani finds such desire, enjoyable," she continued.

The light grew brighter and brighter. Daniel focused on it to glow ever brighter till it filled his mind. He found himself again and opened his eyes. To his shock, he had leaned into her touch. They were so close, her lips were nearly brushing his.

"Jelani's not engaged," he said, feeling the need to defend his friend's honor as well as his own. "Jelani wasn't committed to another. If he was," he remembered to phrase his words carefully, "he would have struggled just like I am to resist your, no doubt, lovely charms." He straightened and her hand slowly fell away. "Otherwise, we would betray those we love most. How attractive would you find us then?"

Saaya grinned at him. There was no disappointment or irritation. It actually looked like an interested expression. The fact that she was not shocked that he'd resisted her made him nervous, though he didn't know why.

"We are of different minds, lovely Daniel, though I understand yours, while you do not understand mine."

Daniel thought it best to steer the conversation in a different direction. "As to our other subject, it turns out that I'm meeting up with Jelani in a bit. He wants to talk."

"That is good."

Her tone was neutral. Daniel wondered if she already knew. He had trouble thinking that much of anything could escape this woman's attention. Perhaps she had come to ensure he would meet with Jelani.

"He is confused and doubts himself. It's a difficult time."

"I'm sure," Daniel said. "What with being turned into a vampire and all.

"I am trying to temper his recklessness but still, you would be proud of him. He is quite capable, young though he is."

"Recklessness?"

"Meet with your friend." Saaya stepped away, and a towering dark figure suddenly dropped behind her. He swept an arm out, holding the side of his coat. "And walk in the light," Saaya finished, and Kafeel swept his coat around her. Daniel was thrown into darkness.

23

After his conversation with Saaya, Daniel had to rush home and get cleaned up before heading out to the boardwalk. He checked his phone. "Five to seven." He looked around but only saw tourists and local joggers. "'Tis the season," he said, thinking of how he and Jelani referred to the beginning of every summer thus.

"Indeed."

Daniel nearly jumped off the bench. He turned to see Jelani standing directly behind him, a smirk on his face.

"You think giving me a heart attack is funny?" Daniel snapped. "I told you not to sneak up on me like that."

The smirk disappeared and Jelani spread his hands. "I'm sorry. It wasn't intentional."

"It wasn't?" Daniel gave his chest a little thump with his fist. "I don't think a cat could've been quieter."

"Mind if I sit down?"

After a moment of hesitation Daniel nodded.

They sat on the wooden park bench in silence for a time, gazing out at the ocean. With the weather finally turning warm, even at night, and the sun making more frequent appearances, joggers, walkers, and cyclists filled the seaside boardwalk. Even at dusk, pedestrians were numerous. Seagulls shouted to one another from overhead while crows roosted on handrails, tree limbs, and walkway lamps, waiting for someone to drop a snack.

Daniel hardly saw any of it. He kept stealing glances at Jelani. He looked the same, yet different. There was an aura about him that suggested a person much bigger than the man sitting next to him. He also sat perfectly still. Unnaturally still. Daniel found Jelani's presence unsettling in a way he couldn't describe.

Despite Daniel's discomfort with the silence, Jelani seemed content to remain so. He looked back out at the water, and North Vancouver far on the other side. Several times Jelani had mentioned moving to the other side of the Burrard Inlet. Daniel had teased him about being a suburb kid.

"Wondering why I wanted to meet with you?"

Daniel glanced at Jelani, who was still staring out at the water. "Actually I was wondering why you didn't choose to come out later." He jerked his head in the direction behind them. Sun's still out."

"We're sitting in the shade of two tall buildings under a tree," Jelani said. "Sunlight's no biggie. Direct sunlight is where the problems happen."

Daniel started to respond, then stopped. *That wasn't awkward at all.* The silence between them returned. Daniel returned his gaze to boardwalk, the inlet beyond, and the tall buildings of North Vancouver on the other side.

"It's a different world, you know." Jelani spread a hand to encompass their environment. "It's like a sub-world that exists right alongside this one. Hidden in plain sight."

"Seems that way," Daniel said. "The fact that we've probably been walking next to ..." he hesitated, "people other than humans, is kind of hard to absorb."

"You can say vampire, Daniel. I've gotten over the initial shock of it. It is what it is, and I am what I am."

"Yeah, maybe you've gotten over the shock, but I don't think I have yet."

"Fair enough."

Another stretch of silence.

Daniel interlaced his fingers and leaned forward, resting his elbows on his knees. "What's it like?" he finally asked. "What's it like to be …"

"A vampire?" Jelani finally looked at him. There seemed to be something more behind those dark brown eyes. Something different. "I'm still pretty new at it, but it does take some getting used to. I imagine some might adjust better than others, but for me it's been rough.

He looked back out at the water. "Imagine everything about you being superimposed. Your strength, speed, dexterity. You're patience, temper, skills. Everything that you are is … increased. Whatever you have an affinity for is increased. It's like being some kind of super human."

"Doesn't sound so bad," Daniel remarked.

"There is another side to it."

Daniel nodded. "Of course. There's always a catch."

"A big catch," Jelani said. "You can never feel the sun on your skin again. Your blood doesn't produce the proper amount of cells to keep you going, so you have to find it elsewhere, if you get my drift."

"Gotcha," Daniel said, making an effort not to squirm.

"Don't worry about it. I'm full. And I'd never harm you. Whatever I've become, I wouldn't put myself in a position for that to happen."

"I'm not worried about it," Daniel replied.

Jelani looked at him and smiled. "Sorry, man, but you're racing heart says otherwise. I understand, though.

"You start to think differently, too," he said, returning to the subject. "Things that would be important to a human are trivial to an immortal. I can think of little that would cause me to be in a rush, anymore. Relationships take on a different meaning, I think, but I'm not really certain about that."

"And apparently you start talking differently, too," Daniel observed.

Jelani nodded. "I don't know why, but there is a sharpness to my thought processes that wasn't there before. And the rage."

"Rage?" Daniel looked at Jelani as if seeing him for the first time. "You?"

Again, Jelani nodded. "When I really stopped to think about what had happened to me, to all of us, it set me off. I wanted to rip Remy in half and run my blades right through that other Hunter's heart. When they weren't available, I settled for wiping out probably a couple dozen vampires at what I can only describe as a vampire rave."

He looked back at Daniel, noticing his best friend had gone rigid. "I've said too much."

Daniel shook his head, but he never took his eyes off Jelani. "No. It's just that I've never heard you talk that way, and I didn't think you could be capable of killing anyone."

Jelani looked visibly hurt by that last remark and Daniel started to apologize. Jelani held up a hand. "No. You're right. I would be just as horrified if the situation was reversed. But allow me to explain. I was beyond anger, but I also reasoned that the more vampires I killed, the less threat there would be to you guys, and humans in general."

Daniel looked out at the ocean beyond the boardwalk. Yacht large and small swayed in the rippling current, while geese and ducks drifted between them as though shopping for a residence. "Sounds like a good cause. Makes sense to me."

"Does it?" Jelani indicated himself. "I've fed on no human so far, I seek to protect you and Wen and Alisha, and the thought of killing a human is repulsive to me. Yet I am a vampire. I'm surely not the first decent person to have been turned. How many immortal lives did I end that may have been decent people? Maybe they were just there to have a good time to help them deal with the lot life had thrown them. I'll never know."

When the silence resumed once again, Daniel tried to think of something to say to make his friend feel better. Was it truly murder to kill a bunch of vampires who probably fed on and killed humans anyway?

"You're probably trying to think of something to say to make me feel better, aren't you?"

"You know I won't sit here and lie to you, but I must admit I'm not sure if this area is as gray as you seem to think it is. You yourself said that when you were out at dusk, a bunch of vampires were staring at you and commenting that they could smell Saaya on you. I think if you had been alone somewhere, they might have attacked you. And don't forget your ordeal on the Skyride up on Grouse."

"A handful doesn't represent the many," Jelani said, "and vice versa. Anyway, I didn't come here to debate the moral gravity of my actions. If what I did was right, then fine. If not, the consequences will find me."

"That kind of talk coming from you scares me, man," Daniel said.

"As I said, you start to think differently. I find myself thinking and speaking a little more different every day. It worries me."

Daniel didn't doubt it. It worried him, too. "So what did you want to talk about?"

Jelani went straight to the point. "Kafeel has been watching over you for the last month. That's why you haven't been attacked."

"Yeah, I noticed that."

"I don't know how long he will continue to do so. It's more a favor to Saaya than out of any interest in keeping you all alive."

"Of course," Daniel said dryly.

"It doesn't matter," Jelani continued. "Regardless of what Kafeel does, I'll be watching over you now. I'll need you to be careful though, until I manage to kill Remy."

Daniel's spine went rigid at that. It wasn't the first time he'd heard Jelani speak that way, but it still made him no less uneasy.

"I'm not going to mince words with you," Jelani said, reading Daniel's expression. "I figure you need to know all this, so I'm putting it to you as direct as I can."

"I hear you," Daniel said. "But if you happen to talk to the girls, you might want to be a little more selective in the verbs you choose. You're making me uncomfortable, but you'd freak them out."

Jelani nodded and continued. "Remy isn't worried about you right now because he's got me, and likely that other Hunter on his trail ..." he faltered.

"What?" Daniel asked.

"Just thinking."

"About?"

"That first Hunter, Yako. You remember him, right?"

Daniel looked at Jelani as though he'd lost his mind. "Barely. He's just a haze in my mind. I'd probably remember him better if he were attached to something more important than trying to kill us."

His sarcasm flew right over Jelani, who was still in thought. "I fought him the night I reawakened. He is formidable."

"Formidable?" *There's a word I never expected to hear in a conversation.* "So you're telling me you went after that guy?" Jelani nodded. "With what?" Daniel asked.

"What else?" Jelani replied.

"You're silver daggers?" Daniel was incredulous. "The ones that are only about twelve inches long? The ones that, if you put them together, are still shorter than that guy's sword?"

"Yes."

"Well, now I'm really relieved to see you here; whole."

"I nearly wasn't. As I said, he's formidable. He could have killed me but he held his stroke. I don't yet understand why. He doesn't give me the impression of a man that would show mercy to anyone, especially someone who attacked him."

"I can't believe you went after him," Daniel said.

"I don't think you'll have to worry about Yako anymore," Jelani continued. "I think he's more concerned with Remy's uncreation."

"You think you can cut the vampire talk?" Daniel said. "It's kinda giving me the creeps."

For whatever reason, this made Jelani chuckle. "Sorry."

A woman with long brown hair tied into two braids on either side of her head walked by with a pug on a leash. The little dog stopped and started sniffing the grass. Catching the cue, the woman reached into her pocket and pulled out a small plastic sack and stuck her hand in it.

"That's exactly why I don't want a dog," Jelani said as they watched the woman wait for the dog to finish its business. "When I was a kid, I didn't even like it on the end of my shovel. I can't imagine the only thing separating my hand from the dump that dog is taking, is plastic bag."

Daniel snickered at that. "You've appointed yourself as our guardian angel, then?"

"Hardly an angel," Jelani said. "But I'll be watching over you all. As best I can, anyway."

As soon as the woman and her pug continued on their way, a man walked by. On a leash trotting next to him was a gray and white schnauzer. The dog glanced at them with dark eyes and a downturned mouth. Jelani smiled at the dog.

"Get that little guy a tweed suit jacket and a pipe, and he'll have the 'dignified old man' look perfectly."

Daniel laughed, and his heart lightened a little bit more at his friend's familiar humor.

"It's true," Jelani said, staring after the dog. "They look like old men."

"Where do you come up with this stuff?" Daniel asked. "Dogs

that look like old men, afghan dogs that you call monkey dogs?"

Jelani rolled his eyes. "First of all," he pointed in the direction the schnauzer and man had gone, "those dogs look like old men, I don't care what you say. Second, I was a little kid when I used to be terrified of afghans. Back then, I thought they looked like monkey dogs. I was a strange kid. I won't deny it."

Daniel pointed in the direction the woman had gone. "And your description of pugs?"

Jelani tilted his head at him. "Are you really going to tell me that those dogs aren't snorting, farting little sausages?"

Daniel laughed again. "You win, man, you win. But keep that to yourself. You know Wen wants to get one."

"Why?" Jelani asked. If it had been the normal Jelani, he might have wrinkled his nose.

"She loves the little bastards."

"Just get her a miniature pig. Less funny looking."

Daniel shook his head. "Seems like there's still a little of the old Jelani in there."

"I hope that'll be true in a few weeks or a month, or a year."

"What are you planning to do?"

"I told you already—"

"Not that," Daniel interrupted. "I know what you said you're planning to do right now, but I'm talking about in the future. Let's say you manage to get rid of Remy, and through some miracle, we're not bothered by any more Hunters. Will you try to go back to life as close to normal as you can?"

"I don't know. It's only been a short time since I've arisen …" he glanced at Daniel, "woken up, again. Things are changing in me. I'm not going to lie to you. A lot of the things that would have been important to me just one month ago are not, anymore."

"Are you planning on staying in Vancouver?"

"I'd like to."

They were dancing around the most important topic aside from survival, he knew it. Daniel finally took a deep breath and decided to jump right in. "And Alisha?"

Jelani leaned forward and rested his elbows on his knees. "I don't know."

"Have your feelings changed at all?"

Jelani shook his head. "No. I still feel the same, but I don't know what can happen now, if anything. I don't know much about my new existence yet, but I'm learning. I don't know if I can be with her, or if she'd even want to be with me now that I am what I am."

"She loves you."

"I know. But I'm not the same person. Not exactly."

"She plays the tough role," Daniel said, "because she's just being careful. I'm telling you that she is really right there with you, man. She loves you. The whole time you were gone, she slept very little, and when Saaya came to give us updates, there were a couple times when I thought she was about to get in Saaya's face." Jelani tensed, and Daniel put a comforting hand on his shoulder.

"Don't worry about it. Wen and I were always there. I'll also have to admit that, despite her being somewhat detached from our worries or our situation, Saaya does seem to have some small measure of sympathy. That she actually went out of her way to communicate with us about you says a lot."

"It says she probably didn't want to hear my incessant whining about all of you if she didn't," Jelani said.

"I admit the girl isn't the easiest to be around," Daniel said, "but I think you may not give her enough credit."

Jelani shrugged. "Maybe. She's been helping me out a lot, but I think there's a price attached I'll have to pay later."

"The whole time, Alisha kept trying to convince Saaya to take her to see you."

"That might not have been a good idea."

"I agree."

"There's something else," Jelani said.

Dread settled over Daniel's shoulders like a cloak. "What could possibly make any of this worse?"

"When I was at that outdoor rave I told you about, this thing happened where everyone raised their hands and stared at the sky. At the moon."

"What's so strange about that?"

"To your eyes, it would have been an extra bright moon. My eyes saw that brightness, but with an orange tint."

"Orange?"

Jelani nodded. "I've spoken to Saaya about it, and this is called a Hunter's Moon. During this hunter's moon cycle, vampires have a variety of reactions. Some become stronger, some more wild. The thirst is stronger in some, while others experience heightened senses and awareness. It only happens every so many years."

Daniel stared at him. "So, what you're saying is?"

"That you should stay inside as much as possible at night. Knowing that this cycle has been going on since our initial ordeal, I'm amazed that we're all still alive."

"I thought only werewolves were affected by the moon," Daniel said.

"There's the grand irony," Jelani replied. "For all that the two like to snub each other, the similarities between vampires and lycans make it almost laughable."

Daniel noticed Jelani still referred to vampires as something apart from himself. His heart broke for his friend. "How long will this hunter's moon cycle last?"

"I don't know. I'm hoping it won't be much longer. It's not like it can last forever." A woman walked by and glanced at Jelani, then at Daniel, and her lips thinned into a half-smile. Jelani stared at her with such hard intensity that she sniffed and shook her head, continuing on.

"What the hell was that all about?" Daniel asked.

"Likely she thought that I was planning to take you somewhere and kill you. Maybe she thought to join in."

Daniel was growing tired of getting terror chills. "So you're telling me that was a vampire that walked by just then?"

"There are more around than you think. The funny thing is, it's the Hunters, and the pureblood leaders of the covens that keep everything in check. If a lot of the *shaquora* like her were left unchecked, they'd kill and feed without any kind of tact, and there would be chaos."

Daniel's head was spinning. "Makes me wonder how many of the girls I've dated were vampires."

"Remember Lisa?" Jelani said. "The one who worked the early evening shift and only ever got off at night? The one that was always doing something on her day off till night?"

Daniel's mouth slowly fell open.

"Yeah," Jelani said. "Knowing what we do now, I'm betting she walks the night."

"Ho … ly … shit," Daniel whispered. "She invited me to her house one night, and the only reason I didn't go was because I had to work."

"The job saved your life, homeboy."

Daniel just stared out at the water, wondering how many times he'd come close to dying in his life. *Sharing the world with vampires. I still can't believe this.*

"Makes you a little paranoid, doesn't it?" Jelani said.

"Nothing you have to worry about anymore," Daniel replied.

"How's Wen?" Jelani asked.

"Putting on a strong smiling face."

"And worried sick."

Daniel nodded. "And worried sick."

"Don't ever forget how lucky you are."

Daniel frowned at him. "You talk like a single guy with no hope."

"That's because I'm a single guy with no hope."

"Quit being dramatic, man. I don't think Alisha is looking to just chuck everything and start dating again. Once you get this all resolved, you can come talk to her."

"I'm not sure that's possible."

"Why not?"

"Would you be able to live with Wen in this situation?" Jelani looked straight at him. "Could you watch her age and eventually die, while you remain the same?" He closed his eyes and opened them again, looking at the ground. I don't think I can do that."

"I hadn't thought of that." Daniel tried to imagine living such a life with Wen. It was not a pleasant thought.

Jelani stood. "Come on. Let's get you back home."

"Thanks. I have to tell you, though that this whole bodyguard thing has me feeling like someone who can't take care of himself."

"You can't. Not really."

"Thanks for making me feel better."

"We've survived this long mostly out of luck, man." Jelani raised a hand and let it fall. "I wish I could tell you something better, but that's what it is. Once I get this mess straightened out, maybe things can get back to a semblance of how they were."

They stopped at their apartment and stood for a while, each wrapped in his own thoughts. Finally, Daniel asked, "What the plan?"

Jelani stared out at the mountains. "You don't want to know."

24

Atop a nearby building Jelani waited until his best friend went back inside their condo. For a while he remained where he was, lost in dark thoughts. He wished he could go inside and see Alisha again, but that might not be a good idea. The future was uncertain, and Jelani wasn't sure he trusted himself. Trusted himself how?

Jelani's thoughts held him on that rooftop long into the night. Below, the occasional couple or solitary person went for a night-time stroll on the lamplit boardwalk. One couple stopped to lean on the rail and gaze out at the dark ocean. On the other side of the walkway, tree limbs swayed in the ocean breeze. Jelani imagined those branches as the arms and curled fingers of a predator slinking their way toward the oblivious pair.

He shook his head. "I've got to get away from here."

The sound of audible footsteps approaching had Jelani spinning on his heels, daggers instantly in his hands. After a moment of recognition he relaxed. "Hello, Kafeel." The towering shadow stared at him in response. Jelani tucked his blades back into his pants.

"You should find something to strap to your body to sheath

those in." Kafeel nodded to Jelani's side. "Stuffing knives in your pants isn't efficient."

Jelani's mouth fell open. He couldn't think of a single instance when he'd heard the big man speak this much. Now he was practically making conversation. "I'll look into it."

"Do what you will, or don't."

Jelani blinked. "Brotha, conversation with you is kinda like a verbal kick in the nuts. You know that?" What looked like a hint of a smile came and went.

"Are all vampires so devoid of emotion?" Jelani asked.

"Not necessarily, but we don't emote in the same manner as a human."

"Seems like you don't *emote* at all."

"Says a newly turned human."

"Hardly a human."

"Hardly a vampire."

The soft chirp of a killdeer pierced the darkness of a lawn somewhere below the building. The only answer came in the soft murmur of the ocean, as the tide bumped against the rocky shore.

Jelani frowned. "So what am I, then, if I'm hardly a vampire?"

"A child in transition. If you survive, you would be unique in some ways."

"Why wouldn't I survive?"

"I don't have time for your insatiable curiosity."

Jelani laughed, though there was no mirth in the situation. "You don't have time? You're immortal."

"My patience is not."

"Okay man, okay." Jelani jabbed a thumb in the direction of Stanley Park. "You know about the um … situation back there?"

This time, Kafeel let out a little chuckle. It was the most ominous sound Jelani had ever heard. "Few who walk the night do not know about that. Less than three full nights old, and you are already quite infamous."

So much for a low profile. "I guess I'm in the crosshairs of every vampire in town then?"

"Perhaps, perhaps not." Kafeel moved to stand beside him and looked down at the boardwalk. "It might happen that a cowardly *shaquora* might try to drive a silver knife through your back, if you are an oblivious fool." His eyes flicked in Jelani's direction, then back down at the boardwalk and the people milling about. "I do not believe you're oblivious."

"Thanks," Jelani said dryly.

"You should be more concerned about Hunters," he continued. "You dispatched six that night. If you are lucky, the coven in which they belong will not discover that it was you."

Once again, Jelani's mouth fell open. "How do you know about that?"

Kafeel's only response was a microscopic grin.

Jelani cleared his throat. "I don't think I was recognized."

"Impossible for you to know," Kafeel responded. "Likely, they will connect the deaths of the six Hunters with your attack at the *Reverence.*"

"*Reverence?* I thought it was called a *dark rock,* or something like that."

"What you saw was a mix of the two. When large numbers of *shaquora* converge upon one location to observe a full Hunter's Moon, they call it *Reverence.* Purebloods call it foolish."

"Looked like a party to me," Jelani said. "You purebloods prefer sitting on couches with wine and stuffy shirts?"

"Purebloods prefer anonymity, which a *Reverence* endangers. That is why those Hunters you killed were there. To keep humans from stumbling upon it, and keep any *shaquora* who become too enraptured from wandering loose and attacking humans."

Jelani nodded. "Fair enough. And what about *Ancestors* and their families?"

"We prefer anonymity from all. Few purebloods know we still

exist. Turned vampires even less so. You are one of the few who have been turned, who know of our existence at all."

"Should I feel privileged?"

"You should feel careful," Kafeel looked down at him. "As I said. We prefer anonymity."

"Gotcha," Jelani replied. He looked at the building where he had lived for years. The light to his apartment was on. Daniel and the girls were probably watching a movie or something. Jelani would have given anything in the world to be there right now enjoying a good movie with dinner and a hot drink, sitting on the sofa with the woman he loved curled up next to him."

"Engaging in the human habit of wanting what you cannot have?" Kafeel asked.

"Engaging in the act of wanting what I already had," Jelani clarified, not appreciating the sarcasm.

"How much of your new immortality will you spend lamenting this former life?"

The lavender glow crept into Jelani's eyes. "Oh, not very long at all. I can only think about what I've lost and what I've been made into for so long before I'm ready to do some hunting of my own." He looked up into Kafeel's hard eyes.

"A dream career, my perfect girl, freedom to live and work wherever I wanted. I worked my ass off to get to where I was and one of those parasites," he pointed at a vampire walking down the boardwalk in the middle of a crowd of humans, "took everything from me and made me a predator of my own species. Former species. Whatever."

He stared at the vampire below their perch and his lavender eyes smoldered. With his newly enhanced senses, Jelani smelled the man's cologne even from his position so high up. Armando Spice Collection. He flirted with a woman who it turned out, lives in the building next to his. He said all the right things, offered a charismatic smile at just the right time. The woman likely would die this night.

"When I finally catch up to that slippery muthafucka I'm going to make sure he feels every tiny second of his un-creation. I want him to have time to remember every bit of the long life his pure-blood ass enjoyed before I take it from him."

The towering vampire looked down at him, clearly unimpressed with the speech. "The pursuit of revenge is more enjoyable than revenge itself."

"What, then?" Jelani demanded. "Just turn the other cheek? Be thankful for my new 'gifts'?"

Kafeel turned away, heading toward the opposite end of the roof. "Find a purpose that will carry you past the day of reckoning."

"Maybe I'll just go for a walk in the sun." He barely heard a chuckle before Kafeel spoke again.

"That, you could do, little fledgling. That, you could do."

25

R emy couldn't remember the last time he wanted to take a woman to his bed yet rip her apart at the same time. Seeing Melinda, his newest re-creation staring defiantly into his eyes, made him want to do just that.

"If I had a way to bring Jelani to you, you know I would." Her voice was so sweet, so earnest. So mocking.

Remy's upper lip curled. She was lying of course. And what frustrated him even more was that the bitch was smart. She knew how to speak without actually alerting his mind to the lie. She couldn't hide her encounter with Jelani from him, but she could lie about what had happened. That she was somehow able to so control her emotions to limit Remy's ability to read her infuriated him.

"You've had the gift for longer than him, even if little more than two months."

It was true. They were both fledglings but Melinda was the older. A month was sufficient time for her to have grown more comfortable with her new existence than Jelani, who had just awakened. Difficult or not, she should have been able to bring Jelani back.

"He's quite strong," she said. "I don't believe I would be able to bring him here against his will."

He thought about it. How could that be possible?

"Of course," Melinda continued, "how would I stand a chance when he nearly killed the Eldest Hunter in a fight?"

Remy stared at her. It was an obvious lie, but why would she bother telling it? No. She was still trying to protect him. More likely, she had found a way to tell Jelani to stay outside of Remy's influence. He started probing her mind and she recoiled, but quickly composed herself. She stared balefully at Remy, who found it amusing. She cocked her head to one side and smirked at him.

"Ah, love of my life. Don't you trust me? What kind of rela-tionship are we going to have without trust?" She put a hand on her hip. "If anything, it's me who shouldn't trust you. I mean, look at you." She waved her hand at him and his amusement evaporated. "All this manly man standing in front of me. With your undeniable courage and masculinity, you must leave countless enthralled women in your wake wherever you go. Your prowess must be legendary—"

He was right in front of her and clamped his hand around her throat. He squeezed and lifted her from the ground till she was eye level with him. "I feel a windpipe begging to be crushed." This time, he saw fear. Satisfied, he gave her another squeeze till she clamped her eyes shut, then dropped her to the floor and turned his back.

She wouldn't die, of course, unless he ripped her throat completely out. But the pain she would have to endure while healing would be excruciating. "Do me a favor, pet, and go away until I'm ready to see you again."

Melinda struggled to her feet. "Can ... I get you ... anything ... while I'm gone?" she rasped, squeezing her eyes shut through the agony as her throat healed. C ... Coffee? A cup ... of tea?" She swallowed, then winced. "Liquid silver?"

He spun and dealt her a backhand across the face that sent her spinning through the air to crash to the ground. He stood over her, red eyes glowing in anger. "Speak another word and I will tear you apart."

Once again she climbed to her feet, nodded to him, then turned and left the room. Remy sent a portion of his rage into her mind and heard the resulting cry of pain and surprise, followed by a thud when she hit the floor for the third time. Satisfied, he calmed and slammed the door shut.

Despite the woman's insufferable defiance, she was weak and stupid. Only an idiot would test the patience of the one who turned them. He was a Hunter of unparalleled skill, and could destroy her with little effort.

Remy cast the thought away. Just like any other creation, she was expendable. He would manipulate her tiny little mind and use her until she was no longer needed. Then she would be discarded.

Remy sat down on the dingy sofa chair in his motel room. An immortal deserved the best life had to offer, not these disgusting dwellings that humans built for themselves. He hated being here, hated having to pay money for such unsanitary accommodations. Massius had been clear, however, that he was to keep a low profile.

Sometimes Remy wished he could just kill the stupid Elder and do things his way. The fool was incompetent and paranoid. What difference did it make whether Remy stayed in a five star hotel or this dive he currently inhabited?

He considered the information he had gleaned from his servant. Either Melinda had told him, or Jelani had somehow discovered that if he stayed a far enough distance away, he would be out of Remy's influence. Whichever it was, he would have to find a way to bring Jelani back to him. He would need both of them at his side when it came time to deal with Yako.

"I'll need to bring him to me before he finds a way to die," Remy thought aloud. A fledgling *shaquora* was at risk of uncreation shortly after their rebirth. Older turned vampires, pure-bloods, and even the occasional werewolf would prey on them.

The red glow of Remy's eyes intensified in the darkness of the musty hotel room. Jelani was staying out of reach, fine. A smile slithered across his face. If Jelani wouldn't come to him, he would go to Jelani's friends. What would he do when he went home and found that he had nothing left? In his anger he would likely come looking for Remy, and then it would be too late.

∼

Melinda was careful to remain quiet. The wall between them would not insulate her laughter. He threatened to kill her, but he wouldn't do it until she was no longer useful to him.

She sat on the bed and thought about their recent conversation. Remy was getting impatient with her, which was what she wanted. The less patient he was, the less likely he was able to probe her mind to any real effect. She shook her head at the humor of the situation to keep herself from crying.

If she and Remy were human, she would have had little difficulty turning him in circles. The fact that he could intuit her thoughts forced her to be very careful about her feelings and what she allowed to occupy her mind. By telling him the truth about Jelani's skills, but then adding the lie about him fighting Yako, she had perfectly hidden the truth from him. Of course he wouldn't believe that Jelani would survive a fight with the Eldest Hunter.

Melinda didn't know whether Jelani had fought Yako or not, but she knew that Remy would see her impressions of Jelani's abilities and had to think fast. It was always like that. If she tried to plan what to say to him, he would know. So she had to rely on quick thinking to keep him away from the truth.

She rubbed the side of her face where Remy had struck her. He knew she was lying to him, but he couldn't prove it and hadn't yet figured out what she was lying about. Once he did, that would be when Melinda's life would be in danger.

She left her room and exited the lobby of the dank motel. Remy was too busy sitting in the dark thinking about his plans to be bothered. She almost laughed. He wanted Jelani and Melinda had every intention of bringing the two together. After witnessing the havoc Jelani had caused at that *dark rock*, Melinda was confident that Jelani would be able to kill her master. If she could find a way to convince that ninja-like Eldest Hunter to join in the fun, so much the better.

26

A lisha tapped her foot, willing the elevator to hurry to the bottom floor. Daniel had tried to hide the truth from her, that he had just spoken with Jelani, but she knew him too well. He'd tried to deflect the conversation, even flat out lie to her about it, and she loved him for it. Daniel and Wen were great friends. They knew that the situation was difficult, and had gone to great effort to help her through it. Still.

If Jelani was out there, she would speak with him. There was so much unresolved between them and she had questions that needed to be answered.

A soft 'ding' indicated the elevator had reached the lobby. As soon as the doors opened, Alisha hurried out of the building and went around the front to the boardwalk. She tried to look casual while scanning the darkened area for any signs of vampires. A few joggers and cyclists passed by, then several couples followed, out for a walk. Feeling at least a little safer, Alisha went out onto the boardwalk and leaned on the rail, looking out at the parked yachts and the quiet ocean, and the mountains shrouded in the darkness beyond.

What the hell is she doing? Jelani thought, seeing Alisha tentatively stepping out onto the boardwalk. It was after nine o'clock and though there were people around, there weren't many. She might have felt safe with people passing by, but Jelani had already seen two vampires take a casual interest in her on two separate occasions.

At first he thought Daniel had foolishly told her they'd met up tonight, but knowing Alisha, she'd read it in his face as easily as she could read Jelani. That was the thing about Alisha. She could read a lie well enough, but if she knew you personally, it was practically impossible to lie to the woman.

He dropped from the roof, silently descending the sixty feet to land in the middle of a clump of trees and a flower garden. He stepped out and moved quickly. The last thing he wanted was for her to be snatched away. He knew it could happen. He could have easily done it himself right now with no one around.

"You walk the night as if it's safe."

She jumped and turned around to face him. "Jelani! Don't do that. You nearly gave me a heart attack."

"Then you know how I felt when I saw you walk out here."

"You saying you're not glad to see me?"

"You know better than that."

She leaned back against the rail, but he could tell it was a show of comfort. It must have taken some courage to come out here and wait, hoping he was still around.

"Alisha, why are you here?"

"I live here."

"You know what I mean."

She turned those beautiful hazel eyes on him that he loved looking into. "I want to know what's going on with us."

Jelani didn't know how to answer. *I'd like to know that, myself.*

"There's a lot going on right now and I don't think the best thing is for us to worry about this."

Alisha stepped closer and wrapped her arms around him. "I know a lot has changed, but I'm wondering if there's something still there for us, and if there is something I can do to help you."

Jelani knew what he wanted. But he wasn't sure if what he wanted and what was right was the same thing. He felt an ache in his chest just looking at her.

"I don't think there is anything you can do to help me, except stay safe. Which pretty much means never step outside at night again until I get this situation rectified."

Alisha crossed her arms. "Judging by your choice to answer my second question first, you're planning on giving me the noble and heroic speech about how it's too dangerous for us to be together."

"Not going to give you that speech at all," Jelani said, trying not to notice that her arms were crossed under her breasts. They were the perfect size to him; not too small and not too large. *I have got to be the biggest pervert alive.* "I'm not going to stand here and tell you that I don't want us to be together, because I do. I'm also not going to tell you that I think us being together is a good idea."

"Do I get a say in this?"

"I don't think so."

"Oh, really?" She shifted her weight from one foot to the other and started tapping her foot. Jelani's super sensitive 'man intuition' told him that he might not have said the right thing.

"So let me get this straight ..." They each took a step back to allow a jogger to pass between them.

"Guess we're in the middle of the sidewalk," Jelani said with a hollow chuckle.

Alisha was having none of it. "You," she jabbed her finger at him, "are going to stand there and tell me that I have no choice in this situation. You're saying that you're telling me that you aren't allowing this to go any further."

Jelani cleared his throat. "It's not like I'm telling you what to do ..." she arched an eyebrow at him. "Not like I could do that anyway. But what I'm saying is that we can't continue like this. I just awoke to find out I'm some new kind of thing that I personally find horrifying, and I'm looking for a Hunter who's also looking for me."

"I can't think of a crazier thing to do, Jelani."

"Not exactly crazy. Things are not the same as they were."

Alisha hugged herself and looked away. "You've told me."

Jelani hesitated, but then figured it might be best if she knew what kind of thing he'd become. "I told you what I'm going to do, Alisha."

"I know. But part of me hoped otherwise." A gentle breeze blew her ponytail to one side as she turned back to him. The lovely sight crumbled when he saw the resignation on her face. That expression was like a cold hand clamped around his heart.

"You're planning to ... kill him."

He spread his hands. "What else can I do? Just like that guy that was after us back then, the one you helped me—"

"That was self-defense," she said.

"What do you think this is? If I don't get rid of this guy, he's going to keep coming after you, whether the coven orders it, or to use you to get to me. As long as Remy walks the night, all of you are in danger."

"I hate that he did this to you," she said, stepping forward again and wrapping her arms around him.

Feeling her body pressed to his made all of his concerns melt away. Jelani returned the hug, closing his eyes and breathing in grapefruit shower gel mingled with her own personal scent. He could have stood there forever, feeling every muscle, every cell in his body, tingling with energy. He felt her chest rise and fall with each breath. He heard each inhale and exhale, felt her heartbeat increase. He also heard the blood rushing through her veins.

"Spend the night with me," she said.

"That's not a good idea."

"I'm not totally clueless, Jelani. I know there's a risk, but I also know you."

"Right now, I don't even know me," Jelani replied.

"Then maybe I know you better than you know yourself."

"I shouldn't go back there. Wen hasn't seen me yet. I don't want to just pop in like this. She might not be comfortable with me and I wouldn't blame her."

"That you're saying things like this to argue against coming home proves my point."

Alisha turned around and leaned back into him. He let out a sharp breath and tried to cover it up by clearing his throat. She let her head fall back against his chest and reached back to find his hands. As always, her soft and strong fingers felt perfect when intertwined with his own.

"I don't want to go in there." He tried to make his voice sound firm.

"Someone down there is calling you a liar, baby." She pressed harder against him, arching her back ever so slightly. A hungry groan escaped him, and he could feel the heat rising in his blood. He felt with the tip of his tongue and found that his fangs were extending, along with other things.

"I didn't say I don't want to go with you," he said, once he trusted himself to speak. "I just don't think it's a good idea."

"You don't give Wen enough credit."

"That's not what I'm talking about."

She started away, but not before dragging his hands across her buttocks as she moved. She held one of his hands and pulled him after her. Jelani allowed himself to be led away, making a valiant—if failing—effort at refusal. The result was walking behind her and admiring the way her waist moved with that little side to side twitch, the shape of her hips, and the roundness of her—

"Jelani."

"Hmm?"

"Quit staring at my butt."

"Huh? No. Yeah. Okay."

"Hmm. Doesn't seem like you've changed that much."

"I have."

"Not completely."

They reached the front door to the building, and Alisha unlocked it. Stirred as she had him, the sound of the key sliding into the lock was a loud echo in Jelani's ears. They stepped in and went for the elevators. He watched the numbers illuminate as the descending metal box drew closer. Each number that lit up and went dark again was like a countdown to a mistake until finally the doors opened.

"Alisha—"

"Please," she stopped him. "I've heard why you think we shouldn't go up there and I understand. But I want to be with you. I need to be with you, at least for tonight."

She pulled him into the elevator and they ascended. Less than a minute later, the doors opened again and they stepped into the hallway. It had been little more than a month, but it felt much longer than that. It was like coming back to a place that was familiar but different.

Alisha unlocked the door and opened it slowly, peeking in. "Hey, girl," he heard from inside. Poor Wen. Poor, gentle-hearted Wen. Never had Jelani heard such sadness masked as cheer. "Are we playing hide and seek, now?"

"Hey, girl," Alisha responded. "Um. I've got a visitor."

There were a few tense heartbeats of silence before he heard her voice again. "Jelani?"

He saw Alisha nod. Wen must have nodded back, because Alisha opened the door and stepped in. She stepped aside into the kitchen and Jelani stopped at the doorway. He and Wen had a clear view of each other.

"Come in, Jelani." Wen's voice was tiny, almost like a child's.

"You're sure?"

She nodded, not taking her eyes off him. He stepped in and closed the door. After he removed his shoes, he walked slowly through the hallway, past the kitchen, and stopped at the edge of the living room.

Wen, who had been standing straight and still, with her hands clamped together in front of her chest, dashed around the couch and ran toward him. Before he could say a word, she slammed into him, wrapping her arms around him in a crushing hug.

"We've been so worried about you," she said in between sniffs. "We didn't know what happened."

Jelani patted her on the back, touched beyond words by his best friend's fiancée; his good friend. He fumbled for words. "Saaya came by to update you guys, didn't she?"

"I don't trust what she says," came the muffled reply. Now they were rocking side to side, and Jelani resisted the urge to laugh. Wen had to be the cutest, most kind-hearted person he knew.

"You making out with my fiancée, now?"

They let each other go and Jelani turned to see Daniel leaning in the doorway. He had a half-smirk on his face, but his eyes and posture were less relaxed.

"Oh, babe!" Wen said, but her cheeks flushed.

Jelani and Daniel stared into each other's eyes. Daniel desperately wanted to trust him, Jelani could see it. "I assure you, all is well and all necks are intact," he said.

Wen looked down at her feet, then at Alisha, who glanced at Jelani and then at Daniel. *Guess that wasn't so funny.*

"Of course they are!" Wen said, walking over and draping her arms around Daniel's neck. He smiled and they gave each other a peck on the lips. Jelani could tell his friend was trying not to look at her neck.

"Go ahead and look, man. I won't be offended."

Wen looked questioningly at Jelani, then at Daniel. When comprehension dawned, she frowned up at Daniel. "Honey. You don't trust your best friend? How could you—"

"Please don't blame him, Wen," Jelani said. "He loves you and he's right to be wary." He nodded at Daniel, who looked down at Wen. "Let him look," Jelani said. "Please."

"Fine." Wen pulled her hair back and held it with one hand. She leaned her head to one side, then the other, allowing Daniel a clear look.

Once he was satisfied he looked back at Jelani, relief and gratitude clear on his face. At that moment, everything felt right. His best friend and his fiancée, and Alisha. It felt right, but wrong. A tiny part of him knew this couldn't continue. *Why am I here?*

"I'm surprised you came up," Daniel said.

"Me, too," Jelani replied. He glanced at Alisha, who turned and went into the kitchen and began rinsing glasses that were already clean.

"Ah," Daniel said.

Alisha had Jelani in such a heated state, he hadn't registered Daniel's absence when they'd come in. "Where were you? Not out—"

"Smooth out your feathers, mother hen," Daniel said, some of the normal ease returning to his voice. I just went downstairs to the gym, that's all.

"I know you didn't just call me—"

"Yup. I think I did."

Jelani's mouth fell open into a smile. "Oh yeah? You got me messed up—"

"Okay, okay," Wen said, rolling her eyes. "I know where this is going. "You two can 'crank it up' later."

Jelani snorted, then he and Daniel burst into laughter. It was always funny when Wen used Jelani's slang.

"Let's go down to the lobby and give these two some time."

"I need a shower," Daniel protested.

"You can have one when we get back." She crossed the room to the coffee table and grabbed a book on interior design, then tossed a fiction book to Daniel. "You and your B.O. can sit on the other side of the room."

"Sounds romantic," Daniel mumbled. "You did just hug me."

"See you later," Wen said, shoving Daniel out the door.

Daniel looked over his shoulder. "At least let me get my—" the door shut.

Jelani stood in the living room, watching Alisha rinse and dry the dishes till she was finished. It felt odd standing there. It was his living room, yet it felt like it wasn't. Alisha finished the dishes and turned around.

They faced each other for a while, Jelani enjoying those hazel eyes, while Alisha made an effort not to fidget. She rubbed her left arm, then rubbed her finger behind her ear.

"You wanna watch some TV?" Jelani asked, and Alisha made a half-cough, half-laughing sound.

"Oh my goodness. Jelani ... just be quiet." She came out of the kitchen and wrapped her arms around him. "Will you listen to me a second?" she asked.

"Yeah."

"I know why you're nervous, because I am, too. But ..." She took a deep breath. "I know I said it before, but ... I'm ... I love you." She leaned back and looked at him.

The words were like pain and pleasure mixed into one. He didn't know whether to feel happy, sad, or furious. He felt all three.

"I love you, too." *This is a mistake.* "I've loved you for a long time." *Why the hell did I say that?* "But I don't know what to do." *Great, Jelani. Indecisiveness. Perfect trait for a strong man. Solid as a rock.*

To his surprise, she rose to her tiptoes and kissed him; soft at first, then more deeply, more passionately.

"Thank you," she gasped, breaking for air.

"For what?"

"Not feeding me a macho line of bullshit about knowing exactly what to do."

Jelani didn't know how to respond. "Um. Yeah."

She glanced in the direction of the bedroom. His bedroom. Their bedroom.

He hesitated. "You sure?"

"I'm sure you're trying to kill the mood."

"You don't know what I am, not really."

"I think I do."

"Do you?" He scooped her off the ground and slipped his arm under her, holding her at eye level.

Alisha's eyes went wide, and she looked down. She was sitting on his arm as though it were a steel bar, her legs dangling above the floor. "You're strong."

"More than you know."

Her chest heaved and he saw desire and trepidation in her eyes. He took her in, head to toe. *Beautiful*, he thought.

She draped an arm around him, leaned back, then looked herself up and down. "You want this?"

"Yes."

27

J elani lay her gently on the bed and climbed over her. He studied her body, watched her chest rise and fall with each breath. His gaze slid down. When he came to her pants, he unbuttoned them and slipped his fingers in the sides. She lifted her hips upward so that he could slide them off.

Slowly, he pulled them down, his eyes taking in every inch of her smooth brown legs. Once he'd gotten them off, he came back over her. Alisha reached her hands behind his head and pulled him down to her. Her kiss was gentle, exploring. Jelani returned the kiss, their tongues slowly finding each other.

She slid her hands under his shirt and dragged her nails down his back. He arched his back, letting out a shaky breath. Alisha slid her hands back up again, pulling his shirt over his head.

Those beautiful hazel eyes moved as her gaze slide up and down his torso. Soft, smooth hands ran slid over his chest and down his abdomen, her fingers gliding over each crease between the muscles in his stomach. Her hands stroked up and down, and her body squirmed beneath him.

Alisha reached down further, unbuttoning his pants and sliding them down. He pulled them the rest of the way off and she immediately grabbed his buttocks with both hands. They kissed, growing more urgent. He pressed against her and could feel the lace of her bra rubbing up and down his chest.

He abruptly broke off away and groaned with pleasure when her fingers slipped into his shorts and found him. He let out ragged gasps as she massaged him, until finally he slipped his hand behind her back. She lifted her back and he unhooked her bra. He took his time, sliding it away, slowly revealing her round, perky breasts.

Alisha pulled off his shorts, and he slid his hands down her body, pulling her panties down to her ankles and slipping them off. Jelani admired her naked body. *Perfect.* He slid his tongue over every inch of her. He explored her small feet and delicate, manicured toes. The hint of muscles in her legs. He moved up, admiring her thighs, between her legs, her smooth, slightly sculpted stomach, her small waist. He continued on, running his tongue under her breasts, then up to her tiny black nipples.

He wanted her. All of her. His fangs gradually extended and his eyes glowed lavender. He saw every tiny colored vein in her breasts, each funneling sweet, delicious blood. What must it taste like, that thick hot liquid that practically sang to him? *No! Yes.*

Jelani clamped his eyes shut then opened them again, but the sight of her beautiful naked body, and those tiny beautiful blood-filled veins called to him. *Dammit, control yourself!* As if something else had subtly taken control of him, his eyes narrowed and he slid the tips of his fangs over her round breasts, heaving with repressed passion. His breath grew ragged, and a primal sound rumbled from deep in the pit of his core.

"Jelani?" Alisha whispered.

The sound of her voice was a beacon, lighting his way back to himself. He shook his head and looked down at Alisha to see her looking into his eyes. "Stay with me. I love you." He looked into her hazel eyes and found not fear, but love, compassion, and desire.

He looked back down to her breasts, waiting to be enjoyed, and he went back to them. Her back arched and she ran her hands over his head as he suckled. He remained there until her hands fell away and went down his stomach. Her tiny, delicate fingers found him again and stroked.

They teased each other, played with each other until it was too much to bear.

Alisha guided him upward till their hips were aligned.

She looked into his eyes again.

"You're sure?"

"Please," she breathed, then guided him. She took in several sharp breaths as he slowly, gradually, merged with her. Their bodies moved together perfectly in a rhythmic dance of passion. Time undefined passed. They were together. They were one.

28

The basket was heavy.

Heavy as the notion that the space Mallika occupied might as well have been empty. Graceful and dexterous, Mallika could have easily slipped through the crowds of couples, families, playing children and foreigners. She didn't need to. Everyone pretended she didn't exist yet gave her a wide berth.

Hawkers spoke of fresh caught fish, hand-woven jewelry, and beautiful handmade saris. As she passed by one shop, she stole a glance at her favorite. It was expertly embroidered, but not over-done and gaudy. It was blue-green, like the ocean. The shopkeeper looked up at her and she realized she had slowed too long to gaze at the beautiful piece. She moved on.

The basket was heavy.

Heavy like a woman's burden, her mother had taught. A woman must have excellent balance and posture. Mama had always said that when she caught Mallika slouching.

"A woman must have proper posture and balance. Never forget that you're a lady, Mallika."

The thought made her spirit smile, though the smile didn't

reach her lips. "What does it matter if I'm a lady or not, Mama?" she had asked once. Her mother ran a hand down her long black hair.

"Because you are, Phool." Phool. It meant flower, and Mallika always felt happier when her mother used her nickname. "One day you will bloom into a beautiful woman."

"I don't feel beautiful," Mallika had said. "We have to live here, while they live in homes with four walls and hard roofs. They have clean water and enough food. We clean up after them, and they look down on us for it."

"It is our karma that places us where we are in life, my little girl."

Mallika was a stubborn child, but also a respectful one. She nodded and silently disagreed. Her mother laughed.

"Oh, my little girl. I think you have more to your destiny than this." She waved a hand to indicate their little three-walled hut. "Maybe there is more for you in the world."

"I don't need more from the world. I'm happy to live here with you, Mama. Or maybe one day we will move away to someplace better."

Her mother smiled and ran her hand over Mallika's hair again. The smile was warm and loving; and hopeless.

Mallika snapped out of her daydream just in time to swerve around a child who had run across her path. The mother grabbed the child and pulled him away, admonishing him about how Mallika was unclean and to stay away from her. Mallika ignored the woman and increased her pace.

The basket was heavy.

Heavy like the plight of the Untouchables who remained in their slums and only ventured out when it was to do some manner of filthy work. The Untouchables, her people, were the dregs of society, who represented all that was unclean and undesirable. No one wanted to look upon an Untouchable, and Untouchables didn't *find it enjoyable to mingle with the rest of society anyway. Who would want to mingle in a society where the old superstitions said it was considered unlucky even for your shadow to pass across someone?*

It was their karma. That's what Mama used to say. Mallika didn't know if her mother actually thought it was true, or just told her that to make it easier to accept. Mama had accepted this life as her karmic existence and had lived it to her last breath with neither jealousy nor animosity toward those whose karma afforded them a better life. Mallika was not her mother.

The basket was heavy.

Heavy like the responsibility placed on a child who was forced to grow up too soon. Her responsibility, and those of many other Untouchable children whose parents had died from illness. It was better in the country. Mallika knew that. She had heard stories of how a family of Untouchables had actually managed to relocate out of the slums of the city and make a life in the country. Mallika had no idea how that could have been possible, given the difficulty of simply surviving day to day in the bowels of society. Was it a story to entertain children? To offer some kind of hope? How could it be? Such a story, true or not, offered nothing more than emotional torture.

The basket was heavy.

Heavy as the hot, humid air, the perspiring bodies, the averted gazes. Heavy as a hard life, cast upon one's shoulders because of their karma. Karma. All her fourteen years of life, Mallika had heard that word, used as a badge of justification by the privileged, and shawl of comfort by the impoverished. A shawl her mother had worn. A shawl her mother had lovingly tried to drape over her shoulders to comfort her from the unfair realities of her life.

Mama.

Mallika turned down one street, then another, thinking of Mama. As long as she had been alive, she remembered Mama coming home with bleeding, cracked hands, sore knees, and a stiff back. But she was strong. Strong for herself and for her daughter when Papa died. Strong to make the best life for her daughter with the little that her karma had afforded her. Never complaining, ever strong and loving till her last breath. Tears welled in Mallika's eyes and spilled down her cheeks, and her silent sobs nearly made her lose the heavy basket filled with freshly washed laundry balanced upon her head.

The basket was heavy. Like her heart.

❧

M emories. *They were her mother's experiences, her mother's memories, yet she felt them, dreamt them, as though they were her own. Pain crept through and forced her to forget the daydream for now. She was hungry, but she wasn't.*

"Mama, I don't understand."

Her mother ran her long gentle fingers through her daughter's raven black hair. "I know, my heart."

"Help me understand, Mama."

"I cannot, little one."

"Why not?"

Her hand stopped, and she pulled little Saaya into a tight hug. "You must ask Baba."

"But why can't I ask you, Mama?"

"I am not the same as you, Saaya. Not quite."

The little girl looked up into her mother's kind, dark brown eyes. A small part of her knew that her mother was the same, but part of her was different as well.

"Sometimes I'm hungry for food. Sometimes I'm hungry for water. Sometimes I'm hungry and thirsty at the same time, but not for food or water."

"I know, my little Saaya."

Despite her confusion, the little girl smiled. Saaya. It was her name, and it meant shadow in her mother's native tongue. "It is because you are my shadow, little one," her mother had once told her. "Because you are a dark and beautiful side of me."

"It hurts when I'm hungry and thirsty, Mama."

"I know little one. But Baba can help you understand. It is very important that you understand your other nature."

She nodded, and her long raven hair fell over her face.

The six year old girl ran through the castle, unbothered by the darkness. Unlike Mama, Saaya could see perfectly in the dark. She healed almost instantly, and was stronger and faster than any adult, including her mother. There were also times her body demanded more than food and water. There were times when her body demanded blood.

Ever since she was old enough, her mother had been adamant that Saaya understand that she was different from other children, and that they would be afraid of her if she revealed her other nature.

Up the winding stairs she climbed until she reached the top floor. Their home was the largest and grandest of any Saaya had ever known, and it was yet another secret that her mother had been adamant that she keep. "Some will be intimidated and some will be envious. Never flaunt the good fortunes of your life to others, Phool. Let people love you for who you are, and not what you have.

Saaya came to a room that was easily larger than the average house, and turned the latch on one of the twelve-foot tall double doors. It groaned open, and the little girl crept in.

Facing the tall window, a figure sat with legs crossed in a plush, high-backed leather chair. In his right hand was a crystal glass of red liquid. Saaya stood where she was, watching the back of the chair.

"You must remember to knock before entering," a deep and powerful voice said.

"I am sorry, Baba," Saaya said, doing her best to sound like it was the truth.

"In the flicker of time that you have been alive, not once have you been sorry for anything."

Saaya grinned, but remained silent.

"Come, Ua. Tell me why you are here."

Saaya loved that she had the same nickname in two different languages. While her mother called her Phool in her native language of Hindi, her father called her Ua, in his native language of Swahili. Her parents often used the two different yet beautiful words to call her their little flower.

She moved to stand beside the chair. *"The thirst is upon you, Ua,"* he said.

"How do you know, Baba?" Her father turned his head to regard her. In the darkness of the room, his lavender eyes practically glowed. On the rare occasions when they ventured as a family into the cities and villages, Baba's eyes were always dark brown. At home, often they were brown, but equally as often, they were that purplish lavender color.

"You are my child, Saaya. You are a part of me, as I am a part of you." He smiled, and the corners of his eyes crinkled. *"If you were not my child, however, one way I may know is by those little eyes of yours."*

Saaya looked down at her feet, confused. *"My eyes?"*

Her father slipped a finger under her chin and lifted her head. *"Yes, your eyes. The eyes tell the irrefutable truth, Saaya. It is what reveals our true nature."*

"But don't you hide things with your eyes, Baba?"

The smile deepened. *"Humans have eyes to look, but rarely do they use them to see."*

Again, Saaya was confused.

"You will understand in time," he said. *"And since the thirst is upon you, perhaps you will share a drink with me."* He handed the crystal glass to Saaya.

She gingerly took the glass from her father, looking from the crimson contents to him, and back. It was only recently, that she had begun to experience this new hunger. When her hearing had become more acute, she had overheard her mother and father discussing what her father repeatedly referred to as the thirst. On her sixth birthday, she discovered it for herself.

"You are the same as your mother and I, and yet different," Baba continued. "Because you are my child, you will occasionally thirst for blood to sustain yourself. As the child of a Count, you will thirst less than others of our kind. As the child of a human, you will thirst even less."

Saaya sipped the contents at first, then drained the glass in one gulp. She wiped a little crimson stream from the corner of her mouth. The result was immediate. Her body felt better, lighter, stronger. Baba nodded.

"For a short time, the thirst will be heavier for you, as your body is changing. As you mature, so too will your body's need for blood change."

"Can we go to the city today, Baba?"

Her father reclined back in his chair. "Not today, Ua. But I recognize your need to be around others. It is the human side of your nature."

Behind her, Kafeel materialized out of the darkness. "Your brother," Baba continued, "will accompany you."

Saaya looked up over her shoulder at her older brother, towering over her like an ominous cloaked sentry. "Hello, brother," she said. As expected, there was no response. Baba rarely spoke unless it was to educate Saaya about her life, and if her father spoke little, Kafeel spoke even less.

"Listen to your brother, for he is and always will be your guardian, your friend, and family. Listen to your sister, Kafeel, for she is your charge, your friend, and family."

"As you say, so shall it be," Kafeel replied. He looked down at Saaya, and though his face was—so much like their father's—

stony and hard, his dark brown eyes were kind. "Come, little one."

Saaya smiled wide. "What are we going to see?"

Kafeel turned toward the door, and Saaya hurried to catch up.

"What are we going to see?" she repeated.

Kafeel glanced down at her as she stepped past him through the door. "The world, little shadow."

29

S aaya opened her eyes. It was finally over. She had to admit that the woman had stamina. They had been at it for the better part of two hours before they'd stopped, then started up again.

When Saaya had felt the first signs of passion it had been as unexpected as the first time, but unlike before, she was prepared. Sitting in the lotus position on the floor of her dark apartment, Saaya had lost track of time till the first rays of light came streaming through the blinds of her room. She hadn't bothered to close and seal the curtains against it, for she knew that Jelani wouldn't be returning today.

She smiled a narrow-eyed smile. She had been speaking with Kafeel when her hips had twitched of their own accord. Then she'd felt a quickening in her body. Kafeel had looked right at her and shook his head, disgusted. "Find me when you are able," he'd said, turning away.

Saaya took a deep breath and slowly unfolded her legs and stretched them. It was more ritualistic than necessity, for she could snap out of her position in an instant if need be. She found the slow movements peaceful, however.

She leaned back on her hands and continued stretching her

legs, wiggling her toes. For three or four hours she had sat in meditation, firmly resisting wave after wave of passion that had come washing through her as the result of her blood connection with Jelani. She thought about that day, seemingly a lifetime ago, when she'd sneaked a tiny sample of his blood by piercing a bruise on his shoulder with her fangs. It had been sweet and perfect, and what had so long sung to her body, had then sung within her body.

From that moment forward, a connection between them had been formed and Saaya could feel the things Jelani felt. It had been an unintentional result of her deviousness, and at the time it had seemed like an unintended bit of good fortune. Now she knew that it had come with a cost that multiplied when Jelani had been bitten by Remy and she had intervened to save him a life of servitude to the Hunter.

Now she and Jelani were irrevocably connected. She wondered when he would truly come to understand that the connection worked two ways, and what that meant. Perhaps once he'd grown more into his new existence.

She opened her window and looked out at the sunny morning. Sunny for now. Dark rain clouds were drifting in, and soon a gray and rainy canopy would settle over the city.

After deciding on a flowing, ankle length skirt and a top that stopped above her navel, Saaya slipped on a pair of sandals and left.

She stood outside her building and closed her eyes. Kafeel was east of her position, likely on the roof of the Shangri-La again. It had been his favorite place to visit since the building was finished.

She turned east and made her way toward the tallest building in Vancouver, drifting through the pedestrians like a rose passing through a field of grain. Many eyes lingered on her as she went, reactions ranging from incredulity at her choice of clothes in such cold weather, to admiration and lust from men, and criticism from women.

She turned up Barclay Street, preferring a quieter path, when she became aware of a presence behind her. She smirked and began turning on the various streets, finding quieter and quieter paths, until she came to the busier part of downtown. Here, there were plenty of alleys and parking lots behind the buildings—usually occupied by the homeless—and Saaya kept going until she found one that was empty.

She walked down the alley and into a parking structure, taking the winding path down until she came to the bottom. She turned and smiled at the approaching figure a dozen feet away.

"No need to be shy," she said. "Come. Be close to me."

The figure, a man looking to be in his mid to late forties, came closer into view. He had a patch of stubble on the middle of his chin, and wore a pair of cop style shades that hid a vertical scar over his left eye. He approached quietly and confidently, stopping only a few feet in front of her.

Saaya gave him a once over. "I'll give you credit for assertiveness, but you're not really my type."

"Shut up, *skiek*, and I may not kill you. Or I may just kill you quickly."

"That's rude."

The vampire hissed and lunged at her. And stopped. Just a few inches away, the male vampire was practically frozen mid-step, a look of confusion and outrage on his face.

Saaya made a casual circuit around him, assessing her catch. "Hmm. Almost muscular build, short leather jacket, jeans that are just a little too tight in the crotch yet still not much on display." She clicked her tongue behind her teeth and shook her head. "You keep dressing like that and stalking and lunging at girls," she rose to her tiptoes and patted him on the head, "you're not gonna get laid very often. But then," she leaned around him and gave his crotch another inspection, "never mind."

A guttural sound rumbled in the male vampire's throat, but it was choked off.

"Now, now, let's not start threatening. You followed me down here. Still, I'll not be impolite and refuse to hear what you have to say." She released her mental clamp on his throat and he gasped.

"Who the hell are you?"

"So rude!" Saaya said, placing her hand over her chest in feigned shock. "I might ask the same question of you." He went quiet.

"I think I can guess. You're little throat is dry and your blood is on fire. You see a half-breed and figure you've found an easy meal." She rose up to her toes and grinned at him. "Am I close?"

The vampire clamped his eyes shut, making a visible effort to break free of her mental hold on him. She laughed, patting him on the cheek. "You better stop that. You're going to burst a blood vessel."

"Dirty-blooded *skiek*," he growled.

Saaya wrinkled her chin. "So says the weakling *shaquora* who came hunting but didn't understand his prey. How long have you walked the night? Twenty years? Thirty? Are you still in contact with the one who turned you? Will he or she care if I delivered you to death right now?"

"How can you do this?" he grunted as Saaya pressed her will against him. "Half-breeds are not this strong."

"That is only partially true," she replied. "It's too bad the one who created you did not better educate you. But then, not many know of the existence of my kind anyway, let alone the *Ancestors*."

"Ancestors?"

"Such a shame," Saaya said. The mock sympathy in her voice infuriated the man. "Do not be angry, my pursuer. Maybe I should educate you on the traits of a *dampeal*." She stepped away and held up a finger. "Lesson number one." A crunching sound echoed through the parking garage, and blood splashed out of his mouth. He fell to the ground and began to rapidly decay. "We are powerful."

J orge stepped out of the shadows and looked down at the pile of clothes the dead vampire had worn until just a few minutes ago. This was getting interesting. When first Remy had approached him about tracking the half-breed and his newly turned fledgling, Jorge had been less than excited. At one point, he'd thought to simply dispatch both of them and be done with this business.

Looking down at the remains and considering what he had just witnessed, he was glad he'd decided against it. Jorge knew he was not the best warrior of the Hunter class, but he was smart. And he also knew two things that Remy did not.

This woman, Saaya, was well beyond anything he or Remy could challenge. Not directly, anyway. Half human she may be, but she had a powerful vampire parent who would have to be capable of things he'd seen no Elder do.

Second: for whatever reason, Jelani was not subject to Remy's influence. He had told Jorge to track him down and that he was likely out of the city and thus out of Remy's range of influence. Wrong. Jorge had stalked Jelani for days now—at a wary distance, considering that towering devil in the trench coat watching over him—and he'd never left Vancouver. It hadn't taken long to figure out that the Remy's *shaquora* was unaffected by his attempts to bring him in. That was interesting.

Jorge pursed his lips. He wondered if Remy knew how capable his fledgling was. Knowing Remy as well as he did, Jorge had to wonder if he would still be so adamant about the death of those two if he'd seen Jelani so decisively overwhelm another vampire after having arisen only one night prior.

He smirked. Or, would Remy pack up and blaze a cravenly trail straight back to Romania. Jorge was sure there was someone powerful in Peles Castle that had an interest in Remy's success.

There was no other explanation for how anyone with such unremarkable skill could be a ranking Hunter in any coven.

He shrugged. It may be annoying to have to take orders from the fool, but judging by the trouble he seemed to be accumulating, Jorge wouldn't have to tolerate it much longer. And on that thought, the Hunter turned away. It was time to meet up with Remy and decide how much about all this he intended to share.

30

T he hallways of Peles Castle were quiet in the day. Not that it was a noisy place in the night when its denizens were active, but it was a different kind of quiet. A sleeping quiet.

Mariska knew she was taking a risk. The same risk she'd been taking for weeks, now. When first Yako had ordered her to remain in Sinaia to gather information, Mariska had silently doubted the wisdom of her task. For all it seemed, Massius and Remy were simply trying to eliminate Yako and his personal history. This would extract the potential thorn from Massius's side about his own history with the coven, and aid Remy's rise in the ranks of the Hunters.

There had still been pieces of the puzzle missing. Why would Massius would actively go after Yako? The Eldest Hunter had no knowledge of the connection between his family history and the Elder. Better to let things remain as they were, and if Yako went digging into the past—which was unlikely—take action then.

Now Mariska knew differently, and she was trying to figure out how to proceed. Massius was responsible for the murder of Yako's family, his lineage was not tied to the Sinaia coven, and he was not even an actual Elder. All of these things were true, but it was only part of the story.

Devious and ambitious, Massius had eyes for a larger place in the order than simply occupying a seat at the High Council of Elders. He wanted to wield its power as his own and the major obstacle to that was not Yako, or his family history, but Vicken.

Massius knew that Vicken would not be easily unseated, so he'd waited and worked quietly, finding allies where he might, and securing trusts with his lycan contacts. Over the last week as things started to come together, Mariska wished Yako would return. This was much bigger than simply killing Remy. If what Meilana said was true, things were moving quickly toward insurrection. Massius was devious and ambitious, but also patient.

She rounded another corner and passed through an indoor courtyard filled with plants and small trees. Massius had spies everywhere, but even they had to sleep in the day. Years of training by Yako had given Mariska the ability to remain functional during the day, so long as she avoided the sun's deadly gaze.

Mariska navigated the various gravel paths until she came to a small bridge. At the other end was a woman, no taller than five feet. The only thing that distinguished her from her identical twin sister was the lack of two small scythes strapped to her sides.

"Hello Second," Meilana said.

Mariska bowed her head in greeting. "You've found something new."

The Hunter smirked. "If not for your obvious differences in heritage, I would be certain you and Eldest Hunter were siblings, so alike, you are." With a visible effort, she straightened. "It still amazes me that the daylight hours seem not to affect you."

Mariska nodded, waiting.

Meilana closed her eyes and shook her head. "Straight to business as always. Very well. Everything we've suspected appears to be true."

Mariska held up a hand. "We are alone?"

"As alone as can be. Not many of us walk the day hours, and those that can, function with little approaching coherency. Do you mind if I sit?" Mariska nodded, and Meilana led her to a wooden bench with black, wrought-iron legs.

Although they were alone, the women still spoke in quiet voices. "Massius has taken years to secure a solid relationship with the wolves and carefully nurturing allies in the coven. It looks like he will make a move soon."

"What lycan in their right mind would oppose the High Council, and with Vicken at its head?" Mariska frowned, staring at the space in front of her. "Relations have been tentatively peaceful, but peaceful nonetheless. Why damage that?"

"It's not just the lycans, Meilana said. "You would be surprised how many grow bored of things as they are. I haven't needed my sister to tell me." She spread a hand to encompass the area. Whispers are everywhere about complacency, and how it wouldn't take more than an attack by the wolves to throw things into chaos."

"That's nonsense," Mariska replied. "It was Vicken who led the Hunters who eventually ended the conflict. It has been Vicken who has kept things in place since then."

"And it is Massius who plants seeds of doubt among the younger members of the coven."

Mariska looked at her. "Younger?" Meilana's face was answer enough, and Mariska's eyes glowed in anger. "Filthy *shaquora*," she hissed. "They were not born of the coven, of this history. They were merely inducted. They know not, nor care about our history."

"For some, that is true, but not all. There are many who were turned to our world that respect who they are and what they have become." Meilana looked disappointed. "The dissenters aren't alone, however."

"Purebloods?" Mariska couldn't believe it.

"Not many, but enough to be a threat."

Mariska blinked, digesting the information. "If some of

Massius's allies are purebloods, and Massius is the one who created the Hunters, then some of his allies ..."

"Are Hunters," Meilana finished for her.

"And if he can find a way to kill Eldest Hunter, it would make things much easier for him to enlist more Hunters to his cause."

"Now you begin to see."

"Traitors," Mariska spat.

"Our job is to serve, not to question, Second. It's possible that any Hunters who have joined Massius's cause have not been told the whole truth. More likely, they believe they are being addressed by a member of the High Council and are being told that the coven is in some sort of danger from within."

"But Yako would refute his claims," Mariska reasoned, "Which is why Massius is bent on his un-creation."

Meilana looked at her squarely. "Not just *his* un-creation."

Mariska's eyes narrowed. "Of course not."

31

J elani opened his eyes and looked around the dark room. He'd
tried to remain awake to spend as much time as possible with
Alisha, but it couldn't happen. It was like his entire body had
fought against him in favor of a deep sleep. He'd lasted about an
hour into daylight before he finally succumbed.

The smell of boiled greens and baked fish drifted into the
room. Jelani remembered it as a smell that would have had him
dressed and nearly breaking his neck to get to the kitchen. Now it
was simply a smell that was neither enticing nor repulsive. He
swung his legs over the side of the bed and looked around. Alisha
had bought several types of curtains, all thick—and unfashionable,
she'd complained—and capable of blocking out the sun
completely.

When he thought about it, he might have been smart to take
extra precaution and sleep under the bed, or in the closet, or even
the bathroom. If for any reason Alisha had had second thoughts
about him, she needed only to tear down the curtains and it would
be over. Not that he thought she would do such a thing to him, but
anything could happen. Maybe Remy would show up and do one

of those mind things to her and force her to do it. The nails could fall out of the walls. Anything.

He took a deep breath and stood, making his way to the bathroom. His toothbrush and shaver and other items of personal hygiene were still where they were when last he'd used them. "Thanks, baby," he said under his breath.

He grabbed the toothbrush and squeezed some toothpaste onto it, then leaned over the sink. Just as he was about to put the brush to his teeth, he stopped. He opened his mouth and clamped his teeth shut, inspecting them. Not a speck of yellow anywhere. Not even a tiny hint of discoloration.

Do I even need to brush my teeth anymore? He turned his head from side to side, marveling at how perfectly clean and white they were. They were even straighter.

Jelani shook his head. What else had changed? With a shrug, he went about brushing his teeth anyway. *I'm not taking a chance on walking around with stank breath; white teeth or not.*

He was rinsing his mouth out when a soft knock came from the door to the bedroom. "Jelani?" he heard Alisha say.

"In the bathroom. I'll be out in a minute."

"Okay, babe. I've got food ready when you're done."

The thought of food made Jelani forget about his initial reaction. He finished rinsing his mouth and went for the door. The aroma was twice as strong in the living room, which was only separated from the kitchen by a half wall with a counter top. Alisha had set two plates at the counter and was waiting for him.

"Hey, sleepyhead. I thought you'd be hungry, so I made your favorite. Baked tilapia and greens."

Jelani kissed her and sat down. He was indeed hungry, almost ravenous. But when he picked up his fork, he hesitated.

"What is it?" Alisha said, noticing his reaction. "Something not look right?"

"No," Jelani said, blinking. "No, everything's fine."

"Then, what's wrong? You've got to be hungry. You slept all

day …" she trailed off, as if realizing what she'd just said and what it meant.

Jelani stared at all that good food on the plate in front of him, not desiring to take a single bite. He looked over at Alisha, thinking to apologize, and saw her flinch away from him.

"What—" then his stomach clenched and he nearly doubled over. He put a hand on the counter to keep him from falling off of his stool. His hand slipped and knocked the plate off the counter. The dish hit the tiled kitchen floor and shattered.

Alisha hopped backwards as bits of ceramic mixed with fish and vegetables scattered about the floor. Jelani hardly noticed the crash, but when he looked up again, Alisha had backed away from him.

"What's wrong?" he gasped. Another cramp. His body was starting to get hot from the inside out, and his blood was like gasoline and someone had lit a match.

"Your eyes," she breathed. He saw her fear and it crushed him.

With shaking hands, he steadied himself on the counter and stood. Every time he moved, Alisha seemed to move a little farther away from him. He grabbed his knife and looked at a sliver of his reflection. His pupils were huge, with a tiny purple dot in the center of each eye.

His blood was turning to lava and he was becoming thirsty, so thirsty. An intense hunger and an insatiable thirst blended into one. It was more than he could stand.

Jelani clenched his eyes shut, fighting the urge. He knew what he needed. He had to have it. There was no choice. He needed blood or … or what? Would he die?

He looked up at Alisha and she flinched away again. His body moved toward her while his mind screamed to get out of the room. He took another step, and his fingers curled. Alisha moved back, and he paced her. His mind was a deafening roar in his head to get away from her, but something primal had taken over. If she turned to run, he would be on her in an instant. He closed his eyes and shook his head, but still took another step forward.

"Jelani," Alisha said. "Jelani, it's me. It's Alisha. You know me. It's Alisha, your girl."

He stumbled at the effort of fighting off the thirst, while the sound of her voice, calm and soothing, helped him to fight back to himself.

"Jelani, hold it together. I know you can—"

He was there in an instant, hand clamped around her throat, face inches in front of hers. He slid his thumb under her jaw and turned her head to the side. Ah, there it was. That beautiful, delicate neck, and that artery streaming all that sweet warm blood. A whimper came from her throat, but it sounded far away.

He turned her head a little father, and his fangs began to extend. A bit of moisture wet his hand and he looked at her face, her eyes, where tears were falling down her face. His grip loosened and she gasped for breath.

When she looked up at him, her eyes were so genuine, so loving, so fearful. "I love you, Jelani. I love you, baby."

He let her go and backed away. The burning pain of the fire in his veins was temporarily cast aside by horror and self-loathing.

"What … what did I just do? What did I almost do?" He looked at the thumb shaped bruise forming on her neck, a bruise he caused. "What …"

"Baby," Alisha said. "Just, hold on to yourself."

He shook his head. "I'm sorry, Alisha," he said. "I've got to get out of here. I'm … I …" He was up and out of the living room, through the bedroom and to the window. He opened it and looked over his shoulder into the empty room. "I love you, too," he said into the darkness, and climbed out.

～

"How long?" Kafeel asked.

"How long?"

"No games, Saaya."

The *dampeal* looked up at her brother and gave him a sour look. "You've gotten to be less fun over the years."

"I've gotten to be less patient over the years."

"If you would open your mind—"

"Not where humans are concerned."

"Oh, Kafeel. Have you ever had any fun in your long life?"

"Yes. But limited to situations excluding humans."

"Less fun."

"Less problems."

"Kafeel—"

He looked down at her. "Less problems for me and for them. When you get bored, you step into the human world and change lives."

"Lives always change. It is an inexorable part of creation."

"Do not think to lecture me on creation, little girl. The years you have lived are but a flicker in time."

"Oh? A flicker, dear brother? A flicker in time, you say? And you are how old? Oh yes. Less than five hundred years old. Actually," she tapped her index finger to her lips, "you are less than four hundred years old, are you not? Is your life but a flicker to one of the *Ancestors* who have walked this earth for thousands?"

"How long?"

Saaya went quiet. Whenever Kafeel's tone dropped and went soft, he was at the end of his patience. "I cannot say, exactly. This may be a more permanent thing."

"Do you not think you've played with that human long enough?"

"Human no longer."

"Little better."

"He is different, Kafeel." Saaya craned her neck and looked up into her brother's dark eyes. "I know you feel it too. There is something different about him."

Kafeel returned his attention to the city that sprawled below. "So you've been telling yourself."

"You know I'm speaking the truth."

"Whether or not you speak the truth is irrelevant, because I don't care."

"Oh, Kafeel," was all Saaya said in response. She knew it was time to back off. He may not be ready to admit it, but Jelani had piqued his interest at least a bit, otherwise he would not have agreed to watch over him and his friends, no matter how disgusted he might act about it.

They gazed out at the bright city lights, Saaya wrapped in her own thoughts, and Kafeel, no doubt, wrapped in his.

"Maybe forever," she finally said. When Kafeel didn't react, she continued. "You want to know how long? I have a blood link with Jelani now, and I am quite fond of him. You may have to get used to his presence, big brother."

"A toy to play with until he is broken."

Saaya winked at him, though he was not looking. "Is that a little humor I hear in your tone? Let me say this. I don't think he is one that will break so easily."

"This is true."

That was unexpected. "Why the sudden agreement?"

"He fought the Eldest Hunter."

"Ah." Saaya remembered. She had been too preoccupied to sense that Kafeel had been nearby to witness the confrontation.

"Anyone who could earn the respect of that one, deserves it."

Saaya raised an eyebrow. "Do I hear a bit of admiration for the Eldest Hunter?"

"He has the heart of a warrior and is a worthy adversary."

"That is why you did not kill him when first you two met?" Saaya said.

"His death was your opportunity first, was it not?" Kafeel replied.

"That is part of it, yes. It would have been a shame for our world to lose such a warrior."

"Would you have killed him to save your human?"

"That is a good ..." Saaya trailed off. She looked over her shoulder toward Coal Harbour. "Oh, Jelani," she said. "My poor, poor reckless fledgling." The thirst was upon him and he was still with that girl. He had to be. She could sense his inner turmoil.

"I think I should go get my 'toy'," she said to Kafeel.

"Then go."

She went.

❧

Over fifty feet Jelani dropped. His feet barely touched the sidewalk and he was running. Running as far away from Alisha as he could. As far away from any human as he could. That's all it seemed like he'd been doing for so long, now. Running from vampires, running from the night, running from day. Now he was running from himself and what he had become.

He saw a jogger coming in his direction and he veered to the left and ran across a patch of lawn and leaped across a pond. The fifteen foot jump felt like nothing, but the gasps from behind reminded him that he was not and never would be human again. He ran faster, making his way to the trees. Maybe if he found solitude he could dig in somewhere and wait out this horrible, primal hunger eating his insides.

Jelani forced himself not to look at any humans he passed. If he did, he would attack someone. This pain had to be similar to a kind of withdrawal. Some were worse than others. A caffeine withdrawal caused headaches. He imagined a drug or alcohol withdrawal caused pain that made one feel like they were dying. Maybe this was something like that. It had to be. He definitely couldn't go around biting and drinking people's blood.

Another jogger turned onto the path directly in front of him. She was fit and toned and completely oblivious to Jelani, who was bearing down on her fast. *Get the hell outta here!* He fought the urge, tried to turn away, but then he heard the blood pumping in her veins, her increased heart rate as it pumped precious, delicious blood through her body. He could practically smell it. Rich, sweet, filled with oxygen. Athletic humans always had the best blood.

How the fuck do I know that? It was the last rational thought he had. Everything around him blurred as he increased his pace. He ran straight behind the woman and grabbed her around the waist, clamping a hand over her mouth. He continued straight toward Stanley Park and flew into the woods, darting off the path and into the trees.

Rain started to fall, and soon he and his captive were soaked through. She tried to struggle, but his grip was like iron. To Jelani, she may as well have been an infant.

A tiny voice entered his mind, warning him to take control of himself but he ignored it. Once they were far enough in the woods that he was sure no one would see, he stopped. The woman was frantic, her screams muffled behind his hand.

He held her so that her back was to him and forced her head sideways to reveal her neck. He closed his eyes and opened his mouth. His fangs extended to their full length. The woman squirmed and thrashed but it made no difference. Her struggles only sweetened and oxygenated her blood even more, and the added adrenaline only made the taste more unique. His mind screamed along with his victim but his body and the primal urge that had taken him ignored them both.

The tiny voice in the corner of his mind became more forceful, more powerful, but he still ignored it. His pain and hunger would be over soon. He brought his head down and the tips of his fangs pierced her neck. Jelani tasted a tiny bit of sweet rich blood, the he stopped. His entire body trembled as he warred with himself. *I ... won't ... do ... this!*

But the thirst. The thirst! It was undeniable. Indomitable. He would kill this girl or he would die. *Better to die.*

No. Something inside of him, whatever it was, would not be denied life because of the screams of a fragile human woman. There were plenty in the world to replace her. How long would she live, anyway? Sixty years? Seventy?

No, Jelani. That voice. It was stronger now. More insistent. *Wait.*

Wait? Wait for what? He could barely stand the pain. His body was burning up from the inside out.

And then she was there. Saaya. A feeling of calm and comfort fell over him. "Hold, *jaan.*" She walked up to them and waved her hand over the girl's face. The woman's body went slack, and her eyes closed. "Lay her down, my love."

Jelani complied, laying the woman gently onto the damp ground. "I can't, Saaya," he said, leaning his head back to stare at the treetops and the rain falling through the canopy to spatter on his face. "I can't endure it. I thought I was strong enough—"

"Silly boy," she said, taking his hand. "You have already pierced her skin, but you do not have to kill her."

"But—"

"Sip, fledgling." She guided Jelani to the woman's neck and he lifted her, cradling her head in his hand, while he supported her back with the other. "You can sip from her without killing her. You have already tasted her blood. If you do not continue, you will drive yourself mad and rip her apart." She indicated the woman's neck with an open hand. "Sip."

He lowered his head to her neck and placed the tips of his fangs over the two red pinpricks in her neck.

"Slowly," Saaya said. "Gently."

He inserted his fangs a little deeper and began to carefully sip the blood from the artery in her neck. Tears flowed down his cheeks as he drank the blood of this innocent woman who had been out for a night jog. The irony was not lost on him.

The woman's body jerked.

"Careful," Saaya instructed.

Despite Jelani's desire for more, the *dampeal* indicated that he should stop. He complied, gently extracting his fangs.

"I will not force you one way or another, *jaan*," Saaya said, "but you have reached a deciding point."

Jelani knew what she was about to say but he listened, needing to hear the words.

"You must decide whether to completely satisfy your thirst and drain her, killing her, or leave her alive while you remain unsatisfied."

Jelani looked down at the helpless woman, still unconscious. He looked back to Saaya, and the beautiful *dampeal* read his intent in his eyes.

"Very well." She nodded toward the woman. "Carefully, insert your fangs again." When Jelani recoiled, she spoke up, impatient. "Do as I say." There was no joking in her voice. No tittering or flirtation, no playful barbs. It was the first time Jelani had heard her speak in such a tone. He did as she said.

"Focus your mind on numbing the pain she will feel. Focus on her body healing from the intrusion."

Jelani swallowed his self-loathing and focused on numbing the pain that the unconscious woman would no doubt feel once she awakened. He then focused on her neck healing. Several minutes passed, and finally Saaya spoke again.

"Good. Now carefully release her."

He did. For a few minutes he sat back, staring down at the woman. Then he noticed that the puncture marks on her neck were closing until the two circles from where he'd bitten her were reduced to tiny dots. A minute later, they had completely healed over, and there was not even a scar.

"Amazing," he breathed, leaning over and running a finger over her neck.

"Mhm," Saaya replied, leaning against a nearby redwood. "She will wake soon. Let her do so alone."

"Not alone," Jelani said. Saaya arched an eyebrow at him. In response, he stood and looked above his head at the numerous branches interconnecting each other like spiderwebs. With a single leap, he was crouching on a limb large enough to support himself. A second later, Saaya ascended and moved beside him.

"Be a gentleman and share your perch," she purred, slinking up close to him. Jelani fought his body's lack of discipline as she slid up against him. When finally she settled, her body was tightly pressed against his.

She glanced over her shoulder and down, then back up. That eyebrow arched again. "Thank you for the compliment, love."

"I didn't say anything," Jelani whispered. It was all he trusted his voice to do.

She smiled and turned her attention to the woman stirring thirty feet beneath them. She moaned, slowly coming awake, and lifting herself onto her elbows. She held a hand to her head but didn't move. Minutes passed until she finally reoriented herself and climbed to her feet. She rubbed a hand over her neck, frowning.

Jelani watched as she looked around. She muttered under her breath, but he could hear her perfectly.

"How the hell did I end up on the ground?" the woman thought aloud. She ran a hand through her sandy brown hair and turned around, looking in every direction till she found her bearings and turned east. At first she was shaky, holding her head. With a bit of guilt, Jelani surmised it was because he'd taken as much of her blood as he had. On somewhat shaky legs, the woman started toward the nearest exit to the woods.

His physical attraction to Saaya forgotten, Jelani leaped from branch to branch, following the woman from above.

Several moments passed when the jogger appeared again. She

cleared the woods and turned right, running in the direction of the brightly lit tennis courts.

They stopped at the edge of the woods and watched till she reached the courts, continuing past and turning left onto a residential street.

Watching her go, Jelani found that he wanted to kill one more vampire: himself.

32

J elani fingered the leather wrapped hilt of the silver blade in his belt. He could do it quickly, before he managed to stop himself.

"Think it through, Jelani," Saaya said from behind.

He looked over his shoulder at her. "What?"

"Do not be so harsh with yourself," she said.

He was incredulous. "I nearly killed that woman and I still fed on her. I'm totally out of control." He shifted his weight and turned on the branch to face her. Saaya looked below them, then signaled for him to follow.

They dropped to the ground and made their way back into the more heavily wooded areas where there were no paths. In the dark of the night it was like a forest in the middle of nowhere instead of a large park at the edge of downtown. Even now, with his mind filled with grim thoughts, Jelani couldn't help but marvel at the majestic beauty of Stanley Park. And now, traveling off the paths, he saw yet another dynamic to the park he'd never seen before.

In front of him, Saaya made her way through the shrubs and fallen trees as though she was a part of it. He didn't want to, but Jelani couldn't help but admire the captivating *dampeal*. She appeared uncaring for humans, more concerned with how they amused her. But that wasn't the whole truth. There was another angle to her personality that he wasn't sure even she knew was there.

Saaya turned to face him when they finally stopped.

"Tell me what good could possibly be served by my remaining alive?" he asked her. "I have to subsist on blood. I don't know how that sits with you, since you're half human, but for me having been born a human, it's a little upsetting."

"It takes time. You will adjust."

"Adjust to what, exactly? Will I become numb to killing people?" He shook his head. "Better to die while I still have most of my humanity intact."

"Humanity?" She tilted her head at him. "No other species has such a difficult time defining itself. What is humane to a human here may not be exactly the same someplace else."

"Please don't wrap this issue up in semantics, Saaya."

"Very well. You are adjusting quickly, considering the circumstances of your re-creation. You were turned by a vampire that was not only hunting you, but those you love as well. Before and after your re-creation, you had a vested interest in Remy's demise. Typically, a human has no knowledge of the existence of a vampire before they are turned.

"You've been dealing with a lot of anger and frustration at your situation, which is understandable. In one night you killed more *shaquora* than most Hunters do in a year, and the thirst has only been upon you three times since your reawakening."

"Oh, that's a relief," Jelani said. "Instead of being a full-fledged demon, I'm just a hell spawn, then. Not quite as bad."

A shadow passed over Saaya's face that chilled Jelani to his core. It passed just as quickly as it appeared, but he knew that he was pushing a line, here. He held up his hands in a placating gesture. "I'm sorry."

"Aside from your little rampage at the *dark rock*," she continued, "you have been remarkably stable. And most newly turned vampires would have ripped their lover apart in the heat of passion, yet you did not."

Despite the possibility of him doing such a thing to Alisha, Jelani couldn't help but be curious about Saaya's detailed knowledge of his whereabouts.

"Really?" he said, staring at her. "And how do you know who I was with?"

"I have some of your essence in me as you have some of mine in you. For lack of a better term that you can understand, we are linked. To a degree, I can feel what you feel."

Jelani's features twisted into a look of horror. He knew she was privy to his mind, but this? "You feel what I feel? So … when me and … you can feel …"

Saaya held up a hand to stop him. "Yes, I can feel it, and no, I am not a telepathic voyeur. I block out most of what you are feeling."

"But not all," Jelani said, thinking. "That's why you knew to find me back there." He pointed in the direction of his attack on the jogger.

"It's difficult to explain, but I'm not constantly tuned in to your thoughts and feelings. For now, I am more conscious of you because I'm trying to help you in your transition—"

"My transition," he yelled. "I fucking hate this. My transition! I didn't ask for any of this shit. I've had Hunters on my back, random bloodsuckers eyeing me like a meal, my friends in danger, now I'm the same danger as the ones who've been hunting us."

He punched a fallen redwood, leaving a considerable hole. "Months running from monsters, now I'm one of them, and the only reason why I didn't murder someone tonight is because you were in my head enough to come stop me. So in addition to being a dangerous monster, I also have no privacy."

A lavender glimmer passed across Saaya's eyes, and Jelani was thrown backward into a tree and pinned against it. Saaya casually closed the distance between them until she stood in front of him. He knew she was strong, that she had some sort of mind powers, but the sheer force of her will pressing on him felt like it could crush him and the tree.

"You have enjoyed your little rant, now listen to me."

Jelani stared into those glowing eyes with a mixture of awe and trepidation. The *dampeal* was amazing and fearsome, beautiful and terrifying.

"You are a newly awakened vampire, child. You have not yet begun to learn what it is to walk among immortals, and it will be some time before you do. The concepts of life and creation within the scope of your new existence are outside your current ability to conceptualize, and you would do better to try to understand than to react."

Saaya moved closer until her breasts brushed against his torso. "Up to this point, you've been a newly turned immortal functioning with the mentality of a human. That will not do, but it is understandable. You have a new world to discover, and endless time to do it so long as you do not let your residual human impulsiveness rule your actions and lead to an untimely death."

She released him and he stumbled forward, but recovered quickly. She walked a few paces away then turned back, and the tension dissipated. "You attacked that woman, yes. You possibly would have killed her. Why is this?"

"Because I'm this thing that I cannot control," Jelani ventured, bracing himself for another backward trip into a tree.

"Wrong," came the reply. "You reawakened a short time ago, and have gone for nearly three days since your last feeding. Then you visit and merge with that girl, someone you share love with." Saaya shook her head at him. Her expression said that he was a fool.

"Physical passion leads to many different appetites, Jelani. You managed not to kill her in the heat of passion, a feat in itself, even for an older vampire. Then you expected to awaken not with the thirst upon you? Foolish child."

"So," Jelani said, "back there?"

"You attacked that woman because you were driven mad by the thirst. If you had not the strength of will that you do, I would not have made it in time—"

"To stop me?"

"To offer you an option."

"Option?"

Saaya looked as if she was on the verge of laughing at him. "But a child, you are. I cannot stop you from becoming the immortal you choose to be, *jaan*. I can only guide you to the intersection in which your path led, in one direction or another. "If you had drained that mortal woman, you would have walked a different path that led to becoming a predator of humans. There are many vampires who travel that path. You chose the path that is more shrouded in ambiguity."

"I still fed on her," Jelani said. "There's no telling what'll happen now. She could wake up tomorrow a vampire, and it would be my fault."

Now Saaya did laugh at him, and the soft tittering made him grind his teeth. He remembered his collision with the tree a few minutes ago and held his tongue.

"Oh, my love. You still know nothing. Your human lore is mostly incorrect. It takes more than a simple bite to turn a human. You must make an active decision to do so, and it involves injecting your vampiric essence into them. What you did instead was focus on extracting just enough of her blood for you to be sustained, then you healed her."

"Is that what I did?"

She nodded. "You will find that your mind is so much more powerful when you learn to focus it, while your body is equipped with tools to aid in your survival." She smiled. "We cannot have humans walking around with tiny puncture marks in their necks, can we?"

"So, what you're saying is ..."

"That you did what is called *sipping*. You extracted just enough to survive, then healed her. She will remember nothing of the encounter."

"You did something to her," Jelani said, remembering the *dampeal* waving a hand over the woman's face.

Again, Saaya nodded. "I made her sleep. It is the combination of the anesthesia and healing fluids you injected into her that will fog her memory of the experience along with the pain."

"How the hell is that even possible?"

Saaya waved a dismissive hand. "Why must you know everything? Suffice it to say that the brain indicates pain, so the fluid you inject goes through the bloodstream to the brain, counteracting pain signals to that area. It also clouds the short term memory of the encounter. Now, I am not going into the scientific explanation because I do not care to do so. Become a scientist and study it if you choose."

"Alright, alright I get you."

"You haven't got me yet." She looked him up and down. "But the night is still here. There is time."

Jelani closed his eyes and took a deep breath. "You never stop, do you?"

She stepped close to him again, and placed a hand on his chest. "Do you wish me to stop, Jelani?"

He swallowed. The rain had long ago soaked through the thin material she wore, causing it to hug her body like a second skin. Even her hair, wet and pressed tightly to the sides of her face, seemed to beckon to him. His heart said yes, his body said no. "Yes." He found that it hurt him to see the look of disappointment marring that perfect face.

"Still you choose that human girl over me?"

"I've been in love with her for longer than even I knew, Saaya. You know that."

"Do not my charms entice you?"

"You know they do, but would I be nearly so desirable if I just flip flopped? How genuine would my love for her be if I betrayed it like this?"

"I don't care about your love for her."

"I do."

"Why? She will be dead and gone before you realize it." Saaya spread her hand out to encompass all around them. "They are so short lived. Some of the trees in this park have seen more than five generations of a single human family walk through here. Do you truly want to endure love with a woman who is subject to such ephemerality?"

"That's what love is," he replied, but a tiny voice in the back of his mind wondered if indeed he could endure it. Watching the woman he loved age and eventually pass from this life while he remained ever the same. But could he stand the thought of not being with her for the years she was here, short though they may be?

"That's what love is," Saaya echoed. "Another concept you do not begin to understand."

To his amazement, she faded from his vision till she was gone entirely. He stood there, the rain falling around him and pattering on his clean-shaven head.

"Forgot she could do that."

33

D aniel stood in the middle of the room, watching the two women on the couch. Wen sat with her arm around Alisha, who stared down at the throw rug under her feet. He and Wen had come home from an early dinner to find Alisha on her hands and knees trying to sweep up a mess of food on the floor. At first they didn't think anything of it, until they saw that her hands were shaking and tears were running down her cheeks.

"It's not his fault," she said. "I made him stay. I didn't want him to go."

Daniel didn't know what to think. The thumb-sized bruise on her neck didn't escape his notice, but neither did the fact that she had no apparent puncture marks in her neck.

"Shh," Wen said, hugging her friend tightly. "You're okay, that's what matters."

Alisha gave Wen a pat on the leg and straightened. "I'm okay because he didn't kill me."

"Looks like it nearly came to that," Daniel said in a voice harsher than he meant.

Alisha looked up at him. "He's still your friend, isn't he? Your best friend?"

Daniel held his hands up in a placating gesture. "I didn't mean that the way it sounded, Alisha. I just don't know how to deal with this." He held his hand out to indicate herself. "And it looks like he hasn't figured all this out either."

"Where do you think he is now?" Wen asked.

Alisha shook her head. "He didn't say. He ran out so fast I barely realized he was gone. He was in a lot of pain."

"I'm glad you're alright," Daniel said, not sure what else to say. He sat down on the opposite couch. "Maybe we shouldn't have left."

Wen looked at him, and her expression said that that was the wrong thing to say.

"I hardly think you should have stayed, Daniel," Alisha said. Despite the situation, she smirked a bit. "We needed the time, even if it almost ended in disaster. I love him. He loves me. She saw the concerned look her friends exchanged, and laughed.

"Quit worrying, you two. This isn't a battered girlfriend talking. I know he nearly killed me. I know it was a risk being with him alone last night, but it is what it is." She looked at each of them. "I'm not planning to do anything crazy, okay? The next time I see him, I'll make sure I'm more careful."

"And how do you plan to do that, lady?" Wen asked.

Alisha shrugged. "For one thing, I'll make sure he's ... had plenty to eat, or drink," she frowned, "or whatever it is he does, before we meet again. And maybe we'll meet in a public place next time."

"What do you two plan to do together?" Daniel said, putting his head in his hands. "Are you going to try to make some kind of life together around this situation?"

"I don't know what I'm going to do. Part of me says that I'm crazy and I should run away as fast as I can. But the larger part of me that knows him, knows his heart, wants to find a way to help him."

"I've been thinking about that for a while," Daniel said, "and

I've come up with nothing."

"There has to be something we can do for him," Wen said.

"Like what?" Daniel replied. "Donate blood." Both women wrinkled their noses at the idea.

"That's just weird," Wen said. "Besides, it's not like you can just go to the hospital and get blood drawn and take it home."

"And I am not doing a home syringe thing," Alisha said, "and packing my blood in a container in the fridge. That's going way too far for me."

"No arguments here," Daniel agreed. "So what, then?"

"I wouldn't spend the rest of my short life on questions like that, if I were you."

Wen yelped, Alisha gasped, and they jumped from the couch, darting around the coffee table. Daniel was on his feet placing himself between the intruder and the women.

"Aw, isn't that brave. Placing yourself between the big bad vampire to give the," Remy glanced around Daniel at Alisha and Wen, and winked at them, "no doubt delicious, damsels a chance to escape."

"Dude, seriously. Why the *fuck* do you keep coming here? Do you truly believe we're going to go talking about all this? You have to know by now that's the last thing we're gonna do. If you'd just leave us alone—"

The Hunter was in his face in an instant. His hand snapped up and grabbed Daniel by the throat in an iron-like grip.

"Let me tell you something, human," the vampire snapped, lifting him from the floor. "Your lives mean absolutely nothing to me. I don't care who you are or what you do, I don't even care that you might or might not go running to your stupid little police, or anyone else. I'm here because your friend has been out of my reach, and you," again he looked around Daniel, whose feet dangled several feet above the floor, "all of you, are the worms I intend to hang on the hook to bring him back from wherever he's hiding."

The vampire's hand squeezed and Daniel was sure his neck would be crushed, slowly. Through the growing haze in his thoughts, he heard a voice that sounded far away.

"Put my friend down."

Remy released him and Daniel fell to the floor, coughing and wheezing as he struggled to get air through his bruised windpipe.

"Oh ho!" Remy said, casually turning to face Jelani. "That didn't take long at all."

"You're not very smart," Jelani said. The sound of his voice sent shivers down Daniel's spine even as he struggled for air.

"I got you here, didn't I?"

Jelani tilted his head to regard the Hunter. "You have no idea what I'm going to do to you."

Remy laughed. "And what could a fledgling fool do to a pure-blood Hunter? Tell me." He took a step backward, toward Alisha and Wen.

Jelani's upper lip curled back. In his peripheral vision, Daniel saw Alisha and Wen's eyes go wide. Remy didn't miss the reaction either. "Looks like the girls have never seen you as the monster you are, hmm?"

He took another step toward them and Jelani exploded into action. So fast was he, that not even the pureblood Hunter reacted in time. Jelani slashed him across the face with his elongated nails and grabbed him by the neck, spinning and hurling him across the room.

Remy landed lightly on his feet and grinned as the two slashes across his face closed and disappeared. He winked at Jelani then bolted through the door to the bedroom.

"I'm sorry you had to see this," Jelani said over his shoulder. In the blink of an eye, he was at the doorway to his old room.

"Hold on!" Daniel said, coughing out the word.

"Keep the windows closed," his best friend said, then he was gone.

34

J elani descended the ten floors and hit the ground running. He didn't know if it was intuition or not, but after Saaya had left him, he'd felt compelled to return to his old apartment.

He looked ahead. He shouldn't have stopped to speak with the others, as now Remy had a good head start on him. Still, for some reason he was able to feel his way along the Hunter's trail, and soon he had the other vampire in sight.

He had to admit that Remy was good. The way he darted in seemingly random directions, and managed to have a knack for picking the least travelled streets certainly had to be some aspect of his *talent*. As he leaped across the street, gliding cleanly over a passing pickup truck, Jelani wondered how much respect a person could command, with an inherent skill that had a lot in common with cowardice.

Remy turned down an alley, then leaped to the roof of a low building. Jelani jumped the twenty feet to the roof and continued to close on in. From one rooftop to the next, Jelani followed the one who had hunted him and his friends for months, killed Daniel's good friend Claire McMahon, and made their lives hell. Jelani wasn't sure exactly what he would do to Remy once he got his hands on him, but it would be unpleasant … at least for Remy.

The Hunter leaped across another gap between two buildings, then as soon as his feet touched the roof, he darted left and jumped back to the street. Jelani cursed, as he was in midair when Remy had changed directions. He landed and skidded to a stop, then went to the side of the roof just in time to see Remy snatch a driver out of his SUV and take off in a cloud of smoke and rubber.

Jelani burst into action, going back the way he came. He went back to the previous building, then banked left and leapt across the street to land on the roof of a low rise apartment. He sprinted across, hopping from roof to roof, all the while keeping the blue SUV in sight.

The car turned onto Georgia Street—a three lane highway—and Jelani knew that at this time of night, there would be less traffic, and Remy would be able to outrun him.

Screw it! He traversed several more rooftops, then launched himself straight out over Georgia street. It was a long way, and Jelani hit hard and fast, rolling with the momentum. He heard the sound of an engine roaring and knew that Remy was barreling down on him. Jelani kept his wits about him and came out of the roll, planted his feet, and sprang backward.

The car closed in, and Jelani tucked his feet up, arms stretched out to his sides for balance. For several heartbeats he glided backward as the car came forward. Finally, when gravity began to pull him down, the hood of the SUV was just beneath him.

The hood folded under his weight, and he glared murderously at the Hunter on the other side of the glass. Jelani's fist snapped back and he punched through the windshield. He nearly got his hands around Remy's throat, but the other vampire slammed on the brakes, and Jelani was thrown backward.

He hit the ground in a backwards roll, all the while hearing the roar of the large vehicle. Jelani slapped his hand to the ground and slid to a stop. Kneeling in the middle of the street, he looked up

just in time to see the charging buffalo emblem on the grill of the
SUV before it slammed into him. Out of reflex, Jelani threw his
hands up. The impact would have instantly killed him, had he been
human. But Jelani was no longer human.

The front grill of the SUV knocked him into a into a violent
roll, and he felt the tires climbing over his legs and one of his arms
as it rolled over him. Jelani let out an inhuman growl against the
pain, even as his limbs instantly repaired themselves.

The pain lit his rage, and the nails in Jelani's curled fingers
extended. He managed to turn flat on his back as the vehicle
passed over him, and punched upward. His clawed hands tore
through the undercarriage and he grabbed hold.

Jelani held on along as the SUV roared down the street, and he
began working his way back up the front, tearing and grinding
metal as he went.

He reached the front and grabbed hold of the bumper, pulling
himself out and up. He slapped his hand down on the dented hood,
tearing five angry scars through the metal. Jelani's fangs extended
through his clenched teeth as he pulled himself all the way up. The
SUV swerved, but he had a firm grip this time.

Jelani lifted himself over the grill and thought he saw a trace of
fear in the eyes of his re-creator. But then, the view was blocked by
the muzzle of a nine millimeter handgun. Jelani dropped onto his
stomach just as a pure silver round passed over his back. He
looked up and saw Remy aiming for his head. He threw his body
right and several more rounds passed, hitting the hood.

Remy was forced to swerve around a car and that brief moment
was all Jelani needed. He punched his hand through the hood,
tearing out wires and parts. He pulled out a piece of broken metal
and shoved it through the hole in the windshield, stabbing it into
Remy's face.

The Hunter cried out in pain, and Jelani reached through the
hole, grabbed the steering wheel, and yanked it to the side. The
SUV made a sudden turn to the left, but overbalanced and tipped

over. Just before the vehicle flipped, Jelani leaped away. He hit the ground sprinting after the still rolling vehicle.

As soon as it stopped, he jumped on top of the door reached in, and grabbed Remy by the hair. With strength that still surprised himself, Jelani yanked the Hunter halfway out of the car. Remy bent his arm, lined up the gun with Jelani's torso, and unloaded the remaining clip of silver rounds.

Jelani quickly released him, dodging to the side, but he wasn't fast enough. One round found his side and passed through his body, front to back.

He screamed and fell away as Remy climbed out. The Hunter grabbed him and lifted him off the ground. "You think you're the Hunter, now, you mixed up son of a bitch?" He pulled Jelani close to his face and he had just enough time to see the deep gashes from the metal closing up and the skin smooth again, then Remy threw him backward.

Jelani hit the street and rolled to a stop. He tried to rise, but the searing pain in his side was agonizing. It burned like acid.

Remy hopped down from the upturned vehicle and strode toward him. "I don't know what you've been doing or where you've been doing it to be out of my reach, but you're mine. You hear?" He looked around. Other cars were slowly approaching now. "But first we'll need to make our exit. Get up!"

When Jelani didn't comply, Remy stopped and tilted his head at him. "That silver must have hurt for you not to be listening. I'll have to punish you later for that." He started again toward the still incapacitated Jelani, then stopped. He turned in a circle, eyes wide with panic. "Shit!" He looked back at Jelani, eyes wild and desperate. "Get up! We've got a fight coming."

Remy growled when Jelani still failed to respond, but by then, two figures came into view behind him. Remy spun around, ejected the clip in his gun and reloaded, firing on the approaching duo. The taller of the two increased his step and, to Jelani's amazement, began swatting the flying rounds aside. So quick did his arms move, that they looked like a blur even to Jelani's sharper vampire eyes.

"What the fuck?" Remy swore, then stuffed the gun back in his pants and ran toward Jelani, kicking him as he passed. "You're in my range, now, fledgling. You will come to me." With that last threat, he was gone.

A second later, the towering figure of Kafeel appeared over Jelani, then Saaya. He felt himself lifted off the street, none too gently, then air rushed around him as they made their retreat.

35

J elani crashed back into consciousness after his body was thrown to the ground. He rolled onto his back, but still didn't open his eyes. It felt like his head weighed a hundred pounds. The burning wound in his side was healing, but it was slow to do so. He heard a voice, not Saaya's, but her brother's.

"That was imprudent."

"Uuh. Uh huh," was all he could manage.

"Remind me why we are preserving this fool?" Kafeel asked. When Jelani didn't hear an answer forthcoming, he opened his eyes and lifted himself up on his elbows. A few feet away, Kafeel and Saaya stood looking down at him. The latter looked much the same as when she'd left him; raven hair plastered to the sides of her face and down her back, her clothes clinging to her curvaceous figure. Kafeel's long coat swayed lazily in the wind, but he didn't seem nearly as soaked through as his sister, or Jelani.

At last the wound closed, but his body continued repairing the internal damage. With an effort he climbed back to his feet. "Thanks for the save," he said. "I thought I almost had him. Turns out he almost had me."

"You use your body well," Saaya replied, "now it is time for you to use your mind equally well. It would be a shame to lose you, *jaan*, but we are not your personal bodyguards, nor are we given to babysitting."

It was the second time Saaya had ever spoken to him in a stern tone. For reasons he couldn't define, Jelani found himself unhappy that he had displeased her. And that displeased him.

"I'm sorry." With a groan at the still burning wound, he forced himself to stand up straight. "Look. I know you two have been watching out for me and I really do appreciate it. It's not like I'm taking it for granted, but I'm still trying to feel my way through this."

"That is understandable," Saaya said, "but going on the hunt so soon after first awakening is foolish enough. That you managed to kill several Hunters during that *dark rock* is impressive, but ill advised. I would have thought you'd learned from your nearly fatal confrontation with the Eldest Hunter himself. Your actions are reckless and foolish, Jelani."

Kafeel's eyes flicked down at Jelani with distaste. "Stupid, would be another word."

The corner of Saaya's mouth twitched. Jelani was *definitely* immune to that smile. He most certainly did *not* want to kiss her at all.

"You hint at a smile," Kafeel said to Saaya while nodding at Jelani, "and that vacuous expression reappears.

Jelani frowned and jerked his head back at the insult. *Vacuous?*

"Would it not be easier to have a dog?" Kafeel continued.

The sound of a honking horn drew his attention. For the first time since he'd opened his eyes, Jelani took a look around. They were on yet another rooftop surrounded by taller office buildings. Most of the windows were dark, save the occasional lit office where some poor bastard put in extra unpaid hours to finish a job. *I swear, I've spent more time on rooftops lately than on the damn ground.* "If you'll please pardon my vacuousness," he jabbed a thumb over his shoulder. "I'll be going, now."

"Where to?" Saaya asked.

Jelani started to ask why it was her business, but that was unfair. "I need to make sure my friends are okay." He looked to Kafeel. "You know, that's why I'm being what you consider reckless. I'm new to all this, but I also have to protect my friends while figuring it all out. I'm not saying I've been the easiest to deal with lately, but maybe you could cut me some slack, brotha." He turned and started away.

"Rest and heal. I will watch after them."

To Jelani's surprise, it was Kafeel who had spoken. He turned around to thank the towering vampire, but those dark brown eyes bore into him.

"If you speak another word, I will recant my offer."

Jelani held a hand up and nodded, backing away. He heard a feminine giggle. When he glanced over his shoulder, Saaya was nowhere to be seen. When he turned back, he found that he was on the rooftop alone.

~

Jelani turned the key and stepped inside the lavish apartment, adorned with paintings and art from various East Indian and West African cultures. He turned on the lights, more out of habit than the need to see. The paintings and sculptures were beautiful depictions of people, natural settings, and famous landmarks. Jelani wished he knew where Saaya had found them. He'd asked her once, but the response had been offhanded and vague.

Jelani snorted. Not that he had a need for any of the stuff now. It wasn't like he was going back to his old place any time soon.

Saaya's voice practically drifted into his ear. "Do you find something amusing, my love?"

Jelani hid his startle by clearing his throat. It didn't work. "Just thinking," he said, seeing her sitting on the couch with her feet tucked at her side. She patted the empty space next to her and Jelani hesitantly moved across the room and sat down.

"Still uneasy around me," the *dampeal* observed.

"I think you know why that is."

"Yes, of course." Her long eyelashes dipped as she favored him with a slow, bored, blink. "You must hold fast to your honor, lest you lose it in a night of passion with me, hmm?"

"Saaya, there have got to be a lot more interesting guys around than me."

She arched an eyebrow. "Oh? I've not found one yet. Are you so sure you wish for my interest in you to wane?"

Jelani thought about that for a moment, then decided maybe that wasn't such a good idea right now. He still didn't know what he was going to do or where he was going to go. The selfish thoughts made him feel guilty.

Saaya laughed at him. "Even now, completely re-created, your mind and heart war with each other as if you are still mortal." She shook her head. Her now dry, smooth black hair swished across her face. How he wanted to kiss those grinning lips!

"Okay, foolish boy. I will give you this. Play with your little mortal girl. Have your fun. When time grows harsh and her mortality becomes more apparent," she shrugged, "see how you feel. Though, as I know you, you would probably still stand by her even if she became decrepit."

"I most certainly would, Saaya."

Her bored expression never wavered, but her eyebrow twitched upward, just a bit. Was that a flicker of respect? The silent compliment caught him off guard.

"When mortality finally claims her," Saaya went on, "you will return to me. More specifically, your heart will come to me."

Jelani raised his eyebrows at that. "You can't dictate where a person's heart will go."

"Of course not, but I can predict where it lies, or would lie." She traced a finger down his jawline, his throat, the middle of his chest. "And I know where your heart would lie if not for a little mortal girl." Saaya looked into his eyes with enticing orbs that glowed lavender, much like his own.

"When the pain of loss claims you, I will be your balm. And when your heart is healed …" she left it at that and stood. Try though he might, Jelani's gaze hugged her body as closely as her clothes.

"Your eyes are your torture," she said, never looking back.

How the hell does she do that? Jelani thought, just as the *dampeal* left out the door.

For a while he sat on the couch. Her words cast a sober pall over his mood. Could he really endure Alisha's mortality? He had asked himself this question several times, but the answer still escaped him. He mentally shoved the matter aside and thought about Remy.

Everything Jelani had been taught up to this point was that vampires lived in secrecy. They rarely used guns because of the noise. When they did, it was with a silencer and as far away from any human being as possible. That Remy had fired on him either indicated that the Hunter had no regard for anonymity, or that he had been desperate. It was an interesting thought, considering Remy was not only older, but a pureblood Hunter at that.

He fished one of his silver blades out of his belt and inspected it. He'd killed many vampires with the knife. Being shot by Remy made it all the more real how lethal silver was. As he studied the weapon, a thought occurred to him. With the tip of a finger, he touched the flat of the blade and quickly withdrew. No burn. He touched it again, a slightly less quick tap. Still no burn.

Jelani stared at the knife, then placed his finger on the blade and held it. The silver did not burn his skin. "Strange," he said. "I wonder if it only burns from inside the body." But he remembered that any vampire he'd seen handling silver always wore gloves. Even Yako. Was he somehow different? "Hey, fine with me," he thought aloud, standing. He looked out the window across the living room at the night beyond. "I could use some air."

He left the room and took the elevator down. As soon as he stepped into the lobby, he knew someone was there.

"You might as well quit playing games and step out," he said, drawing his silver blades.

Around the back of the fireplace on the other side of the lobby, Melinda stepped out. "A little jumpy, handsome?"

He relaxed and put his weapons away. In an instant, she crashed into him and bore him to the floor. "I told you to be careful," she said, straddling him. "Remy has a fix on my mind and can compel me to do things I don't want to do. I told you that!"

"Yeah," Jelani said, "but first off, I'm always prepared." He slowly led her gaze down to one of his silver blades pointed at her side, not an inch away.

"Second, you also told me he has to be nearby. I only sensed you, no one else."

She smirked her signature, razor-tipped smirk. Yet another pair of lips he tried not to want to kiss. She made the choice for him.

Jelani tried to protest, but she grabbed his wrists and pinned them to the floor, kissing him deeply. "You wanna be faithful," she said, "fine. Don't enjoy it. I will." And she kissed him again. Her tongue found his, tickling at first, then more insistent. He felt her body starting to rock back and forth on top of him, and try as he might, he could not stop his body from responding.

"Melinda," he breathed, trying to pull away. "We can't do this."

"Then, let's go up to your place." She looked around. "You moved. Nice, though."

They heard someone clear their throat and both looked across the room to see a grinning, white-haired elderly lady. "Can't say I wasn't so impetuous when I was your age. That was a thousand years ago, of course. Don't mind me." She walked down the hall.

Melinda and Jelani looked back at each other. Melinda's lips compressed together, and they giggled like high school kids.

Reluctantly she climbed off of him and grabbed his hand, pulling him to his feet.

"So, your new place then?" She guided his hand around her waist and slid it down over her buttocks.

"Um."

"Yes?"

"We can't."

"Why not?"

Jelani was silent a moment, then finally answered. "This isn't my place."

Melinda went still. "Then who's place is it, love? I've seen you come in and out ..." she stopped. After a moment, she threw his hand away from her body.

"That girl? That tiny little bitch back from the docks?"

"Hey, hey." Jelani backed away, holding his hands up in front of him. He glanced down at her balled fists. "I didn't call you to meet me here. It's been a rough night, and I almost got myself killed."

"And your sweet little belly dancer came to the rescue."

"That pretty much sums it up."

"Ugh." Melinda turned away. "Why can't you just be spontaneous for once?"

"I got no problem with spontaneous."

She rounded on him. "Why can't you just live in the moment?"

"Because I gotta live with myself when the moment is done."

She glared at him, but her anger had deflated. Jelani saw the need in her eyes. He didn't know what Remy was putting her through, but it couldn't be easy to deal with.

Melinda heaved a frustrated sigh, running her hands through her sandy brown hair. "I don't know what to do, Jelani. He's in my head when he's not with me, and when I'm near him, it's ... you're lucky, you know. He can't press his will on you. Why is that?"

"I'm still working that out. Up till recently I didn't even know it was possible."

"It's very possible." Melinda's voice was bitter. "I'd love to ram a silver knife up his ass."

Jelani laughed and despite her irritation, Melinda laughed with him.

"Will you at least hang out with me for a while?" she said. "He told me to get out of his sight until he 'summons' me again."

"What do you want to do?" Jelani asked.

"Let's just, go somewhere. We've got six hours till sunrise."

Jelani rubbed his injured side. It was still sore, but he would be fine so long as he didn't get into any trouble. "Alright. I'm following you."

W ithin seconds of sitting down at the little table opposite Melinda, Jelani had taken in every detail of Meagan's Teahouse. Long-legged stools lined the serving counter, round tables littered the floor, and more tables lined one long tall-backed booth on which Melinda sat.

The woman at the counter had been friendly, but guarded. Jelani wondered if she'd sensed something to be not quite right about them. He didn't blame her one bit.

"So," he said, sipping his steaming mug of mango citrus. "I see your taste for tea has transitioned into un-life intact."

Melinda snorted. "Unlife. You know that's a load of BS as much as I do." She raised her mug to her lips, careful to sip slowly while he watched. Melinda's pink lips were not as full as Alisha's or Saaya's, but the way they angled into sharp edges when she smiled made them enticing nonetheless. She did so now, and her angular features seemed to brighten just a bit. Those familiar dimples emerged.

"Whatcha staring at?" she said.

"Beauty personified."

"Get lost."

"I'm serious."

She reached out and took the mug from his hands and smelled. "Mmm. Never tried this flavor." She took a sip, considered it, then handed it back. "Smells better than it tastes."

Jelani snorted. "I know it's not as bold and risky as your good old Earl Grey, but I like it."

She raised her mug to him as if in toast then took another sip. "It's kind of funny. I still drink it because I like the taste and it feels good to drink something warm, but it's still not the same."

"I know what you mean," Jelani said. "It's like drinking it out of habit than the actual need to quench a thirst or warm up because you're cold."

They looked around the teahouse. "Different kind of people-watching, isn't it?" Melinda said.

"Yeah," Jelani agreed. "I find myself wondering how often I went into a place and had no idea one or more of the people there could have completely slaughtered me and everyone else."

"Scary thought," Melinda said. "Or at least, it would be if I wasn't actually the bogeyman." That enticing smirk again. "Or rather, bogeywoman, that is."

"Heh. Right."

"You still planning on," she glanced around and lowered her voice, "having a little chat with the jackass who re-created us?"

"Already had one. That was the near un-creation experience I mentioned earlier."

"Oh?" Melinda's eyebrows rose. "I didn't think he was that tough."

"I still don't," Jelani replied, "but he's slippery and opportunistic with a dash of smart. I made a mistake I didn't know I was making till he nearly filled me with silver."

"Ooh. You better be careful, love. I don't want to lose you, even if I don't exactly have you yet."

Jelani didn't know how to respond to that.

Melinda read his face and rolled her eyes. "Unless you plan on

re-creating your little friend whom you chose over me, that is."
She took another sip of tea and eyed him. "Not that I'm planning to
wait around for you forever."

"I wouldn't expect you to."

Her lips twitched to the side. "Such a *good* guy."

"So what's your story?" Jelani said, trying to change the
subject. "You working on some way to free yourself from the
guy?"

"Not much chance of that without simply," she glanced around
again, "relieving him of his life. Right now he's got me spying on
that Eldest Hunter, Yako. I think he's pretty afraid of him. Remy
tries to put up a good front, but I think he knows this other guy
would probably kill him."

"Not probably. Yako would certainly kill him." Jelani took
another sip. "All the better for us if he did."

"Unfortunately, the son of a bitch knows it, and that's why he's
keeping a low profile, sending me to spy."

Jelani thought for a moment. "You may as well go have a talk with
him next time you find him. Maybe he'll work together with you."

Melinda's expression darkened. "I didn't know you wanted me
dead."

"I don't," Jelani said. "Trust me when I say this." He leaned
over the table. "If you can see him, he knows you're there."

Melinda shook her head. "No, there's no way he would know
I'm watching him. I keep a hundred foot minimum distance from
him. Most of the time, I hide behind a wall and watch him from a
couple streets away at the top of a building or something."

Jelani nodded through the whole explanation. "All that is great,
Melinda, but he knows you're there. I've been up close and
personal with this guy. He is aware of practically everything. I
could see it in his eyes, his presence, everything about him. I really
wouldn't be surprised if he was some sort of ninja or something."

Melinda rolled her eyes, but Jelani continued. "You really don't understand, girl." I've experienced firsthand how this guy can be right up on you and you don't know it till it's too late."

"And you were no doubt human at the time, my dear."

"Doesn't matter. I still would approach him if I were you. I wouldn't tell you if I didn't believe it completely."

"Then, why don't you talk to him?"

Jelani looked around the teahouse. As a human, he would have enjoyed the atmosphere, here. The soft murmur of patrons, tables occupied with steaming contents of various flavors. Under different circumstances, he'd be sitting in a corner, buried in a good book.

"We have a more complicated history." Jelani thought about his most recent encounter with the Eldest Hunter and again wondered why the highly skilled vampire had spared his life. "I'm still not sure where he stands with me, or I him."

"Well, figure it out," Melinda said. "Remy is a tough one to get your hands on. You might need each other. Hell, for that matter we might all need each other. Think your little belly dancer would help out?"

Jelani chuckled, looking down into his near empty mug. "Her name is—"

"Didn't ask what her name was, did I?"

That brought Jelani's gaze back up to see Melinda's stony visage. He offered a smile. It wasn't reciprocated. "Um. No, you didn't. And no, I really don't think she would be willing to join in a group hunt of one vampire that is well beneath her."

"You seem to place a lot of stock in her capabilities."

Jelani leaned back in his chair. "Heheh. Believe me when I say you have no idea."

"And her brother?"

"Even more so. I've fought Yako once and he could have killed me. I watched Yako fight Kafeel and he didn't fare well. Let me say that under no circumstances would I ever want to piss off

Saaya's brother. That is one dude you do not want coming after you."

"And unfortunately for us, your super-powered friends are of no use."

"It's not their problem."

Melinda shrugged. "Fair enough." She sat the mug down and stared at him until he became uncomfortable. "Stay the day with me at my place, Jelani."

He sighed. "Melinda, you already know—"

"I know I know," she said, holding up a hand to forestall the incoming argument. "Your whole 'death before dishonor' thing you've got going on. I'm not asking you to come have wild, passionate, sensual, soft, slow, earth-tilting sex with me. Never that!"

Ugh, Jelani thought. *Please stop it, please stop it.*

"I'll even be extra careful you don't see me naked when I have my bath."

Dammit, girl!

Those lips slanted into her dimpled smile. "I'll wear my big robe, not the one that hugs my ... well, you know."

He did.

The smile faded. "Seriously, Jelani. I don't know when the bastard is going to call me back. I managed to piss him off enough that he didn't want to look at me for a couple days. Can we at least enjoy each other's company and sleep the day away?"

There is absolutely no way this can end in any other way than me with a yoke of guilt resting on my shoulders.

She pressed, seeing his indecision. "I'm only asking this once." When he looked at her, he saw a very strong woman with a will of steel, but also vulnerable. Jelani could only imagine what it would be like to have to deal with Remy with no one else to turn to. He had been lucky enough to have Saaya guide him through his first days of re-creation. Melinda had Remy.

He stood from the table and smiled. "Let's go."

The pair left the teahouse and headed toward the west end side of town. It was the first time he had seen Melinda smile earnestly since she had been re-created. Likely, because she was heading back to her little hovel with Remy's other fledgling.

Jorge watched them go and wondered again if he should report back to Remy, or follow the couple. The Hunter had no problem with voyeurism, and it would be a lot more interesting than talking to Remy while those two had their fun.

He rubbed his chin. Of course, seeing Remy go into a fit, and possibly compel her to return while in the middle of pleasure would be amusing. Then again, so would watching him storm out to find the both of them.

Jorge thought about simply following them and quietly dispatching the one named Jelani. Remy had promised Melinda to him, and the last thing he wanted was a fledgling that had been sullied by another filthy *shaquora*.

Jorge decided to follow them. He knew that Remy wanted Jelani returned to him, but he probably wouldn't be too upset if Jorge just killed him. He was newly turned, after all. How much use could he be?

36

E ven the night can have shadows. And if the night could have shadows, then Mariska, Second Hunter, trained by Eldest Hunter Yako, stood wrapped within one. In the absence of light, her teacher had shown her how to remain concealed in the edge of vision, to remain perfectly still, even for a vampire.

It had been two hours since she had taken her position with her back against the tree. As with the Eldest Hunter, Mariska was often followed, but not so closely watched as her mentor. A foolish mistake. If Mariska had been in Massius's place, she would have been certain to keep a close eye on anyone friendly with Yako. Perhaps the Elder hadn't the resources. Likely, he was quietly consolidating his power for whatever strike he had planned.

Mariska scanned the darkened woods, only her eyes moving. Meilana had said that Massius assigned three guards to keep an eye on her, but that he hadn't considered Mariska too great of a threat without Yako's presence. Still, he wasn't taking any chances.

As soon as she'd entered the woods, Mariska had darted between the trees more quickly. Fully disorienting her pursuers, she'd taken the position she now held, more still than the tree she stood against. One of Massius's incompetent goons had walked within but a handful of feet from her. If he had turned in her direction, Mariska would have killed him.

A Hunter would have sensed her presence, at the least. Another reason she wondered why Massius had not sent Hunters to follow her. It seemed like good fortune, but luck such as this, no matter how good, was rarely a boon.

Like a serpent slithering into her nostrils, she picked up the gamey emanation signature to a nearby lycan. She remained in her statuesque position despite the offensive odor. Soon, a fully formed werewolf came stalking into view. Despite her disdain for the hulking beasts, even Mariska had to admit that Darren Lacey's pack was composed of the largest wolves she'd ever seen. Most lycanthropes averaged a little over seven feet in their lupine forms.

The beast standing a few dozen feet away rose to its full height, eight feet tall. And this wasn't the biggest. Some older books had described two species of the beasts that no vampire—Hunter or Reaper alike—would want to encounter. One was a form of lycan born without the severe allergy to silver. As undesirable as that prospect was, the other was far worse. The wargkhull ...

"Oh Miss Mariskaaa!"

The sound of Darren Lacey's jovial voice interrupted her thoughts. She remained where she was. A moment later, Darren appeared and moved to stand beside the giant wolf. "Playing coy, are we?"

She continued silently watching the pair, ready to make a move. Even in his human form Darren was dangerous, but a fully formed werewolf was always the first priority.

As if reading her mind, Darren snapped his fingers. "Of course." He turned to the wolf. "How about you take on a more ... civil presence, hmm?"

The werewolf regarded him with large upward angling eyes and crouched. The sickening sound of bone and cartilage popping and re-forming shattered the relative silence of the woods, and in less than a minute, a naked woman stood beside Darren. As soon as the female lycan had begun her transformation Darren had reached into his pack and withdrew a pair of pants and a shirt and shoes.

He tossed them to her, then turned in Mariska's direction. "Better?"

She stepped a few feet away from the tree and stared at him.

His eyes lit up.

Her eyes narrowed.

"There she is. Second Hunter. I'm glad you came from your place of concealment to speak with us."

Mariska's face hardened. Darren and his—thankfully clothed—companion obviously knew where she was. However good her sense of smell was, a lycan's was far more sensitive, made even more so when in their lupine forms.

Darren let his head hang, then gave her the most disarming look she felt he could muster. "My lovely vampire friend, if your eyes narrow any more at me, I fear I will perish from your projected enmity."

"That your new word for the day?" Mariska quipped.

"Why do you tolerate this?" the female next to Darren asked, "when you could rip out her throat instead?"

Mariska arched an eyebrow at Darren. "Leash your bitch or I will put her down."

The woman snarled, but one look from Darren and she took a step behind him, visibly cowed. It was a quick reminder to the Second Hunter that Darren was a powerful alpha. She wondered how far his influence reached.

"I apologize for my friend's behavior. Your kind are not her favorite."

"Likewise."

Darren laughed. Did anything prod his temper? "So much of your Eldest Hunter I see in you—"

"What do you have and why are there two of you?"

Darren shook his head. "I hope you will see I bear you no ill will, my lady Mariska. As for my accompaniment." He glanced back at the woman. "My pack is well aware of your distaste for us. It was either I come to you with one friend or the entire pack at my back."

"Your pack seems to think little of you."

"Actually, they think little of a blood's ability to uphold a promise of no hostility."

Mariska nodded the point. It was true enough. Her trigger finger was still itching.

"Massius is planning to kill as many of the High Council as he can, except for Alicia. He has enlisted three werewolf packs to aid him, as well as a number of your ilk, though I do not know how many."

Mariska restrained her scowl. Kill the High Council in a power grab? Why?

Darren continued. "The two packs that I spoke to have said that they are on standby for the attack, but that it will be soon. They have been promised a continued treaty and more of a share of the wealth once Peles is taken."

"It always comes down to money," Mariska said dryly.

"Live without the smile of privilege to warm your bed and you may understand."

The retort was unexpected from the normally cheerful man, and Mariska thought that maybe she was being overly rude. He was placing himself and his pack at considerable risk between the Peles coven and the other three wolf packs.

"Very well," Mariska said.

Beside Daren, the female lycan ground her teeth.

"Be calm, Lyska," Darren said, tapping her on the shoulder. "This is the same as a 'thank-you-very-much' from anyone else, I assure you."

"They do not know when this attack is supposed to happen?" Mariska asked.

Darren shook his head. "I'm sure I don't have to tell you that you may want to speed up whatever information gathering you've been doing. I don't think you have a lot of time."

"Why help us?" Mariska asked suddenly.

Darren looked as though he had been expecting the question.

"Old memories and old friendships die hard, Second Hunter." When she frowned, he smiled at her. "A time before your own, Miss Mariska. Good luck to you, and may the night bring you comfort."

"And where does your pack stand?" she asked.

Darren, who had turned to go, stopped and faced her again. "With our old allies, of course." He smiled again and it held a hint of regret. "Though it is unfortunate that many from both our species fail to realize it.

37

Yako's face hardened as he listened to Mariska's report. A takeover of the seat of their power, and three lycan packs siding with Massius. It seemed unreal. Massius was planning to kill every member of the High Council, save Alicia, and rebuild it after his own fashion. Did he really think to do this quietly? Would killing Yako really have been sufficient to eliminate the possibility of opposition? In his paranoia, perhaps Massius estimated Yako's influence a little too highly.

"I'm not so sure," Mariska said, when he'd voiced his thoughts. "Of all the information I've gathered about him, Massius appears to be the careful sort. One that studies his targets." Yako found he couldn't disagree, given what they suspected of the Elder's hand in the fate of Lord Denry Ordine.

A flash of movement caught his eye, but Yako remained still. It headed to the right of his position, likely making a circuitous route to move to behind him or to his side.

"Darren actually said he would stand with us." That was a bit of a surprise. Though Yako and the big lycan had known each other for longer than he cared to remember, he hadn't expected

Darren to pledge the support of his pack beyond information gathering. "That is fine. And the others?"

"Lydia and Barakus have pledged to stand with us, and Lydia has personally pledged to keep Barakus's temper in check. Reed has come to heel as well, and has been discretely gathering information of his own. I almost killed him when I found out, but as it happens, he discovered some of the Hunters and purebloods siding with Remy. He also managed to gain the loyalty of many *shaquora* that scurry in the corners of the castle."

"Whether or not you think of them as rodent pests, it is unwise and arrogant to scorn the one who would stand beside you as an ally."

He waited through the brief pause on the other end of the line. "Is a turned vampire worthy of our trust?" Mariska finally asked.

"Each individual is unique. I do not trust or mistrust until given a reason for either."

"Yes, Eldest Hunter," came the reply.

"Things are moving in an interesting direction here," Yako continued. "There is a possibility that I may be back soon. Remy has made dangerous enemies as only Remy can. Sooner or later he will have to leave this city or they will close in on him."

"The *Ancestor* offspring and the *dampeal*?"

"And the fledgling."

There was a pause before Mariska spoke again. "The fledgling that was once your target? He is newly awakened. How much of a threat could he pose?"

"More than enough," Yako answered. "He is unique. I haven't figured out how, but he is like no newly turned vampire I've seen. He would make a desirable ally, witting or not."

"You think to use him against Remy," Mariska surmised.

"I don't need to use him. He already seeks to kill Remy. Our efforts combined will tighten the noose, and either Remy will die here, or he will begin to feel the pressure and flee to his handler."

"Where I will be waiting."

"Yes, but be careful not to—" Yako jerked his head back, narrowly avoiding a silver tipped arrow that shot by his face.

"Eldest?" he heard Mariska say through the phone.

"I will contact you later," he said, switching off the earpiece. He shifted to a kneeling position, scanning the darkened surroundings of the construction site, high above the city. He had chosen this location because it was an incomplete high-rise and there was no work to be done at night. He knew Remy was having him followed, but he doubted that girl was the only one. Now he was sure.

Yako slowly crept across the giant red beams until he was on solid concrete. He kept as still as possible, only his eyes moving as he continued to scan the rows of beams and half-constructed walls.

Then he heard them. The contracting of a leather glove around a trigger, the drawing back of a bowstring, the whipping sound of a knife spinning end over end through the air. There was the muffled sound of a silencer as a gun was fired.

Yako judged the direction of the sound and ducked. The bullet whizzed over his back, then he dropped to his stomach, allowing two silver throwing knives to pass over him. He came back to his feet and dodging left, as another bullet came at him. With reflexes remarkable even for a vampire, Yako slapped aside another throwing knife.

Another was coming right behind it, and without breaking his motion, Yako grabbed the knife out of the air while spinning backward and down, then launched it back in the direction it had come. The throw was a guess, but his aim was true. A surprised grunt preceded a shadowy form falling from an overhead beam.

Two more silenced guns fired. Yako ducked, turning his body while back-stepping. The shooter finally descended from an overhead beam and charged in, the darkness pierced by the flashing discharge of his handgun.

A skilled vampire might dodge one bullet. A skilled Hunter

might dodge two, or even three. Yako was Eldest Hunter. His enemy could not fire fast enough to hit his target.

The shooter stopped and quickly reloaded, taking aim again. That was enough pause for Yako to charge in with a snapping kick, dislodging the gun from his hands. The Hunter cursed and drew a silver knife, thrusting out with quick jabs, forcing the Eldest Hunter to retreat.

Yako's instincts screamed at him. He dropped to one knee just as a silver tipped arrow sped by the side of his head to embed itself in his attacker's shoulder. The Hunter cried out, but he was strong, and managed to fight through the injury, though his flesh sizzled from the poisonous silver.

He continued to advance, jabbing and slicing. This one was skilled. Yako used the time he spent retreating to study his opponent's movements.

Yako heard the draw of a bowstring. The Hunter stepped in for another jab with his knife. Yako snapped his left hand out and snatched the arrow out of the air. At the same time, he grabbed the Hunter's knife hand, forced it up, then twisted under his arm. He stepped back and around, leading his enemy in a half circle. Yako wrenched the Hunter's arm under the elbow, forcing him upright. The Hunter was forced to straighten, placing himself between the second incoming arrow and Yako, who'd known it was coming.

The second arrow pierced his adversary's chest just as Yako stabbed the silver arrowhead into his back. The Hunter slumped. Seconds later he began to decay. Yako faced the remaining Hunter, who dropped from his perch without a sound. He nocked another arrow, took aim, and shot. Yako whipped his hand up in an outward arc, and the arrow fell to the ground in two pieces.

The remaining Hunter smiled and dropped his bow to the beam, drawing a sword. "I know of your skill, Eldest. I have trained for this."

All the while he spoke, Yako watched his movements, the way

he took his steps, how light he was on his feet, the way he carried his weight. "In body only," he replied.

"We shall see."

"You shall die."

The Hunter held his sword high, leaving his midsection exposed. Yako saw the trap for what it was and merely continued to watch the advancing warrior.

"Draw your sword."

"Give me a reason."

The Hunter snarled and came in, bringing his sword down in vertical and horizontal cuts that no human could hope to follow. Yako was not human. He dodged every attack by simply ducking, sidestepping, or thrusting his hips backward to avoid a forward stab.

The Hunter feinted left with his sword—which Yako didn't react to—then came in again. This time, Yako stepped into the attack, inside the sword's reach, and slammed the butt of his hand into the exposed chest. The attack knocked his adversary backward, but he rolled to his feet.

Not quickly enough.

Yako was already there. He grabbed the other Hunter's sword arm by the wrist, held it out wide, then delivered a series of one-handed chops and palm strikes that had the vampire helpless and jerking wildly as the Eldest Hunter pummeled his torso.

Finally, Yako tightened his grip and twisted, snapping the wrist of his adversary, and kicked him in the midsection. The Hunter flew backward and over the side of the building. Yako picked up the dropped sword and ran after him, jumping over the side.

The Hunter was tumbling in the air, but managed to right himself just as Yako was bearing down on him. He looked up just in time to see his death, as the Eldest Hunter drove the silver blade through his mouth and out the back of his head. Yako held onto the sword as the Hunter began to decay.

Several seconds and two hundred feet later, Yako landed. A

scabbard, some dust particles and bone fragments hit the ground around him. Yako looked down at the remains. "You should have trained another thousand years."

He recovered the scabbard and sheathed the sword, continuing to stare at the place where the remains—now little more than dust —lay scattered. He reached under his left arm, drew a throwing blade, and sent it flying into a nearby tree. There was a grunt, followed by a figure falling from a leafy branch. Yako went to recover the blade and looked over the decaying corpse. A scout, no doubt sent by Remy to report back the results of the attack.

Seeing the fate of his partner, a second scout dropped out of a nearby tree and ran. Yako was immediately after him, but kept his distance. If he was lucky, the scout would lead him to Remy.

38

The kiss was sudden, unexpected, and thoroughly enjoyable. Still, Jelani gathered his willpower and broke away. In the darkness of Melinda's apartment, they stared at each other until Jelani went to a nearby lamp and pulled the string, illuminating the small room.

"Trying to kill the mood?" Melinda asked.

"Yes," Jelani answered. To his surprise, she laughed.

"I'm not sure I don't feel sorry for your girlfriend. You have a very crisp way of telling the truth."

"I'm not going to stand here and lie," Jelani said.

"Maybe I would like it better if you did."

Jelani held his hands up in a warding gesture. "Oh, no no no. Hell no. You're not going to get me with that. You females always talk about guys being liars, and when we tell the truth, you don't like that either. You ever wanna know why most guys don't talk that much? There's one reason."

"Is that so?"

Jelani shrugged. "More or less, but it's not a hard and fast rule."

"Hard and fast?" Melinda smiled. It was the same smile that

he'd always liked, but there was something different to it; like countless years had refined it to a new level of elegance. "That's what *she* said."

Jelani laughed. "You know. The world thinks guys are the perverts, but the real truth is the opposite."

"Oh really?" She took a step closer. "And how so?"

Jelani took a step back. "Okay. How about the fact that the best-selling book right now is an erotica novel? The book is literary porn. There's no getting around it."

Melinda laughed. "Oh, I know what book you're talking about. Several months ago I was thinking of reading it."

"Yeah," Jelani shot back, "and if I told you I was thinking of going to buy a porno magazine, I'd be a pervert."

She shrugged. "That's your business."

"Yeah, right."

She took another step closer. "Are you saying you'd like to go get a magazine or video to help the mood?" She placed a hand on his chest and let it trail down his midsection.

"Um. The last thing I think need any help with, is the mood," Jelani replied.

"Do you want me to strip for you?"

"Yes. But don't." Melinda stopped her advance and looked up into his eyes. He saw frustration there.

"You know. Remy talks about how he's going to torture us by keeping us close together and never letting us have one another. I'm starting to think it's already happening without him."

"I'm sorry. You know me."

"I know you're trying to be this ridiculous, perfect person that no one can be."

"I'm trying to be what's true to myself," Jelani replied.

"A samurai?"

Jelani narrowed his eyes at her. "Funny." She took another step toward him and ran her hand up his stomach to the middle of his chest. "Uh … uh … Melinda," Jelani stammered. "Um …"

"Hmm?"

"You promised to behave, remember? You said you just wanted company."

She smiled. This time there was a hint of the tip of a fang peeking underneath the corner of her upper lip. He couldn't believe he found it enticing.

"Yes," she said. "I did. But unlike you, I'm not above lying." She moved closer until she'd backed him into a wall, then ran her other hand up his chest.

"Come on," Jelani said, his words coming out more labored. "Why are you trying to do this to me?"

"Do what, love?"

"You already know what." Jelani went to grab her wrists, but her hands snapped up and grabbed his. Her fingers were surprisingly dexterous, and she maneuvered his hands up and then laced her fingers between his.

"Melinda—"

"Stop talking, Jelani." She guided his hands down around her back and pressed them against her buttocks. She leaned forward and pressed her body against his, then glanced down between them and smiled. "Mmm. You still enjoy that, I see."

"Yeah," was all he could manage. His mind was screaming at him to stop, but his body was calmly and steadily overpowering it until it was a tiny voice in the back of his head. She turned around and leaned against him, arching her back and pushing her hips backward.

Jelani groaned.

"Still like it back there, hmm?"

"I ..." he placed his hands on her shoulders and closed his eyes. That only made it worse, so he opened them again and leaned his head back. He tried to think of Remy, of the vampires at the *dark rock*, of the Hunters he'd dispatched. He tried to think of anything that might give him the willpower to stop.

He found Alisha in his mind, conjured the image of her face, disappointed and betrayed, and it was enough. He slowly began sliding sideways from between her and the wall. "I can't—"

Before he was able to finish, she spun around and grabbed him by the shirt. With little more than a snarl, she threw him across the room. He hit the floor flat on his back, and she was immediately there, straddling him.

"You can't what? Betray her? Give it a rest, love."

"She's my girl."

"She's human."

"And?" Jelani looked into her eyes. His question was an honest one. What did her being human have to do with it? Melinda had been human not long ago.

"And … I don't know. Ah! You're pissing me off. Why can't you just be quiet and make love to me?" She shook her head. "No, don't even say it. I don't want you to answer that." She looked down into his eyes and her face softened a bit.

Had re-creation so changed her? The human Melinda would never have tried to seduce a committed man like this.

"See what you turn me into?" she said. "You made me hurt you."

"I'm not hurt."

"I've been bad." She started rocking back and forth on top of him. "Maybe you should give me a spanking. I promise I won't moan with pleasure and rip your clothes off."

"More lies?"

"You know me so well—"

Her words were bitten off when Jelani shoved her away so hard she flew across the room and hit the wall. Had he been a second slower, the three bullet sized holes in the couch would have been in Melinda's head instead.

He was instantly on his feet and over the back of the couch. Recovering from her surprise, Melinda swung herself around the wall and gave him a questioning look. She'd heard the muffled sound of the bullets hitting her couch, but clearly had no idea who had tried to kill her.

Remy? Jelani mouthed the words to her. She shook her head and shrugged. They remained where they were, waiting in the silence. Jelani stole another look across the room at Melinda, still hiding behind the wall. She looked more puzzled than afraid, which was good, because he was getting angrier by the second. His brown eyes smoldered lavender, revealing his vampiric nature. If it wasn't Remy, then it had to be one of his friends.

He crept to the side of the couch and peeked around. There had been no sound of shattering glass, so the bullet had to have come through the partially opened window on the far side of the room. Jelani looked back over at Melinda, who appeared to have come to the same conclusion.

"This is pissing me off," he growled. She gave him another questioning look, but he was already around the couch and sprinting toward the window. His instincts sounded and he dove to the side, narrowly avoiding another bullet. The missile had barely passed before he was up and at the window, shoving it open. With a quick glance down, he leapt out. Another bullet fired, this one passing right through his shoulder.

The burning pain was no less excruciating than the last time he'd been shot. The sudden burst of white hot pain caused him to lose his bearings as he plummeted toward the ground. He hit the sidewalk hard, but it wasn't the impact he felt, but the burn from that cursed silver.

"Holy shit!" he heard someone say. A man ran up and squatted beside him, looking up at the window that was far too high for a person to have survived a fall from. "You alright, man? You're lucky to be alive at all." He pulled out his phone. "I'll call and get the paramedics here—"

"I'm fine," Jelani growled through clenched teeth.

"Forget it, man. Don't try to get up."

From the corner of his eye, Jelani saw a figure drop down

behind the man. "There won't be a need for that." It sounded like some kind of British accent, but Jelani couldn't be sure.

"What?" The other man looked over his shoulder and, seeing the gun leveled at him, raised his hands and stood. "C'mon, man. This guy's hurt. He needs to get to the hospital."

"In a few minutes there won't be enough left of him for the hospital to deal with." His hand snapped out and grabbed the human by the throat. From his vantage point, Jelani saw his unfortunate would-be savior's shaking feet leave the ground. There was a sickening 'snap' and the feet went limp.

The vampire tossed the dead man aside like he was a sack of clothes, then pointed the muzzle of his gun in Jelani's face. "I don't much like having to follow stupid fledgling *shaquora* around, but orders are orders. I'm tired of it. I supposed Remy will get over it when he discovers that I killed you when you tortured the information of his whereabouts from your former lover. You just went mad with rage when you found out she was working for Remy, after all."

He suddenly leaped aside, just as Melinda crashed down on the spot where he'd been standing. "Ah! Two in one. Thank you for making this easier—"

He hadn't the chance to finish the remark. Jelani shoved the fiery pain aside and dove into him. He lifted the other vampire off the ground and they crashed into a tree. Jelani rolled away, struggling to his feet.

With an angry hiss, the man swung his gun around. A muffled high-pitched whistle pierced the silence as he fired the weapon. Melinda tackled him from the side and the shot went wide. The sound of shattering glass broke the night silence. Melinda slashed and raked at him with her claws, then punched him in the face.

Jelani had never seen her so aggressive; almost savage. The other vampire dropped his gun and warded off her attacks, quickly turning the advantage. He reacted to her with such skill, Jelani had no doubt that this was a Hunter.

He deflected another of her raking claws and slapped her across the face, sending her spinning to the ground. She was up in an instant and, balling her fist, punched him in the nose.

His head snapped back, and she grabbed his jacket, drew back and punched again. His hand went up and he grabbed her fist. Melinda let out a high-pitched grunt as he squeezed and crushed her hand.

When Jelani saw her dropping to her knee and the Hunter standing over her, leaning to pick up his gun, Jelani's vision narrowed into a tunnel of rage that had only his enemy at the other end.

He was up and across the dozen feet between them in an instant. He raked his claws across the Hunter's face then grabbed the hand that held Melinda by the neck, whipped his other hand up, and slammed it into the Hunter's elbow. A second sickening sound 'crack' broke the silence that night as the Hunter's elbow was violently forced in the wrong direction.

"Auck!" the Hunter growled, and stumbled to the ground. Jelani picked up the gun and pointed it at his enemy, but then hesitated as he saw lights coming on in the apartments and houses up and down the street.

Melinda was on her feet, her hand already mending. The Hunter was healing just as quickly, and came to his feet. Seeing that they had drawn a neighborhood of spectators, he broke into a run.

Jelani shared a look with Melinda, and they went after him.

39

He was being led into a trap. All it had taken was for the scout to glance over his shoulder once, and Yako had gotten a quick glimpse into his eyes. The fool was ensuring that Yako was still behind him. He could either catch the imbecile now and kill him, or leave off the chase and let him report back. Remy knew as well as Yako that the Eldest Hunter would have had no trouble catching and killing his scout. Let the craven make what he would out of the situation.

Yako had just decided to back off when he caught a glimpse of a figure standing with his hands in his pockets at the top of winding stairs connected to the side of a building. A moment later they passed another spectator.

Yako gave a mental shake of his head. This scout was comically oblivious. How could Remy employ such incompetence?

Another figure up ahead was standing across the street beside a building, one hand in his pocket, the other bouncing a large object in his hand. The fleeing scout veered in his direction, and the figure launched the object with incredible force toward the scout.

His aim equaled his strength. The object struck the side of the scout's head, throwing him off his feet to tumble midair to hit the ground in a heap. Before he could rise, Yako was on him, sword drawn, silver tip less than half an inch from the hollow of the other man's throat.

"Where is Remy?"

"What? Who?"

Yako touched the tip of his sword to the scout's throat, drawing a gasp. "Those who know me, know that I do not waste time with nonsense. You do not know me, so I will allow you this one mistake."

As he spoke, Yako sensed the presence of at least half a dozen vampires converging on his position. He decided to leave the situation to his allies for the moment. "Use what little wisdom you command and answer my question."

He watched the scout's eyes look left, then closer left, then right, then slightly farther right, then up and left. "Or what?" he replied, his tone filled with defiance.

Yako drove the sword through his throat and into the concrete beneath him. "Or you will die before your aid reaches you."

He withdrew the sword from the ground as if it were encased in butter and not concrete. He whipped the blade it around to deflect the descending sword of the attacker to his right. He drew the second sword he'd claimed from his slain foe at the construction site and parried another sword stabbing from the left. He dove into a roll, avoiding the bullet discharged from a silenced handgun.

He ran toward the shooter, then dropped and slid as another vampire fired at him. That was the fourth enemy, but the scout's eyes had spoken of five. The silver bullets passed over the Eldest Hunter's head and there was the agonized cry of someone being hit. The fifth attacker.

As he regained his feet, Yako whipped his right sword in an upward arc, severing the arm of the shooter in front of him, then bringing his left sword straight in and stabbing him through the chest. Seeing the life drain from the impaled Hunter, Yako brought his right sword up, tip pointing down, and blocked a horizontal swipe that would have taken his head from behind.

He pulled the left sword free and followed the motion through, slamming the butt of the weapon into the new attacker's nose. The other man stumbled back, and Yako turned and brought his right sword over and down, slicing him down across the face and chest. Before the Hunter could cry out, Yako brought the sword back up, slicing him yet again, then impaled him with the second sword.

He kicked the dying vampire away. Now his enemies numbered three. Beyond the trio that cautiously encircled him, figures darted in every direction as vampires battled Darren's lycan pack. The muffled sound of silenced handguns and dying fighters filled the air.

Yako regarded each of the Hunters that had surrounded him. "Loyalty to this degree for a coward is unusual," he remarked. "You would die for someone who would not lead you in the fight?"

The other Hunters said nothing, just continued to study him. One was visibly favoring his left shoulder. Yako guessed it was the one who'd been hit by the missed silver bullet.

They were hesitating, afraid to engage him. Yako remembered having been told by a laughing Braggus Rayne that his reputation for mercilessness was spoken of by every Hunter in every coven. "I don't even have a reputation like that!" the giant Reaper had said.

"Come, then," the Eldest Hunter said. "Die for him."

One Hunter did step forward to attack. She was the youngest of the group, and thus the one Yako had expected to move first. She brought her slender sword to bear, saluting in the fencing style. She took another half step forward and darted in for a quick strike. Yako was ready.

From the make of her sword, and her salute, she had given Yako all the information he needed. In less time than it took her to step before him, the Eldest Hunter had her dead and decaying on the ground.

The two remaining Hunters glanced at each other, suddenly at a loss for confidence. Yako faced them, casting his gaze from one to the other. "You are Hunters, are you not? The shadow of the warrior is the reflection of death." He lowered his stance and readied his swords. "It is your time. Come and embrace your uncreation as warriors."

Both Hunters had their swords leveled at him, but he could see the fear in their eyes. They were going to run. "Do not disgrace your coven or the rank which you have earned," he admonished them.

They fled. Yako sheathed his swords and went after them. Never, ever, would he allow a cravenly Hunter to live.

He caught up to the closest vampire and leaped forward, drew a silver dagger in midair, and buried it in the other Hunter's back. He went down with little more than a gasp, and Yako launched himself off the other's back, gliding forward to land on the second.

At the moment of impact, Yako buried the dagger in the back of his neck. The Hunter died the instant he hit the ground. Yako rose and looked disdainfully at the decaying corpse. Something needed to be done. Never had he seen so many cowardly Hunters. Disgraceful.

He shook his head when yet another Hunter stepped out onto the sidewalk in front of him. *How many of my own kind must I kill tonight?*

A very large figure dropped from a low rooftop behind Yako's new enemy. The vampire spun on the threat but it was too late. A large hand with elongated claws tore through the Hunter's back and lift him into the air.

With little effort, Imron tossed the vampire aside and approached Yako. He held his hands out. "If you can excuse the remains of your comrade dripping from my hand here, I come in peace."

"I know."

Imron smiled. "Ever the friendly one."

Yako looked around. A few humans were quietly scurrying away. There was no reason to pursue, for the lycans had refrained from transforming. There was nothing about this conflict that spoke of anything more than a deadly fight between two gangs.

The conflict was ending as quickly as it had begun. Yako hadn't the chance to take the number of his enemy, but only four remained, and they were in flight.

Imron saw it as well. "They wouldn't so easily get away if we had more freedom in how we could deal with them."

Yako nodded. "Running through the city in your lupine forms would garner a little more attention than you'd want."

Imron looked back at Yako, a smirk on his rocky features. "You know, I've always wondered what would happen if one of us or the other was discovered. If humans found out you bloods actually existed, would they automatically assume we did, as well? And how about the other way around?"

"Best if we never find out," Yako replied, wiping his daggers on the clothes of the decayed vampire.

"Darren thought to come back tomorrow, but changed his mind," Imron said, as they walked away from the site of the carnage and toward a less busy street. Lycans carried their dead over their shoulders and followed. "He thinks it might be best if he remains in Sinaia to aid Mariska." He glanced at Yako, his face growing serious. "Seems to think what's about to go down might be a little beyond what she can handle on her own."

"He may be right," Yako said. That brought a look of surprise to Imron's face.

They rounded a corner where they met with a few members of the pack and waited for the rest. Unlike vampires, werewolves were a bit more human. When they died, they reverted to their human form, but did not instantly decay.

"You're planning to leave again also?" Imron guessed.

Yako looked up to the rooftops and the cloudy night sky beyond. He needed to find the trail of those who fled the fight. "Yes."

The smirk returned and the hulking lycan looked down at him. "Trouble in the land of the bloods?"

"Yes." Yako jumped, catching hold of a balcony rail and lifted himself up. From below he heard Imron muttering to a friend.

"Humph. He talks too much."

Yako paid the sarcastic remark no mind and continued up. As soon as he reached the roof, he sprinted across and leaped the thirty-foot distance to the next rooftop, angling in the direction the four fleeing Hunters had gone.

Yako focused his hearing, not on the vampires, but their lycan pursuers. Vampires did not require much oxygen and as such, breathed a lot less and had nearly endless endurance. Their lycan pursuers, on the other hand, were faster on the sprint, and had excellent endurance as well, but could not last indefinitely. As they continued the chase, their breathing would become more labored and the Eldest Hunter would hear them if he was close enough.

And soon he did hear them, seconds before they came into view. Two females and a male. They ran faster than any human could ever dream of running, but they were tiring. Yako looked ahead and saw four figures gradually stretching the distance between themselves and their pursuers.

Yako increased his pace, leaping from rooftop to rooftop. He held a tactical advantage from his position. The fleeing Hunters would have been in a better position on the rooftops, but the time it would take them to leap along the side of a building would be enough for the three lycans to catch them. A werewolf could jump much higher than a vampire, and the Hunters would have simply been plucked from the side of the building.

Yako sped past the three tiring werewolves and closed on the other vampires. Traitorous vampires weren't any more unusual than in human societies. But renegade Hunters? Remy and Massius would pay for turning his noble order into this travesty.

Yako readied a throwing dagger and continued to pace them from above, waiting. He didn't have to wait long. One of the Hunters fell behind a few paces. Yako's hand whipped out. A pure silver dagger flew from his hand, straight and true. The tip struck through the back of his target's head. The Hunter fell to the ground without a sound.

Yako continued to follow the remaining three until another fell behind and he dispatched her in the same manner. One of them glanced over his shoulder and saw that there was no more pursuit, but that they were also lacking two of their comrades. With little regard, they wrote off the other two and continued on. Likely, they figured the lycans had caught the other two and they were safe.

Yako had a decision to make. He only needed one of them to lead him back to Remy, or whoever sent them. However, if he dispatched one of them, they would know they were being followed. Yako gave them a little distance.

They finally came to a stop at the underpass of Cambie Street. Yako remained atop a low-rise across the street and watched and listened.

"Looks like they got Larna and Dak," one of them said.

"That's fine," the other vampire said. "They didn't get us. Maybe later, when all this is done, we can get a group together and go hunting."

Such disregard for the fate of their companions. These were not the principles that the Hunters were founded upon. Whether Massius was behind their inception or not, Yako's ancestor had created it. The principles upon which the Shimamoto clan had lived were interwoven into the order of Hunters. Yako had known it to be true the moment he'd read that his ancestor had formed the Hunters at Massius's behest. The signs were everywhere now that he knew to look.

Yako's simmering eyes narrowed. Remy and Massius were

disgracing everything the Hunters stood for. He would follow these two and when they led him to his quarry, he would kill them. Then he would kill Remy and his cravenly master across the sea. Then he would hunt down and kill the ones who served Massius. Every one of them.

40

The name displayed on his ringing phone was not unexpected. "Hey, boss. What's up? Yeah, we lost two, and four bloods escaped. Three of ours went in pursuit, but I don't think they'll catch them." He offered a slanted smile that he knew the pack leader couldn't see. "I think your best buddy went after them, too." A moment later, the smile disappeared. "How many?"

The phone still pressed to his ear, Imron reflexively looked northwest, toward Coal Harbour. "The rest of the pack has gone back underground, but I'll get over there right now." The call ended and he put his phone in his pocket. "Shit."

Concealed in the trees at the edge of Stanley Park, Remy watched the towering vampire who stood sentry on the rooftop facing the home of Jelani's human friends. He needed to get in that apartment but he had no intention of dealing with that one. Massius hadn't gone into detail, but simply warned that the man was well beyond him. Remy hated to admit that it was true, but there was no doubt.

He looked around, wondering where that slinky little sister of his was lurking. She had given Remy more trouble than seemed possible. "Oh, yeah, cutie," he mumbled under his breath, "I'll find a way to take care of you when I get this business done."

His phone vibrated. He read the text message and smiled. They were in place. He typed on the little touch keyboard, put the phone away and waited.

Remy wondered where Melinda had gone. His first thought was to use her in this little plan, but even with the woman under his control, she had an inexplicable ability to squirm around his compulsions just enough to defy him. Best to let her roam around and cry herself to sleep for a few days.

He thought about Jorge and frowned. He'd hoped that Melinda would have led his underling to Jelani and that he would either have brought them both back, or at least given Remy some kind of indication of where the fledgling had been hiding. How Jelani had come out of his hiding place so quickly to attack without Remy knowing he was near was a mystery he would need to unravel.

Several figures appeared on the rooftops surrounding the big vampire, who seemed oblivious to their presence. Remy's eyes glowed. After he killed Jelani's friends, the fledgling would come straight to him in a ball of rage and anguish. In such a state, Jelani's mental guard would be down and Remy would have the pleasure of dominating his mind while allowing him to feel the hurt and anger at the same time.

Seven shadowy figures converged on the tall vampire at once. At first, Remy thought he was just going to stand there and be cut down. He winced when he saw the truth of it. At the last possible second, the big man reached out and grabbed one of Remy's Hunter's by the neck and snapped it, then hurled him into another. The fight was on in earnest, now, and Remy knew he would have to act fast. From what he'd seen, that big bastard might actually kill every one of his Hunters.

Remy dropped from his perch and sped toward the apartment.

Overhead, he saw two more Hunters leading a group of seven vampires from his coven. As the grin slithered across his face, Remy wondered how Yako would react when he found out that one of the North American covens was completely under his control. That was a bomb he couldn't wait to drop on the Eldest Hunter's head.

He looked up and saw the lone vampire, hurling his attackers in every direction. It seemed impossible that anyone could be so powerful. As he neared, he could have sworn he saw one vampire stop in midair. His body contorted in a strange angle, then he flew aside as if tossed. Remy shook his head. He must've seen that wrong. He'd never heard of a vampire being able to do such a thing.

As soon as he arrived at the apartment, three Hunters appeared at his side. Remy snatched the door open, and they went for the stairwell. The four vampires flew up the winding stairs gracefully, coming to the tenth floor in less than a minute.

Remy quietly opened the door, almost sniggering to himself. Oh, how this was going to be fun. Remembering his way from the last time he was here, he easily found the correct door and wrenched it open. His smile vanished when he saw the glowing lavender eyes of that half-breed freak.

"Hello, Remy," she said. An unseen force struck him in the chest and threw him against the far wall.

S aaya had come to warn them not ten minutes before several groups of vampires converged on their apartment. Daniel had grabbed two backpacks and given them to the girls, instructing them to get to Richmond. If they hadn't heard from him by dawn, book a last minute flight some place far away with longer daytime hours.

When he'd first brought up this emergency plan, they had

argued. Now, they crouched in the kitchen, backpacks strapped tight, Wen fighting tears and Alisha looking fearful for him. He'd purchased two small water guns for each of them. Poor Wen held one gun filled with garlic infused water in a shaky hand. Alisha looked only a little steadier.

He waved to catch their attention, then nodded, pointing toward the door. When Remy came through, Saaya would deal with him and they would get out. Daniel felt in his back pocket for the small silver knife hidden there, then clenched his longer silver dagger in one hand and a water gun in the other. The contrast between the two weapons looked ridiculous, but that plastic gun had saved his life at least once already.

Standing in front of the door, Saaya glanced over her shoulder at him and nodded. He hadn't heard anything, but that meant nothing. The *dampeal* likely heard the Hunters the moment they entered the building, for all he knew.

Daniel nodded back, wondering where Jelani was. He'd chased Remy out of here not long ago, and now this. The thought made him fearful for his friend.

The door suddenly flew open. Daniel ducked back around the corner and waited, hand tightening around his silver knife. "Hello, Remy," he heard Saaya say, then there was the sound of an impact farther back into the hallway.

The sound of scuffling followed. Daniel peeked around the corner. What he saw left him in such awe that he almost forgot the danger they were in. Saaya danced in between three other vampires, avoiding every lunge or slash, slapping one aside while kissing the other on the cheek just before breaking his arm and hurling him down the hallway.

Daniel's mouth hung open. He looked over to see the girls equally entranced. He blinked and shook his head, then tried to get their attention. "Psst!" They looked over at him, and he nodded his head at the door. *"Follow me,"* he mouthed, and they nodded.

The fight had moved into the hallway, and Daniel took the

lead. He peeked around the doorway and cursed. The vampires were between them and the elevators. Saaya dealt with Remy and his group with such lethal grace, it was like watching her dance them to death. One Hunter stabbed out with a silver sword and she brought her arm up, knocked the weapon wide while sliding her hand up and around his arm, forcing it straight.

Daniel's eyes widened when he saw what came next. The *dampeal* flipped up and over the Hunter's arm in what looked like a cartwheel. Once she was on the other side of him, Saaya twisted his arm with her movement. The unusual counterattack, forced him into an awkward position while she brought his sword arm up and over his head, snapped his wrist, and grabbed the falling sword.

At the same time this was happening, the other two Hunters had been coming at her from behind while Remy was trying to circle around the side. One of the other Hunters had stabbed out at the same time she had grabbed his comrade. Her sudden counter caused him to stab his comrade at the same time Saaya had snapped his wrist.

The dying vampire opened his mouth to scream, but Saaya, who had grabbed the sword from his hand, stabbed it through his neck. The gurgling vampire slid to the ground, and now there were three. How they managed all this in such a cramped space was beyond Daniel's comprehension.

He looked down the hall to the left, remembering that there were stairs on the other side as well. He beckoned for Wen and Alisha to follow They ran as quietly as they could away from the fighting down the hall.

They turned one corner and ran to the end, but then Daniel skidded to a stop and held up his hand.

"What—" Wen started to ask, but he waved the question off. His instincts were screaming at him. Daniel made a silent pushing gesture with his hand. Wen and Alisha got the hint and backed away a few steps. He crouched low and peeked around the corner.

A surprised woman looked down at him and hissed. Daniel fell to his back and rolled away, but she was right on top of him. He swiped out with his knife, but the faster vampire deflected the attack with a well-placed kick to his wrist. A popping sound preceded a burst of pain. Daniel clenched his teeth to keep from crying out, and brought his water gun to bear. She laughed and stomped down on his arm. Stars danced in his vision from the pain and he let go of the water gun.

"That brings a whole new meaning to fighting with toys," the woman said, looking down at the plastic weapon. She lifted a heeled boot and stomped down on it, crushing the water gun into pieces.

With everything he had, with every ounce of will he could muster, Daniel kicked and kneed the woman, trying to do at least enough to distract the vampire so that Wen and Alisha could slip by. The woman just laughed at him.

"You mad because I bwoke your wittle toy?" she teased. Her claws extended, and she drew her hand back.

This was it, then. After all he had endured with Jelani these past months, it finally caught up to him. Daniel would die, here, in his home. And the girls next. That was his biggest regret. His heart ached at the thought …

The woman's back suddenly arched. Daniel saw Alisha, one arm wrapped around the vampire's neck, the other with the water gun pressed against her throat.

"You like necks so much, you forgot to protect yours, bitch." She pumped the water gun, shooting a stream of garlic infused water into the other woman's neck and the side of her face. The resulting screech was deafening, but it was cut short by Daniel's silver knife that went into the woman's ribcage.

Daniel looked down at the knife and at the trembling hand that clutched it. Wen held the knife in place for only a second, then pulled it away and stabbed again. The vampire lurched, gasping. She grabbed Alisha's arm and squeezed, causing her to cry out and loosen her grip.

The female vampire hurled Alisha over her head as if she were a child. She crashed into the opposite wall and crumbled to the floor. One hand clutching the side of her burned face, the vampire hissed and reached down at Wen, but she had already let go of the silver knife and scooted away.

The vampire turned on her, but Daniel was there. He rained blow after blow of kicks and punches with his good hand, jumping up to knee the woman in the face. The assault would have downed any normal human, but this woman only stumbled under the attacks while still trying to extricate the silver that was burning her insides like acid.

Daniel whipped his leg out and around in a powerful round-house kick that buried the silver knife further into the woman's side. Now fully lodged in her body, the vampire fell to her knees and began to decay.

Wen's eyes were opened so wide, Daniel thought they would pop out of their sockets. "C'mon babe," he whispered, trying not to speak too loudly. He needn't have bothered, for two doors opened, and curious and alarmed neighbors looked out into the hall.

"Everything okay out here?" one man asked. He then looked down at the decaying vampire and his mouth fell open. "What the hell?" He looked from the macabre scene to Daniel. "What—"

A flash of movement and the man was knocked back into his apartment. Another blur of movement knocked Daniel aside on its way down the hall to the second person.

A tall woman with scarlet hair grabbed the unfortunate neighbor by the neck and held her aloft, staring into her eyes. The woman went limp, and the female vampire tossed her back into her room and closed the door.

She spun on Daniel. "You know how much trouble you've caused us, you maggot?" She looked past him at the barely conscious Alisha, then at Wen. "I'd stay right were I am if I where you, honey. I'm required to kill you, but my allegiance is conflicted at the moment." She took a step toward Daniel, then stopped as if remembering something.

"On second thought," she walked over and grabbed Wen by the throat and lifted her.

"No!" Daniel said. He struggled to his feet and rushed the woman.

The instant he reached her, the redhead snapped her fist out and connected a sideways punch to his stomach. Daniel nearly threw up as he doubled over and fell to his knees. He'd never been hit so hard!

The woman looked down at him, then back at Wen. "Remy is a fool, but somehow he controls the coven; for now." She tossed her head, red locks swishing. "Probably with the sweet talk of increasing the coven's status, and the power grab that goes with it. Fools will believe anything if it comes from Peles." She looked over the trio. "I'm supposed to kill you all, but I am a Hunter, not an assassin or a simple murderer." She returned her attention to Wen. "I can do something different with you and her," she nodded at Alisha. "But you," she looked back down at Daniel, and he saw the contempt on her face. "You have caused us no small amount of trouble. You are a problem I will deal with."

Daniel struggled to rise, but the woman walked over, Wen still in her grasp, and kicked him in the stomach again. He rolled away, curled into a ball.

She looked at Wen, then at Daniel. "Best say your goodbyes." When Daniel didn't speak, the vampire shrugged and looked into Wen's eyes.

On his hands and knees, helpless, Daniel watched as his fiancée's eyes glazed over under the weight of the redheaded vampire's stare. A second later, Wen let out a scream that cut off in her throat, and she went limp.

Daniel growled, climbing to his feet as the woman dropped Wen unceremoniously to the floor. "What …"

"The mind's ability to remember depends on the importance of the memory; the depth of the imprint that has been left on it." The woman walked toward him. "Normally, that is."

"What … what did you do to her?" Daniel finally managed.

She grabbed him by the arm and hoisted him up. His feet barely touched the floor. "In a minute, handsome."

She half dragged half carried him over to where Alisha stirred. With a wink at Daniel, she dumped him on the floor, then knelt beside Alisha. She lifted the other woman's chin and looked into her eyes. "I can't tell you how lucky you are that you haven't been just a little tiny bit more involved in all this than you have been. So lucky." A glimmer passed across the vampire's eyes and Alisha fell unconscious.

She shook her head, using a finger to slide a few stray red locks behind her ear, then turned back to Daniel. "Up we go." She lifted him none too gently and muscled him to the stairwell. Down nine flights of stairs she dragged him, till the last flight, which she slung him down. It was a painful tumble down those last rows of metal stairs that left Daniel broken and bleeding at the base. Despite the agony, he still struggled to rise.

"You've got heart, I'll give you that much." She shifted her weight, placing a hand on her hip. "I'm afraid I have to be brief, here, so I'll give you the abridged situation. Your best friend; wrong place, wrong time. You; wrong friend. Several of our kind are dead because of you, and you've had too many direct dealings with us for me to give you a break. Rules are rules, so you die." She shrugged as if it were just that simple.

"Your girlfriend up there and the other one are more lucky. I have a way with minds, so I cleaned out any memory of you and your friend and this whole thing from her mind; same as the other girl. They'll remember each other and their lives, for the most part." She started toward Daniel. "You, on the other hand, no longer exist."

"Why couldn't one of you have done this shit from the start?" Daniel growled, talking through the shooting pain in his body.

"Not all are created equal, human. The gift I have is not present in all. If it had been me that your friend had stumbled on that night," she shrugged nonchalantly, "things might have been different. Life is luck, is it not? You just came up craps."

Daniel listened in a mental haze. At least two ribs were broken, his wrist was busted, and his right ankle sprained. In his twisted and crumpled position, he had fumbled the small silver blade out of his back pocket and held it behind him. The knife was just long enough that if he could stab her at least once, he might be able to overwhelm her.

"You're broken up pretty bad," she said, grabbing him by the arm and lifting him.

"Why not ... turn ... me?" Daniel gasped, gathering his energy.

"Why the hell would I do that?" She stared at Daniel in irritation. Her scarlet hair was perfectly straight, not a single strand out of place. Despite the contrast of her pale skin, bright red hair and glowing red eyes, she was striking. She would have been all the more entrancing if she were not trying to kill him.

"You know, it amazes me that you humans really believe all those bullshit myths and stories." She genuinely looked insulted. "Yes, we consume blood for sustenance. Yes, some of the things about our weaknesses are true, and yes most of us have an aversion to sunlight."

She leaned in closer, impatience clear in her tone. "But contrary to your stupid legends ..."

Daniel stabbed out at her ribcage. Her other hand snapped up and caught his wrist. He felt his wrist snap and a fresh burst of pain followed. The little knife fell from his grasp. She let go of his hand and snatched it out of the air before it hit the concrete floor.

"... we don't need or desire to turn every one of you irritating animals into one of us."

Burning pain crashed into his chest and Daniel coughed. A crimson stream dribbled from the corner of his mouth. He looked down to see the tiny hilt of his silver knife protruding from his chest. He looked up at her, but only managed a wheeze. Suddenly, the pain in the rest of his body was diminishing.

"Hunters only kill when necessary," he heard her say. She sounded oddly far away, though she was still right in front of him. "This was necessary. You have the heart of a warrior, though it will cease to beat in a few minutes ..." she trailed off and looked up.

"Hmm. Sounds like things are ending. Remy is either gone or, if I'm lucky, dead at the hands of that exotic whatever-she-is, up there." She looked back at Daniel and clicked her tongue.

"Such a waste." She dropped him to the ground and stepped over the pool of blood that started to spread beneath him. He heard a loud crash followed by an inhuman roar, and the redheaded vampire cursed and bolted out the door.

In his blurred vision, he saw Saaya's face appear over him, and a large man who was not her brother, standing next to her. Daniel's body convulsed, and he gurgled, coughing up blood and spittle.

"He will die," Daniel heard the stranger say.

An angry glow blazed in Saaya's lavender eyes, and she straightened. "Look after him," she said, and was gone. The last thing he saw was the blurred image of the large man with a thick goatee looking down at him, then there was darkness.

41

Twice, Jelani almost had the slippery Hunter and both times he had been able to wriggle free. He was starting to wonder if this vampire had also been turned by Remy, and subsequently inherited his uncanny ability to avoid harm.

Melinda had circled around to the left to try and cut him off, but Jelani hadn't seen her since then. *Where is she?*

The fleeing Hunter jumped from the rooftop, gliding clear over the street below, to land on another rooftop nearly forty feet away. Jelani didn't hesitate, leaping the distance just as easily. The man looked over his shoulder and winked at him. His anger flared. Jelani drew one of his silver daggers and let fly.

The blade flew end over end, and found its mark in the back of the other man's shoulder. He cried out and fell. Jelani was right on top of the other vampire before he hit the ground. The Hunter found his wits and swept his feet in a scissor motion. Jelani hopped away, then drew his other knife.

"JELANI!"

He looked up and that instant of hesitation cost him. The Hunter snatched the burning weapon out of his shoulder and was on his feet. He threw the dagger at Jelani's face, but Jelani was quicker. He snatched it out of the air, but by then, the Hunter was already gone.

"I seriously hope there's a good reason you're just now getting here, only to distract me from killing that fool."

Melinda came up beside him, ignoring his irritation. "Your old place!" she explained. "It's being swarmed."

"What?"

"I just saw it. There's got to be at least twenty or thirty—"

Jelani was off, speeding back toward Coal Harbour. They hadn't gone far, and in less than a minute, they came in view of a sight Jelani wasn't sure he could bring himself to believe. Atop the building on the other side of the bend in the boardwalk, facing his old apartment, Kafeel fought what looked to be an onslaught of at least ten to fifteen vampires.

The towering pureblood son of an *Ancestor* not only held them off, but punished any who came too close. One vampire was knocked off the roof, while another came in from behind, only to be caught by his neck and have it snapped. Another was punched in the chest so hard, Jelani heard the bones crack even from his distance.

He circled around the building and saw that the lights in the apartment were on and the door was open. Jelani felt his heart sink. There was no one in the apartment. He jumped from roof to roof until he came to the top of his building, and snatched open the locked steel door.

He leaped down whole flights of stairs, Melinda right behind him, and crashed through the door to his floor. They rounded a corner and ran headfirst into a fight between Saaya and two Hunters. And Remy.

Jelani looked past them to the open door of the apartment. Remy spotted Jelani and smirked. That tiny flicker of time cost him. Saaya slapped him across the face, sending him spinning to the ground. Jelani drew his silver knives and went to work.

With the odds evened, the trio would have easily eliminated

Remy's advantage, but then six more vampires appeared from the stairwell Jelani and Melinda had come.

Jelani cursed and turned to meet them. A blur of brown hair and elongated nails shot past him, and Melinda was on one of them. As Jelani went to help, he heard Remy from behind, taunting Saaya.

"So what'll it be, hot pants? Me or him? I'm sure you know your toy cannot fight so many. And my little toy is soon going to switch allegiance."

He was right on both counts. Jelani was already being pressed to his limits. These were not simple vampires like the ones he'd attacked at the *dark rock,* these were trained warriors. If there were only one or two of them, he would have had a better chance. And to his dismay, Melinda suddenly went rigid and ceased her attack on the Hunter she was fighting. She took a step back and looked over at Jelani. He could see the pain and regret in her face as she turned toward him.

"I ... can't stop myself," she said in an apologetic tone. "I ..." she took a stiff-legged step toward him. "I'm sorry, baby." And then she was on him.

The Hunters Jelani had been fighting backed off and watched as Jelani's former lover snarled and attacked him. She slashed at his face and torso with elongated nails, fangs bared, yet agony clear in her eyes. She was surprisingly fast and relentless.Despite the gaps in her defense, Jelani found it hard to hold Melinda off without killing her.

On the other end of the hall, he heard Remy continue to taunt Saaya. "By the way," he chuckled, "my Hunters are just having fun watching. In a moment, they're going to kill him just like one of my other Hunters killed his friends."

Those last words sent Jelani's mind racing. Was he lying, or was it true? Melinda slashed at his face, and he leaned back out of her reach. He had to get away, get to Daniel and the girls.

The other Hunters were joining the fray again and Jelani was in trouble. A searing pain stretched the length of his back, drawing a strangled growl from his throat. He gasped spun away, but had no time to recover. The moment he saw his own blood lining the edge of his attacker's sword, another Hunter almost took his head.

He ducked and stabbed out and to the side, burying his dagger into the Hunter's stomach. He retracted, then stabbed again; one, two, three, four, with both blades in little more than half a second. The Hunter stood dead on his feet for several seconds before he collapsing to the ground where he began to decay.

One threat dispatched but seven more remained. Jelani was surrounded. But then Saaya was there. With a loud slap that resounded through the hall and made Jelani wince, the diminutive *dampeal* struck Melinda across the face and sent her flying across the hall to crash against the wall. He glanced at Melinda, unmoving, and felt a moment of relief. It was a brutal strike, but he knew that Saaya had taken Melinda out of the fight without killing her. Yet another favor Jelani would probably have to repay.

Now the two of them fought the six remaining Hunters, and it was all Jelani could do to hold off the three that were on him. He took two cuts across his back again, then narrowly avoided a cut to his face, still taking a slash that almost took his eye. A kick in the middle of his back sent him lurching forward, and he would have been impaled on the waiting silver sword in front of him, but suddenly all three of his attackers froze.

In that instant, Jelani continued his fall, but slapped the sword aside and spun to his left to avoid it. He hit the ground and rolled to his feet, delivering three stabs up the Hunter's side, from hip to neck. The vampire fell to the ground, where his smoking wounds began to eat at him.

Jelani quickly assessed the situation, and saw that all of their enemies were similarly paralyzed, and Saaya was already past him and down the hall.

"Finish them," she called over her shoulder.

He knew she was faster, and that was why she took off after

Remy, who was surely long gone. Jelani put an end to the remaining Hunters, sending them all into sizzling, decaying oblivion, then glanced over at Melinda. She was beginning to stir, so he left her where she was. She would be fine, but his friends were less durable.

He turned the corner and his already infrequently beating heart stopped. Wen lay on the ground at his feet and across the hall, Alisha. He knelt and felt Wen's neck, and sighed in relief when he felt her pulse. In the blink of an eye, he was at Alisha's side and also felt the relieving beat of her pulse. His vampiric nature stirred at the sensation, but the situation aided him in repressing it. He looked further down the hall. Where was Daniel?

Somewhere in the back of his mind was a feeling of surprise and regret that didn't belong to himself. What had Saaya just discovered?

The pit of his belly gone cold, Jelani looked to the doorway leading to the stairwell and was immediately there, yanking the door open. He looked down the middle of the winding stairwell and his mouth fell open. Ten floors down, a hulking figure was crouched over someone, blood all over the floor. When the big man straightened, Jelani's blood turned ice. There, lying in a pool of his own blood, was Daniel. His friend's eyes were closed, and blood flowed freely from his chest.

Jelani's lavender eyes flared. His lips curled back, revealing fangs. He leaped over the rail. Just before he landed, the man— nearly twice his size—looked up. Their eyes met and he stepped aside. As soon as Jelani's feet hit the floor, he lunged forward and swiped his silver dagger.

The huge man sidestepped the attack, grabbed Jelani by the arm, and hurled him into the wall five feet away. Jelani was up and at him again. Just as before, the big man—much faster than his size would indicate—avoided his attacks and struck Jelani with an openhanded blow, sending him flying into the wall again. This time, Jelani was slower to get up. The guy was much stronger than he was, and the hit had dazed him.

The big man walked toward him. Jelani staggered to his feet and stabbed out with his dagger. The man knocked the clumsy attack aside. With large, thick fingers, he grabbed Jelani by the neck. The man lifted him a full two feet off the ground with one hand and looked up at him. Helpless, Jelani looked down at the man, who smirked beneath a thick black goatee.

"I'll give you credit, little blood. You have no fear. But you must have no brains either to attack me like this. You must be new." He sniffed the air, and it was nothing like what a vampire would do. "Ah, right. You are new. A fledgling. You stink of inexperience. Too bad. You seem strong enough, and you got some skill, too. But attacking me?" He shook his head regretfully. "Not a good idea."

His lips curled back and he opened his mouth to reveal, not a set of fangs, but a mouth full of them. Werewolf.

"Put him down." It was Saaya's voice.

"What?"

"Put him down, my new friend."

"I'm not sure we've made it to friends yet, little one, but why should I spare this blood? He attacked me."

"This scene looks guilty enough, does it not?" She spread her hand to indicate Jelani's dead friend. His brother.

"Umph. Fair enough. He needs to learn to be more careful, though." He dropped Jelani unceremoniously to the floor.

"Jelani," Saaya began, but all he could do was stare at his friend. His dead best friend that was like a brother to him. He looked at the big man standing to the side, blood staining his chin, then turned murderous eyes on Saaya. The small woman seemed unperturbed.

"Why? What did you have to gain?"

"Be calm, *jaan*, and—"

"Don't call me that. Ever." He stood. "You will pay for this,

Saaya." He kept his eyes on them as he circled toward the door and opened it. The cold air was a perfect complement to the coldness he felt inside. *You may be strong*, he thought, *but I will kill you for this*. His icy lavender glare fixed on the big lycan and the *dampeal*, Jelani backed out of the door and fled into the cold, bitter night.

42

A wraith, passing across the rooftops. A wraith, yet whole. Whole, yet empty. The street lights passed below, blurred by tears that might be clear or might be crimson. The sounds, muffled by what might be rage or might be anguish.

Jelani knew not where he traveled as he passed from rooftop to rooftop. The pain of what he had just witnessed was too much for him to bear. His best friend dead. Betrayed by one they had come, hesitantly, to trust. How foolish a mistake that was. How could he have possibly trusted that woman? From the very beginning, she had displayed nothing but amusement for their plight, opting to act only when it suited her interest, her enter- tainment. And they had trusted her, partly because they'd had no choice.

In the back of his mind, Jelani felt pity. Not remorse, not sadness or regret. Pity. He knew it was Saaya's feelings that he was receiving, and he knew that she felt what he was feeling. That she could have such a dismissive attitude about all this showed just how cold she was. It made no sense. The dreams he'd had about her childhood, or even the memories he had of her mother through their link didn't lack their share of human pain. How could someone who was half human be colder than a full-blooded vampire?

The sense of someone following him interrupted Jelani's thoughts. Several seconds later, a cloaked figure came into view. One of Remy's Hunters, he guessed. The figure angled its way toward him, and once he was far enough in front, the man leaped at Jelani, bringing a short sword to bear.

Without slowing, Jelani brought out his daggers. He slapped the sword aside and stabbed the Hunter in the stomach, spinning around him, reversing the grip on his second dagger, and stabbed him in the back. Jelani was gliding over the street and onto the next rooftop before the Hunter had fully collapsed to the ground.

Remy must be trying to cover his tracks by sending his flunkies out to watch his back. If he had to go through every vampire in every coven in the world, Jelani would rip through every obstacle until he got his hands on the coward. And for the first time in his existence, Remy would truly know pain.

Saaya's mind touched his again and he instinctively shut her out. It surprised him, but also gave him an idea. He skidded to a stop and closed his eyes. He opened his mind again and Saaya was there, but she had wisely backed off. Jelani continued to focus. Several minutes passed before another consciousness came into his mind. The thoughts were distinct and completely different than Saaya's, almost like how a voice would differ from individual to individual.

He felt ruthlessness and malice that was unlike anything he had ever felt. Remy's thoughts—he knew beyond doubt that it was him —were wrapped in a selfish, apathetic cloak of immeasurable darkness.

Jelani's lavender eyes narrowed. He knew which way to go. The Hunter was somewhere east, and Jelani knew that the closer he got, the stronger the connection would be. Suddenly there was an awareness of him, as though Remy had physically turned to look at him. He had felt Jelani's connection.

To his surprise, the fool was actually beckoning to him. No, not beckoning; compelling. The tone of the thoughts he received was commanding. The idiot must not realize that Jelani was immune to his compulsion. This must be what happened to Melinda.

The brief thought of the woman distracted Jelani for a moment, but he cast it aside. She was smart. She would be fine. The command came again, more insistent. Jelani laughed darkly.

"You want me? Muthafuckin' you got it."

～

S omething was wrong. He felt it as clearly as he could feel his own thoughts. After all this time, Remy had finally connected with his other creation. Or rather, his other creation had connected with him. He felt the consciousness the moment it touched his mind. Jelani had actually been searching for him.

At first, Remy thought his fledgling had accepted his fate and embraced his vampirism, seeking out his re-creator like a wayward child calling to a parent. But it didn't feel like that. Jelani had sought him out and found him, and when Remy had used his will to compel him to come, the response had been a mixture of amusement and sardonic compliance.

Remy frowned. Could it be possible that Jelani was somehow immune to his compulsion? But how was that possible? Every fledgling was tied to their creator until one of them was dead. This was an irrefutable fact. But the feeling he received from Jelani was clear. The fledgling was coming to him. No. Not coming to him. Coming *for* him.

And where was Melinda? Before Remy had left the fight, he'd compelled Melinda to attack Jelani. After only a few minutes, he'd lost his connection with her mind. Had Jelani cast his feelings for her aside and killed her? Or had that little Indian woman done it? Too many questions. Too much uncertainty.

He scanned the city from the roof of the motel where he stayed. He'd had enough of living in this hovel. It was time for something a lot more comfortable. Now that he had control of the local coven, he had a lot more autonomy to act as he pleased.

"Eldest."

Remy closed his eyes and smiled. How he loved hearing that term when he was addressed. It was the first thing he'd done upon securing the coven. With the help of one of Massius's elite Reapers, Remy had gone in and eliminated the sitting coven leader, declaring him a traitor to the High Council by allowing Yako to remain alive. Next he'd declared Yako and his little crisp tart Mariska traitors to the species. Now, he was officially Eldest Hunter. All that was left was to actually remove his troublesome enemy.

"Yes, Jorge?"

"Your creation is … more capable than we may have thought."

"Oh?" Remy continued to survey the city. "How so? Did you engage him even though I instructed you otherwise?"

"It was unavoidable …"

Remy could hear the lie before the other had begun to flesh it out. He held up a hand and Jorge stopped speaking.

"Best not to continue with your little taradiddle and save us both the trouble of me killing you." He practically felt the other man go rigid with indignation. Good. As long as he remembered his place. "No harm done, my friend. My creation is actually on his way here. He has finally come within my range and I have ensnared his mind. I've commanded him to join me."

"I see. And what would you have of me now, Eldest?"

"He is coming from the west, from his home in Coal Harbour, I presume. Position yourself between him and myself, but do not alert him to your presence. He may have that slinky little bitch and her brother tagging along. Once he's passed you by, follow him back here." Remy had a thought.

"One other thing. Contact the remaining Hunters from the

attack and have them position themselves around this building. Depending on who shows up here, they will be of use." Remy wasn't sure how many—if any—Hunters remained of the force he'd sent, but hopefully it would be enough.

"Yes, Eldest."

"Oh, and one more thing, Jorge. When this is done, if you've sufficiently pleased me with your efforts, I'm in need of a Second."

"It would be my honor, Eldest Hunter."

"Of course it would be. Go."

Remy ran his hand across the butt of the gun, strapped to his leg. The laws forbade using handguns, even silenced, for they still made enough sound to attract unwanted attention. Remy thought it a ridiculous law and would see to it being changed once the dust settled. Let the human cattle know their betters actually exist. What could they do? Vampires were firmly interwoven into society. Humans were just too dull-witted to see it.

Remy considered the situation and decided things were in his favor. If that *skiek* and her brother showed up with Jelani, he was certain he had enough silver bullets in both his guns to deal with them. If Melinda happened to appear from whatever void she'd fallen into—if she was even alive—he would at least have a little fun forcing her to deal with Jelani. All this combined with the aid of the remaining Hunters from tonight's attack, and Remy would have things firmly in hand.

His smile disappeared. There was only one matter that hung dangerously over his head. Where was that tick in his side, Yako?

43

Whether it was the gradual erosion of his order through decadence, or something else, Yako didn't know. What he did know was that there was no excuse for the obliviousness of these two whom he'd been following for the last five minutes.

To his delight, Remy had actually contacted them and summoned them back to him. It was a good stroke of luck, but it came at the cost of the Eldest Hunter seeing just how ridiculously inept Hunters had become. Having only worked with a small group or alone, Yako had not monitored things close enough. There would be changes. Even if he had to scour the order and start it anew with only a handful, it would be better than this pathetic shadow of its former self.

They were heading east. Curious that Massius would order Remy to stay holed up someplace in East Downtown Vancouver, a part of town not noted for comfort. Yako allowed himself a mental chuckle at the thought of the arrogant Remy laying down for the day on a lumpy hard mattress. If humility was the lesson Massius had thought to teach Remy, it may be the only thing the so-called Elder and Yako could agree upon.

Yako knew that not to be the case, however. Likely, it was

more out of necessity. No one would suspect Remy to have taken lodging here. It worked, for Yako had not thought to come looking for Remy in the poorer side of town.

Out of the corner of his eye, he noticed a large number of figures passing over the rooftops, converging on one location. They were moving northwest from his position. Coal Harbour. Remy pulled a lot of resources to make a bold move on Jelani's companions. The craven would know of the *dampeal* and her brother's prowess by now, so he would have sent as many resources as he dared.

Given the little he'd seen of what Saaya and her brother were capable of, Yako doubted twenty or even thirty vampires would be enough for those two. What was troubling, however, was that Remy commanded so large a force. That he could send such a large number out at his bidding didn't make sense. Only the coven leader and the Eldest Hunter had such authority. He needed to confront Remy as quickly as possible.

Nearly fifteen minutes passed when Yako spotted more figures moving along the rooftops, these heading in the same direction as himself. He looked over his shoulder and noticed that some were starting to come from Coal Harbour. It seemed the confrontation had been decided.

He returned his attention ahead, past the two he was following, and saw a solitary figure standing on a rooftop. Remy. Yako drew two silver throwing knives and let fly. Death went spinning from his fingers and into the back of the necks of both Hunters in front of him. They dropped to the ground and skidded to a stop. Yako caught up to the decaying corpses and retrieved his weapons.

He checked the straps on his torso and legs and arms, ensuring all of his smaller blades were in place. Three silver throwing shurikens were strapped to each side of his body, three more to the sides of each lower leg, and two on each thigh. Three more on each forearm, and one on each side behind his waist. As with the clothes he wore, the blades were all black-coated, and practically invisible upon his person.

He moved to the edge of the rooftop and watched as what looked to be at least twenty vampires converging on the spot where Remy stood. Something had happened at the coven. There was no other explanation. If he'd had a bow and arrows or even a gun, Yako would have shot Remy on the spot. He didn't deserve a warrior's death.

Crouched behind the three foot wall, Yako looked to his left and saw another figure, similarly hidden behind a short wall on a building across the street.

Jelani.

Yako nodded in approval. Somehow Jelani had found Remy, but had chosen discretion, to assess the odds. If Yako wasn't forced to kill the fledgling, he could make a fine Hunter.

Finally, the last stragglers arrived, and it looked to be nearly forty vampires present. Not all were Hunters, Yako could tell. As with humans, vampire warriors held themselves and moved differently than civilians.

Yako's eyes moved as he took their measure. He was certain he could have at least ten of them dead before they knew he was coming. He looked back in the fledgling's direction and wondered if he would strike when Yako did. The Eldest Hunter didn't like leaving things to chance, but he knew that this was his opportunity, and he also knew that this confrontation was going to happen one way or another. He just needed to be in front of Jelani at the start so that he could thin their ranks a bit before the real fight began.

His mind made up, Yako was just about to move in when his intuition nudged him. He held his position and carefully studied the surrounding area again. After countless hunts and countless targets dispatched, Yako could feel a situation better than most could see it. There was something missing here, some missing player. If there was one thing he knew about Remy, it was that the elusive Hunter possessed the type of careful planning typical of a coward.

He looked back at Jelani again, then a little farther back. If he were Remy, and trying to bring his newly created fledgling in hand, he would have had someone keeping an eye on him. With the task of dispatching the remaining humans, having his new female creation watching Yako, and causing whatever trouble he was causing in the coven, Remy would have little time to personally deal with Jelani. It made sense that he would have passed that task on to another.

Yako continued to watch the area behind Jelani's position. Soon he picked up a subtle movement in the corner of his eye. He focused on the spot and waited. His patience was rewarded a few minutes later when he saw a man creeping from behind a wall at the top of a penthouse, moving to the edge of the building.

Yako frowned and focused more on the familiar figure. His frown deepened when he finally recognized the Hunter as Jorge. So, Remy managed to gather at least one like-minded fool to aid his cause. Jorge had always been opportunistic and naturally given to subterfuge. As Eldest Hunter, Yako had not the luxury to deal with him personally, as tasks always saw him away from the coven.

Tonight, this would change. Remy, and all who willingly sided with him would be dealt with; starting with Jorge.

Yako slipped away from the wall and made his way in the opposite direction. He leaped from his rooftop to another, making a roundabout path to Jorge's position. In minutes, he was crouched above the Hunter, waiting. When Jorge finally moved away from the wall again, Yako dropped silently behind him.

Jorge looked as though he was about to take another step, but his body went rigid. "Hello, Yako," he said. "As you are the only person I know of who can so freeze a person in their tracks, I'm assuming it's you." There was a hint of trepidation in his voice but he was trying to hide it.

"You are correct."

"Why have you sought me out? The fledgling betrays us and his friends will have been dealt with by now. That *shaquora* is the last loose end to all this."

"Wrong."

"I don't know what's going on between you and Remy, but I only do what I am told."

"You act under the orders of one who would fashion himself as Eldest Hunter."

The resulting pause confirmed Yako's suspicion.

"Why do you say that, Eldest?"

"There are four reasons why I am about to proceed with your un-creation," Yako said. "First, the fear in your voice. I do not tolerate cowardice. Second, your mouth betrays you. If you truly served Remy in ignorance of his personal designs, you would have addressed me as Eldest, first, and not after I revealed my knowledge of your plot."

He circled the other man. "Third, you willingly serving a traitor to the coven and enemy of your Eldest Hunter." Slowly, deliberately, Yako drew his sword. "And lastly, you have gaping holes in your defense and awareness."

Jorge's eyes were wide with fear. "If you would spare me, Eldest Hunter, I am yours to command.

"You were always mine." A blindingly fast horizontal swipe of his sword and it was in its sheath an instant later. Yako turned and leaped from the roof without a backwards glance at the headless corpse decaying behind him.

44

T*oo many.*

Through the rage and pain he was feeling, Jelani still held his wits about him enough to know that there were too many between himself and his enemy. Remy had spared no expense in protecting himself. What amazed Jelani was that he could not recall meeting a single person in his human life that worked so hard at not getting hurt. That this man was a Hunter made it even more laughable.

Jelani stared at the one who had brought him so much pain. Even if it meant his own un-creation, he would send Remy to whatever hell awaited him. The question was how to get to him. More than thirty vampires stood around him, listening to whatever the coward had to say.

Jelani scanned the surrounding buildings. There must be a closer vantage point where he could hear what was going on. He spotted a ledge one street over from the rooftop where Remy and his cronies congregated. *Worth a shot.* He started in that direction, or tried to.

"Remain where you are."

Jelani felt a surge of panic. The low, even-toned voice of Yako had commanded him to remain still, and he was powerless to do otherwise. Jelani took a deep breath and calmed himself. "You have me at a disadvantage, Yako."

"You had yourself at a disadvantage, fledgling. Your negligence to your surroundings is grounds enough for your uncreation."

Jelani forced his voice to remain steady. "Loathe though I am to pay you a compliment, I must admit that you-re better than most at sneaking." To his surprise, the Eldest Hunter chuckled.

"Fair enough. But if you wish to remain alive, you'd best learn to focus through your anger."

Jelani's face tightened. Was Yako somehow involved in the attack on his friends? That seemed unlikely. "How do you know about my anger?"

"I know nothing directly about it. But it is wafting off of you."

Still frozen to the spot, Jelani's eyes moved as he took in the surroundings ahead. Remy stood tauntingly within reach, surrounded by enemies. In his frustration, even the humdrum noise of traffic on the streets below mocked him. "Well, you got the drop on me. You gonna kill me, then?"

"How would that serve me?"

"You tell me."

"It wouldn't."

Jelani would have shrugged if he could move. "Then are you here for my amazing company?"

"You are trying to find a way through Remy's force to attack him."

"You object?" Yet another surprise came when Jelani found the force binding him released.

"I will move in first," Yako said, "and have ten of their number dead. You move in behind me and we engage them together."

Jelani couldn't believe what he was hearing. "And what if Mr. Bravery turns tail and runs?"

"We go after him."

"And all his friends?"

"Be fast."

The Hunter turned and moved into position behind the wall, looking over the top at the group across the street. Jelani had no idea how this man intended to kill ten of them before the fight even started. He noticed all of the black-coated cutlery strapped to the ninja-like Hunter's body. If he hadn't been covertly studying the Eldest Hunter, he would have missed them. He raised an eyebrow appreciatively. This would be interesting.

"Why are you helping me?"

The stern vampire never turned around when he answered. "I'm not. Our goals are aligned."

"And when this is done?"

"We will speak again."

"We will?"

"Twice I have spared your life when I could have ended it. You are indebted to me by the blood in you that I did not spill."

"I don't do the slave thing, man. I'm nobody's servant."

"We will speak later. Come."

Jelani moved beside him. It mattered little anyway. Either something would be worked out, or he would die fighting before living in subjugation. One thing at a time.

"I will move in first. Move in right behind me and we take them at once."

"Remy will be caught off guard at us working together," Jelani said.

"How so?" The Hunter continued to study the group, picking out his targets.

"He's been trying to do some kind of Jedi mind trick on me to force me to come to him. I think maybe he thinks he's supposed to be able to control me or something."

"You have a rare luck about you, fledgling," Yako said.

"How so? And can you not call me fledgling? My name is Jelani. I don't mind if you use it."

"I have never failed in eliminating a target. You were my first failure because a *dampeal* took interest in you. You were turned by Remy, only to have the *dampeal* counter his essence with her own, which is infinitely stronger. You should either be dead or indentured to Remy, yet you remain alive and retain your free will."

"How do you know all this?"

Now the Eldest Hunter looked at him. "There is no other explanation. Your immunity to Remy's influence and your abilities despite being newly turned. You carry the essence of a powerful vampire in you."

Jelani tipped his head at that. "Let's hope it's enough to see me through tonight. If you have my back, I've got yours."

"Agreed."

Jelani peeked over the wall. Remy's group had positioned themselves all about the rooftop while Remy himself—predictably —had positioned himself at the center. He saw Yako's body tense, then he was over the wall.

"Could've at least said let's go," Jelani grumbled, scrambling over the wall after him. He leaped off the roof, gliding across the street. To his amazement, Yako spun in a forward flip and from his curled body rained at least a dozen small blades. The storm of death descended on the vampires below, piercing eyes, throats, and chests.

Just before Jelani landed, he saw Yako touch down and draw his sword in a diagonally downward arc, cutting down another enemy as he foolishly lunged at the Hunter. Yako went right, and as soon as Jelani's feet touched the roof, he went left, drawing his silver daggers and going to work.

They worked in unison, keeping relatively close but far enough away so as not to get in each other's way. Jelani deflected a sword and spun around it, stabbing the attacker several times before completing the circuit around him. He dove to the side just as a silenced handgun fired, the silver bullet striking the ground where he'd been just an instant before.

Jelani hurled the dagger at the gunman and ran after it. The weapon found his throat, just as Jelani stabbed him in the torso. At the same time he withdrew the blade from the gunman's neck and spun around him. In little more than a second, another enemy was down.

Jelani was about to engage his next foe when a powerful mental assault hit him. He staggered, but powered through it and kept moving. That instant would have been the end of him, but Yako was there. The Eldest Hunter decapitated the man who had come in at Jelani with a short silver sword, then launched a shuriken into the chest of another.

Yako gave Jelani a look that suggested he needed to better mind his surroundings, then turned away. Jelani instinctively ducked, and a sword swiped overhead. At the same time he'd ducked, he spun on his heels and drove first one dagger, then the other, into the woman's abdomen. He hated to kill a female, but he didn't have time to think about it, for two more enemies came at him.

A little way off, Remy watched the action passively. The casual look on his face suggested he was sure this would all be over soon. *Yeah, you just stay right there,* Jelani thought, just as he felled another adversary. As if reading his thoughts, there was another attack on his mind. It felt as if a tiny voice in his head commanded him to stop and turn on Yako.

"I've had just about enough of this guy." Jelani jumped straight up and kicked off of the chest of the large vampire he'd been fighting and somersaulted away, landing behind one of the three Hunters that had been fighting Yako. Three stabs in the back and another enemy was dead on the ground.

Jelani turned and saw Remy staring right at him, a mixture of confusion and outrage on his face. "Something wrong?" he asked, smiling as he approached.

"You are mine, fledgling," Remy hissed. "You *will* obey me."

Jelani laughed. "Then come and claim me. You're not afraid,

are you?" When Remy looked past him, Jelani saw the concern on his face. A good number of his flunkies were dead and Yako was probably working his way toward them.

"If you want, you can just stay there and watch—" he hopped to the side just as a sword thrust next to him. Jelani turned and delivered a horizontal swipe, taking the man across the eyes, then came back the other way, taking him across the neck with his other weapon. "—while we kill all your friends," he finished.

"You're overconfident."

"You're dead." Jelani came at him, slashing left, right, diagonal. He stabbed and retracted, using a series of attacks to put his enemy off balance. To his credit, Remy avoided most of the attacks, suffering a few glancing slices that seared his flesh.

"I'm going to kill you," Remy growled.

"Sure you will," Jelani growled back, kneeing Remy in the groin, then connecting a roundhouse punch to the side of his head.

When Remy fell, Jelani reversed the grip on one of his daggers and drove it down. Or tried to. A woman with dusty brown hair tackled him at the waist and they both went down. He rolled to his feet and leaned to the side. When she overextended herself in a follow-up attack, he kneed her in the stomach and drove his dagger into her back.

A short distance away, Remy was moving toward the opposite side of the roof. *No you don't.* Jelani started toward him, but then he saw that Yako was surrounded. The Hunter was amazing, fighting off four enemies at once. But more were moving in. Even Yako's skill could not see him victorious against the group that remained.

Jelani looked back and forth from Remy to Yako, then cursed and went toward the latter. He heard Remy laughing as he went to help his ally. Jelani sheathed one of his daggers, snatched one of Yako's shurikens from the ground and launched it Remy's way. The laughter was bitten off by a muffled curse that told Jelani he had scored a lucky shot.

And then he was with Yako. He drew his second dagger again and together they cut down their enemies. Yako dove right, and Jelani leaped in, bearing a pursuing enemy to the ground. Another vampire came at his side. Yako glided over Jelani and buried his sword in the other's chest, just as Jelani dispatched his foe.

Jelani came to his feet and leaped at Yako's back. The Hunter's intuition was remarkable, and he sidestepped to the left, cutting down an enemy to his side at the same time Jelani drove his foot into the face of the man who had been facing the Eldest Hunter. The man staggered backward and Jelani finished him with a series of thrusts and swipes of his two silver daggers.

Both men back-stepped till they were back to back, and Jelani glanced over his shoulder. "Is it just me, or is this getting a little easier?"

"Four Hunters accompanied Remy," Yako answered. "Our enemies here are not warriors, but fodder."

"Maybe we should tell them that. They might stop."

"They would be fools."

"You'd kill them anyway?"

"Yes."

"What—" Jelani deflected a thrusting sword. He swiped his right handed blade down, cutting the stabbing arm, then brought his left blade around and across the attacker's throat. Their remaining enemies hesitated and Yako was immediately off, bounding in the direction Remy had gone. Jelani sheathed his daggers and went after him.

45

I mpossible. That was the only word that came to mind when Remy thought of his failed attempt to bend Jelani to his will. The fledgling was his creation. It was impossible for one's own creation to deny his will. Something was wrong.

He looked over his shoulder and saw two of his four remaining Hunters trailing him. They would stand against Jelani and Yako, while the two at his sides would stand with him if it came to a confrontation. Not that Remy was worried about that. It would be more convenient for that scenario not to come to pass. Better to deal Yako a crushing blow by allowing him to see his power crumble around him, then the High Council can see to his formal uncreation.

They were moving toward the shipyard when Remy turned west. They would make their way back toward Stanley Park. Let them find him there. Tiny droplets started to fall and in minutes, rain poured from the sky. Remy smiled as the drops spattered across his face. The better to obscure their passage.

He looked over his shoulder again and his smile fell away. In the distance he could barely make out two figures giving chase.

Damn. He hadn't expected them to do away with the distractions Remy had left to occupy them. He didn't know whether to be smug or irritated by his new creation's prowess.

In the end, it didn't matter. There was no way Yako was going to get his hands on Remy, so there definitely was no way his own creation would take him down. He still wondered how Jelani managed to deny him. He wondered if Yako had anything to do with that … or that female half-breed. The latter was even more unlikely. That she was half human negated any possibility of that being the case.

They passed from building to building, heading west. Remy was careful to give Coal Harbour—and by extension that towering pureblood—a wide berth as they passed the area by. His clothes were soaked through, and his sandy blond hair was plastered to his head. He looked over his shoulder again and saw that the two were drawing closer.

He increased his pace, and hope drew nearer with the thick vegetation of the huge park. Again he looked over his shoulder, and again, he saw that his pursuers were closing in. He drew his silenced handgun and fired. The two pursuers dove away out of sight.

Remy smirked and continued on, passing through the tree line and entering the dark woods of the mini rainforest that was Stanley Park.

D espite the irritation of losing Remy, Jelani couldn't help but marvel at the fact that he had just literally dodged a bullet. He had actually seen the tiny black missile coming right at him. It was an odd sensation. They were traveling fast, but just slow enough that he could see them clearly and move out of the way, like someone at a distance throwing a rock. He felt eyes upon him and looked to see Yako regarding him with an expression that looked like disapproval.

"Reserve your self-discovery for later."

Jelani shook his head at the other man. "Ever serious."

"Ever alive," came the retort, then Yako was gone.

Jelani sighed and went after him.

All at once the rain started coming down in sheets. Pissing rain, as they said here in Vancouver. It was one of the many terms people used here that reminded Jelani that Canada seemed like a cross between the UK and the US.

They traversed rooftop to rooftop until the buildings ended. They dropped to the sidewalk, speeding across the remaining distance until they were in the woods. Yako leaped into the trees, and Jelani followed.

Though vampirism had enhanced his existing abilities, it didn't necessarily give him new ones. Try though he might, Jelani could not match the perfection Yako exhibited as he passed from limb to limb, sometimes leaping higher, sometimes dropping a full twenty feet and leaping forward upon touchdown. It was all Jelani could do to simply keep up with the Hunter without stumbling and falling to the ground.

After a few minutes, Yako stopped and held up a hand. Jelani stopped in a tree just behind him. In a rare show of force, the rain intensified and the roar of the showers was deafening. Then something odd happened.

Jelani had always enjoyed the rain. Despite the frequent complaints by most Vancouverites that there was too much rain and it was depressing, Jelani had always loved it. Something about the countless drops of water falling from the sky gave him focus; made his thoughts more keen. That focus amplified.

He closed his eyes for a moment, then opened them again, and found that Yako was staring directly at him. "Left," he heard himself say. One of the Hunter's eyebrows twitched. Jelani knew the Eldest Hunter enough by now to realize it was an indication that Yako was impressed.

Yako nodded in agreement of Jelani's estimation. They moved through the trees, Jelani still struggling to keep up, but managing. Every time a change in direction was needed, they acted in unison.

Finally, they came to a stop and waited. Remy was nearby. Again, Jelani closed his eyes, allowing the relentless drops of rain spattering against his shaven head to sharpen his focus. In one fluid motion, he drew one of his daggers and launched it up to his right. As soon as he released the blade, he leaped up after it.

There was a cry of shock when the dagger found its mark and an instant later, Jelani was there, snatching the weapon free and cutting the Hunter across the neck and torso. He fell from the tree, decaying on his descent.

Jelani's instincts saved him yet again. He dropped from the limb. He heard the muffled sound of a gun firing, and a shower of bark rained down on him. He dove to the left just as more silver bullets came for him.

As soon as he landed, Jelani was set upon by two Hunters. These two carried swords instead of guns. Fortune was with Jelani, for they were no better at moving through the trees than he was. They passed from limb to limb, but as long as Jelani kept moving, they could not directly engage him.

From somewhere in the darkness, he heard the sound of silver clashing, and then a scream. Yako had dispatched another Hunter.

Jelani landed and sidestepped just as one of his pursuers landed beside him. He swiped a horizontal cut that the other man blocked, then brought his other blade in. Again, the Hunter turned and blocked the attack. This one was more skilled than any Jelani had fought so far and the other was closing in.

Jelani doubled his efforts, but the Hunter matched him. He felt a burn along the side of his forearm where the silver sword had cut him. The Hunter snarled and feinted left, then came in straight.

Jelani saw the move for what it was and went in the opposite direction.

He was at an awkward angle for a killing blow, but he managed to hop upward and connect his knee with the other man's face. The Hunter's head snapped back and he fell from the tree.

Jelani dropped to a crouch and ducked a horizontal cut at his head, then turned and deflected a stab at his face. The tip of the sword passed inches in front of his eyes. His hands were a blur as he fought to keep the sword away. This Hunter was even more skilled than the one he'd just knocked from the tree. Just a few moments into the fight, Jelani found himself overwhelmed.

He stabbed with one hand, then retracted and brought the other around for a downward slash. The Hunter deflected the first and cut Jelani across the chest before he could complete the second attack. The pain was so fiery, so acidic, it drained strength from Jelani's legs.

He slipped off the limb. The treetops fled but the Hunter was directly over him, sword in a two-handed grip, poised to run Jelani through the moment his back hit the ground. He slammed into the earth so hard, his back bounced off the ground and his head snapped back. But the end of his life did not come.

A few yards to his right, the one who had bested him was now embroiled in a struggle against Yako, but with the aid of Remy as well. Jelani was surprised the coward had actually chosen to fight. He thought the odds were in his favor, no doubt.

Jelani ignored the molten pain arcing across his chest and started toward them, but then he heard someone coming from behind. He turned and fell back. The first Hunter he'd dislodged from the trees had found him. His movements slowed by the silver injury, Jelani was barely able to defend against the other man, much less offer any kind of offense.

He heard a grunt that he knew came from Yako. Jelani rolled away from his adversary and managed a glance over his shoulder.

Yako was still fighting, but he had taken several injuries. He heard Remy's voice, taunting.

"Such a shame, all this wasted talent. I was hoping to keep your former target and maybe make a subordinate out of you … well, that's a lie. I was actually planning on tormenting your former target and killing you. Looks like I'll just have to kill you both."

Jelani ducked a swipe at his head and kicked out, connecting his foot with the other man's face. He fell backwards, rolling to his feet in a defensive posture.

"Such a shame," he heard Remy say again. "All that vengeance and burning fires of retribution, extinguished in one stroke by yours truly."

Jelani thought of his life for these past months. He thought of the lives of his friends. He thought of Alisha and Wen. He thought of Daniel. His best friend. His brother.

If Jelani's anger was an expression of color, there was no red dark enough to wash it through. The rage inside burned through all other emotions and even fed upon itself, until all thoughts fell away and his mind quieted. His body took control and years of training in his human life, enhanced by his new existence came fully to bear. Sparks lit the darkened woods as Jelani parried and blocked. His movements became faster. His arms were cobras, his hands were the mouth, and his daggers, the venom-filled fangs.

Again and again, the cobras bit, and again and again, the venom poisoned his enemy. The Hunter's movements began to slow as Jelani's movements grew faster. The pain of all he had lost guided him, and soon his enemy was a smoking corpse, decaying upon the wet forest floor.

Jelani turned and saw that Yako still fought. He raced toward the trio, veering left. Though he might not be able to control Jelani's mind, Remy must still be able to feel his thoughts on some level. Just as Jelani was going in for a killing strike, Remy fell away and to the side.

Jelani missed his mark, but it was enough to give Yako the instant he needed against the remaining Hunter. Jelani knew that Yako would soon overwhelm his adversary, so he focused on Remy. The cravenly Hunter must have known the same, for he fended Jelani off just enough to draw his gun.

He fired off several rounds and Jelani was forced to dive aside. When he came to his feet, Remy was in full flight. Jelani gave chase, passing through the trees, not letting his enemy out of his sight. Closer, closer. Remy was fast and dexterous, he was good at changing directions on a dime, but Jelani had gained these same attributes the moment Remy had turned him. There would be no escape this time.

Just as Jelani closed in, Remy turned and fired. Jelani was expecting it. He had already moved to the side as Remy drew the gun, and he brought his right dagger around and down, slicing a deep gash in the other man's arm.

Remy cried out and dropped the gun, cradling his injured arm as he ran. If he had been at his best, Remy could not have outrun Jelani and now he was injured. Jelani kicked his feet out from under him and sent the other man rolling to the ground.

Jelani savored the moment of the kill, not by stopping and taunting his prey. He savored the moment, not by circling his felled enemy, not by delaying the moment, but by drinking in the fear in the eyes of his re-creator as he came down on him. This would end now, and quickly—

A huge form bounded out of the trees and crashed into Jelani. The impact was so hard, it sent him flying away until he slammed into a thick redwood. Far more durable than his human body had been, the vampiric Jelani was not killed, but he was still jarred by the impact. He shook his head and came back to his feet, running toward this new enemy. He skidded to a stop when he saw it. What came stomping into view was the size of a grizzly bear. Jelani wished it was a grizzly. But it wasn't. It was a werewolf.

The beast stalked toward him, then rose up on its hind legs and stared down at him with eyes as black as pitch. Jelani looked up into those eyes, more than a foot above his head. For the time being, Remy was forgotten as he faced this new and more dangerous foe.

He readied the daggers that suddenly seemed quite inadequate against the seven foot werewolf. He lowered his stance and circled to the right. The werewolf tracked his movements. The long muzzle drew back to reveal a row of jagged fangs that would give a shark pause.

Jelani took the last moments he had to consider his enemy. The wolf's weapons were its fangs, its claws, and its size. There were only so many ways it could attack; slashes and bites. He waited for the wolf to make the first move. He didn't have to wait long.

The beast dropped to all fours and bounded toward him. Jelani waited till the last possible instant, and dove aside. While his body was horizontal, he slashed out with one of his daggers. The wolf howled at the burning bite of the silver.

Jelani was fast to his feet, but the wolf was faster. It slammed its huge head into him and sent him flying, then leaped high into the air. Jelani hit the ground and immediately rolled out of the way. As soon as the werewolf hit the ground where he'd been, Jelani jumped at its side and buried both daggers in its flank. It howled again and spun, throwing Jelani away. He hit the ground and was on his feet and diving aside yet again as the beast bore down on him.

Jelani spun and slashed it across its injured side, then leaped up as it curled its body around and snapped at him. He kicked it in the face, pushing himself away, then turned and ran.

He couldn't win this fight. He had stabbed and slashed the thing multiple times with his silver daggers, but all it seemed to do was anger the thing. *Thought these fuckers were allergic to silver, too.*

He heard the thuds of heavy footfalls as the werewolf pursued.

He passed through the trees, using every skill and ability he had gained from Remy's essence to help him escape. He managed to keep his distance for a while until the thuds grew more distant, then fell away.

Jelani took to the trees, leaping from branch to branch. It was slower, but he'd never heard of the giant wolves navigating the treetops—

The massive wolf tackled him mid-flight. Jelani's back hit the ground hard, every bone in his body vibrating upon impact. With an intelligence beyond any normal wolf, the lycan held his arms pinned beneath its giant claws.

It growled deep in its belly and opened its maw, blasting Jelani with its hot, acrid breath. He struggled to get free, but he might as well have been trapped under a mountain. As that gaping maw filled with fangs came down at his face, he managed to lean just enough away that it missed his head. Still, the jagged teeth found his shoulder, tearing through flesh.

It wasn't silver, but it still hurt, and Jelani hollered as the beast bit down harder. He felt the weight on his arms lift, but it didn't matter. The beast hoisted him from the ground by his torn shoulder and shook him side to side like a chew toy. The pain was unbearable and Jelani thought his arm might be ripped off.

The werewolf threw him a dozen feet to crash into another tree. As soon as his feet touched the ground, the wolf plowed into him with the top of its head, knocking him back into the tree. It moved away and Jelani simply rolled to the ground. He screamed when the huge teeth bit into his shoulder again.

With inhuman strength, the beast lifted him from the ground and threw him into another tree. Jelani ricocheted off the immovable redwood and spun to the ground. His shoulder shredded and the injury to his chest still not fully healed, Jelani was slow to his feet.

All he could do was watch as the wolf tore up the ground as it came for him, jaws opened to rip him in half. Jelani struggled upright on shaky legs. He would at least meet his death squarely.

Silent and deadly, a blur passed underneath the werewolf's neck as it ran. The wolf gurgled once, then collapsed into a silent tumble. The momentum sent the giant body crashing into Jelani and pinned him against the tree.

Jelani groaned and tried to push the giant furry body away, but he had not the strength. A black clad figure appeared over him and he recognized Yako's cold visage.

"You are not ready to fight a lycan."

"No shit," Jelani said. "I didn't have much of a choice." He shoved at the body again. "You mind helping out, here? Wet fur stinks like hell."

"They revert to their human forms in death. You won't have long to wait." He started away. "Remy is gone. He'll likely flee across the sea. We will have to travel to Romania."

"Romania? He's going to Romania?" As Yako had said, the giant wolf was beginning to revert to its human form. Jelani tried to ignore the repulsive sound of bone and cartilage popping and re-forming. Soon he rolled a naked male off of him.

"Ugh. I don't know what's worse, having a dingy dog on top of me or some naked dude." He looked down at the dead man and shook his head. "Damn, that was close."

"Sinaia is the seat of the High Council of Elders. It is there that Remy will flee, and there where he will die. Come."

"I told you about that subjugation thing. I don't belong to you, Hunter."

Yako turned and looked at him. "Three times," he simply replied. "I do not seek to enslave you, but you are bound to me in your blood. You will honor that blood binding now, or I will spill it all over the forest floor right here."

Jelani faced the man, and saw no sign of anything other than a promise. He knew that he could not best Yako in a fight, injured or not. "Alright, man," he said, his compliance driven by gratitude, rather than fear. "You've saved me more times than I want to think about. Guess I owe more appreciation than I've shown. Just try to excuse my hesitance, given how we initially met."

Yako turned away. "And I am not a Hunter. I am Eldest Hunter."

46

Mariska passed through the halls of Peles Castle, considering all that would happen. If Darren Lacey was to be believed, an attack upon the Elders and those most loyal to them would happen soon. Yako and those loyal to him were also at risk, placing herself at the top of that list.

After meeting with Lydia and Barakus again and ensuring their loyalty, she had begun discretely confirming on which side of the fence the residents of Peles stood. A good number sided with the current seat of power and the Eldest Hunter, but a disheartening number also sided with Massius.

Lemanda's sprawling suite was not far away. Mariska would need to speak with the Elder as soon as possible before the conflict arose. She was hoping to quell the insurrection before it happened, but it was a thin hope. Beside her, Reed practically exuded anxiety.

"I don't think there is time to warn all of the Elders," he said.

"I doubt they are oblivious," Mariska replied. "A political situation such as this has no straightforward solution. If they accuse Massius openly and deal punishment, they risk sparking the fire."

"The fire has already been sparked."

"Yes, but it must be seen as Massius's doing."

"It is," Reed said.

Mariska hid her impatience. "But it must be seen that way. Massius is not an original member of the High Council. If they attack him, it can look as though they used him for his skills then discarded him."

"That makes no sense," Reed said. "How many centuries have passed?"

"Time is an afterthought in the face of patience. The accusation, though a ridiculous and simplistic one, could have a tight grasp if endorsed by only one other member of the High Council."

"Why in the name of the *Ancestors* would any of the Elders back him?" Reed asked. "Who would back him?"

"Who indeed?" another voice replied.

Mariska stopped, and she and Reed exchanged a glance.

The frosty voice of Alicia drifted in the air and caressed Mariska's body like an unwelcome lover. "Tell me, child. In all the sniffing you have done around this castle, did you think that you would be unnoticed? Did you truly think I would not know?"

Mariska watched as the beautiful and terrible Elder stepped out into the hall before them.

F ailure was a concept the Eldest Hunter did not acknowledge. He'd been delayed from achieving his objectives before, but never failed. Three times he had come close to eliminating the very person who stood next to him as they watching the private jet that contained Massius's cravenly subordinate lift off the runway. It was quite the twist of irony that his former target had not only been turned to the night by the very one he hunted, and was now allied with him against his hated enemy.

And his hated enemy was lounging in the luxury of that jet, gliding across the sky toward their seat of power. Twice he had almost killed Remy and twice the coward had managed to wriggle free. It was not failure, but a delaying of the inevitable. Remy would die or Yako would die in the effort. It was the only way failure would find him; in death.

He would need to make arrangements immediately to get to Sinaia. For the time being, Mariska would need to handle things until he arrived. He had confidence in his Second, but he doubted any one person could deal with Remy and Massius together.

"I need to go. I'll be back soon."

Yako knew that Jelani wanted to check on his companions and see to his dead friend. Hatred and pain burned inside that one. Yako could feel it radiating off of him. He would need to temper those emotions if the fledgling was to be of any use to him. Emotions clouded judgement and dulled focus. He looked to the east. Dawn was upon them.

"Go, but return with the night."

Yako nodded to himself at the other's soundless departure. That one may be a *shaquora,* but he was learning quickly.

"**Y**ou care more than you admit to yourself."

Saaya offered a hint of a smile. "Perhaps, perhaps not."

Kafeel gave her a look that suggested she continue lying to herself if it suited her.

"My heart may be encased in ice, but it is not made of it."

Her brother arched an eyebrow. "And you imply what?"

"That perhaps you could warm yours, just a bit."

"You are not well enough practiced at humor, little sister. You played with that human till he became of the night. Then you played with him more. All the while allowing your heart to entwine with his, while his was entwined with another. Now his heart does burn for you, but in hatred. Tell me about the part you've played in this little drama of yours."

Saaya didn't respond. It was rare when she lacked a response, particularly where her brother was concerned. But she knew he was right. Things hadn't gone as she'd intended. She had thought to have a bit of fun, playing with a human pet. It was a hard thing to admit to herself that she had not the heart for it. Human affairs meant little to her, but individuals were a different matter.

On some level, she knew she had touched Jelani. But he had touched her as well, she just hadn't allowed herself to realize it. Now the question was what to do about it. She felt indebted to him and hated it. His world was gone, his former life destroyed, and Saaya stood in the center of the devastation.

"He hates me because he still has not mastered his emotions. He still does not look with clear eyes. He looks, but does not see, and acts on what he has not seen."

"And you fail to see that this is irrelevant. What he has or has not seen changes not the fact that he sees you as an enemy."

Saaya thought for a moment, then turned to her brother and allowed herself a tiny smile. "He has lost much, but not all is destroyed. He will return to me."

"You are so sure," Kafeel said. He held open his long, flowing coat with one arm.

"All will be fine," Saaya replied. "He will return to me because he must. And the truth will set his heart free. In time."

She stepped in front of her brother and turned her back to him. His coat enveloped her in blissful darkness.

Kneeling on the edge of the rooftop, Jelani stared across the distance through the window of Wen's apartment. The two buildings were close enough together that he could hear their conversation. It was light and cheerful, and totally inappropriate given what they had just been through.

A quick stop by his apartment had told Jelani there was no going back. Police were everywhere. The bodies of several human victims were being carted off to waiting ambulances. Bystanders stood by and watched, some of them speaking to the police. Only the work of vampires could ensure that no one had anything substantial to report; no one except for one of the witnesses who lived on Jelani's floor.

Even her account was meaningless. All of the six police officers were human, but one of the detectives was a vampire. He had been quick to find the female who remembered the attack and had used some kind of mind manipulation, altering her memory. In minutes, she was heading back to her apartment, stripped of any real knowledge of what had happened.

Jelani might not like it, but he couldn't argue with the logic. Better for everyone involved if the woman remembered nothing and told no one. He felt a twinge of jealousy that she was spared the type of nightmare his life had become.

Not all vampires shared the same abilities, though some had them in common. If only he'd been lucky enough to encounter two feeding vampires that had the ability to wipe his memory, or even a Hunter with that same ability, his life could have gone on as usual. He looked back in the window.

Wen and Alisha. Completely oblivious. Neither of them had any memory of anything that had happened. That should have been a good thing. It was, in fact. But the girls also had no memory of Jelani or Daniel.

They talked and laughed and ate dinner as if things were the same as they'd been before Jelani and Daniel had entered their lives. He wondered if it was that detective who had erased their memories, or someone else.

Wen crossed in front of the window, making some kind of gesture in the form of one of her typical bubbly jokes. Seeing her made him think of Daniel and he forced down the grief. If he allowed it to surface now, it would drown him.

"I'm sorry, man. I tried and failed. I failed you and I failed the girls. But I promise you I'll make it right." The voice that answered Jelani chilled his blood.

"You gonna do that all by yourself?"

CONTINUE THE STORY WITH:

∾

Revenire
Final Book of the Hunter's Moon Series

ABOUT THE AUTHOR

Ramón Terrell is an author and actor who instantly fell in love with fantasy the day he opened R. A. Salvatore's: The Crystal Shard. Years (and many devoured books) later he decided to put pen to paper for his first novel. After a bout with aching carpals, he decided to try the keyboard instead, and the words began to flow.

As an actor, he has appeared in the hit television shows Supernatural, iZombie, Arrow, and Minority Report, as well as the hit comedy web series Single and Dating in Vancouver. He also appears as one of Robin Hood's Merry Men in Once Upon a Time, as well as an Ark Guard on the hit TV show The 100. When not writing, or acting, he enjoys reading, video games, hiking, and long walks with his wife around Stanley Park in Vancouver BC.

Connect with him at:

ALSO BY RAMÓN TERRELL

Hunter's Moon

Running from the Night

Hunter's Moon

Revenire (Forthcoming)

Legend of Takashaniel

Echoes of a Shattered Age

Legends of a Shattered Age

Heroes of a Broken Age (Forthcoming)

Saga of Ruination

Unleashed

The Fairies

Our of Ordure